CHOCOLATE SHOES
and
WEDDING BLUES

CHOCOLATE SHOES
and
WEDDING BLUES

Trisha Ashley

LARGE PRINT
Oxford

First published in Great Britain 2012
by
Avon
a division of HarperCollins Publishers

Published in Large Print 2013 by ISIS Publishing Ltd.,
7 Centremead, Osney Mead, Oxford OX2 0ES
by arrangement with
HarperCollins Publishers

British Library Cataloguing in Publication Data
Ashley, Trisha.
    Chocolate shoes and wedding blues.
    1. Love stories.
    2. Large type books.
    I. Title
    823.9'2–dc23

ISBN 978–0–7531–9152–1 (hb)
ISBN 978–0–7531–9153–8 (pb)

Printed and bound in Great Britain by
T. J. International Ltd., Padstow, Cornwall

I would like to thank Angela Dracup for her recipe for Fat Rascals, Linda Long for help with Welsh names and my son, Robin Ashley, for brewing up experimental flagons of the medicinal mead that features throughout the novel. But most of all, grateful thanks must go to my mother, Mary Long, whose enterprise in starting up a little shoe shop in the difficult post-war years inspired me to write this story.

This one is for my friend Nora Neibergall,
distant only in miles.

Prologue: June 1945

Nancy had to walk quite a way to the red call box near the village green, then stand in an unseasonably cold wind waiting for a large woman in a spotted headscarf tied turban-fashion round her head to stop talking and come out, before she could place the call to her sister.

"At last! What kept you?" Violet exclaimed.

"Never mind that now," Nancy said tersely. "I'm in the phone box, so call me back. You're the one with all the brass."

She dropped the black phone back onto its rest, thinking that brass was something her sister had never been short of. But her latest scheme — well, that really took the biscuit . . .

The phone rang almost immediately. "I was starting to wonder if you'd got my letter," Violet said.

"Oh, I got it all right — and Mother and Father got theirs, too. But what on earth are you thinking of, Violet? This mad plan of yours will never work!"

"Viola," her sister corrected her automatically. "And of course it will — why shouldn't it?"

"I can think of at least five reasons off the top of my head. And you might have asked me first."

"We're sisters, so why wouldn't we help each other out of a sticky spot? And I've got it all planned. I'm going to rent somewhere quiet, where no one knows us, and in a couple of months you'll be home again as if nothing had ever happened and can put it right out of your head."

"But something *will* have happened. And if I suddenly vanish like that, then reappear, don't you think there'll be talk? You know how rumours get around in the village."

"Oh, probably no one will notice," Violet said optimistically, "and if they do, they won't *know*, that's the main thing."

"Vi, I can't let you do this — and don't you think your husband might have something to say about it, when he finds out? No, we'll have to find another way."

"Too late, because I've already written to Peter explaining everything, though goodness knows when he'll get the letter," Violet said triumphantly. Despite the recent VE Day celebrations, many men were still fighting out in the Far East, Violet's husband among them.

"You've actually *sent* it? Without asking me first?"

"Of course, because it was obviously the only way out of the situation. So you see, we'll have to go through with it now. Peter will be fine about it when he comes home. I can twist him round my little finger," Violet added. "There's no fool like an old fool."

"You shouldn't speak like that about your husband. *You* chose to marry a much older man when you were barely in your twenties, Violet, no one forced you!"

2

Nancy could almost see her sister shrug her thin shoulders. "So, when are you coming?"

"Violet, we can't possibly do this. You're quite mad to even think it!"

"You mean you won't come, Nancy? You'll just tell Mother and Father the truth? Mother will probably have another stroke from the shock and shame."

"You've got Mother upset already, telling her you'd been ill again and were going to convalesce somewhere quiet and wanted me to keep you company. She was all set to come down herself and look after you, but Father wouldn't entertain the idea for a minute," Nancy said. Their mother had suffered a mild stroke the previous year and, though she had made a good recovery, she was still not fully fit.

"Thank goodness for that! But I didn't think he'd let her. I take it they're OK about you coming, though?"

"Yes, in fact they're so worried about you they want me to go at once. They think you're a frail little flower since the pneumonia, though you only got that from gallivanting about in flimsy clothes in the evening with your fast friends, drinking too much."

"Honestly, Nan, you sound more like twenty years older than me, than two! But the sooner you come down the better, because it's lucky no one's noticed anything yet. There's nothing to keep you there now, is there? I mean, you're not *still* seeing that American pilot?"

"No, he's gone home and, anyway, we were just friends, really," Nancy said. Her fiancé had been killed in the early days of the war and there hadn't been anyone serious since then. Not that Violet was likely to believe that.

"Tell that to the marines!" she said now, rudely.

"But I *have* started seeing someone recently," Nancy confessed.

"This is certainly not the time to get involved with another man!" Violet said severely. "Who is he?"

"The new curate. He's been round to tea at our house once or twice and we've been for walks. Mother and Father like him and . . . well, he's a good, decent man. I know I'll never love anyone like I did Jacob, but I don't really want to spend the rest of my life alone, either."

"A curate? Good grief!" Violet exclaimed.

"He was an army chaplain."

"Honestly, what a moment to pick to go out with a curate! Let's just hope he never gets wind of this, because I don't suppose he'd be very forgiving."

"Amen to that!" Nancy said devoutly. "And I wouldn't have encouraged him if only I'd known . . ."

"Well, you didn't, and with a bit of luck you'll be back home before long, and can pick up where you left off."

"I don't think I could — not without telling him the truth."

"You can never tell *anyone* the truth. And it's not like you can back out of the situation now, Nan, is it? It would finish Mother off if it all came out, and as for Father . . ."

"You don't think that they'll suspect anything eventually?"

4

"They might *guess,* but that's not the same as knowing — and everything will be nicely sorted out by then, no scandals. But you must keep it secret . . ." Violet paused then asked, "You haven't already told Florrie, have you?"

She knew Florrie was Nancy's best friend and there were few secrets between them.

"No, no one knows but you and me." Nancy sighed. "It suddenly feels as if I'm trapped in a horrible nightmare, but I can't see anything else I can do, so I'll be down on Monday afternoon."

"I don't know about nightmare, but it's all a damned nuisance," Violet said. "Tell me which train, and I'll meet it."

A woman walked up to the phone kiosk and stood shifting her feet restlessly outside. "Look, I'll have to go — there's someone waiting for the phone," Nancy said.

Stepping out of the booth Nancy pulled her warm coat around her against the chilly evening breeze. It was made of good but well-worn pre-war tweed with a little fur collar, and was now getting tight over her waist and tummy — but then, Nancy was a typical Bright, like her father, small and dark, and the womenfolk did tend to put on weight in their late twenties. Her sister, Violet, in contrast, was tall and fair like their mother, and stayed slim no matter what she ate.

Normally, the thought of the carrot cake her mother had made earlier would have hastened Nancy's steps home, but now the heavy burden of lies, secrets and subterfuge she was shouldering made her feel distinctly queasy.

CHAPTER
ONE

Christmas Present

My name is Nancy Myfanwy Bright. My father liked the name Nancy and I was called Myfanwy after my mother. I'm ninety-two years of age and I've lived quietly in this cottage behind Bright's Shoes in Sticklepond all my life, so I don't really know why you want to record my memories for your archive, because it isn't going to be very interesting, is it, dear?

Do help yourself to a slice of bara birth — it's a sort of fruit loaf made to my mother's recipe. There's another kind they call funeral cake in the part of Wales Mother's family came from, because it was always served to the mourners after an interment. I've told Tansy — that's my great-niece — that she should do that when I pop my clogs, too. I've taught her all Mother's old recipes . . .

Now, where were we?

Middlemoss Living Archive
Recordings: Nancy Bright.

As I drove out of London and headed north for Christmas my heart lifted with each passing mile. It always did, because West Lancashire — and, more specifically, the village of Sticklepond — was always

7

going to feel like home to me. You can take the girl out of Lancashire, but you can't take the Lancashire out of the girl . . .

I would have moved back there like a flash, if it weren't that my fiancé, Justin, was an orthopaedic consultant whose work was in London, not to mention his being so firmly tied to his widowed mother's apron strings that he spent more time with Mummy in Tunbridge Wells than he did with me. And even when he wasn't with Mummy Dearest, I still came second to his latest passion — golf.

Justin's mother was only one of the many things weighing on my mind — the sharp, pointy tip of the iceberg, you might say. She'd be staying at the flat in London while I was away and I knew from past experience that by the time I got back she would have thoroughly purged my unwanted presence from it by dumping all my possessions into the boxroom I used as a studio to write and illustrate my popular *Slipper Monkey* children's books.

I'd tried so hard to get on with her, but I was never going to be good enough for her beloved little boy. In fact, I once overheard her refer to me as "that bit of hippie trash you picked up on the plane back from India", and though it's true that Justin and I met after I was unexpectedly upgraded to the seat next to his in Business Class, I'm a couple of decades too young to have been any kind of hippie!

I suppose many people did still go to India to "find themselves", whatever they mean by that. In my case

I'd gone to find my father. Now, he *was* an old hippie, if you like . . .

Still, at least I'd *tried* with Justin's mother, which is more than he did on his one and only visit to Aunt Nan in Sticklepond, when he'd made it abundantly clear that he thought anything north of Watford was a barbaric region to be avoided at all costs, full of howling wolves, black puddings and men in flat caps with whippets.

He did condescendingly describe Aunt Nan's ancient stone cottage set in a stone-flagged courtyard just off the High Street, its front room given over to a tiny shoe shop, as "quaint". But then, that was before Aunt Nan made him sleep downstairs on the sofa in the parlour. I told him she disapproved of cohabitation before marriage so strongly that he was lucky she hadn't taken a room for him at the Green Man next door, but he failed to see the funny side.

Still, you can see why we'd spent our Christmases apart during our long engagement, not to mention many weekends too, what with him in Tunbridge Wells with Mummy (and a convenient golf course) and me heading home at least once a month — and more often than that, as Aunt Nan got frailer . . .

Aunt Nan was actually my great-aunt, aged ninety-two, and as she kept reminding me, wouldn't be around for ever. She'd brought me up and I adored her, so obviously I wanted to spend as much time with her as I could, but I also wanted her to see me married and with a family of my own, and so did she. And if I didn't get a shift on, that last option would be closed to me for ever, another thing weighing on my mind.

I knew it could be more difficult to get pregnant after thirty-five, so without telling Justin I'd booked myself into a clinic for a fertility MOT and the result had been a real wake-up call. The indication was that I had *some* eggs left, but probably not that many, so I needed to reach out and snatch the opportunity to have children before it vanished . . . if it hadn't already.

When Justin and I had first got engaged we were full of plans to marry and start a family, yet there we were, almost six years down the line, and he seemed to have lost interest in doing either. In fact, I could see that he was totally different from the man I fell in love with, though the change had happened so slowly I just hadn't noticed. Perhaps it's like that with all relationships and it takes a sudden shock to make you step back and take a good clear look at what's been happening.

I mainly blamed Mummy Dearest for poisoning Justin's mind against me, dripping poisonous criticisms into his ear the whole time, though she hadn't been so bad the first year — or maybe I'd been so in love I simply hadn't registered it.

Justin and I were such opposites, yet until the golf mania took hold, we used to love exploring the London parks together, and before he became such a skinflint, we used to go to a lot of musical theatre productions, too. When I first found out about Justin's secret passion (we must have seen *We Will Rock You* five or six times!) I found it very endearing . . .

As the radio cheered me on my way north with a succession of Christmas pop songs, I knew that when I got back to London we would need to do some *serious* talking.

Aunt Nan's mind seemed to have been running along the same lines as mine, because she decided it was time for us to have a little heart-to-heart chat the very day after I arrived.

My best friend, Bella, was looking after the shop and Aunt Nan had spent the first part of the morning shut away in the parlour with Cheryl Noakes, the archivist who was recording her memoirs for the Middlemoss Living Archive scheme. This seemed to perk up my aunt no end, despite awaking bittersweet memories, like the loss of her fiancé during the war.

I'd shown Cheryl out and returned to collect the tray of coffee cups and any stray crumbs from the iced fairy cakes that she might have overlooked, when Aunt Nan said suddenly, "What will you do with the shop when I'm gone, lovey?"

She was still sitting in her comfortable shabby armchair, a gaily coloured Afghan rug over her knees (she believed overheated houses were unhealthy, so the central heating, which I'd insisted she had put in, was always turned down really low), crocheting another doily for my already full-to-bursting bottom drawer.

With a pang I realised how little room her once-plump frame took up in the chair now. When had she suddenly become so small and pale? And her curls, which had been as dark as her eyes, just like mine, were now purest silver . . .

"Shouldn't you leave it to Immy, Aunt Nan?"

"No," she said uncompromisingly. "Your mother hates the place and she's got more money than sense already, the flibbertigibbet! Anyway, she seems to be sticking with this last husband and making her home in America now."

"That's true! Marrying a Californian plastic surgeon seems to have fulfilled all her wildest dreams."

Aunt Nan snorted. "She's probably more plastic by now than a Barbie doll!"

"Her face *was* starting to look a bit strange in that last picture she emailed me," I admitted. "All pulled up at the corners of her eyes, so they slanted like a cat's. I hope she doesn't overdo it. I didn't realise you could have your knees lifted, did you? But she says you can and your knees show your age."

"She shouldn't be showing her knees to anyone at her age. But there, that's Imogen all over, shallow as a puddle from being a child. Except that she's the spitting image of her mother, you'd think there wasn't a scrap of Bright blood in her . . ."

She paused, as if at some painful recollection, and then said firmly, "No, I'm passing on the shop and cottage to you, because you're a true Bright and you come back every chance you get, like a homing pigeon."

"I do love the place, but I come back because I love you, too," I said, a few tears welling, "and I can't bear to think of you gone."

"You great daft ha'porth," she said fondly. "You need to be practical about these things, because I'm ninety-two and I'll be ready to go soon, like it or not!"

"But do we have to talk about it now?"

"Yes." She nodded her head in a very decided manner, her silver curls bobbing. "I'm not flaming immortal, you know! I'll soon be shuffling off this mortal coil, as I told the vicar last time he called."

"Oh, Raffy Sinclair's *gorgeous*!" I sighed, distracted by this mention of our new ex-rock star vicar.

"He's also very much married to Chloe Lyon that has the Chocolate Wishes shop, and they've got a baby now," Aunt Nan told me severely.

"I know, and even if he wasn't married, he'd still be way out of my league!"

"No one is out of your league, Tansy," she said. "The vicar's a decent, kind man, for all his looks, and often pops in for a chat. And that Seth Greenwood from up at Winter's End, he's another who's been good to me this last couple of years: I haven't had to lift a hand in the garden other than to pick the herbs from my knot garden, and he or one of the gardeners from the hall keeps that trim and tidy, and looking a treat."

"Seth's another big, attractive man, like the vicar: you're a magnet for them!" I teased.

"I was at school with his father, Rufus, and I've known Hebe Winter for ever — has a hand in everything that goes on in Sticklepond, she does, despite her niece inheriting the hall."

13

"And marrying Seth. In fact, marrying the head gardener seems to be becoming a Winter tradition, doesn't it?"

"He and Sophy have got a baby too. There's so many little 'uns around now, I'm starting to think they're putting something in the water."

I felt a sudden, sharp, anguished pang, because when you're desperate to have a baby, practically everyone else seems to have one, or be expecting one.

But Nan had switched back to her original track. "I don't suppose you'll want to keep the shop open. Goodness knows, it's been more of a hobby to me than a business the last few years, and I'd have had to close if Providence hadn't sent Bella back to the village, looking for a job. The Lord moves in mysterious ways."

"He certainly does," I agreed, though I wasn't sure that losing both her partner and her home in one fell swoop, and then being forced to move into the cramped annexe of her parents' house with her five-year-old daughter, Tia, was something Bella saw in the light of Providence. But it had been a huge relief to me when she started working in the shop, because she could keep an eye on Aunt Nan for me too.

"There's been a Bright's Shoes here since the first Bright set up as a cobbler and clog-maker way back, so I feel a bit sad that it'll end with me. But there it is," Aunt Nan said. "Perhaps you and Justin could use the cottage as a holiday home — assuming you ever get round to marrying, that is, because I wouldn't like to think of any immoral goings-on under this roof!"

"Having the cottage as my very own bolthole in the north would be *wonderful*," I agreed, "but I really don't want to see Bright's Shoes close down! Do you remember when you used to take me with you to the shoe warehouses in Manchester in the school holidays? You'd be searching for special shoes for some customer, or taking bridesmaids' satin slippers to be dyed to match their dresses . . ."

I could still recall the heady smell of leather in the warehouses and then the treat of tea in one of the big stores before we came back on the train. Not many shopkeepers nowadays would go all that way just to find the exact shoes one customer wanted, but then again, nowadays anyone but my aunt Nan would be tracking them down on the internet. That, together with vintage clothes fairs, was how I was amassing an ever-expanding collection of wedding shoes — or vintage shoes so pretty they ought to be wedding shoes. I was collecting them just for fun, but I only wished I had somewhere to display them all.

"When you were a little girl you wanted to run the shop when you grew up and find the right Cinderella shoes, as you called them, for every bride."

"I remember that, and though I'm still not so interested in the wellies, school plimsolls and sensible-shoe side, I do love the way you've expanded the wedding shoe selection. I've wondered about the possibility of having a shop that specialises in bridal shoes."

"Would there be enough custom? It's only been a sideline," Aunt Nan said doubtfully. "You don't get much passing trade here either, being tucked away down Salubrious Passage, as we are."

"Oh, yes, because people will travel to a specialist shop once they know you're there. I could advertise on the internet, and my shop would stock some genuine vintage bridal shoes as well as vintage-styled ones, so that would be a fairly unusual selling point," I enthused.

"That would be different," Aunt Nan agreed. "But wouldn't you have the bread-and-butter lines still, like purses and polish and shoelaces?"

"No, not unless I could find shoe-shaped purses! In fact, I could sell all kinds of shoe-shaped things — jewellery, stationery, wedding favours, whatever I could find," I said thoughtfully, "because I'd be mad not to tap into the tourist trade too, wouldn't I? I mean, the village has become a hotspot between Easter and autumn, since the discovery of that Shakespeare manuscript up at Winter's End. The gardens are a draw too, now Seth has finished restoring the knot gardens on the terraces, and then you get the arty lot who want to see Ottie Winter's sculpture in the garden and maybe even a glimpse of the great artist herself!"

Aunt Nan nodded. "Yes, that's very true. And when they've been to Winter's End, they usually come into the village, what with the Witchcraft Museum and then the craft galleries and teashops and the pubs. The Green Man still does most of the catering for lunches and dinners, but Florrie's installed a coffee machine in the snug at the Falling Star and puts out a sign, and she says they get quite a bit of passing trade. You'd be amazed what people are prepared to pay for a cup of coffee with a bit of froth on it."

Florrie Snowball was Aunt Nan's greatest friend and, although the same age, showed no signs of flagging. Aunt Nan said this was because she'd sold her soul to the devil, involved as she was in some kind of occult group run by the proprietor of the Witchcraft Museum, Gregory Lyon, but it doesn't seem to have affected their friendship.

"I'm sure I could make a go of it!" I said, starting to feel excited. Until all these plans had suddenly come pouring out, I hadn't realised just how much I'd been thinking about it.

Aunt Nan brought me back to earth with a bump. "But, Tansy, if you marry Justin, then you'll make your home in London, won't you?"

"He could get a job up here," I suggested, though I sounded unconvincing even to myself. Justin could be transferred to a Lancashire hospital, but I was sure he wouldn't want to. And even if he did want that, Mummy Dearest would have something to say about it!

"I can't see Justin doing that," Aunt Nan said.

"Even if he won't, Bella could manage the shop for me and I could divide my time between London and Sticklepond," I suggested, though suddenly I really, *really* wanted to do it myself! "Anyway, we needn't think about that now, because you're not going to leave me for years yet, and until then, Bella can run things just the way they've always been."

"I keep telling you I'm on the way out, and you're not listening, you daft lump," my aunt said crossly.

"After that rheumatic fever I had at eleven they said I wouldn't make old bones, but they were wrong about that! But now I'm wearing out. One day soon, my cogs will stop turning altogether and I'll be ready to meet my Maker. I'd hoped to see you married and with a family by then, though."

"Yes, me too, and it's what Justin seemed to want when we got engaged . . . yet we haven't even tied the knot yet!"

"That's what comes of living with a man before the ring's on your finger," Aunt Nan said severely. "They've no reason to wed you, then."

"Things have changed, Aunt Nan — and I *do* have a ring on my finger." I twiddled my solitaire diamond.

"Things haven't changed for the better, and if he wants a family he should realise that time's passing and you're thirty-six — starting to cut it close."

"I know, though time has slipped by so quickly that I've only just woken up to the fact."

"I don't know why you didn't marry long since."

"Neither do I, though Justin does seem to have a thing about my weight. I thought he was joking when he said he'd set the wedding date when I was a size eight, but no, he was entirely serious! Only my diets always seem to fail, and then I put a few more pounds on after each attempt."

"He should leave well alone, then," she said tartly. "You're a small, dark Bright, like me, and we plumpen as we get older. And, a woman's meant to have a bit of padding, not be a rack of ribs."

"It's not just my weight, but everything about me that seems to irritate him now. I think his mother keeps stirring him up and making him so critical. For instance, he used to say the way I dressed was eccentric and cute, but now he seems to want me to look like all his friends' wives and girlfriends."

"There's nowt wrong with the way you look," Aunt Nan said loyally, though even my close friends are prone to comment occasionally on the eccentricity of my style. "He can't remodel you like an old coat to suit himself, he needs to love you for what you are."

"If he *does* still love me! He *says* he does, but is that the real me, or some kind of Stepford Wife vision he wants me to turn into?" I sighed. "No, I've been drifting with the tide for too long and after Christmas I'm going to find out one way or the other!"

"You do that," Aunt Nan agreed, "because there are lots of other fish in the sea if you want to throw him back."

I wasn't too sure about that. I'd only ever loved two men in my life (if you count my first brief encounter as one of them) so the stock of my particular kind of fish was obviously already dangerously depleted.

"If I want to have children, I've left it a bit late to start again with someone else," I said sadly, "and although Justin's earning a good salary he's turned into a total skinflint and says we can't afford to have children yet — they're way too expensive — but then, I expect he thinks our children would have a nanny and go to a private school, like he did, and of course I wouldn't want that."

"He doesn't seem much of a man to me at all," Aunt Nan said disparagingly. "But I'm not the one in love with him."

"He has his moments," I said, thinking of past surprises, like tickets to see a favourite musical, romantic weekends in Paris, or the trip to Venice he booked on the Orient Express, which gave me full rein to raid the dressing-up box . . .

But all that was in the first heady year or so after we fell in love. Then the romance slowly tailed off . . . How was it that I hadn't noticed when the music stopped playing?

CHAPTER
TWO

Frosted Knots

I've had my share of sorrows, of course, but I've never been one to dwell on them. Mother always said we should strive to be like the words carved around that old sundial in the courtyard, remembering only the happy hours, though I think being so old it actually says "hourf" and not "hours". The courtyard used to belong to a house that was where the Green Man is now, but lots of houses went to rack and ruin after the Great Plague visited the village, because it wiped out whole families. and there's nothing of it left now bar the sundial. You know about the Lido field turning out to be a plague pit, don't you, dear? It was quite providential in a way, because it stopped those developers building on it.

Middlemoss Living Archive
Recordings: Nancy Bright.

I had my recurring dream that night — or nightmare, I was never sure which. It was a Cinderella one, featuring Justin as the handsome prince and with Rae and Marcia, my wicked stepsisters from my mother's second marriage, as the Ugly Sisters, though actually they're only ugly on the inside.

The dream ran its usual course, with the prince looking up at me just as he was fitting the glass slipper onto my foot, at which point Justin's leonine good looks would morph disconcertingly into the darker, somewhat other-worldly features of my first, brief love, Ivo Hawksley.

Weird, and strangely unsettling for an hour or two after I woke up . . .

So I was up early, and when I looked out of the kitchen window, Aunt Nan's herbal knot garden was prettily frosted with snow and the spiral-cut box tree in the centre looked like an exotic kind of ice lolly.

Knot gardens have low, interwoven hedges forming the pattern or "knot". When I was a little girl Aunt Nan used hyssop and rosemary bushes to make the outline, in the old way, but since this made a rougher effect than box hedging and also had to be renewed from time to time, a few years ago she bought a whole load of little box plants from Seth Greenwood, who is the proprietor of Greenwood's Knots as well as being head gardener at Winter's End, and replaced the hedging with that.

That's when Seth started to take an interest. He helped her to pull out the old hedging and replace it with the new, in a slightly more intricate design, and then afterwards just kept dropping in and doing a bit of garden tidying.

Sometimes he sent one of the three under-gardeners instead, and I expect they were glad of the break, since Seth was so passionate about the garden restoration at Winter's End he seemed to have become a bit of a slave-driver. Aunt Nan would be trotting out with hot tea and Welshcakes for her helpers every five minutes, too.

Each segment of knot was filled with fragrant herbs: lovage, fennel, dill, thyme, several types of mint, clumps of chives and tree onions, sage and parsley. She used several of them in the Welsh herbal honey drink, made from an old family recipe passed down from her mother, that she brewed as a general cure-all. The recipe calls it Meddyginiaeth Llysieuol, Welsh for "herbal medicine", but we always referred to it just as Meddyg — much less of a mouthful!

The gardens behind this and the adjoining cottage were very long, and divided by a wall topped with trellis, while our other boundary was the high wall of the Green Man's car park.

The two seventeenth-century cottages formed an L shape fronting onto a little courtyard accessible only by foot from the High Street via the narrow Salubrious Passage. Both had been extended to provide bathrooms and kitchens, and also, in our case, an anachronistic little three-sided shop window pushed out of the cottage front, like a surreal aquarium. I had to park my car right at the further end of the garden, where a lane turned up behind the pub and ended just beyond the cottages.

I finished my coffee, then put on my coat and boots and went out. Aunt Nan had always been a haphazard kind of gardener, mixing fruit, vegetables and flowers together in chaotic abundance, but most of the beds had been turfed over when it all got too much for her, so by then it looked a little too neat and tidy.

I walked to the far end and on through the archway cut into a tall variegated holly hedge, to let out the hens. Cedric the cockerel, who'd been emitting abrupt, strangulated crows for at least the last hour, ceased abruptly when I opened the pop-door. He stuck his head out and gave me one suspicious, beady glance, but then when I rattled the food bucket his six wives jostled him out of the way and came running down the ramp.

Bella had been letting them out and feeding them lately, when she came to open the shop, but since she had to take her little girl to school first, that could be quite late.

I looked for eggs, more out of habit than expectation since the hens generally stopped laying in winter, and found a single white freckly one.

When I went back in, Aunt Nan told me she'd discovered an early Christmas present left outside the front door when she'd gone to get the milk in.

"Two of them, in fact!"

"What, on the doorstep?"

"No, next to it, one either side. This was attached." She handed me a card threaded with red ribbon.

"'A Happy Christmas from Seth, Sophy and all the Family at Winter's End,'" I read.

"They're still out there — go and have a look, while I put some eggs on for breakfast," she urged me.

"Here's a fresh one." I handed her my booty, then went out to admire two perfect little ball-shaped box trees in wooden tubs on either side of the shop door.

24

Seth must have carried them down Salubrious Passage in the night!

It had been lovely to see Bella again when I came home, but we'd postponed our catching-up until that evening, because it was Christmas Eve the next day, and Aunt Nan was fretting about the state of the house. I needed to embark on the sort of major clean she would have already done herself in times past, until everything sparkled, while Bella minded the shop.

When that was done we decorated the sitting room with paper garlands and put up the ancient and somewhat balding fake tree, made from green bristles on twisted wire branches. I left her hanging glass baubles on it while I went to start off the sherry trifle and bake mince pies and other goodies.

This year's Meddyg, which Nan made in summer and autumn, was long since bottled and stored away, for it was best at least a year after brewing — pale yellowy-green and aromatic. I made it in London too, fermenting it in the airing cupboard, much to Justin's disgust, since he couldn't even stand the smell of it.

It must be an acquired taste. Like Aunt Nan, I always had a glass of it before bedtime . . . and whenever I felt in need of a pick-me-up, for, as she said, "A glass of the Doctor always does you good!" She also insisted she never drank alcohol, so clearly Meddyg, which packs a powerful punch, didn't count.

After supper I left Aunt Nan comfortably established in front of the TV in the parlour and popped next door to the Green Man to meet Bella. Her parents were babysitting, which was not exactly an arduous task, since they only had to leave the door to the annexe open to hear if Tia woke up, but she'd rarely had a night out since she'd moved back home.

"They love Tia, but they don't like it when they have to alter their plans to look after her," Bella said glumly. "At least now she's turned five and at school, working is easier, but if I had to pay a childminder in the holidays it wouldn't be worth my while working."

"I know, it must be really difficult," I said sympathetically. "How is everything going? You look tired." Bella has ash-blond hair and the sort of pale skin that looks blue and bruised under the eyes when she is exhausted.

"I must need more blusher," she said with a wry smile, though having been an air hostess, she made sure her make-up and upswept hairdo were immaculate. Old habits die hard!

"And I *am* tired, but at least my office skills evening class has finished for Christmas, and there's only a few weeks more of it next term," she added. "I'm going to advertise my secretarial services and see if I can get a bit of extra work to do at home."

"It's been a godsend having you helping in the shop and keeping an eye on Aunt Nan for me now she's got so frail, but we'd both understand if you took up a better-paid full-time job offer."

"I couldn't fit in a full-time job around Tia, but Nan's let me close the shop just before school finishes so I can pick her up, which has worked very well. Plus

I love working in the shoe shop *and* I love Nan too. The holidays and Saturdays are a bit of a problem, though, because unless I can arrange a playdate, or Robert's mother comes over from Formby to take her out for the day, Mum has to mind her again." Her face clouded.

"Not good? How are things going with you and your parents?" I asked.

"Oh, Tansy, it's *horrible* living in the annexe!" she burst out. "I know I should be grateful we've got a roof over our heads and no rent to pay, because goodness knows, Mum and Dad tell me that often enough, but when you're used to having your own house and suddenly you're crammed with a small child into a flat the size of a garage, it's not that easy!"

"No, I can imagine," I said sympathetically. "It seemed so unfair that you lost everything."

Bella's partner had been an airline pilot, several years older and separated from his wife when they met. Bella was an air hostess on one of his flights and they got to know each other on a stopover in some exotic location. He'd been handsome and charming, and swept her off her feet, but though their life together had seemed idyllic, and he'd adored Tia, it had all gone pear-shaped after he'd died suddenly from a heart attack and she'd discovered his debts.

"There was very little left to lose. He'd already gambled us deep into debt, though I didn't know it. And he'd never got round to divorcing his wife like he said he would, so she got whatever was left. I even had to sell my car to cover our moving expenses *and* a lot of

27

our belongings, because we couldn't fit them in and I couldn't afford storage," Bella said bitterly.

"But coming back home was the only thing you could do, wasn't it?"

"Yes, and although Mum and Dad have been very kind, letting me have the annexe, you know what they're like, especially Mum. I'm sure she's getting worse."

I nodded. Bella's mother was super-house-proud, to the point where it was becoming an illness. She swept up every microscopic particle of anything that fell in or outside her house with manic fervour, and polished every surface that would take it to a burnished, mirrored sheen.

"She's in my flat cleaning all the time too. There's no privacy! Even Tia's toys are all clean, disinfected and lined up on shelves by order of size or colour or whatever."

"Not an ideal atmosphere to bring up a small child in — it's surprising you turned out relatively normal," I teased.

"Thanks," she said with a wry grin, "but then, neither of us had ideal parents, did we? Your mother dumped you with Aunt Nan soon after you were born and you've hardly seen her since, and your father was a passing fancy who went off to India and addled his brains with drugs."

"He was quite good-natured about having a daughter when I tracked him down, though," I said, "even if I had to keep reminding him who I was every time he saw me, because he forgot. What about your father,

Bella? Doesn't he think your mum's gone a bit over the top with the house-proud bit?"

"He likes a neat house and no fuss too, so he wouldn't understand what I was talking about. They love Tia — don't get me wrong — but they've got even more inflexible in their ways and habits since I was last living at home. But perhaps I can rent somewhere soon, if I get lots of typing work," she said optimistically. "I wonder if the cottage attached to yours will come up for rent. It's been empty for months. Still, even if it does, I expect it would be more than I could afford."

"I don't know what's going to happen to it. It might even become a holiday let again. That was what the owner bought it for. She was an actress, and then Aunt Nan heard that she'd been killed in a traffic accident just after being offered a part in *Cotton Common*," I said, mentioning the popular TV soap that was shot locally.

"Yes, she told me — and your stepsister Marcia's already got a part in *Cotton Common*, hasn't she? She must be living up here too, at least some of the time."

"She is. She's got a flat in the old Butterflake biscuit factory in Middlemoss. Lars said he hoped we'd manage to see a bit of each other, but I would so much rather not get together with either of my wicked stepsisters! I don't know how such a nice man came to have such horrible daughters."

Lars was my mother's second husband — she was now on to number three — and much the nicest of any of them. He'd rung me just before I left London to wish me happy Christmas. There was a large parcel from him awaiting me when I got here, which I knew would be a very lavish present.

"I thought you were getting on slightly better with Rae?" Bella said.

"Not really, it's just she comes round to the flat occasionally if it's the nanny's day off and Charlie isn't at school, because I don't think she has any idea what to do with him. He's a nice little boy, about Tia's age, and he loves my *Slipper Monkey* books — his nanny has to read them to him at bedtime every night. I always make him a pipe-cleaner monkey to take home, too. I wish Rae wouldn't keep dropping in, though, because Justin doesn't like her. He's quite rude to her sometimes."

"At least there's one of your boyfriends who doesn't find your stepsisters irresistible," Bella offered.

"True. It was a huge relief when he met Rae and Marcia and didn't get on with either of them. In fact, I'm starting to think that's the main reason I'm staying with him," I said gloomily.

"I thought you loved him?"

"I do . . . I did . . . I . . . well, we *were* in love. It's totally unmistakable, isn't it? That eyes-meeting-across-the-room thing — or across a plane seat, in our case. It was a real case of opposites attracting, and the first year it was all wonderful: we got engaged, I moved in, we were going to get married and start a family right away . . . as soon as I lost a couple of stone."

"I still can't believe he was serious about that!"

"No, I thought he was joking for ages, but he was deadly serious. And I've put on *another* stone since then," I said sadly.

"You're still only nicely covered. *I* could do with a bit of that."

Bella had the opposite problem, for despite eating healthily she stayed almost painfully thin. People thought she had an eating disorder, but it wasn't that. She always looked very striking and elegant, though, even in jeans and a cardi — a real yummy mummy.

"The only time I looked really healthy and had boobs was when I was expecting Tia. I liked being pregnant, but Robert thought I looked gross, a total turn-off."

"Yes — babies . . . that's another thing I wanted to talk to you about, but somehow I couldn't do it on the phone."

Her face lit up. "You're *not*, are you?"

"No, I'm not — it's the opposite problem, in fact." And I told her about my fertility MOT and the iffy result.

"Basically, my chances of conceiving naturally are limited to a pretty narrow window of opportunity and diminishing rapidly, so I should get a move on."

She hugged me. "Oh, Tansy, I'm so sorry! But surely when you told Justin he must have —"

"He doesn't know yet," I broke in. "I wanted to think things through over Christmas first, because when they gave me the results, it made me look at the last few years with clear eyes and realise how different our relationship has become. Opposites attract, but maybe

31

we're just too unlike each other, and if it isn't going to work out then I can't stay with him just because I'm desperate to have a baby, can I?"

"I suppose not," she agreed. "How have things changed between you, then?"

"Well, all the things about me he used to say were cute or quirky, like my clothes, for instance, now seem to embarrass or annoy him."

"Your clothes are often unusual," she admitted, "but they suit you. I mean, that's just the way you are."

I was dressed in wine-coloured corduroy jodhpurs and a Peruvian jumper covered in green, red and blue llamas. I had a matching Peruvian hat with ear flaps and tassels, but of course it was too hot to wear that in the pub. On my feet were blue Birkenstock clogs.

"In fact, I'm the only one of your friends who wears boring clothes," she said.

"Not boring, understated," I corrected. Muted colours and quiet elegance really suited her. "Justin says you always look nice."

"I'm not sure that's a compliment, from him," she said dubiously. "What does he think about Timmy? His clothes are even weirder than yours, not to mention the hats!"

"Oh, well, being a hat maker, he uses his head as a marketing tool. But Justin's made it clear he doesn't like him and he wouldn't even come with me to Timmy and Joe's civil partnership ceremony."

"That spotted prom dress with the red underskirt you wore to the wedding looked lovely in the pictures."

"Timmy made the dress and the hat — he is so clever!"

"I wished I could have been there," Bella said wistfully.

Timmy, Bella and I had been friends since infants' school, and while Bella had trained to be an air hostess, Timmy and I had headed down to London, to art school — fashion in his case, graphic design in mine.

"Justin's become such a skinflint too. He wasn't like that at first, but suddenly he started saying we had to economise and couldn't afford to get married, couldn't afford to move to somewhere out of town, couldn't afford to have children . . . I mean, he earns a big salary — he's a hospital consultant!"

"And you aren't doing too badly with the *Slipper Monkey* books either, are you?"

"No, I'm doing *really* well. I tried to aim the mix of words and pictures at early readers in the five-to-eight-ish age range, but they seem popular now even with adults. They may even be a minor cult!"

"I'm not surprised. The illustrations are lovely," Bella said loyally. "It's the way you use spiky ink lines to suggest the wiriness of the little monkeys and bright watercolour wash for the soft fuzziness of the fur. They're quite magical."

"It's nice when your best friend is your biggest fan!" I said. "My agent says there's talk of spin-off items, like toys and games now. In fact, I don't really need to do the foot modelling any more. I could give that up and wear decent shoes." Despite the success of the books I still did a little foot modelling for adverts and catalogues. Immy got me into it when I was a student — she said the only beautiful bit of me was my feet — and I signed up with a specialist agency. It was quite lucrative, but I had to take real care of my feet.

"I'm not sure I can imagine you in anything other than Birkenstock clogs and sandals," Bella said honestly. "Do you still secretly wear your wedding shoes?"

Apart from Aunt Nan, Bella was the only person who knew that the first thing I'd done when I'd got engaged was splash out *hundreds* on the ivory satin wedding shoes of my dreams, really girlie ones, with thin crossed straps over the instep, trimmed with lace and crystals . . . And yet several years later, the wedding was still just a dream.

"Yes, when Justin's out — he has no idea! I suppose it's a family tradition, in a way, what with Aunt Nan always taking afternoon tea on Sundays in her wedding dress, like a latter-day Miss Havisham."

"She looks very pretty in it," said Bella loyally, long acquainted with the vagaries of the Bright household.

"My wedding shoes are getting a bit worn," I said gloomily, "but it's not looking like they're going to be carrying me up the aisle any time soon."

"So, Justin's penny-pinching, critical of your clothes, appearance and friends, has gone off the idea of marriage and children . . ." summed up Bella.

"Mummy Dearest doesn't help, pouring poison into his ear all the time. She seemed to loathe me even more about the same time Justin went all skinflint. And Justin doesn't even respect my work; he always talks about it as if it's a hobby, rather than my job."

My compulsive habit of twisting colourful fuzzy monkeys out of pipe cleaners and leaving them hanging about all over the flat also seemed to be driving him mad.

"Well, that's the minus side," Bella said brightly. "What's he got going for him?"

"Apart from being tall, charismatic and handsome? Aunt Nan always said he was like Dr Kildare from some old TV series, and when I looked it up on Google I could see what she meant. Only she also said she'd never trust a man who looked like that!"

"So he's tall, handsome and also a well-paid young orthopaedic consultant — which probably means he can delegate evenings and weekends to some lesser doctor, doesn't it?"

"Yes, it's not really the sort of thing you get called out in emergencies for. But he's actually not so young any more, he's about to hit forty. I do wish he wouldn't go on as if we're practically living on the breadline. He was even miffed when I wouldn't accept an allowance from Lars, though I don't see why the poor man should pay out for me, when my mother was married to him for only a couple of years."

"Nice of him to offer."

"Lars keeps trying to persuade me to change my mind, but I won't. I do accept his lovely presents, though."

"So come on, what other good points does Justin have?"

"Charm — though he doesn't often direct it at me these days. And he can be very affectionate and persuasive. He says he wants me to lose weight only for my own health, for instance . . ."

"Yeah, right."

"But then, he loves my baking and sulks if there's nothing in the cake tin, or I haven't made a fresh bara brith loaf."

"All that baking's not exactly going to help you with the weight loss, is it?" Bella pointed out.

"No, not really," I sighed. "He does think the foot modelling is a good thing. He's quite proud of my doing that, oddly enough, and tells everyone I have beautiful feet. He doesn't even object to my slathering my feet in Vaseline each night and then wearing cotton socks in bed."

"Secret foot fetishist?" she suggested doubtfully.

"Maybe . . . but you can't build a relationship on that! No, I think we've been drifting slowly further and further apart and perhaps he doesn't really love me any more — or not the real me. And I want the Justin I fell in love with, not this version," I said sadly.

"Maybe there's an 'IOU a wedding' voucher in your Christmas present from him?" she suggested.

"I doubt it. I know he gets the wife of his best friend to buy my presents because they're always the caramel-coloured cashmere jumpers she wears herself — the ones I pass on to you, because that's the last colour that suits me."

"I love them, but it would be nicer if you had a present that suited you instead," she said. "Did you leave Mummy Dearest a present? I take it she's moving in for Christmas as usual?"

I grinned. "Yes, and her present is a plastic cactus plant in a pot. It flashes on and off and plays '*La Cucaracha*' if you go near it."

"Justin used to buy you flowers and chocolates all the time, didn't he, and book expensive seats for musicals? Robert didn't do any of that so I was terribly envious!"

"He's stopped that, and though he did give me perfume for my birthday, it was the flowery sort I don't like. I'm strictly a spicy, mellow sort of girl."

"Flowery sounds like the sort of thing Mum gives me, too."

"I think your parents would get on like a house on fire with Justin. He'd live in a minimalist, clinical white box if he could, though you'd think he'd have had enough of that in the hospital during the day."

"His mother sounds almost as bad as mine, the way you told me she clears your things away whenever she comes to stay in your absence. I never feel the flat is really my home when I can never have things the way I want them, and Mum walks in and out tidying things away and rearranging everything."

"She should respect your privacy a bit," I replied sympathetically. "Apart from the intrusion when Mummy Dearest messes about with my belongings, the worst thing is that Justin *lets* her do it! Every last book, ornament, fuzzy monkey, even my shoes and clothes, will be in the boxroom when I get back after Christmas."

"That's so hurtful!"

"Yes, but Justin can't really seem to see it, and when I lose my temper, he's the one who goes all hurt!" I then looked at her and said gratefully, "Oh, Bella, it's been so good to talk it all through with you, because I feel I'm sort of coming to a crisis point, wondering if Justin is the right man for me after all, especially when my heart is up here in Sticklepond. Aunt Nan is worrying about the same thing, going by what she said yesterday. She agrees with me, that I need to have it out with Justin when I get back, not let our relationship drift any further. And that's what I'm going to do."

"I think you're right. And I don't know what I'd do if I couldn't talk things through with you either. I really need to find an escape route so Tia and I aren't living in Mum and Dad's granny flat for ever. But meanwhile, let's try and put our problems out of our heads for the moment and get as much enjoyment out of Christmas as we can," she suggested bravely. "After all, it's Christmas Eve tomorrow!"

CHAPTER
THREE

Trashed

My mother's family moved to Southport from Wales when she was a child. A lot of people think all the Welsh are small and dark, don't they? But that's not so, and Mother was tall, fair and very pretty, with a smile like liquid sunshine, while my Lancashire father was the small, dark one! A big store in Southport employed Mother as a mannequin when she left school. Twice a day she was dressed in the latest fashions and driven along Lord Street in an open carriage as an advertisement, and then she would model clothes and hats in the shop, too. This would be some time in the 1880s, I expect.

Middlemoss Living Archive
Recordings: Nancy Bright.

We had a wonderful Christmas, quiet and peaceful, with the world and its worries firmly shut out. At the back of my mind lurked the fear that this might be my last one with Aunt Nan, and I wanted to enjoy each precious moment just in case . . .

I had some lovely presents. Aunt Nan had knitted me a zipped cardigan in rainbow stripes, Lars sent me a richly coloured carpet bag (something I had always longed for) filled with goodies like chocolates, a purple silk scarf covered in butterflies, and a long string of chunky beads made from semi-precious stones.

I don't know how he can judge what I will like so exactly, and yet Justin, who is supposed to love me, gets it so wrong. I mean, I never wear matching *anything*, even a cashmere twinset, and certainly not in taupe, a colour that makes me look like a dead frog.

Lars rang me from New York, where his daughters and grandson, Charlie, were staying with him, to wish me and Aunt Nan Happy Christmas. Then I rang my mother in California, a token gesture Aunt Nan always insisted on, even though I'm not sure Immy remembers who I am half the time. I suppose I should be grateful my name is on her Christmas card list!

I left Justin to ring me, rather than the other way round, since I didn't want to get Mummy Dearest, but it was so late when he did that I'm sure he had almost forgotten me, which was hurtful . . . and he'd certainly forgotten what it was I'd given him until I asked him if he liked his white silk aviator scarf and the enormous box of Turkish delight, a particular favourite of his.

Luckily he didn't ask me if I'd liked the taupe twinset and he didn't mention the plastic cactus I'd given Mummy Dearest, either . . .

"Miss you, darling," he said in a perfunctory sort of way, before ringing off.

"Me too," I said, though really I just missed the warm place in my heart where I felt loved and wanted by the old Justin, rather than this new, critical one — and anyway, by then I was talking to empty air.

★ ★ ★

Timmy who, along with his partner, Joe, was staying with his parents in Ormskirk for Christmas, visited on Boxing Day. He's a firm favourite of Aunt Nan's. She says he has funny little ways, but he's a kind, good-hearted lad. He'd hand-quilted her a rose-pink bed jacket, though she said it was too nice to wear to bed and promptly put it on over her skirt and cardi. I wore the hat he'd made me, too — I'm not sure how he managed to knit it into a twisted spiral ending in a tassel, but it looked stunning.

Bella popped in with Tia, who wanted to show us some of her presents. She was wearing mine, a lilac fairy dress with matching wings, and since she has Bella's slender build, ash-blond hair and pale blue eyes, she looked as if she'd just escaped from *A Midsummer Night's Dream* and might fly away at any moment.

I gave Bella Justin's present. "It's a cashmere twin set, and though it says taupe on the label, it's more of a snotty grey-green really," I said, "so I don't know if it will do anything for you, either."

"I see what you mean," she said, pulling a corner out and looking at it doubtfully. "Mum might like it, though."

"If not, it can go to a charity shop," I said. "It's a good label, so I expect someone will be glad of it."

We all (except Tia, and Joe, who was driving) had a generous glass of Aunt Nan's Meddyg and got quite merry and Aunt Nan told them all about my plans for turning the shop into a wedding shoe emporium. The idea really seemed to have captured her fancy now she'd had time to think about it. Everyone was enthusiastic and had various suggestions to make though, after a second glass of Meddyg, some of those were not entirely sensible. I mean, there can't be that many tall, handsome princes looking for shoe-fitting jobs, can there?

I set off back to London on the Monday after Christmas, resolutely intending to have things out with Justin, but also secure in the knowledge that if it all went pear-shaped I could move back to Sticklepond.

Perhaps that was part of the problem? I'd been constantly torn two ways, between Justin and home, but if we couldn't resolve our differences and rekindle our love, then I would have to abandon my hopes of a happy-ever-after and a family, which would be a hard thing to do . . .

Bella had suggested going it alone, with a sperm donor, but I didn't feel that route was for me: I wanted any child of mine to be brought up in a loving family relationship.

Even though Justin knew when I was returning, he wasn't there when I arrived at our basement flat near Primrose Hill, but out playing golf. I suppose I should have been grateful he'd remembered to leave me a note.

Even if I hadn't known that Mummy Dearest had spent Christmas there, I'd have quickly guessed, because the flat was back to arid white minimalism, and all the homely touches I'd added, like the brightly coloured throws and the rainbow of fuzzy pipe-cleaner monkeys hanging from every possible place had vanished.

This time she hadn't just pushed them all into the boxroom, but right out of the house and into the wheelie bin, among a lot of expensive discarded giftwrap and the flashing cactus I gave her!

She hadn't touched my work for the current *Slipper Monkey* book, of course, because I'd started locking everything personal or precious in a tin trunk when I was away, after the first time I'd returned to find everything jumbled about and was sure she'd had a jolly good rummage through my stuff.

But even so, she'd gone *way* too far this time! The flat might belong to Justin, but it was also my home — and he'd just let her do this?

My blood boiling, I rang him on his mobile, golf or not.

"Oh, you're back, darling! I didn't think you'd be home until later this afternoon," he said.

"I told you I'd be back just after lunch, but from the look of the flat you'd think I'd never lived here!" I told him furiously. "And this time your mother's not just hidden my belongings away, she's put half of them out with the rubbish!"

Justin disclaimed any knowledge of this. "I realise she tidies the place up, and she knows I don't like clutter, but I'd no idea she'd actually thrown anything out."

"Well, she has, and this time she's gone *way* too far. You'll have to tell her so."

"Look, it's my shot so I'll have to go. We'll talk about this later," he said soothingly.

"*And* the rest," I snapped. "We need to talk about *much* more than your mother, Justin!"

"Later," he assured me, though I'm sure he hadn't taken in what I'd said. "Bye, darling!"

I'd simmered down slightly by the time he'd got home, and he'd stopped on the way to buy flowers, wine and chocolates, so clearly it had finally penetrated his thick skull that I was just a trifle upset about Mummy.

As always, I'd forgotten just how stunningly attractive he was, with his tawny hair and bright blue eyes, and my resolve wavered slightly for a moment when he kissed me . . .

Then he apologised for his mother and I pulled myself together and said resolutely, "It's not just your mother that's the problem, Justin. I've been doing a lot of thinking while I've been away and we have several issues we need to resolve."

"*Issues?*" he echoed, blue eyes wary.

"Yes. We seem to be drifting along, never discussing anything important, and I'm not prepared to carry on the way we are now."

I ran my fingers through my hair, which I'd piled up loosely secured with two pink chopsticks, and it promptly came undone and fell in long, ravelled dark curls down my back. "I popped down to the shops after I rang you, and I ran into Rae with Charlie — it was the nanny's day off — and we had coffee together," I added, which might have seemed irrelevant, except that seeing little Charlie had really brought it home to me that I should have had a family by now, just like we'd planned when we fell in love.

The fact that he didn't like Rae or Marcia had always been one of the best things about Justin and now a cloud seemed to pass across his sunny, good-humoured face at the mention of my younger stepsister's name.

"I'd have thought you'd have run a mile at the sight of either of your stepsisters. You're always telling me how mean they were to you after your mother married Lars and you came to London to stay with them."

"Yes, they were, but I was probably too sensitive and should have stuck up for myself more."

I'd always lived up in Lancashire with Aunt Nan. I don't even remember my grandmother, Nan's sister, Violet, because she'd died when I was only two, but she didn't sound any more maternal than my mother and, goodness knows, I'd seen little enough of Imogen over the years! But Immy's second husband, Lars, was such a sweet, kind man that he wanted me to be part of the family unit and insisted I stayed in his London house (he has a home in New York too) while I studied graphic design. But his two daughters, both older than me, were tall, slim and blondly attractive, just like Lars and my mother, so I felt like an ugly little dark goblin child foisted into the family. They made my life absolute hell too, from criticising my clothes (quirky, black and a bit Goth) to stealing my boyfriends. Lars didn't know the half of it and he was quite hurt when I quickly moved out into a rented flat with Timmy.

"Rae hasn't been so bad since she got divorced and had Charlie — and at least *you* don't find her irresistible, like every other man!"

He looked uncomfortable. "I think you know the sort of woman who appeals to me by now, Tansy!"

"Charlie's lovely," I said wistfully. "He's started school full time and he's very chatty. He looks just like Rae, too. No clues to who the father is there!"

Rae got pregnant about a year after her divorce, simply because all her friends were, I felt sure. She wouldn't say who the father was, though she hinted he was a wealthy married man. Someone must have been subsiding her lavish lifestyle, because I knew for a fact that Lars gave both his daughters moderate allowances and expected them to earn the rest themselves. He was easy-going to a point, but totally inflexible in other ways, as my mother found when she decided to move on to husband number three.

Marcia, the older sister, earned her living as an actress of course, but apart from a little modelling when she was younger (like Imogen) Rae had lived an expensive life of leisure. *Someone* must have been paying for it.

I sighed. "Justin, time's passing and I never thought I'd get past thirty-five and still not be a mother! When we got engaged, we were going to get married and have a family within a few months. What's happened to us?"

"Children are expensive," he said defensively.

"But you're earning loads and I'm doing really well with my books. Other people raise families on much less," I pointed out. "You seem to have turned into a total skinflint over the last few years."

"I've had other commitments — in fact, I've been helping Mummy out with a bit of a loan from time to time," he admitted.

I stared at him. "What? But your father left her loaded!"

"Nothing's worth as much as it used to be, is it? Some of her investments haven't been doing well and she's not very good at living within her means."

"Can't you tell her to draw her horns in a bit?" I asked. Not that I was suggesting she really had a devilish little pair of horns, you understand, though sometimes I'd suspected there might be, under that bouffant beige-blond hair. And maybe there was even a hint of a forked tail under her cocktail frocks . . .

"I'm doing my best," he protested.

"No, you've been putting her before me and any chance of a family," I pointed out bitterly, a bit stunned by this revelation. "Anyway, children aren't *that* expensive. They don't have to go to private nurseries and prep schools, or expensive boarding schools. We could manage. Assuming I can still get pregnant, of course."

"Oh, come on, Tansy," he said impatiently, "of course you can get pregnant!"

"Justin, I'm serious: I went to a private clinic and had a fertility MOT and it wasn't the best result possible."

"You did *that,* without telling me?" he said, looking taken aback.

"I tried to discuss it, but you kept shying away from the subject. Anyway, I did it, and although it showed I still had some eggs, I'm running out of time."

He came over and sat next to me on the sofa, putting his arm around me. "I'm sure they were just erring on the side of caution, Tansy, and things aren't that bad," he suggested. "You're only thirty-six, after all."

I turned to him. "Justin, what's happened to us? When we got engaged there wasn't any talk about waiting for children. We were going to start a family as soon as we got married. Not that we've got married, either, have we? I thought you were joking when you said we'd set a date for the wedding as soon I got down to a size eight, but you weren't!"

"I just want you to slim down for your health's sake. You're carrying a bit too much weight . . . though sometimes it's hard to tell under all those weird outfits you wear," he added, eyeing today's bright pink and orange ensemble critically. "Isn't it time to stop dressing like an art student and smarten up a bit? Mother said you would look quite chic with a decent haircut and in the right clothes."

"I'm surprised she remembers what I look like at all!" I said tartly. "And she wouldn't like me even if I'd been gilded by Cartier and dressed by Gucci. But you used to say my clothes were zany and fun, just like me, and you didn't like skinny women."

"There's something between skinny and overweight, though," he said.

"Well, whatever I am, Aunt Nan says I look fine to her. And goodness knows, dieting never works — it just makes me hungrier, so I go off the rails and eat much more. It's a vicious circle."

"Your aunt Nan doesn't like me. I think she's been poisoning your mind about me over Christmas and getting you all upset," he said, which was pretty rich when Mummy Dearest must have spent the entire Christmas season pointing out all my shortcomings!

"Aunt Nan expected us to get married long before this. She doesn't believe in living together beforehand; it's not how she was brought up and it upsets her. But at least she *wants* us to get married — *your* mother's desperate to get rid of me."

"Of course she isn't," he insisted unconvincingly. "You have to admit, though, that we don't have a lot in common, so naturally she's worried that things wouldn't work out. Perhaps you could try to win her round a bit — wear something a little more ordinary when you see her next."

"I don't have anything more 'ordinary', and the way I dress expresses the inner me — so if you don't like that, or my weight, then maybe you don't really like *me* either?"

"Of course I do — I love you!" he protested. "And if you lost a stone, not only would you be healthier, but it would increase your chances of getting pregnant too — and you wouldn't want to start a pregnancy overweight, would you? You'd never get the excess off afterwards. Look at Leonie!"

Leonie, one of his friends' wives, had gone from being a bonily chic woman, all knobbly joints and neck tendons like a chicken, to a plump, dishevelled mother in the space of a year.

"She looks fine to me, better than she did before the baby," I said.

"Do you think so?" He smiled at me ruefully with a sort of boyish charm and I remembered Aunt Nan's Dr Kildare remark. When Justin looked most trustworthy, was he really the opposite?

"Let's not argue about it any more now, Tansy. I can see what the clinic said upset you, though I'm sure they were being alarmist. And Mother really has been insensitive about your things, so I promise I'll speak firmly to her about it. We can sort things out."

"*Do* you still love me, Justin?" I asked curiously, half-afraid of the answer.

"Of course I do," he assured me, giving me another hug. "Look, perhaps we just haven't spent enough time together lately. I'm working all hours, and what with you off to Lancashire a couple of times a month and Mother wanting to see as much of me as she can, the opportunities have been few and far between."

"And the golf, don't forget — you weren't addicted to *that* when we first met!"

"It's healthy to get out and about. You should try it."

"I don't think so," I said firmly.

We used to get out and about together, taking walks in the park, but it was a long time since we'd done that, and even our social lives had been becoming increasingly separate. I didn't much care for his friends and their wives, and he loathed my more bohemian circle. He wasn't even that keen on Bella, who wasn't arty in the least!

"I can see we both need to make some changes — and some plans. I'll tell Mother I can't keep helping her out financially, for a start," he promised, a new light of determination in his eyes.

He gave me another, enveloping hug and kissed me. "We've been drifting apart, and we mustn't let that happen. Let's go away after the New Year on our own and have a romantic break — talk things through and make some decisions about our future."

"Not at your mother's or somewhere near a golf course?" I asked suspiciously.

"No, some little country hotel we've never been to before."

I relaxed, feeling that perhaps there was hope of rekindling our love after all. "Sounds perfect!"

CHAPTER
FOUR

Philtred Out

My youngest sister Violet — or Viola, as she called herself later, when she turned into little Miss Fancy Pants — was tall and fair like Mother, and so was her daughter, Imogen. She and her husband adopted Imogen, but she was a Bright all right — I'll get to that later, dear. I'm not ready to talk about it just yet. You let me work up to it in my own time. And I'm afraid it's all going to come as a bit of a shock to my niece, Tansy . . .

Now, wet the tea leaves and we'll have another brew, because my throat's that parched from all this talking!

Middlemoss Living Archive
Recordings: Nancy Bright.

We saw in the New Year with the promise of our romantic weekend to come. Justin was much more his old self, but still dropping hints that if we set a date for the wedding, it might inspire me to lose weight, so he hadn't entirely changed back! But when he was being warm, charming and affectionate it was hard to resist him.

Even so, my heart longed to be up in Sticklepond with Aunt Nan. I was worried about how frail she'd become, as if a brisk breeze would blow her away. Just as well I had Bella to keep an eye on her! I rang her every day for an update — and to exchange thoughts on turning Bright's Shoes into a wedding shoe shop.

The shop had been closed for a week after Christmas and now, according to Bella, Aunt Nan had entirely relinquished the day-to-day running of the shop to her and just happily pottered about, chatting to customers and holding a sort of court in the kitchen with an endless succession of visitors, from the vicar to most of the Sticklepond Women's Institute.

Of course I spoke to her every day, too, and she told me that Hebe Winter had been to see her.

"Doing the Lady Bountiful, as usual, even though her great-niece Sophy's the one in charge now up at Winter's End, with *her* daughter, Lucy, learning to manage the estate. She was trying to find out what I put in my Meddyg again, but I'm not telling anyone — well, apart from you, lovey. And you mustn't reveal it, either."

"Oh, no, I'll keep it secret," I assured her. "I've got some fermenting in the airing cupboard now, though it always tastes better made in summer with fresh herbs rather than dried, doesn't it?"

"It works just the same, though, that's the thing," Aunt Nan said. "I credit my daily tot of Meddyg with my getting to this age at all. I've had a good innings . . . That Cheryl Noakes has been again, too. I've told her we need to get a shift on with the recording sessions. I won't be around for ever."

"Aunt Nan!" I hated it when she alluded to a time when she wouldn't be here any more, however cheerfully she seemed to be looking forward to going, as if it was some sort of extended holiday.

"Now, our Tansy, there's no point in not being ready when you can see your time is nearly up," she said practically. "But when you hear the recordings, lovey, I hope you won't think too badly of your great-aunt Nan. Things were different in the war."

"What things?" I asked, puzzled, and wondering if Aunt Nan had a skeleton in her cupboard — though if she had I was sure it would only be a tiny one, because she couldn't have done anything very bad!

"Have you thought any more about the shop, Tansy? I liked the idea of it becoming a wedding shoe shop, if you think it would work in such an out-of-the-way place."

"All the time," I admitted. "I can't seem to stop thinking about it and I've even worked out a business plan. I'll tell you all about it when I come up the weekend after next. I wish it was this weekend, but Justin's booked us in somewhere for that romantic break he promised me, and we're going to have a real heart-to-heart discussion about everything. I think he understands a bit more how I'm feeling now, and that we can't go on like this. We need to set a wedding date and start a family soon, if we're going to do it at all."

"I should think so! And I'm glad you and Justin are getting along better, even if it means you won't be moving back home."

"Sticklepond will *always* be my real home, and if I took over the shop I'd have to spend a lot more time up there, even more than I do now . . . but then, Justin's forever at his mother's house or out all day playing golf, so I expect it would work out."

"It's a funny old world," Aunt Nan said. "But if you're sure he's the right man for you . . ."

"Of course I'm sure," I said, though deep inside there were still sometimes niggles of doubt.

He hadn't yet explained to his mother that he couldn't carry on giving her financial support, for a start, but he insisted he would do it after we'd been away for the weekend. He did sound resolute about it, though, which was surprising considering he was generally like butter in her little red-tipped talons.

But the romantic break never happened, because Bella called me the very day after Hebe Winter's visit to say that Aunt Nan had fallen in the night, bruising herself, though fortunately not breaking anything, and she'd found her when she went to open the shop.

"I called an ambulance and they think she's had a mild stroke," she said, and I told her I'd be on my way within the hour.

Justin was at work, so I left him a note explaining and then a text on his mobile — but I knew he would understand. He'd have to.

Unfortunately, he'd have to cancel our hotel booking . . .

Aunt Nan looked frail and small in the hospital bed, but after a couple of days she was well enough to sit up, attired in Timmy's lovely rose-coloured quilted bed jacket, and criticise the thoroughness of the cleaning and the quality of the food.

Then she insisted on coming home, aided and abetted by her friend Florrie, who was constantly to be found by her bedside, eating grapes and picking the pips out of her dentures.

"Don't make a fuss, lovey," she told me when I suggested she shouldn't discharge herself. "I've got the medicine, though I doubt it'll cure anything that Meddyg can't, and in any case, my heart's wearing out and there's no medicine to stop that."

"I can't bear it when you talk like that, Aunt Nan. What would I do without you?"

"Daft ha'porth," she said fondly.

Once she was home she seemed to pick up and was adamant that she wasn't going to take to her bed all day until she had to, even if she did need help with the stairs. One of Florrie's daughters was a retired nurse, and came every morning to help Aunt Nan to wash and dress. Then she installed Nan in her comfortable chair in the kitchen by the stove, from where she could hear what was happening in the shop if Bella left the door open, or hold court with her friends.

I offered to pay for the nurse, but she insisted she had a little nest egg put by for emergencies. "And for my funeral, of course: that's all planned." Seeing my face, she added, "Now, don't look like that, lovey, because my heart's failing. It's tired, and so am I. I'm wearing out and I'm ready to go."

"Yes, but I'm not ready to let you go."

"You'll have to. I'd have liked to have lived long enough now to see this wedding shoe shop of yours get off the ground, that's the only thing — but then, when you're called, you're called."

She seemed quite happy about the thought of her imminent demise, giving me cheerful directions for her disposal: there was room in her parents' grave and she wanted to be buried in her wedding dress and veil, which was touching: her heart had always remained loyal to her fiancé, Jacob, killed in the early years of the war.

The dress, which was of white silk-satin, simply cut on the bias and with a modest sweetheart neckline, was looking fairly worn by now, since of course she put it on every Sunday afternoon for high tea. Originally it had had a lovely lace coat to go over it which ended in a train, with leg-of-mutton sleeves that buttoned tightly at the wrist and satin inserts to match the dress, but this was now much shorter, since Aunt Nan had at some time let the dress out considerably by using part of the train to make extra panelling in the bodice. But the veil was pristine.

"I'd no ring of my own — we hadn't much brass for a fancy engagement ring — but I've got Mother's Welsh gold wedding ring." She told me where she'd hidden what good jewellery she had — a small gold locket and one or two other family bits and bobs. "Just in case I leave the scene suddenly," she explained.

I opened my heart to Raffy, the vicar, about how upset it made me that she seemed to want to leave me like this, and he said I must respect her wishes and that sometimes the elderly had just had enough. Then he said her firm belief in God and the hereafter was a huge comfort to her.

"Yes, she seems to be positively looking forward to 'getting to the other side' and meeting up with her family, friends and fiancé again, even if it does mean leaving me behind."

"I think she'll always be with you in spirit," he consoled me gently, but I was sure Aunt Nan would be good for a few more years yet, if only she hadn't got it into her head that her time was up!

Having got to ninety-two, why shouldn't she make her century? I simply found it impossible to accept that there was nothing to be done, so one evening I decided desperate measures were called for and I'd go up to Winter's End and consult Hebe Winter.

Hebe's reputed to dabble in the Dark Arts, though that doesn't seem to stop her being a keen churchgoer. But actually, Aunt Nan always said she was more of a herbalist than a witch, unlike Florrie. (And I was sure she must be wrong about Florrie, and Gregory Lyon was really just running some kind of witchcraft folklore group, not a coven at all!)

Anyway, many people made the trip at twilight up to the side door of Hebe's still room at Winter's End and came back with a potion or lotion — love philtres in some cases, I'd heard! Perhaps I should have tried one of those on Justin, who'd said it was too late to cancel the hotel for the previous weekend and had taken Mummy Dearest instead!

I'd told Aunt Nan I was going out to meet Bella, but instead I walked up the back way to Winter's End, cut across the bottom terrace and knocked at the side door to Hebe's stillroom, which she opened as if she'd been waiting for me. She was not at all surprised at my request, either.

"I understand what you want," she said, "but if I knew of something that would prolong your aunt's life, I would already have given it to her. There are things that can help with the pains and aches of old age, but nothing that can cure it."

She herself was no spring chicken, but still tall, beaky-nosed and upright; I didn't think death would be creeping up on *her* any time soon.

"That Meddyg, as she calls it, is probably what has kept her going this long. I'd love the recipe . . ." hinted Hebe, when I asked her about payment for the consultation. "I can guess what several of the herbs she uses are — like mint, for instance — but there's a little extra something in it?"

"I'm sworn to secrecy," I told her firmly. "But perhaps I could do with a love philtre to make my fiancé love me for what I am," I half-joked, "rather than all the things he would *like* me to be."

She looked searchingly into my eyes. "But would you want the love of a man who cannot see your finer points and with whom you cannot be your true self?" she said acutely and accurately, then insisted on mixing up a bottle of greenish fluid for me, because she said I needed a special tonic and I was to take four drops in a glass of water every morning. Then she charged me a huge amount for that and sent me on my way.

I'd told Immy (via email, the main way I communicated with my mother) about Aunt Nan being ill, but she'd shown little interest. Lars, who heard the news when he phoned the flat and Justin told him what had happened, was much more concerned and sent a huge basket prettily planted with pink hyacinths in moss.

Aunt Nan said he was a great daft lump, wasting his brass like that, but I could tell she was delighted and the flowers perfumed the whole house with the promise of spring to come.

I started taking Hebe's tonic, because it was kind of her to give it to me, but it tasted quite foul and I didn't feel any different, so I quickly gave it up.

I'd dashed up to Sticklepond without much thought about how long I would be there, but with Nan fading gently by the day, I soon knew I wanted to stay with her.

I explained this to Justin when I rang him and he was very understanding, though he said he missed me and this time actually sounded as if he meant it! Since I'd explained to him how I was feeling, I thought that he'd stopped taking me for granted quite so much.

Then I asked him if he'd told his mother yet that he wouldn't be funding her extravagant lifestyle any more and he said no, he'd found it impossible face to face, so he'd sent her a letter, instead!

Honestly! Still, at least he *had* done it.

"I'll try and get back for a night soon to see you," I promised. "I need to pick some more clothes up and the stuff for the latest book, if I'm going to be here for a while."

Justin was amazingly quiet for a few days — not even firing off texts asking where his favourite socks were, or his best silk tie, or that kind of thing — so I assumed that Mummy Dearest was giving him a bit of trouble over the letter. I hoped he wouldn't buckle under like he always had in the past, especially without me to give him support, so, since Aunt Nan insisted that she could manage for a night without me, I decided to dash down the very next weekend.

It was, in any case, the anniversary of our engagement — not that *he* would remember that, without prompting!

"You do right to get back and see what that man of yours is doing," Aunt Nan urged me. "It's fatal to leave them on their own for too long."

"I think what with his work, his mother, and his golf, his time is pretty well occupied," I said. "I'm going down more because I need to fetch all the stuff for my new *Slipper Monkey* book than anything, but I still don't like leaving you, even for one night."

"Florrie's Jenny will be in as usual, and then Florrie herself is coming to spend the night, so you've no need to worry about me."

"I'm sure that will be lovely," I said a bit doubtfully, because Florrie was even older than Aunt Nan, though amazingly spry and active. "And Bella will be in to mind the shop on the Saturday, though she will have to bring Tia with her, if you don't mind, because her parents are off to some function or other."

"Not at all: Tia's a sweet little thing, and Florrie and I will amuse her in the kitchen. That's settled, then. In fact, I will enjoy the weekend, because Florrie and I have no secrets and it's good to share memories of when we were girls. Mind you," she added with grim humour, "I've not many secrets left from that Cheryl Noakes now, either! She's a good listener, I'll say that for her, and she's promised to give you a set of the archive recordings when I'm gone."

"I'm really looking forward to listening to them, Aunt Nan."

"I hope you think the same after you have," she said enigmatically. "Now, the sun would be over the yardarm if we had one, so why don't we have a nice glass of Meddyg? Cocktail frock optional," she added with one of her sudden grins.

"I think this dress I'm wearing probably *was* a cocktail dress once," I said, looking down at my gold chiffon layers, "only the original owner wouldn't have worn it with a tapestry waistcoat, striped tights and Birkenstock clogs!"

"Oh, I thought it was one of those Gudrun Sodastream ones you get from that catalogue."

"Sjödén," I said, and went to fetch the Meddyg.

CHAPTER
FIVE

Charlie's Aunt

My sister Rosina, who died of diphtheria as a toddler, had black curly hair and dark eyes like Father and me, and though she didn't grow up enough to tell, I expect she'd have been a bit on the short side, too. Tansy now is very much what I was at her age, so clearly the darker Bright genes are reasserting themselves, just like they said in a telly programme I watched, when they were going on about that monk.

No, I don't mean Rasputin, lovey — he was a Russkie. It was Mendel, and he worked something out about genes by looking at his pet rabbits.

Middlemoss Living Archive
Recordings: Nancy Bright.

There were no parking spaces near Justin's flat, so I had to leave the Mini round the corner and hope to move it closer when I loaded my things up next day.

Justin seemed pleased to see me, sweeping me off my feet and giving me a big hug and kiss, and then he pretended he hadn't forgotten it was the anniversary of our engagement when I mentioned it. He said he'd booked a table at our favourite local Greek restaurant already, which I expect he had once he knew I was going to be home that night, because we often went there on a Saturday anyway.

"And since you've had things out with your mother, we can celebrate being rid of one financial burden, too," I suggested.

"Yes . . . she's gone a bit quiet since I wrote to her explaining, but I'm sure she'll realise why I can't carry on helping her out to such an extent when she's thought it over," he said optimistically. "But you mustn't even hint that you knew about me lending her money, Tansy — promise?"

"Of course I won't. Not that I'll ever get the opportunity anyway," I said, because Mummy Dearest always puts the phone down without speaking if I answered it and she never visited the flat when I was there.

In fact, it had been lovely to come back and not find all my belongings in the boxroom! Justin *had* tidied things away a bit, so no brightly coloured pipe-cleaner monkeys swung from any of the shelves or light fittings, but it was a definite improvement.

This flat had always been his rather than ours, so setting up home together somewhere else would, I thought, be so much better. I could assert my love of colour a bit more and Justin would just have to get used to it.

When I went into the kitchen to make coffee, I thought how little of me there was in this flat even when Justin's mother hadn't been here hiding any sign of my existence. Most of my belongings and the majority of my shoe ornament and vintage wedding shoe collections were stored in my bedroom in Sticklepond.

I was dreamily conjuring up a mental picture of a little country cottage in the Home Counties somewhere, roses round the door and maybe a baby buggy in the hall, when the doorbell pealed, breaking my reverie.

I put another cup on the coffee tray in case we had a visitor and took it through into the living room — just in time to hear the unmistakable high-pitched voice of my stepsister Rae exclaiming furiously from the direction of the hall.

"Justin, you bastard! I've only just got your message because I've been away — and if you think I'm going to let you shirk your responsibilities and cut my maintenance payments just so you can swan off and marry Tansy, you've got another think coming!"

I stopped dead, ice trickling down my spine, and then carefully put the tray on the table.

"*Quiet!*" hissed Justin urgently. "Are you mad, coming round here like this?"

"Oh, come on, Daddy told me that Tansy's up in Lancashire with the old bat, so you don't get rid of me that easily."

She must have barged past him because suddenly she was in the room. She caught sight of me, frozen to the spot, and her jaw dropped.

"The 'old bat' was well enough to leave overnight," I said evenly, in a voice that didn't sound in the least like my own. "What did you mean, Rae, about Justin paying you maintenance money?"

Justin, who'd followed her into the room, flushed angrily. "It's nothing, Tansy. You misheard," he said quickly. "I'd loaned your sister some money and told her I needed it back, that's all."

"As *well* as your mother? Have you taken up moneylending as a sideline?" I suggested acidly, while my mind whirled and computed and came up with an almost unbelievably horrible possibility . . .

"No — actually, I only lent money to Rae; Mother's got plenty of her own. But I didn't like to tell you, because I know you two don't really get on."

I suppose doctors often have to think on their feet, but it wasn't good enough to fool me. Anyway, both their faces gave the game away. Justin looked angry and guilty in equal measure, while Rae looked guarded and slightly worried, creases sharply pointing downwards on her usually smooth forehead.

"Whoever's been doing your Botox, I'd ask for your money back," I told her.

"I don't know what you mean, Tansy, but it's true about Justin giving me a loan, when I got into a financial scrape," she said quickly, backing him up. "I couldn't ask Daddy because you know what he's like — thinks we should stand on our own two feet and earn anything above the allowance he gives us. He'd be furious if he knew how much I'd got into debt. But now Justin's suddenly demanded it back without warning, because you two are finally getting married."

"That's not going to wash — do you think I'm stupid? Rae, you said 'maintenance' and that Justin was

66

trying to shirk his responsibilities. *What* responsibilities?"

Rae threw herself down on the cream leather sofa and sighed. "Well, it was worth a try, but I can see that the game's up. The truth is, Tansy, that we had a teensy weensy little affair a few years ago."

"How many years ago?" I demanded. "You'd never met until you came back over here to live after your divorce and I was engaged to Justin by then!"

"That's right, it was just after I came back."

My head and my heart struggled to take this in. That first year after I'd got engaged to Justin, the time I remembered as full of sunshine, love, happiness and promise for the future, had in reality been just a sham . . .

"Tansy, I can explain," Justin said desperately. "I'm so sorry. But it wasn't an affair, just a mad impulse, and it was always you I loved."

"But you said you didn't even like her!"

"I don't. In fact, I think I hate her. I don't know what got into me."

"I think I can guess," I said. "But Rae, how could you do that with my fiancé?"

She shrugged. "Justin was so indifferent to me when we met, making him change his mind was too much of a challenge to resist."

My world was rocking, shifting onto a different axis, and things were clicking into place with the sound of deadlocks slamming shut. "So, this maintenance you mentioned . . .?"

"Justin's paying for the result of his little mistake," Rae said silkily. "Charlie."

"Charlie is *Justin's*?"

Now my suspicion was finally confirmed, I felt truly sick.

"He certainly is — and it's only right he should support his son, isn't it?"

"And the rest," Justin said bitterly. "You wanted extra to keep your mouth shut about who Charlie's father was and you've got increasingly greedy."

"It's not greed — it's necessity. Charlie needed a nanny, and then private nursery school wasn't cheap . . ."

"And he's at private pre-prep school now, isn't he?" I said slowly. "No wonder you were always moaning about economy and saving money, Justin, and stopped talking about us getting married and starting a family. You already had one!"

"No, Tansy, it's not like that —" he began, coming towards me with the evident intention of taking me in his arms.

I backed away. "Don't you come near me! Everything — *every single thing* I thought we had together — has been one big lie, practically from the moment Rae came back to the UK!"

Rae stood up and slung her Mulberry satchel over one thin, angular shoulder. "I'll be off and leave you two to kiss and make up," she said. "But don't think you can stop paying for Charlie now that Tansy knows, Justin, because if you do I'll take you to court for maintenance."

"Just get out, Rae," I said. "I never want to see you again."

"How many years have you been saying *that*?" She sauntered elegantly to the door and turned. "Ever since you turned up in our midst like a little, ugly dark goblin, and Daddy insisted we treat you as a sister. As if!"

Then she slammed the door behind her, leaving a silence you could cut with a knife.

Justin attempted to justify himself and talk me round, but there were no words that could get him out of this fix. He might look like a big, guilty schoolboy, but this was slightly more serious than who scrumped all the apples out of the orchard, so saying it was me he'd loved all the time, and he'd let Rae bleed him dry so she didn't tell me what he'd done, just wasn't good enough.

"I was doing it to protect you — us!"

"If you hadn't slept with her in the first place, you wouldn't have had to," I pointed out. "And because she had Charlie, you put off marrying me and starting a family all this time . . . right to the point where it might even be too late for me to have a baby!"

I didn't see how I could ever forgive either of them for that.

"I'm sure it isn't too late, Tansy darling. Look, I know I've been stupid, but now that you know — if you can forgive me — there's nothing to stop us. I don't need to pay her through the nose any more and everything's changed."

"It has — changed irrevocably," I said. "I thought you were the only man immune to my stepsisters — the only one who truly loved me." Despite myself, my voice wobbled a little.

"I do," he insisted.

"Justin, I'm not sure you even know the *meaning* of the word, but even if you do, then you don't love me the way I am, or you wouldn't keep going on about my weight, and the way I dress and the things I say, as if I'm suddenly not good enough — just like Mummy Dearest always tells you."

"Leave Mummy out of this. She'd love to see me married."

"Yes, to anyone except me!"

At this inopportune moment the phone on the table between us rang.

"Answer it, why don't you? It's bound to be Mummy Dearest herself!" I said bitterly.

He snatched it up and from his side of the conversation I'd clearly guessed right.

"Mummy, can I call you back? This is a really bad time and — no, of course I care that you're having a heart attack! Listen, Mummy, don't —" He paused and I could hear high-pitched and imperative quacking coming from the receiver. "Yes, all right, I'm on my way," he said resignedly, and put down the phone.

"Summoned to Tunbridge?"

"She's feeling really ill. I'm sure it's nothing but indigestion as usual, but I'd better go. I'll be back later tonight and then we can talk things through."

"I don't think we've anything further to discuss, Justin!"

"Look, I know you're upset —"

"That's the understatement of the year!"

"But you must understand it was just a moment of madness — weakness, vanity — call it what you like." He ventured one of his persuasive, glowing smiles, the one most women found irresistible. "I've been a fool, but I don't want to lose you, darling, and I hope you'll be able to forgive me. I'll ring you when I know what time I'm coming back."

"Don't bother!" I said tersely, then locked myself into the boxroom and cried until I heard him leave the flat. When I went out again, the place seemed even colder and emptier than ever and I felt much the same. I was shivering, though that was probably just with shock.

I washed my swollen red eyes with cold water, then went round the flat collecting everything that was mine and stowing it all away in whatever bags, boxes and suitcases I could find. Then I brought the Mini round to a handy space near the front door and packed as much as I could into it. I suppose it was lucky I'd always stored most of my stuff up in Lancashire in my old bedroom, as if subconsciously I'd known my stay here was temporary.

Only my little drawing desk and a couple of large portfolios remained, and I left those in the boxroom, with a note asking him not to let his mother throw them out until I'd got Timmy to come round with his camper van to pick them up for me.

I took one last look round at the sterile rooms, which resembled a minimalist stage set without all my brightly coloured bits and pieces, and then I was off — straight back north like a homing pigeon.

I could have stayed the night with Timmy and Joe, though they're the other side of London, but I didn't think of that until I was well on the way to Sticklepond, when it suddenly occurred to me that I couldn't just turn up early — it would be a shock to Aunt Nan — so I stopped at a motel chain for the night. I was in no fit state to drive any further that night anyway, really, because I don't think I'd stopped crying since Justin had left the flat and everything just kept playing over and over in my mind.

Justin texted me on my mobile several times, presumably after he returned and found me gone, but I deleted his messages unread. There wasn't anything he could say that could make this better.

CHAPTER
SIX

True Lovers Not

As well as the bara brith and Welshcakes, Mother taught me how to make Meddyginiaeth Llysieuol, which is Welsh for herbal medicine, though really it's a sort of honey mead with herbs and very good for you. I still make it and I've shared the recipe with Tansy, though I'm not giving it to anyone else. I've been asked for it time and again, and that Hebe Winter up at the manor would love to get her hands on it. She fancies herself as a herbalist but even she can't guess what the special ingredient is that Mother put in! Meddyg, as we call it in the family, cures most things except old age, though I expect a glass or two will help to ease me out of this world and into the next.

Middlemoss Living Archive
Recordings: Nancy Bright.

As I drove back towards Sticklepond I thought I should never, ever have left there in the first place. After all, I could have done my graphic design course somewhere close, like Liverpool.

Justin had so not been worth the years in London, which I could have spent with Aunt Nan instead . . .

though she'd been the first to urge me to spread my wings and see a bit of the world.

And if I'd never gone to London I'd probably be happily married to someone local by now, and not even known my wicked stepsisters existed. I meanly wished I could say they were as ugly as the ones in Cinderella, but they weren't, though Rae had certainly done a mean and ugly thing.

I hoped I'd never have to see either of them again, even if Marcia, the older one, was living up here since she'd got that regular part in the cast of *Cotton Common*. But Lars had said her flat was in Middlemoss, a few miles away, so with a bit of luck, our paths were unlikely to cross.

Lars himself was on my mind because he was bound to find out I'd left Justin at some point and ask me why. I was fond of him, so I couldn't tell him what Rae had done, or that Charlie, whom he adored, was Justin's, could I?

I felt a pang in my heart at the thought of the sweet little boy, who seemed by nature to be taking after Lars rather than his mother, which was a blessing. In features and colouring he looked just like the Andersons, very fair and with bright blue eyes, rather than with Justin's Viking tawny hair and ruddy complexion.

Ruddy Justin!

No, I couldn't face phoning Lars up and lying about my reasons for leaving Justin — not right now. Perhaps I'd feel braver later and think up a good story, or edit Rae out, or something.

I was overcome with hunger — emotion gets me like that usually; it was surprising it hadn't happened earlier — so I stopped for a carbohydrate-packed lunch, then called Timmy from the car afterwards and told him what had happened.

"Well, I can't say I'm really surprised, because we never liked him," he said. "He simply wasn't good enough for you, darling, but I'm terribly sorry you found that out in such a horrible way. Those stepsisters of yours were a pair of bitches to you, right from the moment you moved into their father's house. Bit like Cinderella, really, but without a prince to whisk you away."

"I was thinking that, though at least I didn't have to clean and cook, or sleep in the ashes. In fact, my stepfather was quite hurt that I wouldn't take an allowance from him! And you were my prince, letting me share the flat with you."

"No, I was your fairy godmother!" he said, and laughed.

"I'm going to ask you a favour now," I said. "I've managed to cram most of my stuff in the Mini, but I had to leave my small drawing desk and a couple of portfolios stacked in the boxroom of Justin's flat. Could you possibly collect them in your van sometime, and then bring them with you next time you're up here? The desk legs unscrew, so it's not too bulky."

Timmy's parents had moved out of the village to Ormskirk a few years ago, but it was only a few miles away, and he and Joe often visited.

75

"Of course I will, but it might be a couple of weeks because the van's in for repairs and it's going to be very expensive. But as soon as I get it back, I'll ring Justin and see when will be convenient to get them, shall I?"

"That would be great, thanks, Timmy. I'll tell him you're going to fetch them at some point. He keeps trying to call me and he sent me three texts while I was eating lunch, but I haven't read them. I just . . . can't face it at the moment, it's all like some dreadful nightmare. I'm all cried out and my eyes are so puffy I look grotesque."

"I don't suppose you feel at all forgiving. This is not something you can just get over and carry on after, is it?"

"No, it's the end of that part of my life — but a new beginning back with Aunt Nan. She's got really keen on the idea of turning Bright's into a wedding shoe shop and I think it will give both of us a whole fresh interest in life."

"It certainly will. It's a wonderful idea! And I can be your scout at all the vintage fashion fairs, looking for wedding shoes," he offered, because we often went to them together. "You can give me a budget and I'll buy anything I think you'll like or can sell."

"Thank you, Timmy, that would be great — and you know what to look for," I said gratefully, because some of the vintage shoes I bought hadn't been specifically designed as wedding shoes, but were pretty enough to be used for the purpose. "You're a wonderful friend — and Joe and Bella, too — What would I do without you?"

★ ★ ★

It was mid-afternoon by the time I turned off the motorway into the tangle of narrow country lanes that eventually brought me to Sticklepond High Street.

I drove past Gregory Lyon's Museum of Witchcraft (I remembered the days when it was still a dolls' hospital and museum, owned by two elderly sisters, the Misses Frinton). Attached to it was the artisan chocolate shop, Chocolate Wishes, owned by Gregory's daughter, Chloe, who had married the vicar . . .

Then, just before the Green Man, I turned right and then immediately left up the unmade lane to the space at the back of the cottage, behind the henhouse, where I usually parked the car.

It was quiet back there, just the ticking of the engine as it cooled and the crooning of hens. This end of the garden beyond the holly hedge arch was not so neat, and I noticed that the trellis along the top of the low wall dividing it from that of the neighbouring cottage was broken away from its post in the middle and sagged down.

I paused for a minute before collecting the first armful of my belongings and going up to the kitchen door where Bella, who had kindly popped round to see that Aunt Nan was all right, spotted me through the window while she was filling the kettle and opened the door to let me in.

I told Bella and Nan everything over a cup of hot tea and the last of the cherry scones Florrie had brought round with her when she came to spend the night. It seemed easier to tell both at once and get it over with.

77

". . . So I just put all my stuff in the car and came back. And that's it, Aunt Nan," I said, when I'd poured out the whole sorry tale. "I'm finished with him. In fact, I'm finished with love. There's going to be no Cinderella ending to my story."

"That stepsister of yours is evil!" Bella declared.

"Yes, that's what Timmy said, when I rang him to ask him to collect the rest of my stuff."

"She's behaved very badly, but Tansy's fiancé could have said no," pointed out Aunt Nan. "It takes two to tango."

"I desperately wanted children and all the time he was saying we couldn't afford it, he already had Charlie!"

"He's shown himself to be a man of no character whatsoever — and as for that stepsister of yours, she's a slut, there's no two ways about it," Aunt Nan said forthrightly. "I don't know what the world is coming to. It's more like Sodom and Gomorrah every day!"

"I'd pay good money to see Rae turn into a pillar of salt," I said with a watery smile.

"So, you're home for good?" Aunt Nan asked. "What about the foot modelling? And your books?"

"I don't need to be near the publishers, I can write the books anywhere, and I can always go down if they want to see me. Timmy's going to bring my desk and the rest of my art materials up eventually, but I can manage without it for a while. As to the foot modelling, I'd been turning down more and more assignments and I told the agency I was retiring when I got back after Christmas. I did tell you I was going to, because I'd had enough. It'll be lovely not having to put Vaseline on my feet and wear cotton socks in bed, or worry about bashed toenails and stuff like that."

"Oh, yes, you did tell me," she agreed. "I'd forgotten."

"After all these years of having to wear sensible shoes, well, I may go a little wild occasionally with the frivolous footwear, but I think I'm addicted to my Birkenstocks, really."

"And you'll take over the shop now, so Bright's will still be here long after I'm gone, even if it has been transformed into a wedding shoe shop?"

"Of course. And I think it should be called Cinderella's Slippers!" I assured her, giving her a kiss. Even in so short an absence I could see that she'd faded — or perhaps she'd been steadily fading before and I had only just seen then, with fresh eyes? "I just want to settle down quietly here with you now, Aunt Nan."

"That reminds me: we've had a bit of excitement up here while you were away, so it's not been that quiet," Aunt Nan said. "You know I told you about the cottage next door being sold about a year ago as a holiday home to an actress and her husband, though they'd not finished doing it up before she was killed in an accident?"

I nodded. "She'd just got a part in *Cotton Common*."

"So the papers said. Well, now her husband's moving in."

"How do you know?"

"There was a huge removal van blocking the lane most of yesterday and we could hear them — you know the dividing wall's not that thick," Aunt Nan said.

"I took the removal men some tea and biscuits round so I could try and find out what was happening," Bella confessed.

"I sent her," Aunt Nancy explained. "I may be on the way out, but I'm still curious."

"They said *he's* an actor too and he sold the house he shared with his wife down south after the accident, rented a flat and put most of their furniture into storage," Bella went on. "But now he's moving up here."

"If he's an actor, then perhaps he's got a part in *Cotton Common* too?" I suggested. "They do seem to have a large cast."

"The men said he'd told them he needed peace and quiet and that he's an edgy, abrupt sort of man, so maybe he's been ill and is just moving here temporarily till he's better," Bella said.

"What's he like?" I asked her.

"I dunno, he hasn't arrived yet. The removal men are still in there unpacking, but they've moved the van to the pub car park now. I suppose they got permission, because the people in the houses at the back were complaining that it was blocking the lane and they couldn't get their cars in and out."

"I did see him briefly when he came to look at the cottage with his wife just before they bought it," Aunt Nan said, "but I can't remember his name. I do recall he asked me how long I'd lived here and seemed surprised when I said there'd been Brights living on this plot since records began, but really she was the lively, talkative one, and very pretty. Tragic she died so young."

"If he's only seen it out of season, then Sticklepond may not be the quiet backwater he expects," I said.

"He *did* remark how quiet it was, now I come to think of it, and that you wouldn't know there was a shop here if you missed the sign on the wall at the High Street end of Salubrious Passage, so I couldn't have many customers."

"Of course you have lots of customers! Everyone knows you're here," Bella said.

"Yes, that's what I told him."

"What does he look like?" I asked.

"I can't really remember, lovey, except that he was a bit older than his wife and pleasant-spoken."

I pictured some silver-haired, elderly and irascible thespian, retiring to live out his days in the quiet backwater that was Sticklepond . . . except, of course, that lately it was less and less of a quiet backwater. A couple of years earlier, when that alleged Shakespeare manuscript had been discovered up at Winter's End, visitors had started flocking there in droves, and there were other attractions in the village as well, like the Museum of Witchcraft, the chocolate shop, a bookshop called Marked Pages, two pubs, and a whole raft of gift shops, craft galleries and cafés that had opened to cater to the tourist boom.

Sticklepond had once been a much larger and more important place, before the Black Death decided to cull so many of its inhabitants, but it was now firmly back on the map.

"It'll be odd having a neighbour after so long," Aunt Nan said. "The cottage has been empty since last year and just holiday lets for ages before that. But I'll be happier for knowing there's someone the width of a wall away when I'm gone and you're here on your own at nights, Tansy."

"I wish you wouldn't keep saying things like that, Aunt Nan! I'm not going to be here on my own for a long, long time," I told her firmly.

"Well, when you are, I'll still be watching over you — your guardian angel! That Chloe from the chocolate shop was telling me all about those yesterday afternoon. The vicar came to visit first, and then his wife came afterwards with the baby and brought me a chocolate angel. But we ate it."

"Didn't you save me a bit? Her chocolate is supposed to be wonderful!"

"I'm afraid we ate every last morsel — and it *was* wonderful," Bella said guiltily.

"There was a message inside it," Aunt Nan told me.

"A Wish, I suppose," I said, because Chloe specialised in making hollow chocolate shells in various shapes, with messages or "Wishes" inside, like a sort of yummy fortune cookie. "What did it say?"

"That imminent meetings with loved ones would give me much joy."

"It probably meant Tansy coming back," Bella said.

"No, I think it meant heavenly meetings with Mother, Father and little Rosina, not to mention

Jacob," Nan said thoughtfully, "though perhaps it meant Tansy as well."

"It meant just *me*," I said firmly. "I'm back and I'm here to stay — and if we're to transform Bright's Shoes, I'm going to need your help!"

"Well, I can't say I'm not glad to have you home, but I'm sorry it's turned out like this, lovey, because I'd have liked to have seen you married and with little ones. But at least you found out he was the wrong man for you before it was too late, that's the main thing."

"Yes, you're right," Bella agreed. "It would have been much worse to have found out about Charlie *after* you were married!"

"You two should get to work on the plans for the new shop right away," Aunt Nan said. "Because if you're going to do it, then there's no time like the present, and it'll keep you both out of mischief."

Working out the plans for the shop kept Aunt Nan amused too.

Florrie's daughter, Jenny, the retired nurse, continued to help Nan to wash and dress in the mornings, before she went downstairs to sit in her big shabby, comfortable chair in the kitchen, by the stove in its inglenook fireplace.

Here she received a steady stream of visitors, including the vicar, Florrie, her friends from the Women's Institute and even Felix Hemming from Marked Pages, who brought her a gift of one of the sweet, old-fashioned romances of the type she had often bought from him in the past.

Hebe Winter took to dropping in on her way to her Elizabethan re-enactment meetings, too, an alarming sight in full Virgin Queen rig-out, right down to the wig and huge ruff. Aunt Nan said she kept coming only because she liked playing the Lady Bountiful, and was also trying to wheedle the recipe for the Meddyg out of her, but I think they both enjoyed the visits really.

I left most of the shopkeeping to Bella, so I could be with Aunt Nan, because even though I tried to convince myself differently, I could see that my time with her was limited. I baked lots of cakes and biscuits for the stream of visitors, and ate a fair amount of them myself . . .

One afternoon, while Florrie was with her, Bella and I began a complete stocktake in the storeroom that had been partitioned off from the shop. It was cramped and cluttered, lit by one dim bulb, which I quickly replaced with something a bit brighter.

"I'll pull things out and you write them down," suggested Bella. "Looking at the dust, I don't think some of the stuff at the back has been moved for about half a century!"

Bella had to answer the shop bell once or twice, leaving me to rummage alone, and I turned up ancient treasures like plastic overshoes and old-fashioned court shoes made for fairy-sized feet.

Aunt Nan herself had tiny feet which, like people, seemed to have got bigger over the years. I might take after the small, dark Bright side of the family, but I was still several inches taller than Aunt Nan and my feet were size five.

"She really let the stocktaking slide for a few years," I told Bella when she came back.

"She's seemed interested in the wedding shoes lately, but I think the shop was getting a bit much for her before I started working here and she just kept it open out of a sense of duty. She's so much happier about it now that she can see that it has a future."

"I hoped involving her in the plans would give her a new lease of life, but . . . well, even I can see she's fading day by day," I said sadly.

"I know it's upsetting, but she's in her own home, which is what she wants," Bella said. "She's happy enough."

"I just can't bear the thought of being without her," I sighed. "I'm so glad you're living in Sticklepond too, Bella."

"My course starts again tomorrow night. There's only another couple of weeks to go and then I'll get my certificate, though much good it will do me in the current job market! Just as well I've already found work."

The course aimed to update office skills, though, as Bella pointed out, she didn't really have any to start with, except she liked playing with computers. "I've just put a card up in the Spar window, offering to do anything at home like typing or spreadsheets or inputting data, so maybe I'll be able to earn a little extra money."

"I'm sorry we can't give you more — or not yet, anyway," I said guiltily, because she wasn't getting much above than the minimum wage.

85

"It's all right. The shop's barely been ticking over and the short opening hours suit me, so I can spend lots of time with Tia. I'm not going to have any more children so I'd like to enjoy her childhood with her."

"At least you got to have *one* child, which is more than I managed," I said sadly.

"You're not that old yet — you could still find someone else."

"What, and then have one of the wicked sisters come and snatch him away before I could get him to the altar? I don't think so!"

"I don't suppose Rae would ever dare to show her nose up here, would she?"

"Probably not, but Marcia's in Middlemoss, don't forget. Still, I don't expect our paths will cross, and if Lars tries to persuade me into one of his happy family gatherings next time he's over here, I'll be sure and have a good excuse ready!"

"What's happening with Justin? Is he still trying to ring you?"

Justin had spent the first few days trying my mobile and Aunt Nan's phone, but I'd either ignored him or put the phone down on him each time.

"No, he's given that up, but he's still texting and emailing me, and I wish he'd stop. It only just seems to have dawned on him that I've left him for good and he's finding it hard to accept that I won't eventually forgive him and go back. I don't think Mummy Dearest is having that problem, though, because when Timmy collected my desk and portfolios, he said she was in residence and the whole flat looked so sterile you could eat your dinner off the floor. She watched him the whole time, too, as if he might load the Conran sofa into the van, when she wasn't looking."

"Justin must still miss you, if he's constantly trying to persuade you to take him back," Bella said. "But you couldn't forgive him for something like that, could you?"

"No, of course not! I don't know why he thinks he can talk his way out of it, but all his attempts to contact me just upset me even more. That's it — I've given up on love."

"Me too," Bella agreed. "Robert might have betrayed me in a different way by running up huge gambling debts, but I've had enough. He seemed so solid and dependable that I trusted him totally, but I've learned my lesson. No, I'll concentrate on being a mum and you can be Tia's favourite auntie — which you already are — and we'll turn Cinderella's Slippers into an astounding success!"

"I only hope you're right," I said fervently.

CHAPTER
SEVEN

Old Valentines

Another Welsh delicacy is laver bread, which isn't bread at all, but a sort of stewed seaweed. Mother used to say how wonderful it was fried up in a bit of bacon fat for breakfast, but when she brought some back from a trip to see her relatives — well, it was such a disappointment! Father said it looked like seagull droppings, and to be honest it tasted the way it looked. Not that I've ever tasted seagull droppings, of course, dear, that goes without saying . . .

Middlemoss Living Archive
Recordings: Nancy Bright.

Justin's emails and texts had started out all apologetic, persuasive and loving, upsetting me and making me miss him . . . or the man I'd once thought he was.

But then his missives slowly turned sulky and indignant, which was easier to deal with and just strengthened my resolve. He was so used to getting his own way that it must have been quite a shock to his system to find I wasn't going to go running back to him. I shouldn't think any woman had ever turned him down before!

Unfortunately, both he and my first love were still regularly featuring in my recurring Cinderella dream, which was definitely a nightmare now that one prince had dumped me and the next dumped *on* me by making out with my stepsister!

I supposed the whole Cinderella thing was going through my head all the time because I was working on ideas for the new shop, but it's a pity you can't turn your subconscious off at night.

Timmy and Joe came up to spend the weekend with Timmy's parents in Ormskirk, and brought my desk and portfolios over early on the Saturday evening.

Aunt Nan had quickly become fond of Timmy's partner, Joe, so their visit perked her up no end, especially discussing the design, layout and colour scheme of Cinderella's Slippers. Timmy had a really good eye for colour and ambience and Joe was good on practical matters, especially lighting, since theatrical lighting was what he did for a living.

Aunt Nan retired to bed early, as she often did, and when I'd seen her comfortably settled the boys and I went to the Green Man to meet Bella, whose mother was baby-sitting Tia.

"How do you think Aunt Nan is looking?" I asked Timmy hopefully. "Quite perky?"

"Frail," he said frankly. "She does love the idea of you and Bella making over the shop and keeping it going after she has gone, though. You can tell she's tickled pink."

"She was knocked back a bit by the stroke, but she's made a good recovery," I insisted.

89

"But she often goes to bed in the late afternoon now, and she wouldn't do that before," Bella said gently. "You have to accept that she's fading away, Tansy."

"She'll pick up again when spring arrives," I said stubbornly. "It's only that she's convinced herself her time is up, but if she gets *really* interested in Cinderella's Slippers, I don't see why she shouldn't make her century."

"Well, we'll all drink to that," Timmy said, but I could see they were just being kind. Deep down, I knew they were right: I was whistling in the wind.

We updated Bella on the ideas we'd discussed earlier with Aunt Nan and Joe said, "So now *we're* all excited about the shop too!"

"*And* I've just found a great designer online called RubyTrueShuze, who does lots of vintage-style wedding shoes. Some of them have really interesting trimmings made out of lace, feathers, pearls or crystals. They're lovely and very different," I enthused. "I forgot to tell you about her. I've emailed her, to see if we can stock them."

"And you're going to sell actual vintage wedding shoes too, aren't you?" asked Timmy. "Or vintage shoes suitable for a wedding."

"Yes, I thought they'd make a good publicity angle, though I don't suppose I'll sell that many of them."

"I know someone who makes lovely embroidered satin bridesmaid's slippers for children, from toddler size upwards," Joe said. "She can match them to the colour of the dresses."

"That sounds interesting. I do need to stock bridesmaid's shoes."

"She has a website — here's her business card," he said, passing it across. "I brought it, in case."

"Things are really starting to come together," Bella said. "I can't wait to open the new shop!"

"We have to have a big closing-down sale and then a total redesign and restock, before then," I said, but I felt excited about it too — and it was a distraction from my broken heart.

Seth Greenwood and Sophy, who had been playing darts with the other Winter's End gardeners, kindly stopped on their way out to ask how Aunt Nan was doing.

Sophy looked pregnant again to me, so maybe Aunt Nan was right about there being something in the water in Sticklepond! But if so, it was probably already too late for me, even if I tried to find someone else . . . which I wasn't going to do.

Then all our plans for the new shop had to go on hold, because Aunt Nan had another small stroke and then went quickly downhill. She seemed to have suddenly released her grip on life and was preparing to coast down into death quite cheerfully.

I had to concede defeat.

I let my mother know that if she wanted to see Aunt Nan, she'd better plan a trip very soon, but the only reply was a get-well-soon e-card via my email address.

I displayed it on the screen to Aunt Nan as she lay propped up in bed, but with the jingly music turned down.

"Well, I'm underwhelmed, to say the least, lovey! But I suppose it's something that Immy managed to get her mind off herself for five minutes to send it," she said sardonically, then shut her eyes and went back to sleep again.

Aunt Nan no longer left her bed and Florrie's daughter, Jenny, kept popping in to keep her comfortable, while the doctor, an old friend, came daily.

Towards the end she dozed most of the time while I sat by the bed, holding her hand. She woke occasionally, murmuring a few random comments, as though she'd been mentally running through a final to-do list while asleep. You'd have thought she was going on a long cruise, rather than leaving life for uncharted territory!

Well, uncharted to *me*: Aunt Nan seemed pretty clear what was on the other side.

"Remember that I've always been proud of you, lovey, and I've been that pleased about your children's books being such a success."

"I know, and they've certainly turned into a good little earner, providing I keep two new ones a year coming out."

"Money isn't everything, but I've put a bit by for you. You'll need something to live on while you get the new shop going."

"It could take a while to build up the new business," I admitted. "But I have some savings too, because I've always invested the foot modelling fees."

"Very sensible. But you want to keep that for a rainy day."

"I don't think it can get much rainier," I said sadly, feeling the tears spring to my eyes.

"Promise me two things, lovey," Aunt Nan said next time she woke up, after a tiny sip or two of Meddyg.

"Anything!"

"Bury me in my wedding dress and veil."

I nodded, mutely.

"And those wedding shoes you showed me, that you bought when you got engaged — wear them to the funeral."

I couldn't help laughing. "Aunt Nan, I'd probably fall over in heels!"

"And you go on with your plans to turn Bright's Shoes into Cinderella's Slippers as soon as you can. What was that last advertising slogan you and Bella came up with?"

"'Don't trip down the aisle, float down it'?" I suggested. "Or Joe's: 'If the shoe fits . . .' — That's a good one and really ties in with the name of the shop."

"Cinderella's Slippers . . ." she murmured. "Well, I hope one day *your* prince will come to find you, Tansy. Not a tarnished one like that Justin, but a good honest man with a true heart, who'll appreciate you."

"I'm not sure they exist any more, or not outside the pages of novels, anyway," I said sadly.

"They do. My Jacob was one, and soon I'll see him again," she said confidently.

And in fact at the last, though her eyes were open on this world, she seemed to be seeing some other, more wondrous place than the little bedroom over the shop where she was born, for she whispered, "Beautiful!"

Then she sighed happily and my beloved aunt Nan was gone.

But then, it *was* Valentine's Day, and time for lovers' trysts.

CHAPTER
EIGHT

Amazing Grace

We grew up happily enough in this cottage and Father ran the shoe shop. Some people still wore clogs then, and he would mend those and repair shoes, harnesses or anything made of leather, as well as selling work boots, Wellingtons, shoelaces, polish and so on. We're a bit out of the way, tucked in off the High Street down Salubrious Passage, but everyone for miles around knows about Bright's.

> Middlemoss Living Archive
> Recordings: Nancy Bright.

We closed the shop for over a week — I don't think it had ever been shut for more than a day before that. Aunt Nan's friends rallied round, especially Florrie, and so did mine, but it was a dreadful, bereft time in which I didn't see how I could go on, without my great-aunt.

Having my heart broken, and then losing the person who had been mother, grandmother and great-aunt all rolled into one in such a short space of time . . . well, it was almost too much to bear, and I felt consumed by a black hole of unhappiness.

Lars sent a wreath and would have come over for the funeral with the least encouragement, despite only having met Aunt Nan once or twice. He assumed Justin would be there to support me, though, and I didn't disabuse his mind of this idea. I couldn't face telling him the truth just then.

Of course, I'd also let my mother know, though, true to form, Immy made a weak excuse and stayed away. Word somehow also got round to Justin and he emailed and texted sympathetically, wanting to come and support me at the funeral. That just made me cry and feel even more bereft and alone than I had before, because Aunt Nan wouldn't have wanted him there and, when it came down to it, neither did I.

Everything was all done exactly as she had planned it, right down to the rich bara brith I baked, the funeral version that's more like a cake, for the small gathering in the Green Man's function room afterwards. I wore my ivory satin wedding shoes, which probably looked a little incongruous with my dark tapestry coat, and they got so muddy that that was the end of them: I took them off and tossed them into the grave. It seemed fitting. I'd almost worn them out while waiting for the wedding, anyway.

When the vicar called a couple of days afterwards he commented on what a joyous occasion it had been, with practically the entire village turning out for the service. I was running on empty by then, not being able to face food (highly unusual), but alleviating my sorrow with Meddyg. I offered him some, but he settled for a cup of tea instead.

Being a relative newcomer, Raffy didn't know all the ins and outs of my upbringing, but enough to be deeply sympathetic.

"This must have hit you extra hard, Tansy, because I'm told you've always lived here with Nan."

"Yes, Aunt Nancy brought me up, though she was my great-aunt really."

"So you're an orphan? I noticed there weren't any other members of your family at the funeral. But of course your friends were there, and your aunt's closest friends, like Florrie."

I only hoped he hadn't noticed Florrie making some obscure, furtive and presumably pagan sign over the grave at the end, but I had a suspicion he had. And goodness knows what was in that bunch of greenery she'd tossed in after my shoes!

"Oh, no, I'm not an orphan," I said. "But my mother was a young, unmarried model when she had me and I was an encumbrance, so she parked me with Aunt Nan and that was that. I used to spend some of the school holidays with my mother later, but I was always glad to come home again."

"What about your father?"

"Apparently he was quite a well-known pop artist in his time and did a record sleeve for some group that's now a collector's item. He's way older than Immy — my mother — and he lives in India. I went out there to find him a few years ago, but though he was kind enough, he wasn't terribly interested, and drink and drugs had addled his brain to the point where he kept forgetting who I was."

"That must have been disappointing."

"Not really. I'd heard a bit about him before I went and I was just curious. I met my ex-fiancé on the plane coming back . . ."

Raffy didn't comment on this obviously thorny subject. "I can see that your aunt was your rock."

"Yes, I don't know what would have happened to me if she hadn't taken me on. I'd probably have ended up in care, because my grandmother died when I was two and Immy's first husband didn't want to know about me."

"Your mother's married more than once?"

"Oh yes, three times. The second one was a rich American manufacturer called Lars Anderson, who was totally different from the first husband and wanted me to make my home with them and his two daughters by his first marriage. But I didn't want to leave Sticklepond and Aunt Nan, especially after I met my stepsisters." I smiled wryly. "*They* certainly weren't going to welcome me into the family."

"Wicked stepsisters?"

"Yes, but not ugly ones . . . that was partly the problem."

Suddenly I found myself pouring out to him a part of my past I normally preferred not to dwell on. "I did stay in Lars' London house with them all when I went down to start my graphic design course, but my stepsisters made my life such hell that I moved into a flat with some of my college friends instead. Lars was quite hurt, but he didn't understand what the girls were like when he wasn't there. He's always been a bit blinkered about them, though he can be very firm too, especially about them earning their own money rather than relying on him."

"So, your mother divorced him?"

"Yes, but Lars still takes an interest in me and looks me up when he's in London — he's a lovely man. Both daughters have made their homes over here now. The elder, Marcia, is an actress living in Middlemoss, but Rae is living in the London house with her little boy . . ."

I felt another pang and added, "Lars is always trying to get me and the girls together for a big family reunion, but sometimes I wish he'd just let me go."

"So where's your mother now?" Raffy asked.

"Immy married her plastic surgeon a few years ago and moved out to California, where she seems to be trying to turn herself into a Barbie doll. That was another thing with the stepsisters," I added bitterly. "They were tall, fair and pretty — much more like my mother than I was, because I take after the darker side of the family — and they all shared the same interests: men, fashion, clothes and gossip. They were like three sisters and she sided with them even when they were bullying me. She was my mother, yet it was me who felt like the cuckoo in the nest! Rae and Marcia called me an evil little goblin."

"Nice," he said. "That must have *really* endeared them to you."

"They stole my boyfriends when they could, too. Recently I discovered that Rae, the younger one, had an affair with my fiancé, and that her son is his. That's why he is my ex and I've moved back here."

"Poor Tansy, you have been having a time of it," Raffy said sympathetically, his lovely turquoise-green eyes sincere.

I managed a wavering smile. "I feel better for having unburdened myself — that was quite unintentional!"

"That's what vicars are for. Chloe says she'd love to pop in and see you, too, if you felt up to visitors?"

"Of course," I said, thinking that if Raffy, ex-rock star, was the unlikeliest vicar you ever saw, then his wife, daughter of the pagan and somewhat eccentric proprietor of the Museum of Witchcraft (who was not only a self-confessed warlock but the author of many lurid black magic thrillers), was an even more unlikely vicar's wife.

But then, her artisan chocolates were heavenly! My spirits rose slightly as my mind took a new tack.

"Actually, I wanted to ask her if she might make a special line of chocolate shoes for me to sell in the shop when it goes totally bridal."

"I'm sure she'd be delighted. And I'm glad you've started thinking about the new shop, because your aunt was really keen that you should get on with it, she told me so."

"Yes, she made me promise I'd carry on, so I must ... and a Chocolate Wishes shoe would be the perfect wedding favour, wouldn't it?"

"It certainly would. I'll tell her to pop round."

As he shrugged himself into a very un-vicar-like long black leather coat he asked, "Any sign of your new neighbour yet?"

"No, so perhaps he's changed his mind, or his health took another turn for the worse, or something," I said. "Nan said he was an elderly actor."

When Chloe came she brought her baby, Grace, with her, who has the same amazingly greeny-blue eyes and dark hair as her father. Chloe's even smaller than I am and very pretty, with a slightly elfin face, a bit like Kate Bush. I didn't say so, though, because she was probably just as fed up with people saying that as I was with being likened to Helena Bonham Carter, just because we both liked to dress a little differently from everyone else.

Chloe'd brought me a chocolate angel and a geranium in a pot. "It's scented and has red flowers. Red geraniums are for protection," she told me.

"Against what?"

"Sadness, bad vibes," she shrugged. "I just felt it was what you needed."

"Thank you — and I love scented geraniums."

"Do you? I've got lots of different kinds. I'll take some cuttings for you." She sat down, holding Grace, and the baby started trying to push herself upright, as though her mother's knees were a springboard.

"Raffy told me about your plans for Cinderella's Slippers," she said, taking a firm grip on her lively offspring, "and that you'd thought of selling chocolate shoes?"

"Yes, I want to stock all kinds of shoe-related things and they would make lovely wedding favours, wouldn't they?"

"I'm sure you're right, but I'd have to have special shoe-shaped chocolate moulds made — though that would be a one-off cost, of course," she explained. "Then I hand-make my Wishes from the best criollo chocolate, so they'd be quite expensive."

"People seem prepared to pay for the best, when it comes to a wedding, and they'll be very exclusive. Could they have a special Wedding Wish inside each one?"

"I don't see why not."

We discussed the design — a high-heeled shoe — and then the packaging, with each to be in its own little transparent box. I wrote it all down; Chloe needed both hands for the baby.

Before she went I thanked her for the chocolate angel.

"There's a Wish in it, but I don't know what it is, because I fold them and pick one out of the jar," she said. "But I'm positive this one will have come directly from Nan, because she's your guardian angel now — we all have one."

She seemed dead serious, and I remembered Aunt Nan saying she had talked about guardian angels with Chloe. It was a very comforting thought . . .

"It does feel as if she's still here," I admitted. "In fact, I keep talking to her, forgetting she isn't!"

"That's because she *is* in spirit," Chloe said.

I didn't tell her that I was sure I'd actually heard Aunt Nan's voice that very morning, telling me to stop moping around like a wet weekend. Grief plays strange tricks on your mind.

★ ★ ★

Later, I ate the chocolate angel, which was also very comforting. Chocolate so often is, and Chloe's was the most delicious I'd ever tasted. In the village rumour has it that her grandfather has put some sort of spell on it.

The message inside urged me to make good a promise, which I supposed was Nan's way of telling me to get on with Cinderella's Slippers, and also, possibly, my next book, which would be well overdue if I didn't get a shift on.

CHAPTER
NINE

Barking Mad

My sister Violet was a clever girl and went to the Grammar, but I left school early, as you often did then, and went to work for the village dressmaker, Jessie Sykes. I loved sewing and I was a sort of apprentice, you might say. I learned a lot from Jessie, and I made my own wedding dress — I'll show you later, I still have it. Jessie gave me the silk-satin for the dress itself and then Mrs Winter — Hebe's mother — gave me an old white lace evening gown and I managed to make a lace and silk coat with a fluted train out of it, like I'd seen in a magazine.

Middlemoss Living Archive
Recordings: Nancy Bright.

Bella reopened the shop and we started getting ready for the closing-down sale, set for 6 March, when everything except Aunt Nan's stock of satin wedding shoes, which were the sort of mid-heel classic court shoes that some brides still preferred, would be sold off at knock-down prices. We advertised in the local paper, and once word got out we didn't have a lot of customers, since everyone was thriftily waiting for the sale.

Bella and I, having already made a start on the stocktaking before Aunt Nan's final illness, now got on with it in earnest, making long lists and marking down the prices. I had to leave a lot of it to Bella, though, since there were a hundred and one things to be organised or sourced before Cinderella's Slippers could open, and as fast as I ticked one off the list, another three took its place.

I drafted adverts, commissioned cards and flyers, and contacted everyone I could think of for publicity — newspapers, Lancashire magazines, wedding magazines, local radio stations — you name it, I tried it. Bella set up a Cinderella's Slippers website, learning how to do it as she went along, and I set about trying to persuade Ruby, of RubyTrueShuze, to let me stock her shoes.

Then there were things like choosing paint colours (I needed several long phone calls to Timmy for that one), finding display stands, talking to Aunt Nan's accountant and organising the book-keeping.

Suddenly it dawned on me that we had left a bare two weeks between the sale and the reopening in which to transform the shop and I realised that I'd need a magic wand to get everything ready in time!

Still, once the die was cast, the panic and adrenaline *really* kicked in, and anyway, keeping frantically busy was one way of coping with my grief . . .

I missed Aunt Nan at every turn and I was looking forward to hearing the archive recordings of her memories when Cheryl Noakes, the archivist, gave me a copy. She'd been at the funeral and said she'd come round and see me soon.

One evening, feeling particularly lonely, I fetched down Aunt Nan's box of treasures, looking for comfort. She'd never been a great hoarder, so everything fitted inside the tin trunk she kept under her Victorian brass bedstead. When I lifted the lid a familiar scent of lavender filled the air and there were all my school reports and photographs, an album of faded family snaps and a ribbon-tied bundle of letters from her fiancé.

I didn't read the letters, but it did make me aware that I was about to become a spinster of the parish too, turning my back on marriage and children, with my life revolving around the shop. Of course, unlike me, Aunt Nan's decision was forced on her by the death of her fiancé in the war, while mine was forced on me by the death of my love.

Well, OK, perhaps it wasn't quite dead, but it had certainly shrivelled away to a poor little creature whimpering in the naughty corner.

At least Aunt Nan had been truly loved by Jacob, whereas I didn't think Justin could have truly loved me, or he wouldn't have wanted me to change. He still seemed to think he had — and still did — since, despite receiving little encouragement, he kept sending me sympathetic emails asking me how I was and telling me how much he missed me, and even all my bright touches about the flat and little fuzzy monkeys!

However, reading between the lines, I could tell that Mummy Dearest had practically moved into the flat with him and he was overdosing on smother-love, but it was his own fault for letting her.

His emails unsettled me and made me even sadder, especially when he begged me to let him come up. I was sure he was convinced that once I'd set eyes on him I'd fall into his arms, weeping glad tears, and he seemed incapable of grasping the fact that he'd done the unforgivable and that because of his actions I'd missed my chance of marriage and children. There could be no going back unless I was suddenly struck by selective amnesia.

Aunt Nan's solicitor called to say he'd had an enquiry as to whether I would consider selling the shoe shop and cottage.

"Your aunt turned down one offer from the people who bought the next-door cottage, and I know you have your own plans, but of course I had to inform you of the new enquiry."

"Of course, but *I'm* not selling either," I told him. "We thought the man who'd bought the cottage next door was finally going to move in, but he hasn't, so perhaps he's changed his mind and you could suggest that they might be able to buy that one instead? Unless they particularly *wanted* a shop, of course. They wouldn't get planning permission next door, because the whole building is listed now."

"I'll pass that to the solicitor who contacted me. You still intend to carry on the business, presumably? You did mention after the funeral that you had plans for it."

"Yes, only I'm going to specialise solely in wedding shoes."

107

"Solely," he said. "Ha, ha — good one!" and put the phone down.

Trust Aunt Nan to choose a mad solicitor.

I hadn't felt in the least like working on the next *Slipper Monkey* book, but I forced myself because of the looming deadline and, once I'd started, I found it very soothing to slip into a fuzzier, brighter world for a bit.

I was very into Japanese woodcut prints when I was at art college, which I think influenced my illustrations, and I still used a combination of spiky, fine black ink lines to suggest the underlying structure, and bright washes of watercolour.

I'd taken over one end of the big pine kitchen table, but I thought eventually I'd move into Aunt Nan's front bedroom and turn my old room, looking over the garden, into a studio. My little white-painted bed should just squeeze into the boxroom, in case I had unexpected visitors.

But for the moment, sorting out the shop took all my time and propping a drawing board against the edge of the table was fine.

Two days before what we hoped would be the Great Clearance we were almost ready for it, with "Sale Saturday!" posters in the window and pasted over the Bright's Shoes sign fixed to the wall of the High Street end of Salubrious Passage.

Bella had marked rock-bottom prices on everything, and we'd put out boxes of purses, laces, polish, suede brushes and tartan sponge inner soles.

Festoons of handbags swung from the hooks over the old wooden counter, which stood in front of the sliding door dividing the shop from the kitchen, and a line of umbrellas was hooked along the dado rail. All we needed now was a horde of customers hungry for a bargain!

I opened the shop that Thursday morning (we were still getting the odd customer for shoe polish, laces and things like that), because Bella was going to be late. Tia's hamster had developed a bald patch and so she was taking it to the vet first.

She was much later than I expected. I'd just come back into the shop with a mid-morning cup of coffee and was sitting behind the counter with paint charts and fabric samples spread out, trying to visualise the shop transformed into Cinderella's Slippers, when she finally turned up — and not alone. She had a large, unkempt and wild-eyed Border collie with her, tied to a bit of rope, which she more or less dragged over the threshold. The dog sat quivering on the welcome mat and refused to come any further.

"What on earth . . .?"

Bella looked hot, flushed, harassed and unusually dishevelled, with wispy strands of ash-blond hair hanging around her face. "Sorry I'm so late *and* about the dog, but I simply didn't know what to do with it!"

"Whose is it?" I asked, trying to coax it to stop shivering and come to me. The dirty-white tip of its black tail thumped tentatively on the mat, but it ducked away from my hand as if I was about to smack it on the head.

"Well, that's the thing," she said distractedly. "I was at the vet's with the hamster and a man came out of the surgery dragging this poor dog with him. He was really angry and yelling at the vet: 'You told me to bring him down here if I was going to destroy him, you didn't say you were going to charge me an arm and a leg to do it for me! I could do it easy enough myself, for the price of a bullet.'"

"How horrible!"

"Yes, it was. He was very aggressive. The vet followed him out and told him that just because the dog was useless at herding sheep, it didn't mean that he couldn't be rehomed as a pet and suggested he take him to the RSPCA kennels. But the man said he'd wasted enough time on him."

"He might at least have given the poor dog a chance!"

"That's what *I* chipped in and said, and that he couldn't possibly shoot the poor thing, because it wasn't his fault he couldn't herd sheep and someone would give him a good home." She smiled wryly. "Me and my big mouth! He said if I felt like that, then the dog was mine. He tossed the end of the rope at me and left."

"So — are you going to keep him?"

"How can I? There's no room in the annexe to swing a cat, and Mum was bad enough about the hamster — she'd go berserk at the sight of a dog hair or muddy paw marks. Dad would go into meltdown if he messed up his immaculate garden, too. It was a huge concession letting Tia have a sandpit in the corner behind the compost bin."

"I see what you mean," I said, and we contemplated the dog, who shivered even more and held one paw up in a very pathetic way. "So, *are* you going to take him to the RSPCA kennels?"

"I suppose I'll have to. The receptionist at the vet's offered to phone them and see if they would come and pick him up, but something came over me and I told her I'd keep him. Only, of course, once my sanity came back, I realised Mum wouldn't let me — and anyway, I've got enough on my hands trying to make a living and look after Tia."

"You certainly have," I agreed, then crouched down and made soothing noises to the dog. He let me stroke him, even though he flinched every time my hand approached him. "But I'm sure the kennels will find him a good home. He seems a nice dog even if he is a bag of nerves."

"I did wonder . . ." Bella said tentatively, "since you are living alone now and have that long back garden, if *you* might like him?"

"Not really," I said frankly. "I'd like a dog eventually, but I was thinking of something small and easy to manage, not a big, traumatised rescue dog!"

"Oh . . ." she sounded disappointed. "It's just I remembered you'd adored that spaniel you had when you were a little girl, and you're much more of a doggy person than I am."

The dog was by now leaning trustingly against my legs, but still holding up a front paw, alternating left and right.

"Why does he keep doing that with his feet?"

111

"The vet said he'd been injured just after the farmer bought him and while he was being treated the vetinary nurses had all made a big fuss of him, so now he thinks he might get a bit of sympathy if he holds his foot up. I don't suppose that horrible man would have paid for that treatment if he'd known the dog would be useless with sheep. But the vet said the foot had healed fine, and he's pretty healthy generally, just a bit neglected."

"He'd still cost a fortune in inoculations, insurance, micro-chipping and all the rest of it," I pointed out, fondling the dog's rough, matted head. "Bed, bowls, food, lead, brush . . ."

"He's called Flash," Bella said. "Perhaps it's because of the white tip to his tail."

At the sound of his name, the dog wagged his tail and then lowered his head quickly as though he'd done something wrong.

We both contemplated him.

"I don't know that he *would* have a big chance of a new home," Bella said, after a minute. "People seem to want puppies or small dogs mostly, don't they? And he looks as if he's been living outdoors, so I'm not even sure he's house-trained."

"Oh, great!" I said gloomily.

"Why, you're not going to take him on, are you? I mean, as soon as I asked I could see it was just as impossible for you as it was for me, and I must have been mad to suggest it when you're trying to start up a new business and everything."

"Yes, the last thing I need at the moment is to take on a neurotic, half-wild Border collie," I agreed, but then I really *must* have run mad because, to my utter horror, I heard my voice adding that I would give it a go and see if Flash and I could get on together.

I had to leave Bella holding the fort — and the dog — and dash out to buy all the things Flash would need. I returned an hour later with a hole in my bank account and a Mini piled high with dog bed, blanket, brush, food, dishes . . . you name it, I had it.

Bella must have put the "Back in Five Minutes" sign on the shop door, because she was in the kitchen with the dog, who was hiding under the table, though he thumped his tail at the sight of me staggering in through the back porch under a mountain of doggy essentials.

Bella said she'd pushed him out into the garden earlier, where he'd peed desperately on the nearest pot plant (probably killing it — there's nothing like dog pee for that) and then when a big, scary hen appeared through the privet arch at the bottom of the garden, he'd turned tail and fled past her back into the house again and hidden under the table.

"Oh, have the hens found another way out? I'd better round them up and block up the hole before a fox gets them." I put down my burden and added, resignedly, "In fact, I'll have to fence off the herb garden, fruit bushes and where I'm going to grow vegetables, or Flash will pee everything to death. But I suppose at least I could have the hen run reinforced at the same time."

"He's not at all snappy, just scared," Bella said. "He seems to like you, though!"

She went back to the shop while I coaxed Flash out from under the table and fed him. In fact, I hand-fed him, since he seemed to have a fear of his new dinner bowl, though he lapped up the water thirstily enough while I was putting his dog bed into the corner near the stove.

Then I got the brush and untangled his long black and white coat, cutting out the worst of the snarls. He suffered my ministrations patiently enough, though quivering with nerves throughout, so it was probably just as well it was a bit too cold for baths, even if I could have managed to get him into one. I gave him a good going over with some big aloe vera doggy wipes I'd spotted in the supermarket where I'd bought his equipment and that seemed to clean him up almost as well.

Bella said he looked like a changed dog when she shut the shop up and came to see how we were getting on.

"He's very handsome, now he's black and white instead of black and mud," I agreed. "I like the stripe down the middle of his nose and the white tip to his tail, but he seems petrified of everything — even his new dinner bowl!"

"I expect he'll soon get over that," she said optimistically.

After she'd gone home, I found the fugitive hens in the knot garden and lured them back into their run with food, then blocked the latest escape hole. The hens were all big white fluffy ones, which only Aunt Nan had been able to tell apart. But she always said it was

Josephine who found the escape routes and Jocasta, Jasmine and the rest followed. Cedric, being henpecked and timid, was usually last out.

When they were secured I went back and put the new collar and lead on Flash and persuaded him to follow me down the garden path, past the scary hens and my Mini, which was pulled in behind the plum tree.

My intention was to walk him up the little lane at the back, and round the streets to the green, but since I had to coax him past every new thing, from wheelie bins to a flapping bit of branch overhanging a wall, we didn't get more than a few yards from the back gate.

He had this really smart way of stopping me pulling him forward: he braced three legs and then clamped the lead to his chest with one front paw! I'd never seen a dog do that before, and although it was annoying I thought it was pretty clever. Then he'd just look at me, afraid and defiant all at once.

"You daft dog!" I said. "This is supposed to be a walk, not a drag."

The only sign of interest he showed was when the vicar walked past the end of the lane with his own small white dog, though they didn't notice us and, as soon as they had gone, Flash turned tail and towed me back to the safety of the garden.

CHAPTER
TEN

Cat Flap

Of course, after Mother had her first stroke I had to leave off the dressmaking, because I was needed at home, and then during the war we all had to do our bit, in one way or another. I'd had rheumatic fever as a child and my heart was supposed to be not very strong, so I wasn't sent to work in the factories or anything like that — and yet you see I've outlived both my sisters and almost all my contemporaries!

Middlemoss Living Archive
Recordings: Nancy Bright.

I went downstairs in my bare feet next morning, which was a big mistake, since I discovered *way* too late that Flash had had the Galloping Gourmets all over the quarry-tiled kitchen floor. The feel of it coldly squishing up between my toes was grim, to say the least.

Flash was in his new basket curled into the smallest possible space, a cowed, shivering and petrified jelly of a dog, but there was no point in being cross with him, since I was sure he hadn't been able to help it. I just hoped he didn't make a habit of it, because there wasn't going to be a lot of time in the near future for house-training.

I made reassuring noises while tossing newspaper down over the mess, then broke out the disposable vinyl gloves and disinfectant wipes and gave my feet a good going-over, after which I encouraged Flash out into the garden.

He stayed just outside the door while the mopping up was going on and stared anxiously at me through the glazed lower pane with his slightly mad amber eyes throughout this proceeding. Then he followed me down the garden when I went to let the hens out: it was getting late, and for the last half-hour Cedric the cockerel had been emitting a steady volley of high-pitched crows like a cheap travel alarm clock.

He shut up abruptly as I opened the pop-door to the run and then was unceremoniously jostled to the back of the queue by his wives, as usual.

Flash had hung back a bit, but once he'd grasped that the hens were staying inside their pen (I'd blocked up where I thought yesterday's escapee had got out) he got quite cocky, sniffing at them through the wire mesh — until one of the matrons gave him a hard stare and he put his ears down and slunk off behind the plum tree.

Bella had arrived and let herself in when we went back to the house. She was very apologetic about the dog's lapse, which I told her she might well be, seeing she'd foisted Flash on to me!

"I feel even guiltier now," she said contritely.

"Well, it wasn't the best start to the day, *or* to our relationship, but I'm sure he couldn't help it," I assured her. "He's certainly not going to be an easy dog, though, because he seems terrified of everything."

He even had to be encouraged to eat his breakfast, because he had such Acute Fear of Dinner Bowl syndrome that I'd started to wonder if there was anything that he *wasn't* afraid of!

Not surprisingly, I'd forgotten to check for any eggs when I let the hens out, so Bella popped down to do that while I made us some coffee before we flung ourselves into the final day of getting ready for the sale.

I also intended going out later to buy paint, brushes, filler and a hundred and one other things we'd need for redecorating, plus a certain kind of spotlight fitting for the window, which Joe had suggested.

Bella brought back two speckled brown eggs and the news that a red vintage Jaguar had gone past our gate and pulled into the parking space at the end of the garden next door, closely followed by yet another removal van, albeit a small one this time. "But it's still blocking the lane, so no one further up can get out."

"Sounds like the owner's moving in at last, then."

"He must be, but I couldn't see him without going up to stare through the trellis when he got out, which might have been a bit rude, so I don't know what he looks like."

"You'd probably have had a long wait anyway, because I expect the poor old thing is as vintage as his car," I told her. "Come on, it's ten — we'd better get going."

We'd shut today in order to make the final preparations without interruption — but as we filled the small window with odds and ends of shoes, boots and slippers with the practically pre-war prices clearly displayed, quite a lot of people gathered to peer in.

It was a relief to retire back into the shop itself, where we crammed as much as we could of the remaining stock onto the stands, along the shelves and even in rows along the floor in front of the wall, three deep. Handbags were hung in clusters on the ceiling hooks behind the counter, and I put all the purses and wallets in a big wicker basket just in front of it.

There were still stacks of boxes in the back room, but we pulled them near to the door, ready to replenish the stock in the shop as it vanished. I so hoped that the shop and stockroom would be nearly empty by the following evening, ready for a Cinderella's Slippers magical transformation!

As I laid out a stack of the unexciting gusseted brown paper bags with pinked tops that Aunt Nan had always used, I suddenly exclaimed, "Carrier bags! Of course, we need some really classy ones with the Cinderella's Shoes logo. Why on earth didn't I think of it before?"

"Or me," Bella said. "You'll need them in various sizes too, and perhaps you ought to get a stack of tissue paper, to wrap smaller items in."

"Just as well I've already worked out the logo for the shop sign," I said, and went off to surf the internet for suppliers, then place an express order for reams of white tissue paper and ivory glazed paper bags with ribbon handles and the name of the shop, enclosed inside the outline of a high-heeled shoe, all done in a rich gold. At least, I *hoped* it was a rich gold, because I wanted to create a subtle and slightly sumptuous ambience, rather than an opulent and slightly tacky one.

When I went back to the shop, Bella said one or two brass-faced women had already knocked on the door wanting to buy items in the window, but she'd said no, tomorrow was first come, first served, and to get there early.

"Quite right too: it wouldn't be fair otherwise."

"I didn't recognise them as local people, so they must have seen the advert in the paper or one of the flyers, and come to look."

"I expect they'll be back tomorrow — and it does seem as if we might have a bit of a rush first thing, doesn't it? I hope we clear a lot of the stock!"

Bella made us a late sandwich lunch and kept an eye on Flash while I popped out for my paint supplies. When she'd helped me carry everything in, we were just about ready. I made sure there was a good float in the till, then, as an afterthought, made some little signs to dot about, saying that we only took cash, not credit cards, but that there was a cash machine in the Spar by the green. A card facility was something I was urgently looking into. It would be vital for Cinderella's Slippers. So would a proper till rather than the old-fashioned wooden drawer sort we had now. It would make life so much easier if I got one that not only calculated the cost and printed a receipt for the customer, but kept a record of every purchase for the accounts.

By then we were both feeling pretty exhausted and it was time for Bella to collect Tia from the birthday party she'd gone to straight from school. I saw to the hens, then gave Flash a little run up the lane, though actually, to be truthful, it was more of a drag again than a walk: I dragged him up the lane to the turning place at the end, and then he dragged me back again.

I noticed in passing (twice, the second time fast enough to leave furrows) that the red Jaguar was still parked at the back of the next-door cottage, but there was no sign of the new occupant. He was probably exhausted by the whole moving-in process, poor old thing.

If I hadn't been so tired myself, I'd have taken him some of the Welshcakes I'd made yesterday to welcome him to his new home and also warned him that next day might be surprisingly busy in the courtyard . . . or so I hoped!

His cottage, however, didn't front directly onto the paved courtyard, as ours did, but was set back slightly behind a low wall and further concealed by rampant rose hedging, so perhaps he might not even notice. Or if he did, maybe he'd come in and introduce himself at some point.

I persuaded Flash that his bowl wouldn't suddenly jump up and bite him if he dared to eat his food by standing next to it with one finger in his dinner (not something I really wanted to do twice a day), and then slumped in front of the TV in the parlour with my own supper.

After a few minutes, Flash timidly followed me in and lay heavily asleep on my feet, though every so often one eye would open to check I was still all present and correct.

I literally had to push him out into the garden at bedtime and he had what must have been the fastest pee ever before dashing back in again. Then I spoke to him sternly about asking to go out if he needed to go during the night, handed him a bone-shaped biscuit and went up to bed.

I had the Cinderella dream, only this time it was a disturbing variation. Ivo, my first love, was the prince and then Justin turned up just as he'd fitted the glass slipper to my foot, and tried to wrench it off again. I was still resisting when I suddenly awoke, kicking my legs like a rabbit.

I wasn't quite sure how to interpret that one: fear that success would be snatched away from me?

"*You great daft lump! You get up and get on with it,*" I heard Aunt Nan's voice say in my head.

"On my way," I replied out loud.

This time I entered the kitchen more cautiously, but Flash hadn't made any kind of mess, which was a relief. For the first time he was keen to get outside and seemed to favour peeing on the nearest rose bush, which was better than the herbs in the little knot garden but might not do anything to cure the black spot. The sooner I could have a bit of fencing put up to divide the garden into food-producing and dog-piddling areas, the better. One or two of the potted plants outside the back door were looking a bit sickly already.

I wouldn't need to fence much of the garden off, since I wouldn't have a great deal of spare time for gardening. I'd just concentrate on nurturing the fruit bushes that were already there, the plum tree and the rhubarb patch, and then have a strawberry bed, and lots of tomato plants and a bit of salad . . .

I came out of my dreamy little trance realising that not only was time ticking on, but Flash was staring back dolefully at me through the glass door, love locked out.

Bella arrived early, since Tia had gone to spend the day with her other granny, who luckily lived in Formby, not so far away, and Hilda was happy to collect her and bring her back. She and Bella had always got on well and Tia was her only grandchild.

I was more than glad to see Bella, for a queue of early-bird customers looking for bargains had started to form well before nine, and once we'd braced ourselves and opened the door, it was mayhem.

After that, a constant stream of customers trooped up and down Salubrious Passage and the little shop was so crowded, we had to let customers in a few at a time.

Luckily Florrie Snowball had come expressly to buy a pair of Cuban-heeled court shoes in a size so small they would have fit a fairy, and she declared that she would stay for a while to marshal the customers into an orderly queue. "I can keep an eye on them shopfitters too," she added darkly.

"Shoplifters?" I suggested tentatively.

"Them's the ones. Always a bad apple or two in every barrel."

"We're selling the stock so cheaply, it's hardly worth anyone's while to steal it," Bella said.

"You'd be surprised," Florrie said. "I'll stand here by the door, letting people in and out, where I can watch the purses and bags. They'll make a beeline for those, you'll see."

And she did too, making sure that anything picked up was brought over to the till and paid for.

The old brass doorbell on its spring was going like the clappers and so was the stock of years — possibly even *centuries*! It was amazing what people were prepared to buy if it was cheap enough: brown canvas sneakers (which Aunt Nan always called galoshes, for some strange reason), with thick, black rubber soles, clear plastic ankle boots made to go over Cuban-heeled shoes to protect them from the rain; black velvet mules with slightly moth-eaten red marabou trimming, tartan slipper booties with pompom ties; sturdy Wellington boots; soft, white leather button-strapped baby shoes, slightly yellowed with age . . .

With each purchase we popped into the bag a business card and flyer for Cinderella's Slippers, with an invitation to the opening day, plus a voucher for ten per cent off a first purchase. It was all free publicity, but also slightly scary in that I would now actually have to make sure Cinderella's Slippers was up and running in time!

I gave Florrie a free pair of the clear plastic rain shoes and a fat red purse as a bonus later when she had to go back to the Falling Star.

"It'll be hotting up for lunch now, and though that Molly can manage to microwave a Cornish pasty all right, neither she nor Clive has got the hang of the coffee machine yet," she explained.

The Falling Star had always been the less trendy of the two village pubs, catering for locals in search of a quiet pint and a game of darts. The newer (by a century or two) Green Man was much larger and upmarket.

Things quietened right down by one, and we were so whacked I put a notice on the door saying "Closed for Lunch — Open Again at Two", and we went to slump in the kitchen over a sandwich and coffee and what was left of the Welshcakes.

"I know your aunt Nan always closed for lunch — which she had to, really, working on her own, or she'd never have got any — but I think we should keep Cinderella's Slippers open all day," Bella suggested. "A lot of people who work dash out to the shops in their lunch hour, so I think it would be worth it."

"You're probably right, and we could try it. I'll cover for you while you have a break," I agreed.

Once the shop was up and running, the plan was that Bella would manage it on her own till about three — though I would be within call, if it was busy — and then I could take over until four thirty, when we would shut. This would mean I could work on my illustrations during the quiet times, and Bella would be free to collect Tia from school.

On Saturdays her mother would usually look after Tia, or she could go to her other granny, as she had today.

"Hilda offered to have Tia every Saturday, which was very kind, but it made Mum jealous, so they'll have to take it in turns. Really, Tia would rather go to Granny Hilda, because she can do messy things like baking and painting, or go to the beach, while Mum generally just wants to visit a garden centre, look at plants and have lunch, which isn't terribly exciting for a little girl."

That reminded me how much time I would have to spend on the gardening too, because I didn't suppose Seth or his henchmen would be popping down any more to keep the garden trim and tidy, as they had for Aunt Nan.

I ushered Flash outside while Bella washed up. There was no sign of any escaped hens to terrorise him, though they were sure to find another way out eventually. But to my surprise, this time he boldly shot off towards the far end of the garden and vanished through the holly arch in the direction of the henhouse.

I followed, afraid for the hens, but quickly realised it was a different quarry he'd scented, for there was a sudden crescendo of barking and a loud and unearthly yowl.

I arrived just in time to see a large, sleek black cat shoot out of the gooseberry bushes behind the henhouse, hotly pursued by Flash. Now I could see how he had got his name, and it wasn't just for the white tip to his tail.

The cat scrambled with more haste than elegance through the broken bit of trellis that topped the dividing wall between my garden and that of the one next door, and Flash followed suit with one balletic, twisting leap, like a canine Nureyev.

After that, it sounded like a small war had broken out and the noise clearly attracted my new neighbour's attention for, in a voice of fury that would have reverberated right to the back of the largest of theatres, he exclaimed, 'Out, damned dog — and stay not upon the order of your going, but go at once!' "

"I'm coming to get him!" I called out, hastily unbolting the gate between the gardens and rushing to the rescue, though next door it was so overgrown I had to push my way through a jungle before I saw Flash. He'd managed to scare the cat up a tree and was leaping up and down vertically, as if someone was jerking him on elastic, while keeping up the high-pitched barking.

"Down, *down!*" shouted the man, even louder, if anything and as threatening as thunder. Poor Flash finally came to his senses and cowered, shivering with fear, tail between his legs and ears flat to his head.

"Just stop shouting like that, will you?" I snapped, running across to comfort Flash.

"Poor thing! Was that scary?" I crooned, giving him a hug. He pressed against my leg and I could feel him shaking like a leaf.

"I think it was my poor Toby who was scared," my new neighbour said, slightly more quietly. "He isn't used to being assaulted in his own garden."

"He was in *my* garden first, Flash's territory," I told him, slipping the red patent leather belt off my dress and looping it through Flash's collar.

"Well, now you're both in mine!"

"Not for much longer," I snapped, giving Flash a last stroke before I stood up. "I'm sorry, but I didn't even know there was a cat — how should I? And he's not hurt."

"Well, no — and I only meant to scare your dog off, not scare him to death," he conceded more reasonably. "What's the matter with him?"

"He was cruelly treated by his past owner," I said, and now that all my attention wasn't on Flash, I suddenly realised there was something horribly familiar about my new neighbour's voice.

Slowly I rose, turned to face him — then stood, transfixed.

He was most certainly not the aged actor of my imagining, only a little older than I, and about six foot tall, slender in build and with darkest chestnut hair that clung to his well-shaped head like silk. His pale face was hollow-cheeked, the luminous, haunted light grey eyes deep-set and the skin beneath stained with dark circles. He didn't look as if he'd eaten a decent meal or slept any time recently and there were signs of strain around his wide, sensitive mouth . . . a mouth I had once kissed.

Well, to be quite truthful, an awful lot *more* than once.

My heart did a leap to challenge Flash's Nureyev performance, then landed with a soggy thud and died.

Unflatteringly, recognition was not instantly mutual.

"'Disdain and scorn ride sparkling in her eyes,'" he quoted sardonically, then narrowed those smoked-glass eyes at me, cold as a merman, before adding, frowning, "But don't I know you?"

Now that he'd stopped shouting, his voice was mesmerisingly mellow and beautiful — had I been in the mood to be mesmerised, that is.

"Or maybe it's just the whole Helena Bonham Carter thing with the crazy clothes," he mused, taking in today's outfit of a full-skirted green tartan dress over a longer red net petticoat, worn with red Birkenstock clogs (old shoe habits die hard, especially if you're going to be standing around in a shop for hours on end). I'd put temporary green and red streaks in my hair too, piled it high and stuck in a favourite selection of brightly-coloured butterflies on long picks.

"I do *not* look like Helena Bonham flaming Carter in the least!" I snarled furiously. "And, what's more, I was dressing like this *years* before I'd even heard of her!"

"No, come to think of it, apart from the clothes you look more like a Renoir painting," he agreed, "dark, plump and healthily rosy. But I'm sure —" He broke off, then said uncertainly, "*Tansy?*"

"Yes," I replied between my teeth, because even with a gap of more than fifteen years I'd recognised Ivo Hawksley, the first man to break my heart, while he'd obviously forgotten all about me. And I might have put on a couple of stone since he last saw me, but that "plump" bit rankled.

I turned my back on him and led the by-now meek and cowed Flash towards home without another word. I'd have liked to have stalked off in a dignified way, but since I was half-dragging the dog, it made that slightly difficult. Then Flash made a sudden sprint for the safety of his own garden and towed me through the open gate at speed, which was even less of a good exit.

I released my belt from his collar on the other side and bolted the gate in the wall, feeling really, really unsettled and upset: hadn't I had enough to cope with already, without old ghosts rattling their chains at me?

Though come to think of it, he had more the appearance of the skeleton at the feast.

CHAPTER
ELEVEN

Cross Patch

My sister Violet wasn't just clever, she was so sharp I was surprised she didn't cut herself. She was determined to better herself and she said she wasn't going to get tied up with any of the local boys, though they were all after her, because she was so pretty. She did take up with the son of the local garage owner for a short time, but looking back I think that that was just because it was the only way she could learn to drive! My father never did and I've never bothered, either — the bus and train were good enough for me.

Middlemoss Living Archive
Recordings: Nancy Bright.

"I was just about to open up — you've been ages," Bella said. "Had Flash got out?"

"He chased a cat over the wall into next door's garden, so I had to go after him. I suppose it was just instinct but, Bella, it was the actor's cat and he was really cross!"

"I thought you looked a bit upset, but there's no way you could have known he had a cat, is there?" she asked reasonably. "Anyway, it must have been in your garden to start with."

"Yes, that's what I told him and I don't suppose Flash could resist chasing it. There's a broken bit in the middle of the trellis on top of the wall near the henhouse, which is where he got through. I've just shoved a bit of board across it, but I'll have to get something more solid put along there eventually."

"Or *he* can," she suggested. "If he's an actor, he's probably loaded."

"I don't know — I don't suppose they all are, and didn't he tell Aunt Nan he was with the Royal Shakespeare Company? Are they paid a lot?"

"I expect so. I don't suppose he's short of a few bob. Did he introduce himself?"

"He didn't have to. I recognised him instantly, though it took him a bit longer to recognise me. I must have changed more than he has." (That "plump" was still rankling!)

"You mean, you've *really* met him, you don't just know him from the telly or films?"

"Yes, and I don't think he's been in films or anything. His name is Ivo Hawksley."

"Sounds slightly familiar," she mused. "So, where do you know him from? Was he one of your mother's friends?"

"No, he's not much older than I am — two or three years. I met him that first summer when I moved down to London to begin my graphic design course. We went out for a couple of weeks — and I *did* tell you about him, only you'd just started working for British Airways at the time, so you've probably forgotten."

132

"I do remember you were pretty upset because you'd broken up with some boy you'd been going out with, but next time I saw you was ages afterwards when I came down for that visit, and you never mentioned him then. Was that him?"

"Yes. Mum used her contacts to get me on the books of a specialist agency as a foot model the moment I got down there, because she said the only beautiful bit of me was my feet." I smiled wryly. "I struck lucky with my first assignment, because it was a TV advert for shoes, based on the Prince Charming and Cinderella story. You must remember that, at least?"

"No! You were Cinderella?" she asked, impressed. "How did I miss that?"

"Of course I wasn't Cinderella, I was only her feet! There was a proper actress for the rest, with golden hair and blue eyes — just like my Wicked Stepsisters — but she didn't have perfect feet, so that's where I came in. Ivo was the young actor they'd hired for the prince. He kneeled down to put the glass slipper on my foot and when I looked down into his eyes . . . well, that was it."

Those smoke-grey eyes, the edges of the iris ringed in smudgy black, the angles and planes of a face that would have looked perfectly at home under an Elven crown in a Lord of the Rings film and that beautiful voice proclaiming, "Whoever this shoe fits, I will marry" — well, they all might have had something to do with my head-over-heels tumble into first love. *And* my subsequent recurring dreams.

I realised that Bella was staring at me, eyes wide. "It was serious, wasn't it? And I must have been too self-obsessed at the time to realise! I'm so sorry."

"Oh, it was only puppy love, really. I took it so seriously because I'd never been in love or had a serious boyfriend. But he asked me out and he did seem to feel the same way. The only fly in the ointment was that Mum had taken me to the studio when we met and she told my stepsisters I'd got off with the actor playing the prince. They teased me horribly about it."

"What a pair of cows they've always been to you," she said sympathetically, because she'd spent a weekend with me in Lars' London house soon after I moved in, so she'd seen me get the full Rae and Marcia treatment. "Still, never mind, you soon moved in with Timmy. What happened with Ivo?"

"Not an awful lot, looking back," I said frankly. "Maybe I quickly bored him. We were meeting during the day, because he was understudying a part in a West End play, and mostly we sat in museums and coffee shops talking, or went for walks in the park. It felt as if we'd known each other for ever. It was quite intense, but then after a couple of weeks he went off somewhere for an important audition . . ." I frowned in recollection. "And you know, now I come to think of it, that might have been for the Royal Shakespeare Company!"

"Well, that would fit. Presumably he passed the audition."

"He must have done, but I never saw him again, so I didn't find out. We were to meet in the Tate Gallery café for lunch so he could tell me all about it and I waited *hours* for him but he never showed. I never heard from him again, even though he knew where I lived and had my phone number," I finished.

"But what if something had happened to him?" she asked, pale blue eyes wide. "Didn't you try ringing him?"

"I didn't have his number. He was in digs, and we didn't all walk about with mobile phones permanently glued to our ears then, if you recall, because this is, what, seventeen or eighteen years ago?"

"No, I suppose not. It's odd how quickly you forget it hasn't always been like this," she agreed. "I'm sorry I wasn't much support at the time. I must have been too wrapped up in my own career!"

Bella had always wanted to be an air hostess, though when she did finally achieve her dream, she said she felt like little more than a glorified waitress. Of course, you saw lots of other countries, but you were generally too exhausted by the time differences to do anything other than slump in your room and to try and remember what day it was.

"I did actually see him once more, a long time later — just across a crowded café. He was with Marcia."

"What, your stepsister Marcia?"

"That's the only Marcia I know. They had their heads together and were talking very seriously."

"Probably just shop, because she's an actress too," Bella suggested.

"Who knows? I hadn't completely got the measure of Rae and Marcia when I first moved into Lars' London house with them all, but later I wondered if Marcia had somehow managed to meet Ivo and get off with him and that's why he stood me up."

"I suppose it's possible."

"It was certainly the pattern of it after that. They managed to take any boy who ever showed any interest in me, even when they didn't want him."

"They're a right pair of cows," Bella said passionately. "I don't know how such a nice man as your stepfather could have had children like that!"

"I've often wondered that myself." I shrugged. "Still, it was all a long time ago and I'd almost forgotten about Ivo."

That was a bit of a porkie really, since I don't think you ever do quite forget your first love and the might-have-beens. Or I hadn't, anyway, or I wouldn't keep dreaming about him. But clearly it hadn't been as serious on Ivo's part.

"I expect you were well out of it really," she said. "I mean, he might have had a good reason for standing you up, but there isn't one for not calling to explain why. And if it was because he was seeing Marcia instead, then he's not exactly a nice man, is he?"

"I certainly don't think he's going to be the perfect neighbour. He frightened poor Flash half to death by shouting at him, and he looks dreadfully strained and edgy. I wonder if he's had a nervous breakdown."

"That would account for why he was so ratty, I suppose," she agreed. "Or perhaps he's still grieving for his wife. I mean, the accident was only last year, wasn't it?"

"True, it could be that. It's odd that his wife had just been offered a role in *Cotton Common* when she died in that accident, and Marcia was already playing a part in it: perhaps she's known them both all these years and never mentioned it?"

"You've hardly seen each other, though, Tansy, so she wouldn't have had much chance for small talk about what ancient boyfriends were up to, even if she remembered you'd once gone out with him," Bella pointed out, which was true. I'd mostly managed to avoid meeting up with Rae and Marcia unless Lars was over here and insisted we all had dinner together.

"Oh, well," I sighed, getting up, "it's ten past the hour and we'd better go and open before people start to think we're never going to! There's still loads of stock to shift."

Another queue had formed and the afternoon proved just as busy as the morning.

Then, when it got to three o'clock and we put a big sign up in the window saying that everything was now half the sale price to clear, utter pandemonium broke out.

Word quickly spread and half the village (and many total strangers) began fighting over the most unlikely things. By four thirty, when the last customer departed, triumphantly clutching a bargain box of Meltonian shoe creams in strange colours to his bosom, we just looked at each other, exhausted and amazed, among the debris of discarded boxes.

"My God, but they like a good bargain round here!" Bella said limply.

"They certainly do, but thank goodness that's the last one," I said, and then we both groaned as the door was flung open, setting the brass bell on its spring bracket jangling.

"Spoke too soon," I muttered.

But this time it was no customer but Ivo who stood there, a dark and glowering figure against the light, the Demon Prince, rather than any kind of Charming.

"What in the name of hell's been going on in here?" he roared. "There've been crowds of people outside the windows all day, chattering and giggling, children screaming, and then in the last hour it sounded as if World War Three had broken out!"

"I suppose it has been a bit like Blackpool on a Bank Holiday," Bella admitted, but he ignored her, his ireful gaze fixed on me.

But as he opened his lips to speak again, the bells of the nearby church of All Angels sent out yet another merry wedding peal to quiver on the air and when the last reverberations faded, he said wildly, " 'Can no one silence that dreadful bell?' "

"It is late in the day for a wedding," I agreed, "especially at this time of year. I haven't been counting, but I'm sure there have been at least three today, so Raffy must be doing them on special offer, or something."

" 'I do begin to have bloody thoughts'," he quoted, "and who the hell is Raffy?"

"The vicar," I began to explain, just as he took a hasty stride forward and, being too angry to notice that there was a step down into the shop, fell headlong into a pile of empty cardboard cartons.

CHAPTER
TWELVE

Summoned by Bells

That's how she became a driver when she joined the Wrens, where she spent all her time driving the top brass about, it seemed to me. Anyway, the next thing we knew she'd gone and married one of them, Commander Poole, a man more than twice her age, and without a by-your-leave. Mother and Father were that upset — especially Father, she was the apple of his eye. I wasn't upset, but I was surprised she didn't hold out for an admiral.

Middlemoss Living Archive
Recordings: Nancy Bright.

"Boxed in," I said, without meaning to.

"Great corrugated catastrophes!" added Bella, sounding like the old *Batman* TV series.

Ivo emerged like some chancy-tempered mythical beast from its lair, and Bella and I instinctively drew together for support.

But dusting himself off, he said quite mildly, "'The portrait of a blinking idiot.'" Then the emptiness of the shop seemed to strike him for the first time and he suggested, hopefully, "Closing-down sale?"

"Well, yes, in a way —" I began.

"We've been having a big clearout of the old stock at knockdown prices, that's why it's been so busy today," Bella explained.

He stared at her, frowning. "This is *your* shop now?" he suggested. "Tansy's working for you?"

"No, it's the other way round," she corrected him. "Bright's was Tansy's great-Aunt Nan's shop and now it's hers. I just work here."

His attention — and those lucent grey eyes — switched to me. "Oh? Then you must have got the offer from my solicitor about my wanting to buy the premises. Are you going to take me up on it? It's very generous."

"I didn't know it was you who wanted to buy it, but it's as I told my solicitor: I'm not selling."

"But if you're having a closing-down sale, you obviously don't intend keeping the shop going, and I don't suppose you actually want to *live* here, so what if I up my offer? It would be worth paying through the nose for the sake of peace!"

"I *do* live here: this is my home, and we may have closed Bright's Shoes down, but there'll be a grand reopening as Cinderella's Slippers, wedding shoe specialists, in a couple of weeks — March the twentieth, if you want to write it in your diary."

"'Don't trip down the aisle, float down it,'" Bella said, helpfully quoting one of our slogans.

"Cinderella's Slippers?" Ivo repeated blankly, then light seemed to dawn, for he added, "Oh, right, I suppose that's a dig aimed at me, since we met while they were filming the Cinderella advert?"

"Oh, don't be so daft, it's not all about you," I snapped. "I thought of the name months ago and I didn't even know you'd bought the next-door cottage until I saw you in the garden! And why would I have a dig at you, anyway? I haven't given you a second's thought for years."

Well, that was almost true: I'm not responsible for what my subconscious gets up to in my dreams.

"But you must have known I was Kate Windle's husband, because it was in all the papers after the . . . accident," he pointed out, the short pause and small break in his voice reminding me that he had lost his wife only the previous year.

"I was away in Italy with my fiancé at the time, and though Aunt Nan told me about it when I got back, she didn't mention you by name. So I really didn't have a clue. I'm so sorry about your wife," I added.

"And I'd never heard of you and didn't know Tansy knew you, so your name wouldn't have meant anything to me, either," Bella said.

"We bought the cottage as an investment and for holidays. It was my wife's idea, because her best friend lives up here. She's an actress with a part in *Cotton Common*, and Kate was offered a role too, but then —"

He broke off abruptly, his expression bleak and anguished. Clearly the accident that killed his wife was still too terrible to talk about.

I wondered if his wife's best friend could be my ex-stepsister, Marcia. It's a small world . . .

He seemed to brood on dark memories for a moment, eyes flat as silver pennies, and then, just as I was starting to feel a little sorry for him, he went back into Attack Mode. "When we viewed the cottage it was very quiet down in this little courtyard, so when I needed some peace and quiet, I thought it would be the perfect place to come . . ."

He stared at us in an intensely antagonistic way, as if we were conspiring to drive him mad. Maybe he was halfway there already, or he *had* had a nervous breakdown, because he was thin to the point of gauntness and the dark shadows under his eyes revealed a lack of sleep.

I certainly didn't want to be responsible for tipping him over the edge, and Bella obviously felt the same way, because she said soothingly, "It's not likely to be as noisy as this in future; it's a one-off. There's nothing to be done about the church bells, though, but I expect you'll get used to them."

" 'For this relief, much thanks,' " he said sarkily.

"I love to hear wedding bells, it's such a joyous sound," I said.

He looked at me broodingly. "I didn't think I would ever see you again," he said, but not as if he was glad he had. Then he turned on his heel and left, slamming the door behind him, so that the brass bell clanged merrily for ages.

"Was that Shakespeare he kept quoting?" Bella asked me. "You're the one who had the Bard drummed into you in Miss Harker's class, while I was doing Extra French."

"Yes, though he paraphrases it a bit, to suit the context. I suppose it's an occupational hazard."

"He's rather gorgeous, in an angry sort of way, isn't he? But he seems very fine-drawn and edgy, to say the least," Bella commented. "Do you think he's had a nervous breakdown?"

"If he hasn't already, then he probably will, the way he's carrying on."

"I expect he's still traumatised by his wife's death. It must have been quite a shock," Bella suggested.

"I suppose so, though he seems to have carried on working afterwards, doesn't he?"

"Delayed shock?"

"Maybe. Something's clearly wrong, or his nerves wouldn't be so very frazzled. But I expect it has been very noisy all day, even if it wasn't as bad as he made out."

Bella giggled suddenly. "You know, I thought those two women were going to come to blows over the last pair of glittery plastic overshoes, didn't you?"

"Yes, though I can't imagine why either of them would want them."

"I expect they each wanted them because the other one did," Bella guessed shrewdly. "People bought the strangest things!"

"The Friends of Winter's End said those really long white tape laces would be perfect for lacing their buskins . . . at least, I *think* it was buskins," I said. "The shy, balding man with brown eyes said his role was to play Shakespeare at Winter's End on open days, so perhaps we should introduce him to Ivo?"

"Then they could fling quotes at each other," she agreed.

I locked the front door and put the Closed sign up. When I turned round the shop looked dark, bare and empty, with only the lingering, familiar smell of leather to comfort me.

"It looks so desolate now, doesn't it? Oh, Bella, do you think I'm doing the right thing and I can make a success of Cinderella's Slippers?"

"Yes, of course you can," she assured me. "It's a brilliant idea! And you can draw in the tourist trade as well as the bridal one, with all the shoe-inspired gift items you've ordered — the silver charms and stuff."

"And the Chocolate Wishes shoes," I said. "If the shop fails, I can always eat the stock!"

"It won't come to that, you'll see."

"Come on," I said, "you'd better get off home and remind your daughter what you look like."

"Yes, her granny should have dropped her off with Mum again by now. I'll be back on Monday to help you with the redecorating, though. I love doing that."

"Same rate of pay as minding the shop," I said, "though I think really it should be more."

"I'm just grateful for any paid work, the situation I'm in. I'm hoping to get a little bit more that I can fit into my own time through that card I put up on the village notice board, advertising my home secretarial services."

"I'm so glad you can work in the shop, so I can carry on with my books. I love doing them, and they've been my bread and butter for years. But I don't miss the foot modelling — all that faffing around making sure they looked their best and worrying in case I bruised them or bashed my toenail!"

"Are you *ever* going to break out into silly shoes?" She looked down at my sensible Birkenstock clogs.

"I will eventually — occasionally!"

"There's another thing you could stock — those glittery plastic dressing-up shoes for little girls, and maybe wands."

"No, I think one of the gift shops has those, and anyway, I want the shop to be an upmarket bridal one rather than a branch of Tinkerbells R Us."

Before she left we quickly Googled Ivo Hawksley: I don't know why I hadn't done it before!

He seemed to have spent his entire career with the Royal Shakespeare Company, apart from one or two brief forays into cameo roles in West End plays and an obscure film. We found pictures of his late wife, and details about the accident, which I quickly scanned, noting that they alluded to him as the "acclaimed Shakespearian actor, Ivo Hawksley". Kate was rather unkindly described as a bit-part actress who'd just unexpectedly landed a plum role in the hugely popular *Cotton Common* series and was driving home from a meeting with the directors when the accident happened.

It also turned out that she'd been staying up here with Marcia at the time, who was quoted as saying that her friend had been under the weather, but insisted on setting off home that day, and she would be a huge loss to the acting profession.

146

So I was right, Marcia *was* the best friend Ivo referred to — and she must have known him for years too, yet never mentioned him to me.

"The web of our life is of a mingled yarn, good and ill together," as Shakespeare put it, one of the many snippets Miss Harker had inserted immovably into my brain at school. Marcia had always seemed to have a suspiciously Iago aspect to me: good at stirring things up behind the scenes. I bet she had something to do with Ivo standing me up.

When I was in the kitchen later I could hear faint strains of gloomy classical music coming from next door. Because the building was all once one, the dividing wall wasn't as thick and solid as one might expect.

I hoped Ivo's taste in music was not always quite so sombre.

CHAPTER
THIRTEEN

Fresh as Paint

On his next leave, Commander Poole came to see us and he seemed a very steady, kind sort of man, though more my father's age than Violet's. Many men who'd been in the forces and taken early retirement came back again during the war, and he had a lot of knowledge of the Far East, which is where he ended up . . . but all that came later.

Anyway, he expressed himself very well and said all the right things, and Mother and Father thought he'd be a steadying influence on Vi, because once she'd left home it was evident even to them that she'd become a bit of a giddy kipper.

What? No, lovey, I don't know where the phrase "giddy kipper" came from, it's just one of those sayings.

Middlemoss Living Archive
Recordings: Nancy Bright.

I was still pretty exhausted when I woke the next morning, but by the time I'd drunk several cups of coffee I'd recovered a bit of bounce, and dragged Flash as far as the village green, stopping every few minutes when some alarming sound or sight had caused him to clamp his lead to his chest and refuse to go any further.

On the way home, he towed me and I considered trying his technique, though I suspected it only worked if you had four legs.

The black cat, Toby, appeared while I was cleaning out the hens and taunted Flash by sitting on the fence post and staring down at him, until I shooed it away.

What with Cedric having been in such a perky mood that he'd been shrieking out a strangled crow every five minutes since dawn, and Flash's furious barking, my neighbours couldn't have been having a terribly quiet Sunday morning. Mind you, apart from Ivo, everyone else was some distance away, the other side of the lane at the back of the cottage, with our long gardens between us. The car park of the Green Man bordered the other side of our garden to Ivo's, also separating us from the pub.

The church bells loudly ringing for the service were obviously the straw that broke the camel's back as far as Ivo was concerned, for an upstairs window in his cottage suddenly slammed shut, but at least the church bells weren't *my* fault!

I had a bacon and egg brunch to fortify myself, then girded up my loins, metaphorically speaking, and gave the desolate and empty shop and stockroom a jolly good clean, squashing all the empty boxes flat (though Ivo had inadvertently made a good start on that) and bundling them together, to go out with the recycling bin.

Then later a moonlighting joiner came and removed the old wooden sliding doors between the shop and the stockroom, opening the space up. He made such a neat

149

job (he even borrowed the vacuum cleaner afterwards!) that I booked him to return and put up some shelving when we'd redecorated. Instead of having a separate stockroom, I was going to have open storage units beneath the display shelves, so I could see at a glance what styles and sizes we had in.

The joiner was inexpensive too, which was a consideration, because my financial resources weren't infinite: Cinderella's Slippers really would need to start making a profit pretty quickly . . .

I did some more calculations while eating a modified version of the high tea that Aunt Nan had always taken on Sunday afternoons, attired in her wedding dress, though she would unbutton the tight cuffs of the lace coat and turn them back, in case they got in the butter.

She had so loved to talk about her fiancé, Jacob, who had been her childhood sweetheart, and who sounded such a kind man that it was not surprising that she never got over losing him in the war.

In tribute today I was wearing a pair of vintage wedding shoes from my collection — Salvatore Ferragamo strappy open-toe stilettos in cream leather and ruched pale pink satin, with pearl and crystal flower detailing — and I felt like a little girl wearing dressing-up shoes as I click-clacked to and fro across the quarry-tiled kitchen floor.

Financially, my books gave me my basic income and the foot modelling had provided some sporadic icing on the cake. I had a little nest egg put by, but Aunt Nan had been able to leave me little more than the property, though she had been putting money by for years for

150

what she called "a good send-off". I'd made sure she'd had that, right down to the buffet for the mourners afterwards, in the function room of the Green Man.

I'd ordered a lovely stone angel, which she hadn't asked for, though that wouldn't arrive for quite some time yet.

"*Waste of good brass!*" I could hear her saying severely in my head, but when I'd asked Raffy about it, he'd said a churchyard could never have too many angels, and to go ahead if that was what I wanted.

There was such a lot to do to the new shop, which would be almost twice as big now it incorporated the stockroom, and though Bella and I could manage the repainting, I'd certainly need an electrician to put new lighting in.

It ought to have carpeting too, and I decided what I could afford for that, bearing in mind it had to be hard-wearing, but also go with the colour scheme. I'd have to try haggling with the nearest big carpet store next day . . .

My musings were interrupted by a crescendo of mad barks from the garden, which had been a recurring theme of the day — every time I'd let Flash out, in fact. I'd assumed Ivo's cat was purposely taunting him again, but at least Flash had come back to the house when I'd called him.

But this time he didn't, so I went down there and found Flash doing his leaping-up-and-down-on-elastic thing, trying to get at Toby on top of the post.

"Go away, you silly creature," I said, trying to shoo the cat off, but he just stared at me balefully — a bit

151

like his owner had the previous day, in fact. And, speak of the devil, there he was, emerging from his overgrown jungle of a garden like a pale wraith of Mr Rochester and looking more wound-up than a clock spring.

"Look, all hell broke loose in your shop yesterday, and today it's been nothing but hammer, hammer, hammer, yap, yap, yap! Can I not even have an hour of peace? Can't you shut that dog up?"

"Your cat is just sitting there winding him up. You don't think I *want* him to bark non-stop, do you?"

"I don't believe you have any control over that animal."

"I've certainly got more than you have over your cat."

"Cats roam about, it's in their nature."

"And dogs bark at cats on their territory; that's in *their* nature too," I snapped back.

"He'll be through that trellis in a minute!" warned Ivo, distracted, as Flash made one of his balletic leaps upwards. "'*O villainy!*'"

"Don't be so melodramatic! He can't get through now I've stuck that piece of board across the broken bit, and I'll have something stronger put up as soon as I can."

"Don't bother, I'll have it properly fenced all along my side," he said shortly, then scooped the indignant cat off the post and went off back into his cottage, slamming the door behind him, which I heard but couldn't see through his garden's impenetrable jungle.

152

It took Flash a moment or two to realise that his quarry had vanished, but when he did, he came to sit at my feet, ears down and tail flapping anxiously.

I patted his head and he flinched, as usual. "It's all right, I understand," I told him. "When that cat is winding you up, you just can't help yourself."

I wasn't entirely sure Ivo could help himself either. Grief must have sent him half crazy, because I don't remember him having such a short fuse. In fact, he was a sweet boy.

Now he seemed set to turn into the neighbour from hell, though I expected he thought *he'd* already got one of those.

Bella arrived bright and early next morning and, attired in cheap overalls and with plastic shower caps over our heads, we got on with painting the shop ceiling before tackling the walls.

I'd got the joiner to remove the bit of existing shelving, but refused to allow him to take down the tiny shelf, held up by brass brackets, above the shop door. You could hardly see it there, but it held a deep green glass bottle with a marble stopper, full of mysteriously-shaped objects.

"Aunt Nancy said it was a witch bottle," I explained to Bella. "A charm to protect the shop and cottage. Florrie Snowball gave it to her and she put it there to please her, so I want to keep it. I don't suppose it'll matter if I take it down for long enough to paint the wall behind it, though."

"Do you think Florrie really *is* a witch?" she asked.

"Aunt Nan said Florrie herself certainly *thought* she was, but it was all a lot of tomfoolery thought up by Gregory Lyon. But there's a long tradition of witchcraft in the village anyway, isn't there? Only think about the Winters, what with Hebe brewing up her potions and lotions and Sophy calling her little girl Alys, like the family witch!"

"There seem to be lots more little girls than boys in Sticklepond," Bella observed. "I think three-quarters of the babies in Chloe's Mothers' Circle are girls, including hers."

"Yes, that's true, now I come to think of it. And there are so *many* babies and toddlers, too."

It had already forcibly occurred to me that Sticklepond had become a seething mass of fecundity, which rather rubbed in the painful fact that motherhood was never likely now to happen to me.

For the next few days we renovated and repainted, using the chosen colour scheme of cream and old-rose pink, with touches of gold and deep raspberry red here and there, to set it off.

Carpet was selected and laid, and an electrician came to put in new light fittings, including the spotlights in the window that Joe had suggested. They would be angled to highlight the old tilting-topped round wooden stand, now painted gold, where I would display a different shoe each week. The idea was to make the whole window look like a little stage with curtains at the back and I'd already bought yards of deep raspberry-red furnishing velvet and oodles of gold cord and tassels from Ormskirk market, ready to run those up.

The hanging wooden shop sign outside, and the one fixed to the wall at the High Street end of Salubrious Passage, had been removed and taken away to be repainted with "Cinderella's Slippers", though I'd also asked them to letter "Bright's Shoes" around the top too, because I thought Aunt Nan would like this link with the past.

And it was not only the shop that was transformed, for we got carried away and repainted the interior of the rest of the cottage in the same cream and old-rose pink colour scheme too, though without all the gold trimmings.

I also gave the cottage a good clear-out and spring-clean while I was at it, and Florrie Snowball, who had been popping in and out daily with good advice served up with lashings of curiosity, volunteered to help me sort out Aunt Nan's clothes and personal effects.

Many things went to her favourite charity but I asked Florrie to choose any little mementoes she would like, and she picked out some costume jewellery, and a dressing table set of tortoiseshell brushes and a mirror, which I thought was *hideous*.

I'd already found the good bits of family jewellery in the bottom of Aunt Nan's tin trunk, but her mother's Welsh gold wedding ring hadn't been with them and although I'd hoped we might discover it somewhere else in the room, there was no sign of it. Florrie had no idea where she might have put it, either. I only hoped it would turn up at some point!

There was not so much of Aunt Nan in the front bedroom by the time we had finished, but enough so that when I moved into it, I still felt comforted each night, just as I did when, as a frightened child, I had slipped into the tall, brass bed with her. And I slept deeply there each night, probably from exhaustion — and dreamlessly too, for the Cinderella dreams had stopped dead from the moment I saw Ivo again.

Strangely enough, I found I missed them . . .

Ages ago, when Timmy and Joe had brought my tilting-top drawing desk from London, I'd got them to carry it upstairs to my small bedroom overlooking the garden and we'd just managed to fit it in, even if I did have to climb over the bed to get to the window.

But now I set about turning the room into a studio, squeezing my white-painted wooden bed into the tiny boxroom ready for any unexpected visitors, though they'd have to share with me the even tinier bathroom on the half-landing, a later addition built out at the back.

While Aunt Nan had not hoarded personal possessions, one kitchen cupboard was crammed full of tins and jars of food, some ancient for, like many, the privations of the war years had turned her into a squirrel.

I fear I'd been making an awful lot of noise — and so had Cedric, who seemed to be increasingly revving up his crowing for spring. And then there was Flash, barking at the cat, of course, though I'd got quite used to that. Besides, it gave him something purposeful to do, seeing the creature off our garden.

Despite all this racket, however, there had been no more sudden Demon Prince appearances. In fact, I'd seen nothing of my neighbour for the entire week, though I heard his back door slam late each evening, after I'd returned from my dog-drag, so he must have gone out for a walk then. Perhaps he was a vampire. He was certainly pale enough for one.

But then on the Friday I caught sight of the vicar being admitted through Ivo's front door, so maybe not ... Also, supplies were delivered one day by an upmarket supermarket chain, so presumably there *was* food in the house, even if he didn't look as if he was eating any of it.

Since the Saturday between the sale and the reopening was the only one Bella was likely to have free for quite some time, she'd decided to take Tia to Blackpool for the day. I would have gone with them, except that Timmy and Joe were up in Ormskirk for the weekend and were going to come over and see how things were going.

They brought me presents of a sparkly "glass" pantomime Cinderella slipper, a string of fairy lights like little crystal shoes, and a wall clock with shoes marking the hours ... I could see a certain theme developing there.

They also gave me lots of good advice on how to "dress" the shop, and Joe adjusted the spotlights in the window for me. Then, since they were in their camper van, they kindly drove me to the nearby Ikea store (bribed by the lure of a Swedish meatball lunch, followed by those lovely green marzipan cakes for dessert), so I could buy two glass display cabinets, a long free-standing mirror in a white frame and a few other bits and pieces, including some light fittings for inside the cabinets, which Joe fitted before they left.

That was quite late, because once I'd told them Ivo was living next door, they'd hung around the garden for ages, hoping to catch a glimpse of him. They said he was a renowned Shakespearian actor, just as the newspapers had put it, and if I'd ever mentioned to Timmy that Ivo was the boy who'd broken my heart in a previous existence — one when I was very much younger and also very much thinner — then he'd entirely forgotten and I didn't remind him.

Timmy did ask me if I was missing Justin, and I said quite truthfully that for days I'd been either too busy or too exhausted even to think of him, though every time I checked my phone or emails there were messages from him, which I deleted unread.

Immy had never been any kind of mother to me — it just wasn't in her — so it was Aunt Nan I thought of on Mothering Sunday. I even made one of my rare appearances at the church for the special service. But then all the services were special — and packed — since Raffy became our vicar, not just because he was once a famous rock star, but because he was so charismatic.

I'd put a little pot of those miniature Tête-à-tête daffodils on Aunt Nan's grave before the service, and the bright yellow blooms nodded bravely in the brisk, cold March breeze. She'd always like daffodils. I was sure she would like her stone angel when it arrived too, whatever she thought about the expense . . .

Later, my moonlighting joiner came back and put up some shelves, fixed the curtain track around the window and moved the heavy, glass-fronted counter (the old one, with the woodwork repainted cream) into position.

The new clock ticked on the wall: it was ten past sparkly pink stiletto time and I felt as if, despite all the loss and heartbreak, I was standing on the edge of something magical.

CHAPTER
FOURTEEN

Bell de Jour

My fiancé, Jacob, was killed on a convoy quite early on
in the war. A direct hit, his ship took, and not many
were rescued. It was a hard blow and for a time I was
inclined to resent Mother and Father for persuading us
not to marry until after the war — though of course
they meant it for the best, and none of us knew how
long it was going to drag on for or we'd all have acted
differently. But after a while I picked myself up, as you
do, and carried on, because it was easier to keep busy
and help others. Moping about wasn't going to do
anyone any good.

Middlemoss Living Archive
Recordings: Nancy Bright.

First thing on Monday morning the new electronic till
arrived and I left Bella trying to work out the
instructions while I was running up the deep raspberry
velvet window drapes on Aunt Nan's old Singer sewing
machine, the sort with a handle and a little metal
footplate that made a cheerful chinking noise against
the needle holder as it sewed.

I'd made curtains before and it wasn't hard, but each
time I began hurtling down a straight seam, the handle

would drop off and I'd have to stop and screw it back on again with the end of the butter knife.

While I was sewing I heard a few deliveries arriving and when I went into the shop later I found that Bella (who's much more technically minded than I am) had sussed out the till and unpacked a carton of our printed carrier bags, which looked *very* swish.

"There're packets of shoe-shaped confetti in that small box over there, and this one's the tissue paper, reams of it," she said. "Are you expecting any more deliveries today?"

"A small consignment of silver shoe charms — remember, I showed you the picture on the internet? The enamelled bluebird ones should come with them. I thought they could either be sewn inside the wedding dress or worn on a chain as the 'something blue'. There'll be some handbag charms, too. But the initial consignment of RubyTrueShuze will arrive later."

"All those smaller bits and pieces had better go in one of the glass cabinets, hadn't they?" Bella said. "Do you want me to explain how to work the till?"

"No, let's postpone the evil moment until later in the week. It terrifies me," I confessed. "Let's put my shoe ornaments out, instead."

I'd had a high narrow shelf put up around what had been the stockroom specially so I could display all the decorative shoe-shaped items I'd collected, or been given, over the years, most of which had been languishing in boxes under my bed here in the cottage, since Justin was so averse to what he called "clutter". Minimalists don't collect anything except empty spaces.

As we unwrapped them I discovered forgotten treasures: flowered china shoes, brass slippers with upturned toes, a wooden pincushion boot from Bavaria and a pair of exquisite fairy-sized high-heeled shoes in deep green glass.

"They're all so pretty," Bella said, standing on the step-stool to put them on the shelf as I handed them up.

"You've given me several of them over the years, and so have Timmy and Aunt Nan. I started with just one or two and it quickly snowballed."

"Like me with my china pigs — I've got about a hundred of them," she agreed. "But the shoes are certainly coming in useful now. They look lovely in here."

She arranged a little embroidered Eskimo shoe next to a gilded porcelain one. "Where are the chocolate shoes going to be displayed when you've got them?"

"In the bigger glass cabinet, I think," I said, "because they'll be quite breakable, even with the special packaging. Did I say I've also decided to stock my own books and ordered a small revolving rack for them? I thought I might as well, starting with *The Slipper Monkeys and Cinderella's Slippers*."

"Oh, I'd entirely forgotten that one. Anyone would think you'd written it especially for the shop!"

"I suppose I did always dream of opening a wedding shoe shop, even if I never thought it would happen, so I expect that gave me the idea for the book. The stand is another expense, though. I'm going to have to be careful with the money now until the shop takes off — *if* it does!"

"Of course it will, it'll be a huge success!" she assured me. "Think about it — you'll be the only stockist for RubyTrueShuze in the whole Northwest, and probably the only place in the country where you can buy *real* vintage wedding shoes."

"It was really kind of Ruby to let me start with such a small order — and some on sale or return too! But I won't have a big range of genuine vintage shoes, because you can't buy many in good condition, or large enough sizes."

"But you've got enough to make a fun display here and on the website, when I've got it properly up and running," Bella said. "It's something different, good for publicity. And you've got adverts going in the county magazines, haven't you?"

"Yes, and all the local newspapers. Oh, and *Lively Lancashire* magazine emailed earlier to say they were going to cover the opening on Saturday and run an article with pictures — in the May or June edition, if they could shoehorn it in — because Cinderella's Slippers sounded different and I had the additional angle of being an author."

"It's not just going to be different, but *unique*," Bella said loyally. "And with all the publicity, brides will come for miles to visit the shop, plus you'll have the casual tourist trade for the jewellery and stuff. Really, I don't see how you can fail."

"Justin doesn't seem to share your opinion. I actually opened the email he sent me yesterday, and he said he didn't think such a specialist shop could ever work in a village location, but if it folded to remember he would always be there for me."

"That was really big of him," Bella said drily. "He doesn't give up, does he?"

"No, but I wish he would, because it just upsets me all over again to be reminded of him. But I've made my decision," I said resolutely. "No second thoughts."

I finished the curtains by working on late into the evening, haunted by the dreary music from Ivo's cottage. It was odd to think of him in his living room next door and I wondered what he was doing — if anything. But I supposed he loved his wife deeply and so was simply wallowing in grief and melancholy, which would account for his look of exhausted strain.

At least things were quieter on my side of the wall by then, so he wouldn't be so disturbed . . . apart from Flash's occasional barking fits when he spotted Toby the cat, and Cedric's dawn chorus. There wasn't a lot I could do about either of those.

I draped the curtains over a chair-back when I'd finished. I'd already made a fat, gold-tasselled cushion in the same velvet to put on the gold tilting stand in the centre of the window, where I would display one wonderful shoe each week. The very first would be the "glass" pantomime slipper that Timmy had given me, with some of the silver shoe-shaped confetti sparkling around it . . .

And by now we'd swapped the old amber plastic window blind for a cream cotton roller one. I would have liked to have replaced the old patched green canvas pull-down awning outside, too, but that would have to wait.

Next day I left Bella putting the curtains up and listening out for the first shoe delivery, while I popped out. I'd remembered seeing a print of old shoes in one of the boxes outside Marked Pages on the High Street and thought if it was still there it would make a nice decorative touch to the shop.

Marked Pages was usually one of my haunts anyway, since I loved old detective novels — Sayers, Christie and Ngaio Marsh especially. I'd been a bit too occupied to visit it lately, so when I'd found the print of Victorian shoes and went in to pay for it and the new doorbell blasted the Beatles tune "Paperback Writer" loudly in my ear, it was a bit of a surprise, to say the least.

I knew the owner, Felix Hemming, and his wife, Poppy, who ran the riding stables just out of town, in a casual sort of way, as you do know many people in a village this size, but today I seemed to have walked in on some kind of marital argument.

"I'm not ill, so I really don't see why I shouldn't carry on riding till the last minute. And Honeybun is *totally* safe," Poppy was stating with great determination. I hadn't seen her for a while and there was no mistaking the pregnant bump, even with a long quilted gilet over her jodhpurs.

"But he could be startled by something, and throw you," Felix pointed out reasonably. "Come on, darling, it's only a couple more months and it isn't like I'm asking you never to ride again, is it?"

"No, but —" Poppy began crossly, then broke off when she noticed me standing, rather embarrassed, in the doorway.

"Sorry," I said awkwardly.

"It's OK, I'm just on my way out," Poppy said.

"But, Poppy —" Felix said urgently.

"Oh, all right, Felix, I won't ride — don't fuss!" Poppy snapped, then brushed past me and went out. I closed the door behind her, silencing the music.

Felix gave me a wry smile. "The confines of late pregnancy don't exactly suit Poppy's chosen lifestyle," he said. "She's never usually cross."

"I suppose it must hamper you a bit," I agreed, feeling distinctly jealous. I showed him the Victorian print. "I thought this would be nice in my new shop."

Of course he knew all about Cinderella's Slippers — who in the village didn't? — and immediately went and found me a hand-tinted bookplate of Prince Charming actually fitting the glass shoe onto Cinderella's foot, which couldn't have been more perfect. So I bought that too, and left them with him to be framed.

"Cream mounts and gold frames," he noted, when I described the shop's colour scheme. "No problem, and I'll drop them in later. I keep stock-sized mounts and frames in, and I'm sure I've got something suitable."

"By the way, I adore your new doorbell," I told him. "I'd love one that played something just right for *my* shop — something bridal."

"That's easy enough because I got it from a friend of mine, Neil Seddon, who's just set up a company making them to order. I'll give you his card and you can ring him and tell him what you want."

"Would it take him long?"

"I expect he'd do it as a rush order. In fact, I could ring him for you now, if you know exactly what you'd like it to play?"

"That 'Here Comes the Bride' music — you know what I mean?"

"Yes, it's 'The Bridal Chorus' from *Lohengrin,* by Wagner," he said knowledgeably. "We had it at our wedding." Then he called his friend and explained exactly what I wanted.

When he passed the phone to me, Neil said it was no problem and if I gave him my address, he'd be round to fit the bell on Friday afternoon.

In fact, he was so eager I had the feeling I might be his first paying customer.

On the way home I glanced at the card Felix had given me, and discovered that Neil had called his company Bell de Jour, Pour la Door.

Back at the shop, stock had been arriving thick and fast, including the first exciting consignment of RubyTrueShuze, which Bella had waited to unpack with me.

We'd decided on a system of writing all the shoe stock down in a book to keep by the till, so we could tick off each pair sold: that way we'd see what was selling best and what needed reordering.

The boxes and tissue paper were silver and purple, and the shoes inside mouthwateringly gorgeous, ranging from classic satin with crystal studding, to forties- and fifties-inspired strappy leather. There were a few in mouthwateringly bright jewel colours, but most were white, ivory or soft sugared-almond shades, and with medium-to-high heels, though there was a small range of flat sandals and sparkly ballerina shoes, too. What with Aunt Nan's stock of classic satin bridal pumps, my vintage collection and a small range of Goth-style black, purple and deep red shoes I'd ordered from another supplier, there should be something at Cinderella's Slippers to suit every bride.

I was hugely grateful to Ruby for letting me have some of this first consignment sale or return — so long as they remained in pristine condition, of course!

"These are all going on the higher display shelves in the back room, where we can keep an eye on them," I told Bella, "and no children are allowed to touch them!"

"It might be an idea not to let children into the shop at all," she suggested. "I'm sure wedding dress shops wouldn't let them in, because they could wreak havoc with all the delicate, white fabric!"

I shuddered at the thought of grubby fingers on the expensive satin shoes. So much of what had been my rainy-day nest egg was tied up in the contents of so few silvery boxes.

"Or perhaps we could just let child bridesmaids in, by appointment?" I said thoughtfully. I'd already stated in the advertisements that I would open out of shop

168

hours by arrangement. "But we can be flexible if brides just turn up with young bridesmaids, and they seem well-behaved."

By now, Bella was trying on a pair of vintage-style ivory satin shoes. "I want these *so* much," she sighed, "and I've almost got enough money saved up . . ."

"But that's your deposit for a place of your own," I pointed out.

"Yes, I know — and Tia and I can't live in a pair of shoes, like the Slipper Monkeys do, can we?"

When Aunt Nancy died I'd spoken on the phone to Lars, my last-but-one stepfather, and then once or twice since, when he'd assumed I was still up here sorting things out.

I still hadn't told him that I'd left Justin and moved here permanently, because it was more than a little difficult, what with his younger daughter being the cause of our break-up, not to mention my fiancé suddenly turning out to be the father of Lars' adored grandson, Charlie! Not that I'd any intention of telling him *that,* of course, but I wasn't sure if I could come up with any convincing lies if he asked me outright why I'd broken off our engagement.

However, I got a chance to find out that very evening when he called me from New York.

"Tansy? I tried to get you at the flat, thinking you'd be back there by now, but Justin told me you'd had a bit of an argument and were staying up in Lancashire for the time being."

"For ever," I amended.

"That must have been quite some argument, honey."

"It certainly was, but things weren't working out, anyway," I told him cautiously. "It wasn't heading anywhere."

"Justin seemed very cut up. He told me it was his fault. He'd made a serious error of judgement, which he deeply regretted."

"He certainly did that, all right!" I said unguardedly.

"He hopes you'll forgive him when you've had time to cool down."

"I might forgive him eventually, but I won't be going back. In fact, it's just as well he kept stalling about setting a date for the wedding, because it made it much easier to split."

"Has he been messing around with other women?" Lars guessed shrewdly.

"One, at least, and there was a bit more to it than that . . . But there's no point in raking it all up again, Lars. It's over, and I'm staying here and turning Nan's shop into a bridal shoe emporium!"

I told him all about it and, being a canny businessman, he asked lots of interested questions and made useful suggestions.

"We've organised lots of publicity and we're going to have the grand opening on Saturday."

"Sounds like a great idea to me," he said, "though it may take time to get the business off the ground and you'll maybe have to plough most of the profits back in for a while."

"I know. Just as well I've got my books to fall back on!"

"It's a big undertaking on your own."

"Bella's helping me. You remember, my friend who came to stay with me at your house in London once?"

"Oh, yeah, nice girl. Is she living back in the old village too, then?"

"Yes, her partner died and it turned out that he ran up a lot of gambling debts. He'd never divorced his wife, so she got the house. Bella and her little girl have had to move back in with her parents."

"That's a shame," Lars said. "Well, if you need a loan, honey, you only have to ask, you know that. I always think of you as one of my own."

"I know you do. It's really kind of you and I promise if I get into difficulty I'll ask you for your advice and help."

I'd never wanted to take Lars' money, just because my mother was married to him for a few years — especially after she'd moved on to the next husband.

"You be sure and do that. And I'll come and see you and this shop of yours next visit. Now I'm taking more of a back seat in the business I don't get over as often as I'd like and it's way too long since I saw Rae and little Charlie. Marcia's living quite near you, isn't she?" he added.

"Yes, over in Middlemoss, but I don't suppose our paths will ever cross."

He sighed. "I sure wish you girls all got on together better!"

"I expect we met at an awkward age and it went downhill from there," I said, "and we've never had much in common."

"I'd have liked to have seen all three of you happily married and settled long ago, but things don't seem to work that way any more. Rae divorced, then got pregnant and wouldn't say who Charlie's father was, and Marcia's never even made it to the altar. When *you* got engaged, I thought you'd be married and starting a family in no time at all, and buck the trend."

"Yes, so did I."

"You'll find someone else, once you're over Justin. He can't have been the right man for you."

"I'm over Justin now, but the only really nice men around here are not only married, but completely out of my league even if they weren't."

I thought of our gorgeous vicar and the equally attractive but somewhat scary head gardener up at the hall, Seth Greenwood . . .

"No one is out of your league, honey," Lars said kindly.

"Aunt Nan used to say that, too," I said wryly. "But it's OK, I've given up on the idea of finding my Prince Charming, what with Justin turning into a toad before my very eyes."

He laughed. "Never say never. But if you're happy, that's good enough for me."

"Oh, yes," I assured him.

I mean, doomed to spinsterhood, with only a neurotic dog and a few scraggy hens for company, and a gloomy actor drowning in the sweet syrup of melancholy next door, who wouldn't be happy?

CHAPTER
FIFTEEN

Luscious

Next time Violet came home on leave, she was full of herself, and I think wanted to show off her fancy engagement ring and wedding band, not to mention her new clothes and boast about all her smart new friends. In fact, even though her husband was about to be posted abroad, she seemed more concerned with finding decent clothes on the ration books — or off them, for she loved pretty things and I'm sure wouldn't balk at black-market goods.

Middlemoss Living Archive
Recordings: Nancy Bright.

I practised for *hours* before I mastered the till and new credit card machine . . . well, sort of mastered them, because I still kept jamming the till, then had "to void the transaction", as the instruction manual put it, and start all over again. Also, replacing the two paper till rolls looked like an almost impossible task, so I was cravenly hoping they only ever ran out when Bella was there.

I'd put Bella in charge of the accounts, and she said this was where the spreadsheets she'd learned about in her night-school class would come in useful, though I'd no idea what those were: it was clearly all going to be a steep learning curve.

I *still* hadn't seen any sign of Ivo, though I could certainly *hear* him whenever I went outside, because he seemed to have decided to work off his grief (which I assume was what was eating him) by single-handedly hacking down the jungle that had once been his rear garden.

By the Thursday before we opened, I'd finished making matching curtains for the entrance to what had been the stockroom and was now a sort of inner sanctum dedicated to my RubyTrueShuze stock, so Bella hung those while I finished hand-lettering a couple of signs with my calligraphy pens.

We were really down to finishing touches by then and, call me immodest, but it all looked wonderful: a sumptuous cavern of cream and old-rose pink, highlighted with touches of muted gold and curtained in bullion-edged raspberry-red velvet.

The lighting was subtle and artfully placed, the tall white mirror at the end of the inner room seeming to extend the shop for ever. There were cream bentwood chairs and a small and ancient red velvet-covered chaise longue, donated by Florrie Snowball, in front of the display of vintage shoes.

There was more lighting in the glass cabinets, where jewellery and the boxed Chocolate Wishes shoes were lusciously arrayed, and the little white rack of *Slipper Monkey* books was tucked in by the counter.

The two prints I'd bought from Felix hung below the clock with its shoe numerals. Timmy and Joe's other gift, the string of crystal shoe-shaped fairy lights, was wound among a tall white pot of willow twigs by the door, shedding some illumination onto the step down. I didn't want any of my paying customers to plummet down head-first, as Ivo had.

Friday was a really busy day, with lots of coming and going. In the morning I baked millions of tiny fairy cakes for the opening — plain, but with a spoonful of pink water-icing and a silver sugar ball on top.

Flash watched me hopefully from his bed and, when a cake dropped, bounced off the table and shot in his direction, it was gone with one snap of the jaws.

I hadn't intended giving him any because I'd suddenly noticed he was looking a bit fat, like a fur-covered coffee table. He needed more exercise and less food: I think I had been trying to make up to him for his horrible past by feeding him titbits, but I didn't want to kill him with love.

I was feeding myself titbits too — I seemed to be doing more and more baking, and eating — since moving back to Sticklepond, but oddly enough *I* seemed to have lost weight!

Florrie's son, Clive, dropped off the boxes of champagne flutes which they were loaning me and also a crate of inexpensive fizz, which I crammed into the tall, old fridge.

Then Cheryl Noakes, the archivist, finally called in with my copy of Aunt Nan's memoirs.

"Here you are, a complete set, just as I promised her I'd give you," she said, handing over a substantial

175

cardboard slipcase. (Aunt Nan must have rambled on for *hours!*)

"Oh, great — thank you! I've so been looking forward to hearing all her memories."

"Well, yes, I'm sure you have," Cheryl said, looking slightly uncomfortable, "but the thing is that your aunt insisted on making an extra recording, just for you. She said you must listen to it after all the others, because it wouldn't make sense otherwise, and she hoped she'd done the right thing by telling you."

"Telling me *what?*" I asked, puzzled.

"Oh, most families have their little secrets," Cheryl said breezily. "She was undecided whether to leave things be, then decided to be completely open about her life."

"Now I come to think of it, she did once or twice drop some hints that there might be a little skeleton in the family cupboard, but I can't imagine what."

"I'm sure it's nothing to worry about: that generation had totally different ideas of right and wrong from ours, after all, and I think I've guessed what it is . . ." She paused, then added, "Still, she left it up to you whether or not to make the final recording public. You'll let me know some time, won't you?"

"Yes, of course," I agreed.

I'd given Bella the morning off, but after lunch I showed her the recordings and told her what Cheryl had said.

"So, *are* you going to listen to them in order, or go straight for the secret?" she asked, almost as intrigued as I was. "I know which it would be if I were you — but then, I never could resist a mystery."

"If Aunt Nan wanted me to listen to the rest first, then that's what I'll do," I said firmly. "I'll start tonight and ration myself to short instalments, to make it last longer."

"Then I'll just have to be patient until you find out what the secret is," Bella said. "If it's something you can tell me, of course!"

"I expect it will be. I'm sure it must be someone else's little secret *they* confided to *her,* and I'm more interested in Aunt Nan's own life."

"Maybe Florrie had a racy past and blotted her copybook in some way?" Bella suggested.

"That sounds more likely than Aunt Nan doing something wrong, and they've always been the closest of friends, despite being so different."

We went into the shop and started putting price tags on the last of the jewellery, which was fiddly, because they were tiny and you had to thread one bit through the other.

Neil Seddon turned up with my new doorbell just as we were in the middle of that and, while he was telling me about it, I could see that he was surreptitiously eyeing Bella in an interested kind of way. She was looking especially attractive today, in a pale blue tunic top that matched her eyes exactly.

Bella glanced at him and away a couple of times too. Actually, he was just her type: stocky, shortish and muscular!

Hoping he wasn't married, I left them both in the shop and went back to the kitchen, where I arranged my fairy cakes on pretty old china plates and an orange Bakelite cake stand, covered in clingfilm.

I could hear the doorbell wedding peal from the kitchen as Neil was fitting it and it sounded *perfect,* not at all jangly, but just like the real thing, but by the time I took some coffee through, he'd already gone.

"He had another bell to fit," Bella explained.

"But I haven't paid him yet!"

"I expect he'll send you the bill, then, or drop in again. In fact, he said he could come back any time and adjust the volume on the bell, if you want him to."

"I thought it sounded about right." I opened and closed the shop door a couple of times. "It *is* louder now I'm in here . . . but then, it's bound to sound loud in an empty shop, isn't it? When the place is full of customers, you'll hardly notice it."

"That's what Neil said. And then, just before he left, he asked me out for a drink," she added.

"Are you going?" I asked, thinking he was a quick worker.

"No, of course not. I told him I wasn't interested in the least."

"He seemed very nice," I offered tentatively.

"Well, so did Robert, didn't he? I totally trusted him and look how that turned out! For all I know, Neil could have a secret vice *and* be married, too."

"There is that. You certainly don't want to rush into a new relationship."

178

"Frankly, at the moment, I don't even want to *walk* into one," Bella said. "And anyway, I'm feeling too excited about tomorrow to think about anything else!"

"Me too, but nervous as hell and I keep thinking I must have forgotten something. But the bubbly's in the fridge, the borrowed glasses have arrived . . ."

"And the fairy cakes," Bella said. "They'll be a revelation to anyone who thinks cakes are those giant, heavy, greasy muffins!"

"I've baked squillions of them in tiny paper cases, so they're only mouthfuls. I expect we'll be vacuuming up crumbs for hours afterwards, though."

"Couldn't we have a cake now to celebrate?" Bella suggested. For a willowy person, she certainly puts away a lot of food — way more than I do, which is a bit unfair!

"I was just going to suggest it — *and* we'll open a bottle of bubbly to toast our hard work!"

I was a bit tiddly when I took Flash out for his drag later, but dogs are quite non-judgemental. So long as I didn't seem angry with him, Flash was happy.

The mad machete man was still hacking at his garden next door when we left, and Flash didn't really want to walk past the end of the garden where the red Jaguar was parked, presumably in case he came out and had a hack at him, too. Who knew what was going on in the poor dog's head?

Anyway, he firmly hooked his front paw over the lead and I had quite a job to get him past. But finally I half-coaxed, half-dragged him onwards and by the time we'd got back there was no sign of Ivo, though faint strains of miserable music were, as usual, filtering through the dividing wall into the kitchen.

I listened to the first instalment of Aunt Nan's memoirs while I was preparing and eating my supper and it was lovely to hear her voice again. It made me cry, but also smile, because she was talking about handing down the recipe for Meddyginiaeth Llysieuol. That was one tradition I intended to keep going.

I'd inherited Aunt Nan's recipe notebook, written in her lovely copperplate handwriting, though of course I'd long ago copied out the recipes for favourites like the Meddyg, Welshcakes and bara brith . . . and now I came to think about it, I realised I'd left six bottles of Meddyg in Justin's airing cupboard.

He'd always declined even a taste of the drink, which was a pity, because it might have made some semblance of a man out of him. Mummy Dearest had probably found it and thrown it out by now.

Justin actually caught me on the phone later and said he'd called just to wish me luck with the opening the next day, which was big of him considering he thought the shop would bomb . . . or maybe that should be *hoped* it would, so I would go running back to him.

Then he said that he missed me, before ringing off, leaving me feeling edgy and unsettled and wishing he hadn't bothered.

CHAPTER
SIXTEEN

Blessed

During the war Father did a lot of fire-watching, being too old and unfit for active service, and he was also involved in the St John Ambulance Service. I stayed home to look after Mother and run the shop. We had the hens, and grew a lot of our own fruit and vegetables, and the family who lived in the cottage adjoining ours kept bees, so we had honey too . . . Mother brewed Meddyg with some of it. People would barter almost anything for a bottle of Mother's Meddyg during the war.

Middlemoss Living Archive
Recordings: Nancy Bright.

I was too excited to sleep properly the night before the opening and was up at the crack of dawn to sort out the hens and take Flash for a quick drag round the green. He was getting a little braver about going out for walks, though any sudden noise or the appearance of a man bearing anything stick-shaped, from a fishing rod to a garden hoe, set him yanking me in the direction of home in a mindless, scrabbling panic.

When we got back we had breakfast and then I changed into a quite demure (for me) dark red dress with an interestingly draped top, which I'd bought from what Aunt Nan had always called "your Gudrun Sodastream catalogue".

Bella and I had debated some kind of uniform, then decided against it, apart from a Cinderella's Slippers name badge and a sparkly bridal tiara apiece, so the customers knew who was in charge.

By the time Bella arrived I'd already switched the lights on in the shop and put the white rope across the inner sanctum where the RubyTrueShuze were displayed, together with the sign saying, "If you wish to try on wedding shoes, please ask a member of staff for assistance."

We set up a pasting table in front of the shop, covered in a white sheet, ready for the refreshments, and Bella decorated the two ball box trees on either side of the front door with ivory satin bows. We hadn't liked to do it the day before in case it rained and the bows wilted, but luckily today looked set to be a lovely fresh bright March morning.

In the kitchen I filled a white plastic bucket with ice and stuck in the first two bottles of pink fizz to chill. I only hoped Flash's nerves would be able to withstand the popping of the corks! I think he was feeling my nervousness, because he was very edgy too, staring at me anxiously with his mad amber eyes.

Half an hour before the official opening time, the journalist and photographer from *Lively Lancashire* arrived to do an interview and we all had coffee and fairy cakes in the kitchen while I told them about the history of Bright's Shoes and Aunt Nan. Initially, Flash had been so scared by these strange intruders that he managed to squeeze under the settle near the inglenook fireplace, though greed got him out eventually.

The journalist was still taking notes when Raffy arrived the back way in full vicar gear (as opposed to his everyday garb of black jeans and a black T-shirt printed with a dog collar), because I'd asked him to declare the shop open and bless the new enterprise.

"Raffy Sinclair, our vicar," I introduced him.

The journalist's eyes widened. "Oh my God — so it is!" she exclaimed, and her biro went into overdrive while I was pouring him a quick cup of coffee and shoving the plate of cakes in his direction.

"Chloe's coming, with her grandfather and Zillah," Raffy said, "and she says she'll be happy to help if you'd like her to do anything? Zillah can mind Grace."

"If she could keep an eye on the refreshment table, that would be wonderful," I said gratefully.

"I'll tell her — and I'm sure Felix and Poppy will help for a while too, though I expect Felix will want to open Marked Pages, and Poppy will have to get back to the stables, eventually. I'll have to leave fairly soon myself, because I've got a wedding later."

"That's very appropriate, really," Bella said. "But let's hope all the Sticklepond brides from now on will be wearing shoes from Cinderella's Slippers!"

The clock was inexorably ticking towards the hour and I felt a flutter of nervous excitement in my stomach. "Right," I said, getting up and dusting off a scattering of crumbs, "we'd better go and open up."

They all helped carry plates and glasses and the fizz in its bucket out to the courtyard, where quite a crowd had already gathered. In fact, as well as a goodly number of unfamiliar faces, I think at least half the village was there — Bella's mother, with Tia; Florrie and her middle-aged son, Clive; Felix and Poppy; Chloe, with baby Grace in her stroller; the tall, imposing figure of her grandfather, Gregory Lyon, his long white hair blowing in the slight breeze; and Chloe's gypsy aunt Zillah, small, beady-eyed and dressed in shrieking pink and lime green, like an exotic parakeet.

I spotted the local reporter George Turnbull, too, and his photographer was snapping away just like the one from *Lively Lancashire* magazine was doing.

Then there was the Winter's End contingent of Seth, Sophy, their little girl, Alys, and Sophy's grown-up daughter, Lucy, not to mention all of the indoor and outdoor staff, together with *their* families . . .

And Hebe Winter too, of course, for nothing ever happened in Sticklepond unless she had a hand in it! She'd rung me a day or two earlier to inform me that the Friends of Winter's End Elizabethan Re-enactment Society would provide the entertainment, though I'd no idea what form this would take. They were all there, though, and in full Elizabethan dress, with Hebe as a very convincing Virgin Queen.

There was a hubbub going on, but everyone quietened and listened intently as Raffy blessed the shop and then cut the ivory silk ribbon I'd pinned across the door. Then Chloe handed baby Grace to

Zillah and came over with Poppy to help remove the clingfilm from the cakes, while Felix opened the first bottle of fizz and started to pour it into the champagne flutes.

"This is really kind of you," I told them.

"Not at all," Poppy said. "It's fun! Anyway, I got my satin wedding shoes from your aunt and they're the prettiest shoes I've ever had."

"You looked pretty all over on our wedding day," Felix said, and she blushed under her freckles.

Bella went in to keep an eye on the shop and Hebe told me that in a few moments she and the other Friends of Winter's End, would perform.

"Perform?"

"An Elizabethan courtly dance or two," she explained, as though I was half-witted. "Laurence has the music."

Indeed, her elderly steward, Laurence Yatton, was inserting a CD into a small portable CD player, which he'd placed on the end of the refreshment table.

Miss Winter's piercing blue eyes wandered over to the next-door cottage and a calculating gleam entered them. "I hear that your new neighbour is a renowned Shakespearian actor. I must call on him and see if he would like to join our little group. We had been thinking of enacting some scenes from the plays as a further draw for visitors to Winter's End."

"I think he's been ill — he's certainly a bit of a hermit," I warned her. "He may only be living here while convalescing." I didn't know how word had got out about Ivo's being an actor, but I was pretty sure that once he'd recovered he'd be back off to Stratford again like a flash.

She looked a little disappointed. "Oh? I had thought he had retired here."

"He's not old enough to retire — only in his late thirties. He did lose his wife last year, though, so I expect he's come here for peace and a bit of time out."

Not that he'd *had* a lot of peace so far, what with the rumpus during the sale, and then all the hammering and drilling during the renovations — and now today there was even more of a racket, not to mention the way the shop bell sent out a merry wedding peal every time the door was opened.

It had occurred to me that perhaps I'd better warn him what was going to happen, so I'd pushed an invitation to the shop opening through his letterbox the previous evening, though I hadn't really expected him to join us . . .

But maybe he was hacking at his jungle of a back garden, ignoring the rumpus? I hoped so, anyway, seeing he had such a short fuse for any disturbance.

While the Friends were tripping their stately measures, lots of people came to wish me every success with my new venture, including Seth Greenwood, who admired the bows on the box trees and then told me more than I really needed to know about the history of knot gardening until his wife, Sophy, dragged him away.

Gregory Lyon, Chloe's grandfather, informed me it was the day of the vernal equinox so very auspicious, and that he'd recited a charm for success and protection on his arrival, which was kind of him . . . if weird. So what with Raffy's blessing, it looked like all my angles were covered!

Even Zillah, who was in charge of Grace's stroller, offered to read my tea leaves one day soon.

My helpers carried the glasses and plates back into the kitchen and then had to leave, while I joined Bella in the shop. The doorbell played "Here Comes the Bride" about every five minutes for the rest of the morning, and sometimes the people coming in would like it so much they stood there, opening and closing the door for five minutes or more.

Most people came in from curiosity, but many then made small purchases of silver shoe charms, chocolate shoes and even *Slipper Monkey* books. One future bride asked to try on shoes in the inner sanctum, too — and I made my first RubyTrueShuze sale! I thought she'd faint at the price of the rose suede court shoes with satin bows that she'd clearly fallen in love with, but she didn't even blink a mascaraed eyelash.

The shop suddenly emptied about twelve and I'd just said to Bella, "I think we could close for a quick bit of lunch, don't you? And I'd better ring Neil and see if he can come and turn the volume down on that doorbell, because I can see now it's *way* too loud!" when the door was flung open, setting off "Here Comes the Bride" yet again. Ivo burst in: this was getting to be a habit.

"*'What fresh hell is this?'*" he roared, clapping his hands over his ears.

"I know it's a bit loud, but surely you can't hear the doorbell through the stone wall?"

"You could hear it in Timbuktu!"

"Well, there's no need to shout. And actually, I've realised it's too loud and was about to phone the man who installed it to come and adjust it."

"It's not just the bell — I work in the adjoining room and it's sounded like bedlam in here *and* out in the courtyard!"

"Couldn't you work somewhere else?"

"No," he snapped.

"And what work?" I asked. "I thought you were an actor and 'resting'?"

"I *am* an actor, but I need a bit of peace and quiet because — not that it's any of your business — I'm writing."

"Your memoirs?"

"Something like that," he said stiffly.

"I don't suppose you want someone to type them up on the computer for you?" Bella interjected eagerly.

He gave her a look that said pretty clearly that he'd certainly prefer not to employ my best friend and co-conspirator in ruining his peace.

"I'm afraid I've already left a message with someone who advertised on the village notice board. She sounds very suitable — if she's discreet."

"Why, is your autobiography terribly scandalous?" I asked, but he just gave me a cold look from his grey merman eyes.

"*I* put the card there," Bella confessed. "I could do with some extra work, and I'm terribly discreet, honestly."

"A clam," I agreed. "Your secrets would be safe with her."

He looked uncertainly at her, then ran one long slender hand through his dark chestnut hair in a very elegant gesture of resignation. "I suppose you'd better come and talk about it."

"If you like, you can go now, Bella, while it's quiet. I'll ring Neil about the bell and make us some sandwiches."

"Quiet — ha!" snapped the actor, and stalked regally out, followed, after a wry look at me, by Bella.

CHAPTER
SEVENTEEN

Typecast

As the war dragged on, rationing became more and more extreme, though living in a village we were probably better off than most, for we had vegetables in the garden, and the hens, and all sorts of bartering went on behind the scenes. But we all learned make do and mend — my sewing skills certainly came in handy and Father could repair and patch and make shoes last and last, until sometimes there was more patch than original leather!

Middlemoss Living Archive
Recordings: Nancy Bright.

Barely ten minutes later Bella let herself back in and I poured her a cup of coffee and passed her the cheese and tomato sandwiches.

"So — how did you get on?"

"Well . . . OK, I suppose, though he took a bit of convincing that I'd keep what he was writing confidential. He also wants me to drop in my references."

"Which references? One praising your air-hostessing abilities isn't going to be very relevant, is it?"

"Character references, which is OK, because I can easily get a couple of people to say I'm honest, sober and truthful. I think he was quite impressed when I told him about the office skills course and that I had a certificate."

"You told me everyone who turned up to more than six classes got that."

"Yes, but there was no need to tell *him* that, was there? And anyway, I'm quite good with computers and can touch-type, so I've got everything he needs."

"What *does* he need?"

"His manuscripts typed up — he likes to write longhand."

"Then you've got the job?"

"Yes, so from Monday I'll call in on my way home from here and collect whatever he's written, then type it into my computer. I can do it after Tia goes to bed, I'd only be slumped in front of the TV otherwise. Then I'll drop it off next day when I pick up the new lot . . . and so on. I told him I worked here part-time, because of picking my little girl up from school."

"Doesn't he have a computer? I thought everyone had one these days."

"Oh, yes, he has a really nice laptop, but he only seems to use it for the internet. I'll transfer his work onto it eventually, when he's finished the first draft."

"Of his juicy memoirs?" I pried interestedly, but Bella looked mysterious.

"My lips are sealed. He said if I told anyone what he was writing — including you, he mentioned you specifically — I'd not only be instantly fired but also pierced by 'the slings and arrows of outrageous fortune', or something Shakespearian like that."

"*Mis*fortune, in your case. And do you mean you're really not going to tell me?" I demanded, incredulously.

"Of course I am! I mentally crossed my fingers when I promised I wouldn't, because telling *you* doesn't count. We always keep each other's secrets."

"So, what's he writing that's got to be kept under wraps?"

"Crime novels under the name of Nicholas Marlowe."

"Oh, I've seen those! Their covers look like Elizabethan stage sets."

"Yes, he told me they were contemporary and set in a Shakespearian acting company, with a parallel historical back story," she said, sounding quite knowledgeable suddenly.

"But there *is* only one contemporary Shakespearian company, the RSC, isn't there?" I said, thinking about it. "And since he's one of their leading actors, you can see why he'd want to keep it quiet, in case people thought he was basing his characters on them."

"Yes, that's more or less how he put it."

"I must have a look in Marked Pages for Nicholas Marlowe's crime novels, just from sheer curiosity."

"He has a deadline soon for the next, so he has to get on with it even though he obviously has other things on his mind. He's written the first few chapters and he's going to give me those tomorrow."

"He didn't tell you what was biting him? Grief, mourning — general nervous breakdown?"

"No, he only told me as much as he thought I needed to know, and that was that. He's not exactly the chatty type, is he? But I did tell him you were an author and wrote and illustrated very popular children's books."

"Only because they're small and affordable."

"And brilliant," she added loyally. "What happens in the new one?"

"It's called *Slipper Monkeys' Safari*. All the animals in a toy zoo have escaped and the Slipper Monkeys go on a safari with them, to find a new home. But go on — I take it Ivo wasn't noticeably impressed when you told him I am an author, too?"

"I'm not even sure he took it in," she confessed. "I think he just wanted me to go, by then. He'd barely let me over the threshold of his living room anyway, though I could see it was full of lovely old furniture and rugs — and bookcases, loads of bookcases."

"He'll probably be spending lots of money in Marked Pages then, if he ever goes out when it's open. So far, he only seems to walk around the village in the dark, though he has started clearing his garden in the afternoons."

"It'll probably do him good. He's very pale and gaunt," Bella said.

"He was always pale. He has that kind of translucent white skin, but he's way too thin and he's so edgy."

"I expect he's had some kind of nervous breakdown because he did say he couldn't take any more noisy and intrusive days like today," she said.

"Well, that's OK, because it should be quieter from now on, with just a steady stream of brides beating a path to our door — I hope."

We reopened the shop and Neil turned up and adjusted the volume on the bell as low as it would go, which I hoped would be audible without being intrusive. I was positive that Ivo couldn't hear it now, anyway.

Neil lingered for a while afterwards trying to chat up Bella between customers, but she wasn't being very encouraging, even though I'm sure she liked him. He did seem very nice.

I made a note to find out from Felix if Neil was married, because you can't be too careful when it's your best friend's possible future happiness at stake, especially if she already has a bruised heart.

The afternoon was much quieter than the morning, though we still had a steady stream of the curious, friends of Aunt Nan and people just after a free glass of bubbly and a fairy cake (we had put the last of both on a small white Lloyd Loom table near the counter). But there was also a confetti-sprinkling of brides-to-be, who tried on shoes, and an enquiry from a mother-of-the-bride about booking a private opening session, so I was hopeful things would snowball from there.

At five I swung the sign to "Closed" with a sigh of relief, and then we just stood and looked at each other in exhausted triumph.

"I'm shattered, but I think you could say that was a pretty successful opening," Bella said.

"I hope so. It's certainly been a long day."

But of course we still had to cash up and print out a till reading. Bella was so much better at these things than I, but I expected I'd get the hang of it eventually.

The float for Monday was put in little plastic coin bags and stored in a locked tin box in the kitchen, just like Aunt Nan had always done. A little safe might be a better idea, if I started selling more of the small goods and my cash takings increased, I decided.

Bella went home with the last of the fairy cakes for Tia and a bottle of Meddyg for her mother, which I thought might sweeten her up a bit. Aunt Nan always said that Meddyg could cure anything except old age, so I hoped it took a little of the acid out of Bella's mother.

Bella had generously offered to come in next day, Sunday, to help clean up, though she'd have to bring Tia with her. But I thought she'd done enough and said I would manage and I'd see her on Monday.

A huge wave of tiredness hit me once she'd gone, so poor Flash didn't get a decent walk that night, just up the lane and back. The cat was sitting on top of his usual gatepost staring down at Flash when we were on our way home, but Flash only gave a token bark and lunge, before trotting up towards the house. He seemed to be losing interest, unless it was all a cunning plan in his devious little Border collie brain to lull the cat into a false sense of security . . .

I continued listening to Aunt Nan's voice telling me her life story that evening, while preparing and eating an easy supper of cheese on toast, followed by half a packet of Jaffa Cakes, which had just happened to jump into my wire basket in the Spar the other day.

Cheryl Noakes' technique seemed to involve asking Aunt Nan a direct question at the start of each session and letting her ramble on, only prodding her occasionally if she lost the thread of the story.

There was a lot about food, but that wasn't surprising since, like me, Aunt Nan took a keen interest in all aspects of cooking and eating, right up to the moment when she made up her mind to pop her clogs.

In the recordings she became a time traveller, moving effortlessly between the past and the present, and sometimes speculating on the future (usually mine), though she seemed to see herself as still being here in some form.

And it *did* feel as if she was still nearby — in another room, perhaps, but ready to pop in and comfort and console, if necessary. My guardian angel . . .

Although I was physically so very weary, my mind was still running round in circles like a hamster in a wheel when I went to bed, and I just couldn't go to sleep. So, despite all my good intentions about rationing Aunt Nan's archive, I ended up fetching the CD player and listening to a bit more in bed.

She'd done one of her sudden time-shifts right after where I left off listening, and was now telling Cheryl all about my books and how proud she'd been when the first one was published and she could hold it in her hands.

That was certainly different from Justin, who'd always referred to them with indulgent dismissal as

196

"your little children's books" even after they proved so very successful.

"*My great-niece, Tansy, that I keep mentioning, she's very talented,*" Aunt Nan's voice, with the familiar flat Lancashire vowels, told Cheryl. "*She writes children's books about little pipe-cleaner animals called Slipper Monkeys — have you heard of them, dear? She paints all the pictures for them, too. That's what she did at college, she learned how to do book pictures. I've got the first one here to show you — in fact, I'll read you the start of it.*"

"*That would be lovely,*" Cheryl's voice said.

"*Right, here goes,*" said Aunt Nan, clearing her throat and then reading, "*'There was a little boy called Freddie who lived in a big square house with so many rooms no one had ever managed to count them all. One Christmas he got a packet of brightly coloured pipe cleaners in his stocking, with pictures showing how to make a fuzzy monkey. Freddie made a blue monkey before he got bored and went off to play with something else.*

His mother thought the little monkey looked sad, so she gave it a nose and a pair of eyes made from tiny beads as black as berries . . .'"

There was a snap as Aunt Nan closed the book. "*When she was a little girl I used to make things with her out of pipe cleaners. My father smoked a pipe, so there were always packets of those white ones in the house when I was growing up, but later you could get bigger ones in bright colours and I always put packets of them in Tansy's Christmas stocking. I expect that's* what gave her the idea in the first place. In fact, I still do make her a Christmas stocking up. You can't get a proper tangerine wrapped in tissue paper for love nor money any more, though."

I turned off the CD player. Aunt Nan and I had fashioned all sorts of things from the pipe cleaners, from bouquets of flowers to long-tailed birds, but making monkeys became a passion with me, I don't know why. And then I started to weave stories around them, as only children often do . . .

So then, when I'd started my graphic design course, the skill and the words sort of came together suddenly in my head and I was off.

Slipper Monkeys for ever!

CHAPTER
EIGHTEEN

Dead as my Love

I was never that close to my sister Violet, but blood is thicker than water, so I went down South to nurse her when she had pneumonia, though if you ask me she caught it gallivanting about at night with her so-called friends. A fast lot she seemed to have fallen in with while her husband was away, with plummy accents and posh clothes — but the type we used to call "all fur coat and no knickers", dear; it was all show. Vi sounded right posh, too — but then, she'd worked to get rid of her good Lancashire accent since she was a little girl.

Middlemoss Living Archive
Recordings: Nancy Bright.

I spent Sunday morning vacuuming and cleaning up the shop: fairy-cake crumbs were *everywhere*, but luckily no bubbly had been spilled. I polished the glass cabinets, already marked by fingerprints and, while I was at it, gave Cinderella's slipper on its cushion in the window a polish, too, so it would sparkle when the spotlight hit it.

Then I washed all the borrowed champagne flutes and put them on tea towels to drain, before repacking them in the boxes to be returned to the Falling Star.

I had a large freshly-baked bara brith loaf (bread-making machines make life so easy), so I buttered some of that for lunch, while I made a note of what had sold well on the first day, and also which shoes had attracted most attention: I hoped to email another order off to RubyTrueShuze before long.

Buying shoe stock was a bit different from in Aunt Nan's day. When I was very small she still went to Manchester on the train every Thursday afternoon, her half-day, to tour the shoe warehouses and make her selections, or drop off satin bridesmaids' shoes to be dyed to match their dresses. In the school holidays she'd taken me with her, which was a big, exciting treat, and the lovely Jewish family who owned her favourite warehouse always gave me sweets and, once, a little pink handbag with a clear plastic handle, which I still had, packed away in tissue paper among my treasures.

I'd have to go down to London some time soon to the RubyTrueShuze showroom, but I didn't suppose Ruby will be handing out sweets and handbags . . .

After lunch I dragged Flash out for a good long walk, to boldly go where he had never gone before, to quote *Star Trek*. Although improved, he was still difficult on the lead, frightened of everything and everyone, and nervous of new places, so I had to stop and unclamp the paw holding the lead to his chest every few minutes.

However, once we were across the green and had started to walk up the path through the fields that led to the Winter's End visitors' car park, he became a lot perkier. He stopped slinking along looking beaten, and up went his ears and the tail with its jaunty white tip.

The car park was deserted, of course, since the house wouldn't reopen for the tourist season until Easter, so I let Flash off the lead to see if he would come back to me. He did, too . . . eventually, after he'd jumped into a small stream and covered himself in mud and a streak of green slime.

I think we both felt better for the fresh air and exercise. The walk had also given me time to think about Ivo — to feel both sorry for him and guilty for my lack of sympathy. He was obviously not himself and couldn't help his bad temper, and *I* could have been a little more understanding. After all, yesterday must have sounded like the circus had come to town, poor man!

And every time I saw him, I felt this huge urge to feed him up, which I'd probably inherited from Aunt Nan, so if I didn't watch myself, I thought I'd be posting bits of buttered bara brith wrapped in clingfilm through his door.

Not long after I'd got home and had finished cleaning up Flash with a handful of those invaluable aloe vera doggy wipes, Bella rang to say Neil had asked her out for a drink again.

"What, Bell de Jour, Pour la Door Neil?"

"The very same. He called me just now."

"How did he get your number?" I asked, surprised.

"I gave him the one for my mobile yesterday," she confessed. "He wouldn't go away until I had."

"You kept that quiet! But I *thought* you liked him."

"He seems nice," she admitted, "but I really don't want to get involved with anyone and complicate my life all over again."

"A drink and a chat isn't *involved*," I encouraged her, because there was no need for us to turn into twin Miss Havishams if there were better alternatives. "When does he want to meet?"

"He suggested tonight, early evening, because of Tia, but Mum and Dad are going out. Bridge night," she added, as though they indulged in some kind of satanic ritual on a regular basis.

"I didn't think people had bridge parties any more."

"Oh, trust my parents to be still in with a set that does!"

"No problem anyway, because *I'll* baby-sit," I offered.

"It's OK, Neil's going to pick us both up this afternoon and take us to Martin Mere instead. You know Tia's mad about swans. I hope she isn't getting some kind of Leda complex."

"Perhaps she'll turn into a ballerina and dance in Swan Lake."

"I don't think so, because I'm sure she'll be very tall, like me. In fact, I'm going to try to steer her away from ballet and towards riding instead, because she loves horses. I was talking to Poppy about riding lessons yesterday. She has a small class for beginners, which Tia could join."

"Is it very expensive?"

"Not more than ballet, and she can borrow a riding hat to start off with, until I see if she likes it."

202

"I expect she will," I said, then told her I'd been thinking things over about Ivo.

"We'll have to get along together a bit better if he's going to be living here for a while. I've been rather mean to him, just because he stood me up years ago, when he was little more than a teenager and I should have been more understanding."

"He hasn't exactly made that easy, has he?" Bella observed. "But I suppose his dodgy temper is all part of the grieving process. How are you going to approach him?"

"Probably with caution, much like I did with Flash, holding out a sticky bun and making encouraging noises," I told her.

While the spirit of conciliation still filled me, I packed a bottle of Meddyg and several slices of buttered bara brith, and went to beard the lion in his den.

I had to take a deep breath before knocking at the door and for five long minutes I thought Ivo wasn't going to answer it, which would have been a relief, actually, because then I could have left my offerings on the step.

But just as I was thinking that, the door was suddenly flung open.

"What?" he demanded shortly, evidently under the impression that I'd come to complain about something, though so far the complaints had all been from *his* side. He had a pen in one hand and his hair was attractively ruffled, though the three-day stubble wasn't doing the line of his jaw any favours.

Then his eyes fell on the basket, which I thrust towards him. "Look, I've been thinking and I'm terribly sorry that I've been disturbing your peace when you're convalescing, so I've brought you a bottle of the honey liqueur that my aunt Nan taught me to make. It's good for bad nerves."

"I haven't *got* bad nerves," he snapped. "I just need a bit of peace and quiet!"

"That's all right. It's good for pretty well anything, really," I said, biting back a sharp answer. "And there's some bara brith in the plastic box. It's a peace offering."

He looked taken aback and muttered ungraciously, "Oh . . . well, sorry if I snapped your head off." He looked doubtfully at the bottle and then added reluctantly, "I *suppose* you'd better come in."

"Oh, no, that's all right — you take these and I'll leave you in peace . . ." I began, but he'd already turned and gone, leaving the door wide open, so after hesitating a moment I followed him in, closing it behind me, and went on into the long room that adjoined my cottage.

I knew it, of course, since before the house became a holiday home it had belonged to a family who, like the Brights, had been here for ever. But now, apart from the huge beams across the ceiling, it was transformed, full of lovely small pieces of furniture and mellow old rugs in muted rich shades.

Ivo walked across to the further window and placed a blotter over the papers that lay on his desk, as if I might rush over and read all his secrets. There was what

204

looked like an old pink leather-bound diary too, open and face down . . . Maybe he was writing his memoirs as well as the novels, but just hadn't told Bella that?

I set the basket down on the carved chest that served as a coffee table and took out the Meddyg and plastic box.

"What did you say that stuff was?" he asked, eyeing the bottle dubiously.

"It's an old Welsh remedy called Meddyginiaeth Llysieuol, passed down from the Welsh side of my family."

He took the bottle and held it up against the light, so that it glowed a pale, oddly greenish amber. " 'Thy tongue makes Welsh as sweet as ditties highly penn'd,' " he said absently.

"We usually just call it Meddyg. It's a kind of mead with herbs infused in it and it's very good. Aunt Nan always gave it to invalids, and her friend Florrie Snowball from the Falling Star says it's what's kept her fighting fit into her nineties."

Aunt Nan always reckoned it was pure cussedness, though, and said it was a wonder Florrie'd never caught her death of cold long before, prancing about outdoors naked from time to time with the other members of her magic circle until recently, when these events had begun to be held indoors.

"I've heard of mead, but not Meddyg."

"Then you try it and see what you think. And the bara brith is a type of fruit loaf, sliced and ready buttered."

"Your friend Bella said you'd written one or two children's books," Ivo said, suddenly seeming to lose interest in the food and drink.

"The odd one," I said modestly, since the latest would make it well over twenty. "They're the *Slipper Monkey* books — I don't know if you've come across them? Probably not, if you don't have children."

A sharp spasm crossed his face, so I seemed inadvertently to have hit on a nerve.

"No, I haven't heard of them," he said shortly. "So, did you go to art college when you left school?"

"What do you mean, 'when you left school'?" I demanded, surprised. "I was nearly nineteen and about to start art college when I met you!"

He looked at me strangely. "No, you were only sixteen — your sister told me."

"What? *Which* sister?" I demanded. "I don't *have* any sisters!"

"Stepsister, then — Marcia Anderson. She said we'd met at an audition, though I didn't remember it. But oddly enough, a couple of years later, when I got married, it turned out she was my wife's best friend . . ."

"She's my ex-stepsister now; my mother's remarried again," I told him. "And are you saying she told you I was still at school? Was that why you stood me up and I never saw you again?"

"I didn't stand you up," he insisted. "I rang your house to tell you I couldn't meet you that day after all, and that's when I spoke to Marcia."

"And you believed her when she told you I was practically jailbait?"

He ran a hand through his hair again. "You did look young for your age, so yes, I believed her. I mean, why would she lie?"

"Because she and her sister, Rae, delighted in making my life a misery from the moment I moved down to London to live with them. And even if you believed her, why on earth didn't you *tell* me you weren't going to see me again, and why?"

"I . . . couldn't," he admitted. "Marcia said she'd tell you I'd rung, and pass on the message that since I was moving out of town, I thought it would be better if we didn't meet again."

"Well, she didn't say anything at all — and I sat in that café the whole afternoon, waiting for you. They threw me out when they closed. I couldn't believe you'd stand me up."

"I'm really sorry — I'd no idea," he apologised. "Blame my 'salad days, when I was green in judgement' and with a head crammed full of dreams of becoming part of the Royal Shakespeare Company. But I did think of you from time to time later."

"Big of you!"

"No, really," he insisted. "I even called your house again, a couple of months later, thinking we could just chat . . ."

"And got the lovely Marcia again?" I guessed.

"No, someone who told me you'd moved in with 'the boyfriend'."

"That would be Rae, then, my other ex-stepsister," I said bitterly. "And I *had* moved in with one of my oldest friends, Timmy — and note 'friend', not 'boyfriend', because he's gay."

Ivo shrugged. "Oh, well, it's all water under the bridge now."

"If Marcia was your wife's best friend, you must have seen quite a bit of her. Didn't she ever mention me?"

He shook his head. I expect I'd been long forgotten by the time he'd met his future wife and her best friend, Marcia.

"She's been very kind, since the accident," he said. "Too kind, in fact — a bit smothering. When I felt I needed to take a break from the acting world and decided to move here, she offered to come and help me settle in, but I didn't want any visitors, especially someone reminding me of the past . . ."

"Yes, I'm sorry about your wife," I said awkwardly. "She'd just been offered a part in *Cotton Common*, like Marcia, hadn't she?"

"Yes. She'd been angling for one for a long time, so that was another of life's little ironies, that she should be killed just as she'd got what she most wanted." A dark shadow seemed to pass across his face.

"Tragic," I agreed sympathetically.

"Marcia means well," he continued, following his own train of thought, "but I'm taking a six-month sabbatical from the theatre world to think things through."

"You do look as if you need a break," I agreed frankly.

208

"After Kate was killed I put everything into storage and moved into a flat, then went straight back to work. I thought it was best to keep busy . . ." Again that introspective, haunted look visited his eyes. "And it seemed to work . . . Then suddenly one night, right in the middle of *A Midsummer Night's Dream*, I dried."

"Dried?"

"On the stage — forgot my lines. It's not something I'd ever done before and it wasn't just once. In fact, it seemed to be a vicious circle, because after a few times I started to worry about it, which seemed to make it even worse." He stopped and looked surprised. "I don't know why I'm telling you this!"

"Well, it's not like you've just confessed to a crime, is it? Delayed shock can affect you in different ways, that's all. I expect you're quite right about a change of scene doing you good. You can rest and recuperate — and write your autobiography," I added brightly and he looked at me enigmatically.

"I didn't recognise you right away. You wore your hair loose and were going through some kind of Goth phase when I last met you."

"Oh, yes, I'd forgotten about that," I said. He didn't mention that I was also currently a couple of stone heavier, too, but that might have been tact. Not that he'd shown a lot so far . . .

"Have you been angry with me all these years for standing you up?"

"No, of course not! I'd hardly thought about you," I lied, because him intruding into my wedding dreams didn't count, did it? It wasn't like I'd invited him in to play the role of princely spouse. "It was all such a long time ago."

"And even if you were eighteen, that was still way too young, so I expect it would have ended badly," he suggested.

"Yeah, well, thanks for helping me avoid that, then," I said sarcastically, getting up (though until that moment, I hadn't actually realised I'd sat down — he must have thought I'd settled in for the day). "I'll leave you in peace."

I knew I'd chosen the wrong word the moment it left my mouth. His face went all tense again and he said, "Peace? That would make a nice change! Even without all the shop noise, your damned cockerel crows for hours every morning and that insane dog yaps incessantly."

"Cedric's just greeting the dawn, and Flash hardly barks at the cat at all now."

"I've got workmen coming this week to put a solid fence up above the top of the wall, so I won't have to worry about your dog chasing Toby in his own garden," Ivo said.

"Good — though that isn't going stop your cat hopping over and tormenting Flash and messing in *my* flowerbeds, is it?"

He gave another of his shrugs. "I expect we'll just have to learn to rub along with each other — and so will Toby and Flash. I'm sorry I've been shouting at him, because he's obviously got a nervous disposition," he added unexpectedly.

"He was badly treated by his previous owner," I explained. "He seems to be afraid of everything except your cat! But well before your six-month sabbatical is up you'll probably be dying to get back to work, so the problem is short-term. What will you do with this place after that — keep it as a holiday cottage?"

"I don't know. It's certainly not the quiet haven of tranquillity I was expecting!"

"You did buy a cottage in the middle of a large village, right next to a shop," I pointed out.

"Yes, agreed — but a run-down shop with hardly any customers, in a quiet courtyard well off the main street."

"Aunt Nan had lots of regular customers *and* she did a steady trade in satin bridal shoes," I began. But he carried on over me,

"A shop that my estate agent assured me I would be able to buy eventually."

"He'd no reason to do that. Bright's has been in the family for generations, but I expect he just wanted to make a sale."

"Then suddenly the place is heaving with people and noise — especially that damned doorbell playing 'The Wedding March' every five seconds."

"That was only a technical hitch. It drove me and Bella mad, too," I admitted. "It's turned right down now to muted mode, and I doubt you'd hear it even with the windows open. But things won't be so hectic from now on. And look on the bright side: no one can park in the courtyard, they have to walk down Salubrious Passage to get here."

"I suppose that's something. And my front garden means no one can see directly into my windows."

"There you are, then."

"Right."

"Right." I picked up the empty basket. "I've got to go: I've a dog to walk."

I left, not sure how solid our truce was, and brooding over the past and might-have-beens. I also really, *really* wanted to kill Marcia . . . and then Rae, slowly and horribly.

I'd have rung Bella up to discuss it all, except I remembered she was out with Neil and Tia, so I rang Timmy and told him instead.

"Oh, yes, I remember you being heartbroken about some boyfriend just before you moved into the flat with me," he said. "I hadn't realised who it was, though!"

Then he was suitably indignant on my behalf and said all the right things, like that both my stepsisters were cows. Then he added that when he and Joe had seen Ivo's Hamlet they'd thought he was sooo dishy *and* a very good actor.

"If he's that good, why have I never heard of him all these years, or seen him in any films?"

"Because he's stuck firmly to the RSC, I expect, though he's been in one or two West End theatre runs that you've obviously managed to miss. If I'd *known* you'd had this boy-girl thing, I'd have told you," he said helpfully. "Oooh, star-crossed lovers, just like Romeo and Juliet!"

212

"Step-sister-crossed lovers, and no one died, they just moved on," I said sadly, though actually, someone *did* die in a later act: Ivo's wife, Kate Windle.

When I got home I put Mortal Ruin (Raffy's old group) on the CD player and listened to "Dead as my Love" while hardening my heart and deleting unread the latest batch of emails and texts from Justin.

CHAPTER
NINETEEN

Overtures

Violet was glad enough to see me when she was poorly, but ashamed of me once she felt more herself. When I left, I told her to think of her good name and of her poor husband, out in the Far East, still fighting for his country.

Middlemoss Living Archive
Recordings: Nancy Bright.

Monday, our first real day of trading, started quietly. We'd expected that, though we hoped business would quickly pick up through word of mouth, adverts, the coverage of the opening ceremony in the local papers and also the website, which was already giving us an internet showcase and point of contact, even if Bella was still constantly tweaking it.

I expected when the article and pictures in *Lively Lancashire* finally came out that would give us a boost, too. And then Winter's End was due to open to visitors at Easter, and the Witchcraft Museum, then open only at weekends, would open for five afternoons a week: so there should, with luck, soon be much more passing trade.

214

I opened up the shop with Bella, and then left her to it while I went to do some work on my latest book. Whenever the shop door opened I could hear "The Wedding March" playing so I could tell if Bella was busy and needed help.

Ruby (of RubyTrueShuze) rang me to ask how the opening had gone, which was really kind of her, and I told her how much interest her shoes had aroused.

"I sold one pair of the Roaring Forties in cream leather, and two other brides tried shoes on and said they'd come back. I hope they do."

"In my experience, brides like to visit every possible shop for the dress, shoes and veil before they make up their mind," Ruby said.

"That's understandable: they want their day to be extra special — and *I* want them to be wearing extra-special shoes!"

"Well, that's the thing," Bella agreed, when I related this conversation to her over mid-morning coffee, while the shop was empty. "Her shoes not only look wonderful, they're so well made that they feel comfortable too, so they'll still look and feel good when the bride has danced the night away at her reception. That's more than you can say for some *much* more expensive designer shoes!"

"You keep telling that to the customers," I urged her.

"I have sold one of those expensive purses printed with high-heeled boots, two boxes of confetti and a silver shoe handbag dangle," she said. "That's not a bad start."

215

"No, but we need more brides-to-be before we really get into full wedding season."

"They'll come," she assured me. "How are the illustrations going?"

"It was a bit hard to concentrate with the doorbell ringing as if crowds were rushing in when it's people trying out the bell. I think we need some sort of buzzer thing on the shop counter connected to the studio, so you can alert me when you're really busy."

"Good idea. I should be able to manage on my own most of the mornings — except possibly Saturdays, because I think then we'll be much busier, don't you?"

"It seems likely. Do you think Neil might be able to install the buzzer thing for us, or should I ask an electrician?"

"Oh, I think Neil can do it."

"Perhaps you could ring him and ask?" I suggested, then grinned. "Notice the careful way I haven't asked how your date went yesterday!"

She blushed slightly. "It wasn't really a date: after we took Tia to Martin Mere, we went on to the Botanic Gardens at Churchtown to have tea in the café there."

"That sounds fun to me."

"Yes, it was. Neil's a very nice man . . ."

"A very nice *unmarried* man, I hope?"

"He said he'd never been married, and he broke up with a long-term girlfriend last year, because she met someone else. An Australian someone else, so she's emigrated, which was a bit final. Not that it matters, really, because I explained about Robert and that I

216

wasn't ready for any kind of relationship with him or anyone else. And probably never would be."

"And how did he take that?"

"He was very understanding and said he'd just settle for being friends. Tia likes him," she added.

I thought Bella had also liked him a lot more than she would let herself admit, but I understood why she didn't want to rush into a new relationship: she was putting Tia first and working hard to be able to provide a home of their own as soon as she could.

While I didn't think there was any hope of me finding *my* Prince Charming in Sticklepond (or anywhere else, really), that didn't mean I wouldn't like my best friend to find love and happiness with the right man.

I left her to ring Neil and went back to work until lunch-time, and she promised to shout if she actually needed me. Then I took over just before three, while she went to pick Tia up from school.

On her way, she had to collect Ivo's manuscript for the first time: another new beginning. She was going to type into her laptop all the chapters he'd done so far, print them out, put them in a folder and push it back through his letterbox in the morning on her way to Cinderella's Slippers, so she had a long night's work ahead of her.

I couldn't see Ivo's door from the shop, even if I went out onto the step, because of the roses hedging his front garden, but she was back through the gate so quickly, clutching a large manila envelope, that she can't have got even one foot over the threshold.

She turned, guessing I would be watching, gave me a wave, and then vanished up Salubrious Passage.

I closed at four, and since practically no one had come into the shop during the last hour, I'd already given the place a quick clean and tidy by then, and managed to cash up and print out the till roll solo for the first time. (Bella had helpfully written out little tip cards this morning, for cashing up and till jamming, in terms a four-year-old could understand. It said "Don't Panic!" in large letters across the top of each.)

Flash refused to go upstairs, so had spent the morning lying at the bottom of them while I was working. He'd had a little bark or two whenever I'd let him out into the garden, presumably at Toby the cat, but each time he'd stopped quite quickly and I hoped eventually they'd just ignore each other . . . unless Toby came right into the garden when Flash was there, of course, when I would expect all hell to break loose again.

I let him out again when the shop was shut and could hear Ivo (I assumed it was Ivo) in his garden, chopping down the jungle.

He must have been still at it ages later when I went to shut up the hens because he nearly gave me a heart attack by suddenly looming up on the other side of the trellis and intoning sepulchrally, " 'You come most carefully upon your hour.' "

"I have to: dusk is the worst time for foxes and you get them even in the middle of the village these days," I explained, getting my voice back. "You startled me!"

"Did I? Sorry," he apologised, then told me that the new fencing was being installed on Wednesday morning.

"I've decided it's still going to be trellis, but higher and that heavier stuff, securely fixed," he said, which was a surprise, because I'd expected him to go for a nine-foot solid wooden stockade with lookout posts and armed sentries. "Otherwise, it would make this side of your garden pretty dark for half the day."

"Yes, that's true — thank you!" I said, surprised at his thoughtfulness and wondering if the Meddyg had already begun to work its magic on him.

But if so, it hadn't *entirely* done the trick, because he added, before he turned to go, "By the way, that doorbell of yours is still *way* too loud," then walked off before I could reply. He must have ears like a bat if he can still hear it!

While the workmen were installing the fencing on Wednesday morning the gate between the two gardens was open and Ivo, to my surprise, came in and made friends with Flash.

I was out there because I'd just struck a deal with one of his workmen to come back in his own time (and on the cheap), to fence off my herbal knot garden and fruit and vegetable beds before Flash peed them to death, so I expect I looked a little guilty.

"I thought you didn't like dogs," I said as Ivo made a fuss of Flash who, after a nervous few moments, suddenly lay down and rolled over to have his rather fat tummy tickled.

"I do — in fact, I'm more of a dog man than a cat one, really. Toby was my wife's cat." Again that shuttered look at the mention of his wife: he must truly have adored her. "I'm sorry I lost my temper when he chased Toby."

"They seem to be mostly ignoring each other these days," I said. "Flash has a token bark when he sees Toby, then he pretends he isn't there."

"I can see now that Toby's purposely winding him up," Ivo admitted.

"Yes, he gives him the evil eye from on top of the post. Why did you call him Toby? I always think it's a benign sort of name and it certainly doesn't suit him!"

"He was a stray kitten who wandered into our kitchen one night and we couldn't decide whether to keep him or not — it was a case of 'to be — or not to be.'"

I groaned and he gave me the faintest ghost of a smile.

Flash was now leaning against Ivo's legs, gazing adoringly up at him, which made me feel slightly jealous. He'd also left a generous covering of white hairs on Ivo's black moleskin trousers, I noticed.

Although I was very conscious of Ivo living next door, just the other side of the wall (especially when the faint strains of melancholy music drift through), he was still leading a semi-hermit existence. I certainly hadn't seen him out in the village during the day and nor was he letting anyone in his front door that I'd noticed, apart from the vicar . . . and Bella, of course, in the afternoons when she collected the manuscript, though she didn't actually go in. Even Hebe Winter hadn't gained admittance and she was highly indignant about that!

I suppose he was working off his excess energy hacking back his jungle of a garden in the afternoons and then going out for his solitary walk at dusk like a lonely vampire.

"He seems in good condition, if a bit plump," he said, stroking Flash's well-padded ribcage.

"I think I may have been overcompensating for his bad past with food — killing him with love," I confessed. "He could do with a lot more exercise than he's been getting lately, too."

"I've seen you taking him out for a walk in the evening," he said, and it was a bit disconcerting thinking of him standing at his upstairs window, noting my comings and goings. That's the only place he could have spotted me from.

"We only get as far as the green, usually," I admitted.

Then Ivo *really* surprised me by offering to walk Flash in the evenings himself. "I might as well, since I go for a long walk anyway."

"He's not easy," I said doubtfully. "The least noise startles him and makes him want to bolt for home, so you have to reassure him. And if he panics, he clamps the lead to his chest with one paw, so you can't pull it."

"Really? That's very clever!" Ivo said admiringly. "But I expect I could cope. I grew up with dogs."

He seemed genuinely keen to walk Flash, so it was agreed that from tonight he would collect him at the kitchen door each evening, which would do the dog a lot more good than a quick drag round the green — and I resolved to repay Ivo with small gifts of home-baked morsels, because if ever a man had forgotten how to eat properly, he was staring me in the face.

If Ivo was surprised when he returned Flash after his first dog walk, and I silently handed him a plastic box of fruit fairy cakes, he didn't say anything, just vanished with it back into the darkness of the garden.

I suspected he'd been roaming the lanes in a Byronic gloom but Flash seemed cheerful enough and had obviously been in a stream at some point, if not the small duck pond by the Spar.

The following morning I gave him his short early trot up the lane with less of a bad conscience, then got on with my latest illustration once Bella had arrived to open the shop. *Slipper Monkeys' Safari* had got as far as the shag-pile rug, where the lions took up residence, and I'd almost finished putting the finishing touches to it when Neil called up the stairs to ask where I wanted him to install my end of the buzzer.

"Bella's got a button to press just under the counter by the till," he explained.

"I'd like it up here in my studio, because if I'm in the kitchen I'll hear her call anyway."

When he'd finished, I followed him back into the shop to see how Bella was doing, and while I was there, Neil asked her if she would like to go to the Green Man for lunch with him.

"I can't, we don't shut for lunch," she said firmly.

"But it's Thursday, our half-day, so we shut at twelve," I reminded her, and she gave me a look as if to say, "You traitor!"

"Well then, if you aren't doing anything else . . .?" Neil suggested diffidently.

"Oh, I suppose I *could*," Bella said ungraciously. "I'll just have to pop next door and pick some papers up first, though."

"And Tansy's welcome to come too, of course," he said politely.

"Oh, not me, thanks. I'm going to have a quick lunch and then go and have my tea leaves read. Zillah Smith at the Witchcraft Museum invited me," I said quickly.

I wasn't actually due there until two; I just didn't want to play gooseberry!

A delivery had arrived mid-morning, including some lovely white umbrellas printed with pastel-coloured shoes, which Bella had unpacked, and I price-tagged those after they'd gone.

Gregory Lyon was in the kitchen when I went round to his house, which was attached to one end of the museum. He told me that the forces in my courtyard were very strong and with my permission he'd like to walk about in it at dawn.

I said that was fine with me, and it only occurred to me later to wonder if he would do it with or without his clothes on . . . and also to wonder what Ivo might think if he looked out in the early hours and saw an elderly and imposing eccentric communing with invisible powers outside.

I'd taken a pile of flyers for the shop with me and suggested they display them in the museum. In return, I'd take some of theirs back to the shop, which they agreed was a good idea.

Then Gregory Lyon wandered out of the room, carrying a cup of tea with two Garibaldi biscuits balanced in the saucer and Zillah urged me to drink mine (which was very strong) so she could read my leaves.

She was wearing big hooped gold earrings engraved with an intricate pattern, layers of bright pink cardigans and a lime-green skirt, shot through with spangly bits. In comparison, my own favourite red tartan dress over green net underskirt and matching tights looked positively bland.

"Interesting," she declared, after staring down into the cup for quite some time. "Your life seems to be about to come full circle. There are forces at work, both good and ill."

"I don't know about full circle, but I do seem to be running round in rings," I said. "Does it say whether the shop will be a success?"

"Not specifically: there will be great challenges in your life, but you'll overcome them and, in the end, get what you long for. Your love life is . . . complicated," she added.

"My love life is non-existent and likely to stay that way! Prince Charming had feet of clay so we never even got as far as the glass slipper."

She gave me her glinting, gold gypsy smile. "You've got your own glass slipper now: I've seen it in the shop window!"

I thought what she was reading meant that the shop would be a big success, because that's all I really longed for now . . . well, apart from a baby, of course, but I knew that wasn't in my stars or my tea leaves.

Florrie Snowball was standing in the doorway of the Falling Star looking like a small wooden Mrs Noah when I came out, and beckoned me across, then gave me coffee in the snug from a hissing and steaming monster of a coffee machine. She seemed to take great delight in operating it and I was quite glad of something to take the taste of Zillah's tea away.

I told her I was listening to Aunt Nan's recordings of her memories and how sad it was that she'd lost her fiancé in the early days of the war.

"She was always one to make the best of what life gave her," she said. "She just got on with it. And she was a good friend to me, my whole life."

"You can't pay her a bigger tribute than that," I said, and she offered me another frothy capuchin, as she called it, though neither monks nor monkeys were harmed in the process.

CHAPTER
TWENTY

Sister Act

I didn't think I would ever fall in love again like I had with my Jacob, but after a couple of years I did start to go out with my friends once more, to the cinema or to dances, and even walked out with a young man once or twice. But there was nothing serious on my side, and it never seemed fair to go on letting them get fond of me if I couldn't return their affection.

Middlemoss Living Archive
Recordings: Nancy Bright.

One night's instalment of Aunt Nan's memoirs wandered off into a description of how she'd made her friend Florrie a wedding cake during rationing, but then suddenly, just when I was about to turn off the CD, she switched to a tantalising bit about how she'd eventually resumed her social life and even gone out with other men, though her heart wasn't in it.

I switched it off there, but I kept mulling over it next morning while I was working on an illustration. She'd been so young during the war, and it was just a pity that she didn't get a second chance at love. But then, so many others didn't either . . .

226

I went downstairs around ten thirty to let Flash out and make Bella some coffee, and as I was carrying both cups through on a tray, I heard the pealing of wedding bells, so knew we had another customer.

"Good morning, can I help you, or would you just like to browse?" I heard Bella ask brightly. Then she added in surprise, "Oh, but it's Marcia, isn't it — or Rae? I'm afraid I never did learn to tell you two apart when I came down to stay with Tansy that time."

"You were right first time, I'm Marcia — the actress," said my elder stepsister in her familiar, slightly husky voice.

And there she was — tall, thin as a rack of ribs and very elegant, her skirt short and her white-gold hair long and loose, though she was well the wrong side of forty. She had on a military-style winter jacket and high black patent Louboutins — you can always tell by the red soles.

She hadn't seen me yet because her attention was fixed on a pair of cream sandals with criss-cross straps and high heels. "These are nice! I wonder if I get a family discount . . .?"

"No," I said, "and those are vintage and size five, so they won't fit you anyway."

She spun round. "Oh, there you are, Tansy! Your big sister's come to say hello."

"Hello," I said discouragingly.

"Well, actually, I came to call on that dishy actor you've got living next door, but he must be out because there was no answer."

I was quite sure Ivo wasn't out, since to my knowledge he hadn't yet been further than the garden in daylight, and that generally in the afternoons (presumably he wrote in the mornings — or in the evenings after he got back from his walk, while playing that miserable music), so he'd meant it when he said he didn't want to see her.

"Ah, yes! That would be the dishy actor *I* was once dating, until you told him I was sixteen and he stood me up," I said coldly.

"Oh . . . did I?" She looked blank. "You know, I'd quite forgotten that." Then she gave an empty, tinkling laugh, like a cheap tin bell.

"Really? *I* hadn't."

"You're not still holding a grudge over it, are you?" Her blue china-doll's eyes opened wide. "It was such a long time ago. He married a friend of mine eventually — but you know about her, don't you? She's the actress who was killed in an accident — and what terrible timing, when she'd just wangled herself a part in *Cotton Common.* So unlucky!"

"I don't know about *unlucky,* but it was certainly very tragic," I said drily, wondering how she could speak so flippantly about Kate when she was supposed to have been a close friend.

"I've been consoling her widower, but he's turned very elusive. Still, now he's living practically on my doorstep, this is my big chance!"

"I think he *vants to be alooone,*" I said, all Marlene Dietrich. "And as far as you're concerned, so do I."

"Are you still mad that I told Ivo you were sixteen? It was just a bit of fun, and your little romance wouldn't have come to anything anyway."

"Thanks to you, it never got the chance! And you didn't let me know he wasn't going to meet me, so I waited for him for *hours*."

A faint illumination dawned. "He's been talking to you about it, hasn't he, or you wouldn't know what had happened. Have you . . . seen a lot of him?"

"Hardly anything. He's almost a recluse and I think he's here for a rest. But of course we recognised each other and I asked him why he'd stood me up."

"Right," Marcia said thoughtfully.

"He told me he'd rung the house again a few months later, and that time someone else — presumably Rae — told him I'd gone to live with my boyfriend."

"Oh, yes, Rae did always call that gay friend of yours 'the boyfriend', didn't she? But only joking."

"Ha, ha!" I said.

"Come on, Tansy, none of that matters now, does it? Are you feeling ratty because you've broken up with Justin?"

"Did Rae tell you that?" I demanded.

"Daddy told me about your great-aunt dying and that you and Justin had broken things off, so you'd moved back here. I rang Rae for the inside story and —"

"I expect she told you what she'd done, so you could both have a good laugh about it?" I interrupted bitterly.

229

She stared at me. "You mean, *Rae* had something to do with you and Justin breaking up?" Then she laughed again, and I could have hit her with the nearest shoe.

"You just can't keep a boyfriend when either of us are around, can you?"

"It would appear not," I said through gritted teeth.

"Look, Tansy, why don't we go into the cottage and talk it all through," she suggested. "You and Justin are made for each other, I've always thought so, and I'll help you to get him back."

"I don't *want* him back, thanks very much! And I'd rather you just went, because you're neither friend nor family. I love your father, but I just can't understand how you two turned out so shallow, selfish, malicious and hard-hearted."

She flushed slightly. "Oh, come on, Tansy! We may not always have got on —"

"Ha, understatement of the year! When I moved down to London I was only eighteen and you were both old enough to know better, but you *bullied* me!"

"Well, you were always such a quiet, geeky little wuss, you provoked us into it. And even your mother preferred us to you!" she snapped, turning nasty.

"That was pretty clear — you were three of a kind. And now I really don't see why I should ever have to put up with you or Rae again."

Marcia reluctantly put the shoe she was still fondling back on its stand (though it would never have fitted her, unless she'd cut her toes off, like the Ugly Sisters in the more extreme versions of Cinderella). "If you feel like that, I'll go," she said, and swept out to the peal of

The Wedding March, a joyous paean to a welcome departure.

"Well, do you feel better after that little outburst?" Bella asked.

"Yes, lots," I said, and grinned. "She's had it coming for quite a while."

"I'd forgotten what she was like, and that perfume she was wearing was almost as invasive as she was — only it's still hanging about," Bella said.

"I expect she'll be back eventually, because she's got the hide of a rhinoceros and if she's set her sights on Ivo Hawksley, which it sounded very much like, then we're handily placed for her to stalk him from here."

"It did sound as if she fancied him."

"Yes, and she always gets her man, though she may have to let this one get over his wife, first!"

"He doesn't look or sound as if he's ready for a new relationship yet, that's for sure," Bella agreed.

When I went back to the *Slipper Monkeys* I picked up the pale yellow pipecleaner monkey I'd been painting earlier and crumpled it up into a ball.

Then I realised what I'd done, and carefully unknotted its furry limbs and rendered it unscary again, because it was all a bit too voodoo doll-ish.

My dog-walking vampire came to the back door and collected Flash at dusk.

"'Light thickens and the crow makes wing to the rooky wood'," he said when I opened the door. I thought that was from *Macbeth*, which it was unlucky to quote. But then, I expected he felt he'd already had all the bad luck possible.

"Marcia Anderson was here earlier and said she knocked at your door," I told him, but I wasn't sure if the news even registered, because he just held out his hand for Flash's lead and then turned and went.

I baked some Welshcakes while listening to Aunt Nan, and when Ivo finally returned with a wet, tired and muddy dog an hour or so later, I handed him a tinfoil parcel of them, still warm from the oven, in return for the lead.

Seeming to feel that some slight social exchange was necessary, he asked me how my book was going.

"Oh, fine," I said, then almost slipped up and asked him how the novel I wasn't supposed to know he was writing was coming along, but just managed to choke the words back in time.

Flash wolfed down his own bodyweight in dog food, and then went to sleep on the rag rug by the stove, while I put a malt loaf in the bread maker.

I'd switched Aunt Nan off when I'd heard Ivo at the door, but now I listened to a bit more, where she did one of her sudden digressions from the narrative thread of her life into the realms of chutney production, before wandering back to the subject of her sister's shortcomings.

I wouldn't say Violet sounded quite as bad as Rae and Marcia, but she certainly seemed to be an early prototype.

CHAPTER
TWENTY-ONE

Fat Rascals

I started seeing an American airman towards the end of the war, which worried my parents a bit even though I assured them it wasn't anything serious. Hank was a nice boy but homesick and lonely, so we had a bit of fun together — we both loved to jitterbug, for a start! You wouldn't believe it now, but I was a slip of a thing then, full of energy.

> Middlemoss Living Archive
> Recordings: Nancy Bright.

"My mother's getting worse," Bella said gloomily when she arrived for work in the morning. "The wind blew all the blossom off the cherry tree last night and she's been out since dawn, picking each petal up individually."

"Her behaviour's getting very extreme, isn't it? Do you think she needs therapy?"

"I'm sure she does, but she and Dad don't seem to think it's a problem and that she's just house-proud."

"I think Flash needs therapy too. In fact, I'm starting to think he's autistic," I said. "He gets upset if everything isn't exactly the same every day — his bowls in the same place, the same walks at the same times —

anything at all different throws him. Sudden noises panic him and so do men holding anything remotely resembling a stick — even a fishing rod."

"Can dogs *be* autistic?"

"I don't see why not. But maybe he's over-anxious because of his hellish life before you rescued him. He still cringes when I pat him, so that gives you some idea of what his life was like."

"He'll learn to know that he's safe now you've rescued him from all that. And I need to rescue Tia from Mum's example, before she thinks her granny's behaviour is normal," Bella said. "Only renting's so expensive."

"Is Tia with her today?"

"Yes, I left her helping to pick up blossom, but I should think the novelty will wear off pretty soon."

"You could have brought her with you — you can do that any time."

"No, that's OK, because Dad's offered to take her up to Stirrups for her first riding lesson later today and she's wildly excited about that. I wish I could have been there, though!"

"Well, you can if you want to," I offered. "You know you can take time off whenever you like."

"That wouldn't be fair. I'd feel I was taking advantage of our friendship if I kept skiving off. Besides, I think we're going to be quite busy today, what with getting all that local newspaper coverage during the week, and we've already decided there needs to be two of us in the shop on Saturdays."

"I hope you're right about it being busy and we sell lots of shoes, before all this year's brides have bought them somewhere else! Did you realise, it's British Summertime tomorrow?" I asked. "The clocks go forward, so we're getting into the peak wedding season already!"

"Or do they go back?" Bella said doubtfully. "I can never remember."

"*Spring* forward, *fall* back," I said. "Easy!"

"Good one."

While we were opening up I described what Aunt Nan had been saying in the latest recordings.

"Cheryl obviously had her work cut out trying to make her stick to the narrative thread, because she wanders off all the time. One minute she's talking about what she got up to during the war, and the next about the best way to make plum jam! And although I love hearing about all the cooking and preserving, and the old village customs and so on, it can get frustrating when she leaves some interesting reminiscence half finished!"

I told Bella how Aunt Nan used to love to jitterbug with her American friend. "Can you imagine that?"

"Not really," Bella said frankly, "but it's good that she managed to have some fun, because she was very young when she lost her fiancé, wasn't she?"

"Yes, and that's what I think, too. I expect she never quite got over losing him, but she had to get on with her own life."

And it occurred to me that I was echoing that, because although my fiancé hadn't died, I had most definitely lost him and was now striking out on a similar path to Aunt Nan. But without the jitterbugging, of course.

Speak of the devil, Justin rang me up just after the shop had shut and Bella had gone home, and on the house phone, rather than my mobile, so he caught me on the hop.

"Tansy darling, I've got you at last!" he exclaimed. "You never seem to answer your mobile, or my texts and emails."

"What do you want, Justin? I've been really busy all day and I'm shattered."

"Just to know how your new shop is coming along. It sounds as if it might be doing really well."

I told him that after a slow start it was picking up and I was cautiously optimistic of success.

"Today we've been rushed off our feet. I've sold four pairs of really expensive shoes and a pair of vintage white kidskin ones, as well as lots of giftware," I said proudly.

"That's great!" he said, sounding so genuinely pleased that perhaps I'd been wrong thinking that he'd expected (or hoped) that Cinderella's Slippers would bomb. He asked me all kinds of questions about it, too, so that I found myself telling him one or two funny things that had happened . . .

In fact, he was so much more like the man I first fell in love with that I forgot for a minute that he wasn't. He was even wry about Mummy Dearest when I politely enquired how she was.

"She stayed here for weeks while her house was being repainted, and my life wasn't my own!" he confessed. "Honestly, you'd think I was still a child and needed my mother to organise my life, the way she goes on."

Well, that was pretty much what I'd been telling him for years, so it was good to hear him admit it, even if somewhat too late.

"I do miss you, Tansy," he added softly. "Please, won't you let me come and see you? I could drive up tonight, in fact and —"

"No!" I said, more sharply than I'd intended. "No," I repeated, softening my tone a bit. "I really am tired and I've got lots to do tomorrow. Besides, I couldn't put you up here, because Aunt Nan wouldn't have liked that at all — and it would be a pointless trip, Justin."

He sighed. "Not pointless to me, because I still care about you and hope we can at least still be friends. Look, what if I get off early in the morning and just come up for the day? I've found a few more of your things you might like to have," he added enticingly, "like your big pottery mixing bowl with the glazed pink inside and several bottles of mead."

"Meddyg."

"Whatever. I can't drink the stuff, so it will only go to waste otherwise."

"Timmy could call in and collect the rest of it."

"I'd rather bring it myself, because I'm longing to see you again. Honestly, I'm a shadow of my former self since you left," he said persuasively, but if that was true, then it was only because he didn't have me filling the house with cakes, pastries and pies any more.

I did my best to persuade him not to come, and *he* did his utmost to persuade me I'd feel differently when I saw him, so even by the end of the call I wasn't sure whether he was going to drive up tomorrow or not.

I *really* hoped not . . .

Unfortunately, I *hadn't* managed to put him off. Next morning while I was out feeding the hens, he left a message on my answering machine saying he was on his way and should be here mid-morning.

I felt cross, put out and upset in equal measure, because once I'd cleaned the shop I'd intended spending most of the day working on my illustrations . . . not to mention a bit of baking, including trying out the recipe for Fat Rascals that Timmy, who shares my interest in cooking, had emailed to me the previous night.

It sounded like a kind of super-duper rock cake and I already had all the ingredients.

So now, since I was too unsettled to work, I began the baking instead and had just taken a cheese and onion pie out of the oven, to join the cooling racks of Fat Rascals (I'd eaten one hot, and it had been yummy), tomato and cheese tartlets and butterfly cakes (basically just fairy cakes — slice a piece off the top, blob on jam and cream, then cut the slice of cake in half and stick it back into the cream like wings), when Flash started barking at the back door.

Justin was standing there, looking his familiar tall, solid and handsome self — and as dependable as I had once thought him. But he also looked nervous; I'd forgotten he wasn't keen on dogs.

Flash didn't seem too keen on *him*, either. When Justin handed me the large cerise orchid in a white pot he'd been clutching to his hand-knitted Aran jumper and would have kissed my cheek, Flash took this as a sign of aggression and broke out into loud barking, hackles raised. I was quite impressed by this demonstration of protectiveness!

"I forgot to tell you I had a dog now, but he just barks, he doesn't bite," I assured him, though I wasn't *entirely* certain about that in Justin's case.

I soothed Flash down while Justin went to fetch the box containing the rest of my things from the car, which he'd parked next to mine at the bottom of the garden. Flash retreated under the kitchen table when he came in, making a menacing low, throaty, rumbling noise.

Justin took hold of my shoulders and gazed lovingly down at me. He always has that Viking glow about him — the fresh skin, blue eyes and tawny hair — so he seemed larger than life, especially in the small cottage. I kept the potted orchid between us, so he couldn't move in any closer.

"You're looking *great*," he said, where once he would have been really critical of the asymmetric orange cardigan I was wearing over a long pink paisley corduroy dress, teamed with a pair of my favourite Birkie clogs.

"Thanks, but you really shouldn't have come, I told you so," I said, then sighed when his face fell and suggested he might as well sit down, now he *was* here.

"If you're sure the dog will be OK?" he asked, with a nervous glance at the table.

I wasn't, but he sat down as far away from Flash as he could get and reached for one of the Fat Rascals on the cooling rack.

"Mother called me just after I'd left the message for you," he said through a mouthful of cake. "She wasn't feeling too well and wanted me to go down to Tunbridge, but I told her I was more than halfway to Lancashire and I'd call her when I got back."

I was amazed: the old Justin would have turned the car round and belted off to Tunbridge Wells and Mummy Dearest at the first slip road! It was a pity he hadn't shown this kind of resoluteness when we were together.

I poured him a cup of tea and offered to butter him some bara brith, but he said he was fine with the cakes.

"What *are* these?"

"Fat Rascals."

"Never heard of them — but they're good. I've missed all this," he added, indicating the array of home baking spread to cool all over the table. "But then, I miss everything about you."

"Including those failings you used to point out to me, like my total lack of dress sense, social skills and not being a size zero clothes hanger like your friends' wives?"

"I didn't mean to be critical! I really do love all your eccentric little ways."

"What about the way I invaded your flat with clutter and bright colours, and hung pipe-cleaner monkeys everywhere?"

"All of it," he insisted. "I don't know what got into me, I must have been mad not to have appreciated you more. It's like that old Joni Mitchell song — you know, the one about not knowing what you've got till it's gone." He gave me a wry smile. "You've left a huge hole in my life, Tansy."

" 'Big Yellow Taxi'," I said, softening for a moment — until I recalled exactly *why* I'd left. "But perhaps you should have thought about all that before you had a fling with Rae!"

"I know I was really weak, but she did do all the running — and it was only a couple of times."

"Oh, well, if it was only a *couple* of times, then that's all right, then," I said with heavy sarcasm, which bounced right off him.

"Really?" he said, glancing up from his third Fat Rascal hopefully.

"*No*."

He looked crestfallen. "I realised the fling with Rae was a big mistake almost at once, because she made it clear she just wanted to carve another notch on the bedpost and crow over you."

"Yes, she and Marcia never really wanted my boyfriends for themselves, they just enjoyed the fact that they could take them away."

"As soon as I came to my senses I told her it was over and I hoped you'd never find out. But then she hit me with the news of the pregnancy and I've been paying her off ever since to keep quiet."

"You'd have to pay maintenance for your own child anyway," I pointed out.

"Of course, but she wanted much more than that."

"Yes, and it's because you were paying her through the nose that you turned into a skinflint and kept putting off the wedding, and saying we couldn't afford to have children. I can see that now."

"I'm really sorry about that, too."

"You should be, because the outcome is that your actions have cost me my chance to have children."

He reached across and took my hand. "Not if we get back together," he said softly. "I'm sure it's not too late. They only told you your fertility was declining, which it would be at your age, and we could always try IVF if it doesn't happen quickly."

I removed my hand. "That would be even more expense."

"It doesn't matter, I just want you to be happy. And anyway, I'm not giving Rae any more money because she's had more than enough from me already!"

"But Charlie's still your son," I reminded him, a knife seeming to turn in my heart. "You have to think about him, he's the innocent party in all this."

"Oh, I suppose I'll have to pay her some maintenance eventually, but it will be the minimum amount." He leaned forward and this time seized both my hands.

"*Please* come back to me, Tansy! I promise to do anything it takes to make up for what I did."

He looked so handsome, appealing and sincere that had it been anyone but one of my stepsisters he had been unfaithful with, I might have wavered momentarily at this point.

"It's just not possible, Justin, because the thought of Rae and the child would always come between us. I'm never coming back, I'm here in Sticklepond for good. In fact, I should never have left."

"Then how about if I move to a hospital up here, instead? Manchester or Liverpool or somewhere."

"Don't be silly! You hate it up here, you know you do."

"I've heard Manchester isn't so bad."

"Manchester is a thriving metropolis with loads going for it," I told him.

"There you are then — and it's quite close to here, isn't it? Commutable."

"It's not commutable to Mummy in Tunbridge Wells, though," I pointed out.

"She'd understand and she could get on a train and visit us."

Yes, I could really see *that* happening!

"Justin, there's no 'us' any more. There's really no point in even discussing it, because we're never getting back together," I insisted.

He went a bit sulky after that, seeming to think he had made the ultimate sacrifice in suggesting he leave London. I'd intended giving him lunch and then attempting to get rid of him, but he wanted to take me out somewhere so we ended up at the Green Man next door.

He came out of his sulk while we ate and was warm and funny about his work and his colleagues, and back to being the man I fell in love with . . . only every time I found myself forgetting, the picture of him and Rae together would suddenly slide between us like frosted glass.

It didn't help his cause that Mummy Dearest rang three times during lunch, either.

"I was hoping to stay longer, but I suppose I'd better head back," Justin said reluctantly, when he'd seen me back to the cottage. Flash seemed no keener on the sight of him the second time than he had the first.

I packed up some cakes for him and then saw him out to the car, feeling relieved and wrung out in equal measure, which I suppose is how he managed to catch me off guard, suddenly pulling me close and kissing me.

His embrace felt treacherously warm, safe and familiar for a moment, and then I pulled sharply away. "You'd better get going, Justin: it's a long way to London."

He got in, grinning as though he had scored some victory with his snatched kiss. "Bye, darling!" he called cheerily through the open window as he reversed out and then headed off down the lane.

As I turned to go in, I noticed Ivo standing next to his Jaguar, Toby in his arms. I wasn't sure how long he'd been there.

"Boyfriend?" he asked, his face shuttered and inscrutable.

"Ex-fiancé."

"That kiss didn't look very ex."

"It *was* from my side. He's ex because he cheated on me and I intend being a singular woman from now on."

He half-smiled and, disconcertingly, the ghost of the handsome boy I once fell in love with appeared on his face. "I think you always were pretty singular."

"I meant *single*," I said with dignity.

"I'll be round for Flash later, if you still want me to take him?"

"Of course I do — why wouldn't I?" I marched off, Flash snapping at my heels as if I were a recalcitrant sheep.

Men!

CHAPTER
TWENTY-TWO

April Fool

VE Day came and we all celebrated — there were tables and bunting and a brass band in the High Street — you've never seen such a grand sight! But of course, Violet's husband was still fighting on in the Far East, because the war there didn't end until a few months later. VJ Day, they called that one. My American friend had gone home by then and the new curate, who had been a chaplain on active service but invalided out, asked me to walk out with him . . .

Middlemoss Living Archive
Recordings: Nancy Bright.

Aunt Nan's latest memoirs rambled back to her wartime admirers — and she had obviously not been short of them! But then, her pictures in the family albums show her to have been very pretty: slim and bright-eyed, with the same dark, curling hair that I had.

She started to put weight on in her twenties, like I did; must be a family trait! Or maybe it was just because we both loved baking so much? (And, of course, eating!)

I wondered if she did walk out with the curate. Because if so, it obviously never came to anything. I was looking forward to finding out.

When Bella arrived for work I told her about Justin's visit and that I just couldn't seem to get it into his thick head that he'd done something so unforgivable that I wouldn't eventually give in and take him back.

"He even suggested he get a job in a hospital up here and move north!"

"Gosh, he must miss you!" she said, impressed, because Justin had never made any secret of the fact that he thought Lancashire a cultural wilderness inhabited by escapees from the *Coronation Street* and *Cotton Common* TV soap series.

"I think it was more due to having forgotten quite how smothering Mummy Dearest could be when I wasn't there to stop her trying to monopolise his time. She's been staying in the flat for weeks while her house was repainted and I got the feeling it was a big relief when she went home. She called him on his mobile several times while he was here, too."

"I am sure he *has* missed you . . ." She looked at me. "You don't think you ever *could* forgive him?"

"No," I said, firmly but sadly. "There were moments yesterday when I remembered why I'd loved him — I mean, he's so big, fair and *glowing* that he's like a Viking invasion rolled into one person! But then an image of him with Rae would flash across my eyes and turn me to cold stone. And there's always going to be Charlie as a reminder, isn't there?"

"Yes, and he'll have to support him, until he's eighteen, at least."

"He said Rae had had more than enough money out of him because she'd been blackmailing him! But I'm

247

sure he'll have to carry on paying her the minimum of maintenance for Charlie, or she could take him to court. Poor little Charlie! He's the innocent victim in all this."

"Not your problem any more, though, is it? I wish I'd been savvier about money when I was living with Robert," she added. "If I'd paid towards the mortgage and bills when I moved in, I'd have had a claim to part of the house, at least, so his wife wouldn't have got everything."

"It sounds like most of it went to settle his gambling debts anyway."

"True . . . and it just shows, however nice and trust-worthy men seem to be, like Justin and Robert, they can still be secretly deceiving."

"'One may smile and smile, and be a villain'," I agreed. I must have caught Shakespeare-itis from Ivo.

"And now there's Neil, who seems very nice — but who knows, really?" she said darkly.

"Have you seen him again?"

"No. He wanted to take me and Tia somewhere yesterday, but I put him off. I said I was doing something else . . . which I was, really, because I had lots of Ivo's typing to catch up with."

"Is his book any good?"

"Yes, brilliant! In fact, it's really frustrating reading it in bits like this, but also quite exciting, wondering what's going to happen next. This one's called *Tempest in a Teacup*, so I think you can guess which Shakespeare play the plot is based around."

"I think I'll have to read one of his books from sheer curiosity. He collects Flash every evening now and takes him out for a walk," I added. "I told you about that, didn't I?"

"No!" she said, staring at me from large blue eyes. "How long has that been going on?"

I shrugged. "A few days, after he apologised for frightening Flash and made friends with him. Then he suggested that since he liked to walk in the early evenings, he might as well take Flash with him. I'm really glad, because it gives Flash lots more exercise than he was getting."

"That seems very kind," Bella commented, then looked at me closely. "Are you two getting *friendly*, then? I mean, he's so not my type, but I can see he's really attractive, though in a much more subtle way than Justin."

I laughed. "No way! We hardly speak, except a few words when he collects Flash or brings him back." I didn't tell her about my attempt to fatten him up by forcing food parcels onto him every time he returned the dog. He'd never said whether he ate them or not — but then, he hadn't so far refused to take them, either.

Business began to pick up steadily in our second week of trading, as word spread about Cinderella's Slippers. Bella could generally manage on her own in the mornings, while I got on with my illustrations. I was making a dummy book of *Slipper Monkeys' Safari* now to see how it looked. This involved photocopying my illustrations and then literally sticking them into a little book in the right sequence. It wasn't just the action in the pictures that had to flow from frame to frame, but the words, too.

I illustrated in line and wash, and there was no way I could create on the computer screen like some artists. I need the connection between hand, eye, brush, pen and paper. I admired those who could, it just wasn't for me.

Anyway, *Slipper Monkeys' Safari* was finally almost finished, despite everything else that had been happening, and part of my mind was already engaged with the next idea.

Justin texted me about some investigations he'd done about transferring to a post in a Manchester hospital, and I texted him right back and said plainly that it would be pointless if he thought that by moving up here I would ever get back with him.

After that, there was silence, so I assumed he was sulking.

I'd given the orchid he'd brought with him to Bella to take back for her mother: it looked the sort of thing she'd like.

When Ivo returned Flash after his walk on Tuesday evening, he actually said he'd liked the cheese and onion pie I'd given him the night before!

"Good, because I don't think you're eating enough," I told him. "Especially now you're working so hard in the garden."

"I seem to have lost the hunger mechanism," he said. "I just . . . forget to eat."

250

"I can't imagine *ever* forgetting to eat," I admitted. "I suppose that's why I'm so fat!"

" 'O, that this too, too solid flesh would melt'?" he suggested. "But you're not fat!"

"I'm certainly not thin."

"You look just about right to me," he said to my surprise, giving me that rather mesmerising smile, then he vanished back into the darkness, though not before I'd thrust my latest food offering into his hands: there's nothing as sustaining as a little hotpot pie with a shortcrust pastry top and a chunk of good, solid fruit cake to follow.

I found myself staring absently after his vanishing form until I gave myself a mental shake and shut the door. Then, since I'd forgotten to switch Aunt Nan's CD off when I let Ivo in, I had to go back a bit. She'd seemed about to confide something interesting but instead, I discovered, she did her usual trick of diverging into describing some local custom or a recipe!

Curiosity got the better of me and next day I slipped off to Marked Pages in the High Street to see if Felix had any of Nicholas Marlowe's novels, leaving Bella to hold the fort.

"Nicholas Marlowe? Yes, there are one or two in the back room on the crime shelves," he said. "They're very good. It's so clever the way he weaves Elizabethan back stories in with the current plot, set in a contemporary Shakespearian company, and then uses a theme from one of the plays to hang the whole thing from! Genius!"

251

"Someone told me they were a good read; I just hadn't come across them. Anyway, you know me — I tend to stick to Agatha Christie, Ngaio Marsh and Dorothy Sayers."

"I'm sure it's worth giving Nicholas Marlowe a go," Felix said.

I asked after Poppy's health and he said she was fretting at the bit but they were both looking forward to the baby's arrival. Then he asked me how business was doing and told me he does much of his via his website, both buying and selling.

"I'm using my website more as a showcase and first point of contact, at the moment," I said, "though I do hope to buy and sell genuine vintage wedding shoes on there too. Bella's just working on that page."

"Now we get so many more tourists in Sticklepond, there's a lot more passing trade — though only from spring to autumn, of course, so the internet sales are still very important in winter."

"I think brides probably plan their dress and shoes months in advance, so winter might actually be a good time for me," I said thoughtfully.

I went to look at the crime novels and had just come back out into the front room of the shop carrying a stack of books with one of Nicholas Marlowe's on top — *Midsummer Night's Scream* — when damned if I didn't come face to face with the author himself!

I'd heard the shop doorbell jingling out "Paperback Writer" a couple of times, but hadn't taken any notice. I mean, why would I expect to bump into Ivo, when to my knowledge he hadn't been off his own property, except for his evening strolls?

"Erk!" I squawked, juggling the slipping pile of books and thinking it was just my luck he decided to make his debut in Marked Pages when *I* was there — caught in the act.

But then I noticed that the book Felix was slipping into a paper bag was *Slipper Monkeys Go Bananas*, my very first one, so evidently curiosity had got the better of him too.

"Hi," he said, deadpan, though his grey eyes were fixed on the books I held and I was sure he'd spotted his own there. Then he turned back to Felix, picked up his purchase and said, "I'll have that coffee another time, if you don't mind: I've just thought of something I really should do."

After he'd left, with a short "Paperback Writer" serenade, Felix relieved me of my slipping stack of books and said, "So that's your new neighbour? He introduced himself, but word has it he's a quite renowned Shakespearian actor."

"Apparently so, but he's resting at the moment. Resting as in *really* resting, not out of work," I explained.

"He seemed pleasant enough, though he left very suddenly. I thought he was going to stay and have a cup of coffee."

"I think I scared him away. Was that one of my books he was buying?"

"Yes, he asked for one specially and I was just about to ask him if he knew they were written by his neighbour when in you walked!"

"He does know, because Bella told him, so I expect he was buying one from curiosity."

As was I, too, about his! Though of course I couldn't tell anyone that Ivo was Nicholas Marlowe . . .

I paid for my books and put them in my nice, eco-friendly orange silk shopping bag, then darted across the High Street and back down Salubrious Passage to the safety of Cinderella's Slippers.

That evening Ivo didn't mention buying my book and I certainly didn't mention buying his.

Instead, he said he liked the look of my herb garden and thought he would create one just like it.

"Seth Greenwood up at Winter's End is the expert on knot gardens. He runs Greenwood's Knots and he's restored two lovely ones on the terraces behind the house, one in the form of a Lancashire rose and the other a love knot like mine, only more intricate. His are full of flowers rather than herbs, though."

"I'd like to see them."

"The house and gardens open this weekend — from Good Friday — for the season, so you could," I told him. "There's a Shakespeare garden on the lower terrace, so that might give you some ideas."

"I saw one of those once in America," he said, interested. "That's an idea!"

This was all quite chatty, for Ivo. And I might be deluding myself, but I don't think he looked quite as hollow-cheeked and starved, even if his eyes were still haunted.

You know, it's odd that I should have fallen in love with two such very different men. Justin's attraction is blatantly obvious to everyone, and he draws the eye in any room, but Ivo has an attraction of his own that sneaks up on you: something to do with the elegant bone structure of his face, his resonant and beautiful voice and his translucent, merman-grey eyes . . .

Just before twelve on our half-day, when we had cashed up and were about to flip the sign over to "Closed", we had a customer. She was a sharp-eyed redhead in her thirties, wearing the kind of thin, tightly fitted woollen skirt suit that looked as if it had been sewn onto the wearer, and I couldn't place her.

She definitely wasn't a tourist, she wasn't local and she certainly wasn't about to become a bride, for she was entirely lacking any of the expressions I had now come to associate with imminent wedlock. These ranged from dewy-eyed bliss to determined gold-digger (that had been a soon-to-be WAG), but all with an element of excitement.

She had a good look round and then began to ask Bella some very intrusive questions about when we'd opened and what our turnover was like.

"I only work here, I'm afraid I can't tell you that," Bella said.

The woman looked back at me. "So are you the owner, then?"

"Yes, I'm Tansy Poole. Can I help you?"

"Not really. It's just that someone told me about the shop, so I thought I'd come and have a look. But I can see it's no competition," she added, with a disparaging glance around.

"*Competition?*" I said quickly. "You mean you're opening a bridal shoe business in the area?"

She looked at me pityingly. "In a way. Haven't you heard? There's going to be a new out-of-town retail business park on the site of the old Hemlock cotton mill between Sticklepond and Ormskirk."

"What, you mean a big shopping mall place?" I asked, stunned. "I hadn't heard a thing about it, so no one else locally must know, either!"

"It's a retail park, rather than a mall, but it *will* include a big branch of the One Stop Bridal Shop chain — and *I'm* being parachuted in to get it up and running. Have you heard of it? We've the best selection of bride and bridesmaid's shoes in the country."

I nodded, numbly.

"Still, never mind, you can always diversify as a gift shop."

"Thanks," I said, getting my voice back. "What else is going to be on this retail park?"

"A giant supermarket, Grocergo, and one or two chain stores." She shrugged. "The usual kind of thing. Fast-food outlets too, I expect. Our bride shop will be the biggest one in the North."

She cast another slightly scathing look around the shop and said, "Well, nice to meet you. You must come and say hello when we open the new store." Then she left on her teetery-tottery stiletto court shoes. I hoped they were as painful to wear as they looked. In fact, I hoped she had hammer toes and bunions.

Bella and I immediately flipped over the Closed sign and locked the door, as if she might try and burst back in again and steal the stock. Then we looked at each other.

"The One Stop Bridal Shop is super-cheap and they provide everything you could possibly need, but it's all very tacky," Bella offered consolingly. "I mean, they're right the other end of the bridal market to us and they only do a limited range of footwear."

"You've been in one?"

"Yes, just once, in the days when I believed Robert was going to divorce his wife any minute and marry me," she said slightly bitterly. "I wouldn't have been seen dead in any of their dresses, though, let alone walk down the aisle in one."

"They must have kept the whole scheme under wraps, or we'd have heard about it by now."

"That mill site is nearer to Ormskirk than here, so I expect that's why no one knows about it locally," she suggested. "But I wouldn't have thought the traders in Ormskirk would be that keen on the scheme, either."

"Grocergo stock everything, don't they? Food, drink, books, toys, furnishings, gifts, hardware," I said. "So that will hit all the other little shops here in Sticklepond. And those that were thinking of moving in will think better of it."

"I don't suppose anything can be done to stop it," Bella said. "Happy April Fool's Day!"

"I expect it depends on whether planning permission has already been passed or not."

I mused for a minute and then said, "Since it's Good Friday tomorrow and the shop is shut, I'd already decided to go up to Winter's End to see how the garden restoration is looking, so I'll try and spot Hebe Winter and tell her about it. If anything can be done, *she's* the one to organise it!"

CHAPTER
TWENTY-THREE

Well Knotted

The curate was a quiet, serious kind of man, a bit older than me. Although I didn't fall in love with him, I liked him very well and, had things been otherwise, might well have settled for marriage and a family with him and been happy enough.

Middlemoss Living Archive
Recordings: Nancy Bright.

It was only with a huge effort of willpower that I stopped myself from carrying on listening to Aunt Nan's recordings late into last night, since once she'd finally returned to the subject of her clerical admirer I was riveted. I mean, I knew she'd never married, but not that she had turned down a second chance. Clearly something had happened to throw a spanner in the works and I was dying to find out what it was.

What with that, and the threatened opening of the One Stop Bride Shop, I had a largely sleepless night. When I did finally fall asleep I plummeted straight into a strangely muddled version of my Cinderella dream, in which Prince Justin turned into Ivo, who seemed intent on cramming my foot into a meat and potato pie instead of a glass slipper.

No wonder I woke up next morning feeling like death warmed up and served with wan relish!

I was really looking forward to visiting Winter's End for the first open day of the season, to see how the gardens were getting on since I'd visited them the previous year. And now I had an extra incentive to go, because I hoped to run into Hebe.

But my visit was a bit like another nightmare really, because I kept catching distant glimpses of her elusive figure, clad in full Elizabethan dress and accompanied by Friends of Winter's End attired as courtiers and ladies, but every time I got to where I'd last seen them, they'd vanished again.

I spotted Shakespeare twice, too, scurrying about furtively like the white rabbit in *Alice in Wonderland,* his chin tucked well down into his ruff and clutching a quill pen and a roll of parchment.

I gave up on Hebe, deciding to ring her later instead, and started a more leisurely tour of the gardens. While I had enough to puzzle me at the moment without trying to find my way through the extensive yew maze, I loved the earthy-smelling darkness of the fern grotto and enjoyed wandering round the new rose garden with its central sculpture of *The Spirit of the Garden.* This had been created by Ottie Winter, Hebe's twin sister, who is a noted artist, and, although very modern, somehow fitted wonderfully into its setting. I supposed that showed her genius.

In the little tearoom, I had coffee and one of those delicious vanilla slices full of confectioner's custard and stickily iced on top, and bought a postcard of Ottie's sculpture. Then, fortified, I visited the terraces at the back of the house. Seth Greenwood had only recently finished recreating them to the original plans the previous year, and he'd added one or two little extra flourishes, like the Shakespeare garden and the wall with the quotes from the Bard carved on the stones.

I was standing on the middle terrace looking down over the stone balustrade at the box-edged true lovers' knot below me, and marvelling at the way it had already grown together so that it looked as if it had always been there, when a familiar, deeply resonant voice said in my ear, "Excuse me, miss, but are these the famous hanging gardens of Sticklepond, eighth wonder of the world?"

I might have gone straight over the balustrade, like a too-eager Juliet, had not Ivo grabbed my arm and apologised for startling me.

"Not at all — I just didn't expect to see you here."

"I wanted to see these knot gardens you'd told me about and get inspiration for mine." He looked down and added, "The flowers look nice in the different segments, especially the primroses, but I think I'd prefer herbs in mine, like yours. "'Have nothing that is not beautiful and useful,'" he added.

"That's not Shakespeare, is it?"

"No, I think it's a paraphrase of William Morris."

"That makes a change! Have you seen the Shakespeare quotes cut into the wall holding this terrace up?"

"No," he said interested, "but I'd like to. I *have* just seen the alleged Shakespeare manuscript — behind

261

reinforced glass about three inches thick, in a wall safe — though I understand the jury is still out on the authenticity, and probably always will be."

"At least they're not about to argue over whether he carved his own quotes in the terrace wall," I said, and Ivo laughed.

"Nothing would surprise me in the world of Shakespeare!"

It was the first time I'd seen anything other than the faintest Banquo's ghost of a smile on his face, so it was a bit unnerving. He might be the Prince of Darkness to Justin's Sun King, but the smile was none the less fascinating.

His face soon returned to its usual sombre expression again and he said, "Come on, show me this wall."

It was there that Hebe finally found me, rather than the other way round, and there was no escaping introducing her to Ivo. In fact, I suspect someone had recognised him and told her where he was, for however reclusive you are, you can't entirely escape being noticed in a village.

"At last!" she exclaimed, not so much shaking his hand as seizing it in a bejewelled claw. "I have tried to call on you more than once."

"I'm so sorry to have missed you, but I expect I was out, Your Majesty," he lied, sounding terribly sincere — but then he *is* an actor. Then he gave her a courtly bow, which softened even her up a bit.

"Since we share this great bond of Shakespeare, I thought perhaps you might like to join the Friends of Winter's End," she said.

"They're an Elizabethan re-enactment society," I explained, seeing his puzzled expression. "They also help out up here as volunteers when the house and gardens are open, wearing Elizabethan dress. You must have noticed them?"

He nodded. "It would be hard not to."

"It would be a huge draw to visitors if we had a genuine Shakespearian actor reciting from one of the plays — perhaps even a special performance . . ." mused Hebe.

"I'm afraid I'm on a six-months sabbatical, for some peace and quiet," Ivo said quickly.

"And then I expect you'll be off back to the Royal Shakespeare Company and we'll hardly see you again after that," I suggested and his face went all shuttered.

"Perhaps. We'll see. But I certainly don't want to join anything — and today I just want to enjoy the gardens like any other tourist," he said, with that sudden and unexpectedly sweet smile.

She'd started to look affronted but now melted slightly, though I was pretty sure she'd still try to change his mind, so I said quickly,

"Hebe, I'd hoped to have a word with you today, if you have time."

"No time like the present," she said, so I explained about the woman coming to the shop and what she'd said about a retail park on the old Hemlock cotton mill site.

As I'd thought, Hebe was flabbergasted. She'd heard nothing about it either but quickly appreciated how it could hit local businesses.

263

"Grocergo? That kind of large chain isn't needed in the area, for everything you could possibly want you can get in this village or in Ormskirk. It will hit local traders hard!"

"Yes, that's what I thought."

"But maybe it could be a good thing, bringing in jobs and providing some competition?" Ivo suggested. I'd forgotten he was there, listening in.

"On the contrary, it has the potential to wreck the community," Hebe told him scathingly, so he had clearly quickly plummeted from favour. Then she turned her aristocratic, hawk-nosed face back to me.

"I'll find out about it. We need a plan of action! It's a nuisance we should only have heard of it over Easter weekend, when it will be hard to get hold of anyone."

"If they've already passed the planning permission, I don't suppose there's much we can do about it."

"Oh, there is always *something* that can be done!" she assured me, then rearranged her ruff, took a martial grip on her sceptre and strode off, shouting, "Shakespeare!"

Mr Glover, who had been scuttling furtively along the top terrace clutching his rolled parchment, gave a great start and then shot into the tearoom. Hebe set off in hot pursuit.

"I wonder what she's going to do with him when she's got him?" Ivo mused thoughtfully. "I feel I've had a lucky escape."

Ivo and I wandered around the terraces and I showed him the fernery and maze, then we went in search of

Seth, whom we discovered replenishing the plant stall outside the shop and tearoom.

"'I know a bank whereon the wild thyme blows,'" I said, and he straightened and turned with a smile.

"Hi, Tansy."

Once I'd introduced him to Ivo and told him that he was interested in creating a knot garden, I knew there would be no stopping him for hours, so I left them to it and sloped off home.

CHAPTER
TWENTY-FOUR

Sweet Music

But it was not to be. Violet and I may not have always got on well, but she was still my sister, and when trouble came she sent an urgent message saying she was ill and asking for me to go down and stay with her. But I knew that whatever story we put about to cover for my absence, I would be gone so long that malicious rumours about the reason for such an extended stay would be circulated and my good name lost.

> Middlemoss Living Archive
> Recordings: Nancy Bright.

Well, Aunt Nan's revelations last night were a bit of a stunner! And now, of course, I suspect what her secret is . . . and it's the last thing I would have expected of her! But she *was* still very young, so I can only think she was friendlier with that American airman than she let on . . .

I was hugely tempted to skip to the last recording and find out what *really* happened, of course, but forced myself to carry on and let her tell me in her own time, rambling diversions and all.

I didn't have much opportunity for brooding anyway, since Easter Saturday turned out to be our busiest day since opening, with lots of brides-to-be in serious shoe-buying mode, early guests for that day's crop of weddings at All Angels in all their finery popping in for silver shoe-shaped confetti, and a steady stream of tourists following the sign up Salubrious Passage to our door.

Many of the latter loitered in the courtyard, taking photographs on their phones (it is quite quaint, especially if you get the ancient sundial in the picture), drinking from bottles of water or even, in the case of one family, picnicking. There was still quite a chill in the air despite the sunshine, but the courtyard was sheltered.

I had a sprinkling of complaints from them about my "No Children" sign, but it is a wedding shop, after all, full of pale, expensive, easily marked shoes, so when I explained, most people were all right about it. Many left their children to run riot around the paved courtyard instead, their yells echoing off the walls, though that was much better than them running riot in the shop.

What with the doorbell constantly belting out "Here Comes the Bride", and the bells of All Angels literally going like the clappers, not to mention all the noise in the courtyard, Ivo couldn't have been having a terribly quiet day again, and I felt a little guilty about that . . .

The Green Man must have been catering for one of the wedding receptions, too, because there was a marquee in the car park next to the courtyard and you could hear sounds of revelry and, later on, a disco.

The music was still going strong when Ivo came to collect Flash that evening, which presumably accounted for why he was back to looking so grim-lipped and as if he hadn't slept for a week.

I commented brightly that business had been surprisingly busy today, but I hoped he hadn't been too much disturbed (or not more than he clearly already was), to which he replied coldly, "You must be joking! Apart from your damned door chimes playing "Here Comes the Bride" every five seconds, the church bells hardly seemed to stop long enough for the vicar to run through the wedding service in between. Then there seemed to be a mass riot in the courtyard, and we've had this thumping music for hours!" He gestured angrily in the direction of the marquee.

"The Green Man doesn't very often have large receptions, but they need the marquee if they do," I explained. "Their function room holds only about fifty people."

Flash also seemed to be put off by the unaccustomed sound of music from the garden and hung back when I tried to hand his lead over to Ivo, clamping it to his chest with an expression of canine determination.

"Look, even your poor dog has had enough!" Ivo pointed out.

"He just doesn't like anything to be different. But the music will stop at ten: they don't carry on late at the Green Man."

"Ten *is* late," Ivo snapped and turned to stride off, though his exit was ruined when he had to stop to reassure Flash, who had firmly clamped his lead to his chest again.

I bet Ivo's now secretly hoping the retail park will put me out of business!

When Ivo returned he only seemed to have walked off a little of his temper, for he said, resuming the conversation where we had left off, "Do you have to have a cockerel? He's so loud he wakes me up in the morning."

"Cedric isn't as noisy as most of them," I said coldly. "If you move into a village, you should expect chickens and church bells and noises like that!"

"And Bach fugues played full volume on the church organ at any time of the day or night?"

"A local foible. The organist is blind and says day and night are all one to him."

"Well, 'I am never merry when I hear sweet music . . .' particularly at two in the morning."

"You need to chill out and adapt to village life, not expect it to adapt to you."

"Thanks for the lecture," he snapped and strode off. He'd automatically taken the parcel of sticky ginger parkin I'd shoved into his hands, but I'm sure he hadn't consciously realised he'd done it.

Wherever he'd hidden that sweet-natured boy I'd fallen in love with so long ago, I wished he'd let him out again.

I decided to keep the shop shut on Easter Monday, though both Winter's End and the Witchcraft Museum would be open, so I supposed I would lose some tourist trade.

But since the wedding shoes were my primary concern, it seemed reasonable, and it gave Bella and me a bit of a break.

We took Tia to the Easter Egg Hunt, which Raffy and Chloe had organised after the morning service at All Angels, though if I'd known Neil would turn up, I'd have given it a miss.

"Neil! Neil!" shrieked Tia excitedly, jumping up and down and waving when she spotted him, and he grinned and started to weave his way towards us through a lot of over-excited little Easter egg hunters.

"Did you tell him you were coming today?" I asked Bella suspiciously.

"I might have mentioned it," she admitted, "but I didn't expect him to come."

I thought she looked secretly pleased that he had, though, and Tia seems to like him already. What's more, it was immediately clear from Neil's slightly sheep-like and adoring expression that he'd fallen head over heels for Bella.

Anyway, I felt a bit of a spare part, so after a while I said I was going to go home and get on with some work.

"I need to tidy up the cover illustration for the new book, and then I can finally pack it ready to post on Tuesday."

"Are you sure you don't want to stay?" Bella asked doubtfully. "I thought we could have lunch at one of the cafés afterwards, as a treat."

"Or I could drive us all to Southport, if you were up for another Easter egg hunt?" Neil suggested. "There's one at the Botanic Gardens this afternoon and we could have lunch there first."

"Ooh, yes. Mummy, can we?" Tia begged.

"I don't think you should eat any more chocolate today, you'll be sick," Bella said, but I could see she secretly wanted to go.

"She could save them for another day," I said.

"I suppose I could confiscate them as she finds them," she agreed.

As I walked home alone, I couldn't help feeling a bit sad that Bella and I would no longer be singletons together, because even though she was resisting I knew she was very smitten by Neil. But I also felt happy for her, because I liked Neil and if it worked out, then my best friend would have another chance at happiness — and I could at least walk up the aisle as a bridesmaid!

I'd actually already finished *Slipper Monkeys' Safari*; it just needed carefully parcelling up. But there was something that needed doing that I'd been putting off for ages: excavating Aunt Nan's big chest freezer, which took up so much of the walk-in larder that you had to sidle sideways past it to get in.

I suspected the lower levels hadn't been disturbed since early last century, so I should probably have asked the county archaeologist to be present . . .

I switched it off, then put the good stuff from the top in cold bags, or wrapped in newspaper on the stone larder shelves. As I worked down towards the bottom I discovered a whole, long-forgotten stratum almost welded together, formed from frozen garden fruit, burst packets of peas, endless trays of liver or tripe and

271

onions (neither particular favourites of mine, even if they hadn't looked ancient and desiccated), and bread rolls so long-frozen that they crumbled to icy crumbs practically at a touch.

I had to chip the last layer out of the permafrost before I could bag it and bin it, and hanging over the freezer for that long made me feel quite dizzy. But at least this deep-frozen Tutankhamen's tomb came with treasure: Aunt Nan's mother's wedding ring of Welsh gold, nestled inside a cottonwool-padded plastic box!

I had been flagging a bit, but this find spurred me on to finish the job. Then Flash asked to go out, though he deliberated in the doorway when he spotted Cedric leading his wives up the garden before suddenly bouncing out, barking. That sent them running back through the holly arch towards the safety of the hen run!

I followed them down and, watched by a pot-valiant Flash, blocked up the place under the wire where they'd got out again. Then I went in and had a well-deserved rest with a cup of coffee and a slice or two of buttered bara brith.

Fortified once more, I set to again and scraped the ice off the inside of the freezer (I'd loosened it with a special defrosting spray), then cleaned it all out, before switching it back on again.

When I put what was worth keeping back into it later, it practically rattled around, but soon there would be a glut of fruit from the garden and I could start batch-cooking and freezing portions of things like pizzas, shepherd's pies, rhubarb crumble and curries, not to mention loaves, bara brith and buns, so I expected it would quickly fill up again.

I'd heard Ivo hacking and digging in his garden earlier, but he'd vanished indoors by the time I'd finished with the freezer and gone out for a late potter round the garden, remembering how it used to look when Aunt Nan was younger. There had been neat rows of cabbages and carrots, tall wigwams of runner beans and sweet peas, clusters of snapdragons and red-hot pokers between the onions, and a tangle of salmon-pink geraniums behind the old stone bench.

She'd always mixed the decorative and the edible up together (though some, like nasturtiums, were both, of course), and it had looked magical. I'd like to recreate some of that effect, but on a smaller scale.

I had a peek through the trellis to see what Ivo had been up to and saw that his garden was looking quite bare now and all the old crazy paving paths had reappeared. I wondered where he was going to put his knot garden.

When I'd fed the hens and shut them up in their house for the night, I'd told Cedric not to dare voice one single crow until he was let out in the morning, but he'd just given me his blank, beady stare.

I certainly wasn't getting rid of him and, since you can't have cockerels fitted with silencers, Ivo would just have to get used to the dawn chorus.

Ivo was uncommunicative when he came to the back door for Flash that evening, nor was he any less taciturn when he returned him an hour later, wet, muddy and happy.

But that suited me, because I'd started to suspect what Aunt Nan's skeleton in the closet was, I just wanted to carry on listening to her story . . . except that I now was having to listen to a long digression on the way to make a proper Lancashire hotpot pie, before she started to divulge anything more interesting — if she intended to at all.

"*Of course, we were lucky to have scrag end of lamb to make hotpot pies. One of the boys at school, his family were that poor that he never had enough to eat. I remember him telling me that he would catch small birds like sparrows, and bake them inside a potato he would steal from the fields,*" she told Cheryl. "*No dear, I don't know if he took their insides out first, I never asked him.*"

And people today think they're hard done by if they can't afford a flatscreen TV or the latest computer game!

Still, fascinating as all these asides were, the urge to fast forward would have been almost irresistible had not Cheryl somehow managed to nudge Nan back in time, to the point when she had returned from the visit to her sister Violet. I strongly suspected that by this point she had been feeling as curious and frustrated as I was!

CHAPTER
TWENTY-FIVE

Good in Parts

The curate I was walking out with, lovey? Oh, that came to nothing. He never even asked me for the truth. In fact, he just turned and went the other way when he saw me in the street, which was very hurtful. My best friend, Florrie Snowball, was the only person I completely confided in and she was — and always has been — a great comfort to me. I'm not saying she isn't a little strange in her ways, mind, but her dabbling in magic never did anyone any harm that I ever noticed, and we all need a hobby, dear, don't we?

Middlemoss Living Archive
Recordings: Nancy Bright.

I spent most of Easter Monday morning cleaning out the shop. It's odd how the glass showcases and the door pane become covered in greasy fingerprints, when I rarely see anyone actually touching them.

Once everything was clean and sparkling I replaced the "glass" slipper on the cushioned stand in the window with a gloriously forties-looking silvery satin shoe that had been embellished with a row of sparkling Swarovski crystals up the strappy front — my very first Bridal Shoe of the Week.

"Don't trip up the aisle, skip up it — in a beautiful pair of Cinderella's Slippers!" I exclaimed, inspired, jotting this new and improved version of our slogan down to see what Bella thought.

Then I answered a few queries that had come through the website, which were mostly about opening times, even though they were clearly displayed on the home page! But someone also wanted to sell me a pair of vintage button-strapped cream leather shoes. They looked to be in good condition from the attached JPEGs, but possibly more bridesmaid than bride. Still, I said if the seller halved her (ridiculous!) asking price, we might have a deal.

After lunch I got a notebook and, accompanied by Flash, went out into the garden to make a plan of what needed doing before lusty spring stirred it up and it all got out of hand — only to spot Ivo through the trellis, seemingly doing the same. His big Moleskine notebook was somewhat more upmarket than my cheap spiral-bound one.

He looked up and caught sight of me but his mood seemed much improved, for instead of scowling and turning his back, which was about what I expected, he came over and said he could do with some advice and then invited me into his garden! I left Flash on my side, though, since I didn't want to strain the truce he seemed to have established with Toby the cat by letting him invade his territory.

"You've worked really hard," I said, having a good look round. "It's come from an overgrown jungle to bare earth in only a couple of weeks!"

"It was bindweed, nettle and bramble heaven, so though at first I was picking and choosing what to pull out, in the end it was easier to dig practically everything up and start again. But I've left some well-established looking things alone, like those espaliered trees over there on the side wall, until I find out what they are."

"Oh, those are quinces."

"I've no idea what quinces are," he admitted.

"They have fruit that looks a bit like a small pear and they're very good for jams, jellies, relish and wine, so they're well worth keeping. I expect they'll take on a new lease of life now you've given them more space. If you don't want the fruit, I'll have it and give you jam and wine back in exchange."

"And the trees at the bottom there?"

"Apple — I think one's a cooker and the other an eater." I surveyed them doubtfully: the years of neglect had made them look a bit past their best. "If I were you, I'd put a lot of compost or manure around the roots and see if they perk up. But that sapling next to them is a sycamore and you need to take that out straight away, before it gets any bigger."

"Right," he said, making a note. "Seth Greenwood's coming later this week to design and make my knot garden. I told him I wanted one just like yours, that I could fill it with herbs — 'hot lavender, mints, savory, marjoram: the marigold, that goes to bed wi' the sun and with him rises weeping' and I suppose he might have some suggestions about what I should put in the rest of the garden."

"Knowing Seth, he'll probably try and persuade you to turn it *all* into a knot garden or parterre!" I said. "But he's a lovely man, even if he does have a bee in his bonnet about knots, and he was really kind to Aunt Nan in her last years, making sure her garden was always neat and tidy. He wouldn't take any money for it, either. She used to grow most of her own fruit and vegetables right up to her mid-eighties, but then it all started to get a bit much for her."

"What are you going to do with the garden now?" he asked.

"Slowly turn it back to an easier-to-manage version of how it used to be. She liked to mix flowers, fruit and vegetables together in a hotchpotch, which always looked amazing. My tree at the bottom near the hens is a plum, by the way."

"I think it looks dead," he said critically, looking up at it.

"Oh, old plum trees just like to fool you, but if you look closer, you'll see signs of life and soon it'll take off and produce loads of fruit, you'll see. Some of the lower branches get so heavy they have to be propped up."

"What will you do with all the plums, then?"

"Jam, wine, plum crumbles and pies, dried or candied plums — there's no end to what you can do with them! Aunt Nan often bartered baskets of them for other things, like honey for the Meddyg, though of course she would give the hive-keeper a couple of bottles of it too."

278

"I've been drinking the Meddyg, one small glass in the evenings," he told me, to my surprise. The way he'd been looking at the bottle when I gave it to him, I'd imagined it had gone straight down the sink. "It tasted weird at first but now I quite like it."

"It's an acquired taste, but it'll do you the power of good. I'll give you another bottle," I promised.

"You don't need to — or all the food."

"Call it payment for the dog walking," I suggested, and he let that go, so I'm sort of assuming he likes the home cooking really and doesn't want me to stop!

It was only after I was back in the cottage that it struck me that for a man on a six-month sabbatical, he was making some expensive and long-term plans for his garden! But I supposed he'd use it as a holiday cottage, and meanwhile all the gardening was keeping him amused and occupied. He certainly looked healthier now, if still just as haunted, which must show how much he had adored his late wife . . .

I made myself a lavish but very late high tea, just as if it was a Sunday, and then donned the Day of the Dead pinafore that Bella had once brought me back from a trip to Mexico (black background covered in very jolly little skeletons dressed in brightly coloured fiesta gear) and embarked on a frenzy of baking: peanut biscuits, Welshcakes, a plum jam tart (from last year's bottled fruit) and a big batch of Cornish pasties, all frilled along the top like the backs of dinosaurs in children's picture books, most of them destined for the freezer.

While I worked I was listening to Aunt Nan, who had once again determinedly sheered off into stories about her childhood.

"Oh, we did look forward to Whit Walking Day! We'd all get dressed up and march through the village with a band and banners!" she told Cheryl. *"Then there'd be a picnic and games with prizes on what they call the Lido field, down by the river. We had a grand time. Proper champion, it was!"*

I was just about to take the tart from the oven when Ivo collected Flash for his walk, so I just pushed the dog out, handed him the lead and dashed back in before the edges caught.

I listened to a lot more of Aunt Nan than my daily ration while they were out. She'd been wandering all over her childhood and teenage years, and by the time I opened the door to let Ivo and Flash back in again, she was describing skating on the lake up at Winter's End one very hard winter with her friends and Ottie and Hebe, and how the cook had sent down a warming pan full of hot roast chestnuts.

"A warming pan?" queried Cheryl faintly. She sounded as if she was losing the will to live.

"That's right, lovey," agreed Aunt Nan.

"Something smells good," Ivo observed, as Flash shot past my legs into the kitchen in the direction of his food bowl, which seemed to be having a non-scary day.

"I've been baking and I've wrapped some biscuits up for you, but I thought you might like a hot Cornish pasty now. I've just taken the last batch out of the oven. Come in."

He looked uncertain, a bit like Flash when he's convinced there's a big scary monster hiding in the garden, or behind his food bowl, but then followed me in.

Aunt Nan was still talking: "*You can still buy cough candy, but it's not the same. I've a good recipe, though . . .*"

I flicked the switch and her voice vanished. Ivo was looking around curiously.

"You know, this is the first time I've been over your threshold — apart from the shop, of course."

"Is it? I suppose it is. Did you know that your cottage and mine started out as one building originally, the sort with the living accommodation at one end and the cattle byre at the other? Then after the Black Death had passed by it became two cottages and they've both been added to and changed over the years."

"I'd no idea, but I suppose that's why the dividing wall between the two cottages isn't as substantial as you might expect."

"You can't really still hear the doorbell playing 'The Bridal March', can you?"

"Yes, if I'm in the sitting room next door."

"Well, *I* can hear this really gloomy classical music from your side in the evenings," I countered, "and that's not *my* cup of tea at all."

"'I can suck melancholy out of a song as a weasel sucks eggs'," he said gloomily. "Sorry if it disturbs you, though."

"It isn't loud enough to bother me, so I don't really mind, except that I wish it was something cheerier," I told him. "Look, sit down a minute while I wrap your pasty up. There's some tea in the pot too, if you'd like a cup?"

He didn't say one way or the other, but he did sit down, so I poured him some and shoved the milk jug towards him, before taking my pinny off and hanging it behind the door. I noticed in the little mirror that also hung there that my hair was half-down and there was a smudge of flour across one cheek, but I wasn't about to start primping under Ivo's gaze.

"Have you heard any more about this retail park?" he asked.

"No, not yet, but Hebe Winter will get to the bottom of it, and if anything is to be done, she'll organise it. I'm *really* worried about the new bridal shop, because I've gambled everything on Cinderella's Slippers and I'd feel I'd let Aunt Nan down if the shop folded when I was running it."

"Wasn't that your aunt's voice I could hear when I came in, or was I just imagining it?" he asked curiously. "I mean, I only heard her voice once, but it was very distinctive."

"Yes, it was. She recorded her memories for the Middlemoss Living Voices Archive and they gave me a copy. It's fascinating stuff," I told him. Then something came over me and I found myself confiding, "She said she had a guilty secret, which she'd tell me about in the last recording, a private one, but she wanted me to listen to the rest of it first."

"Sometimes it's better not to know the secrets at all," he said very seriously, and that haunted look came into his grey eyes.

"Perhaps, but she wanted me to know — and actually, I'm sure I've already guessed what it is. She had a little fling with an American airman and . . . well, I think she got into trouble. But I'm just guessing really."

"Don't you want to skip ahead and see if you're right?"

"Bella asked me that too, but I want Aunt Nan to tell me in her own time, so mostly I'm rationing myself to a session of half an hour or so in the evenings. Only she keeps rambling off the subject and meandering on about all kinds of things, so it's been really hard not to skip forward and find out for sure. It might be nothing to worry about these days, but that kind of thing was a big deal then, a catastrophe."

"My wife wrote a diary every day of her life," he confessed abruptly. "She was no Pepys, so mostly it's just short entries about meeting friends, appointments, that kind of thing. She often left it lying around the house, but of course I never even opened it . . ."

He looked up suddenly, but he wasn't seeing me, he was looking back down the past. "Now I wonder if perhaps she wanted me to open it, to read it."

"So, did you read it after the accident?" I asked cautiously, and into my head popped the image of the old leather diary I had seen lying open and face down on his desk the day I had taken him the Meddyg. It had been a very girly pink . . .

"Not immediately. I just put them all in the small wooden chest she kept her papers in and put it into storage with everything else, and it ended up here. I thought I'd better see what papers she kept in there and saw the diaries again . . . and that's when I started reading them."

"Well, that seems a very natural thing to do, to me. Have you finished reading them all now?"

"No. Oddly enough, *I've* been rationing them each evening, much as you have been doing with your aunt's recordings . . . and I too have been reading things that have made me want to cut to the last one, the unfinished diary."

He didn't elaborate on what that might be, but since his face took on that shuttered look again and he left abruptly, as if sorry he'd said even that much, it can't have been anything good.

I wondered what his wife had been up to: was his grief mixed with anger? Is that why he was so edgy and tense?

And what a strange coincidence it was that we should both be discovering the secret lives of those we loved at the same time, bit by bit, both more than half afraid of what we might find at the end!

I went back in the recording to the bit I'd missed while I was letting Ivo and Flash back in, and it was a real effort of will to turn it off after that, for Cheryl had finally managed to prod Aunt Nan back to her narrative thread and my suspicions began to crystallise into conviction.

CHAPTER
TWENTY-SIX

The Birds and the Bees

Yes, of course, my parents did hear the rumours eventually, dear, but they didn't ask me any questions either. I suppose they were afraid to. Despite all Vi's scheming I expect they guessed the truth, but it was a case of least said, soonest mended. My poor mother had another stroke soon after I came home, though, and that was that. Then it was just Father and me.

Middlemoss Living Archive
Recordings: Nancy Bright.

Bella arrived at the shop, after first pushing through Ivo's door the wad of typescript that she'd typed up some time over the long weekend.

"He's speeding up now," she said.

"I expect he's got a deadline looming. There's nothing like them for making you get a move on. I've read all three of those novels of his that I got from Marked Pages and they're very good."

"So is this new one, and I'm dying to know who did the dastardly deed. I haven't the faintest idea."

"It's very clever the way he has the two stories going, the Elizabethan one and the contemporary one," I said. "And then to be able to tie it all together with a theme from one of Shakespeare's plays really is an amazing feat."

"He's really done his research too, but of course he is part of the Royal Shakespeare Company and knows the Stratford area, where they're all set," Bella said.

"I expect that's why he wants to keep his identity secret, because although he's created a second, smaller Shakespearian company in the books and called it the King's Players, everyone in the RSC would assume *they* were the characters."

"Perhaps some of them are?" Bella suggested.

"All the more reason to hide behind a pen name!" I said. "Ivo actually came into the kitchen and had a cup of tea last night, and we talked a bit, then I gave him a Cornish pasty to take home with him."

"He could do with fattening up. He's obviously lost weight because his clothes are loose on him. What did he say?"

"Well, I had the archive recording running and he asked me if that was Aunt Nan's voice, so I told him about it. In fact, I'd just got to a bit that made me think I'd guessed her secret right and I expect that's why I ended up telling him about it. But the amazing thing is that it turns out that he is reading his late wife's diaries, and spinning them out each evening to make them last longer, just like me with Aunt Nan's memoirs! Isn't that a weird coincidence?"

"Truth always does seem stranger than fiction. Except for Stephen King's novels," she added, being a big fan of his. "His fiction is always far weirder than the truth. But what did you find out about your aunt?"

"You remember I told you I thought she might have had a bit of a fling with that American airman she was seeing towards the end of the war?"

Bella nodded. "The one she went jitterbugging with."

"I think they may have done more than jitterbugging, and she might have found herself pregnant just after he'd gone back."

"Oh, poor Nan, if so!"

"She hasn't come out and actually said so, but there was some kind of trouble, and she went to stay with her sister for long enough for rumours to get out. I suppose she'll tell me all the details in the final recording."

"I still don't know how you're managing to keep your hands off that one! I'd have given in and listened to it long before now."

"It's really tempting, but I'm going to do it the way she wanted."

"Did Ivo say anything about his wife's diaries?"

"Not really, though something about them seems to be troubling him. They're obviously painful reading and I'm starting to wonder if he's finding out that he loved her more than she loved him. But I think he surprised himself by telling me about them at all!"

"He must be coming out of himself a bit. I mean, he hadn't even crossed the threshold before, had he?"

"Not apart from the shop, and he does seem to be less tense, so maybe you're right. His face doesn't look quite so gaunt, either, so I'm sure he's put on a bit of weight since I began giving him food parcels!"

"He probably just forgot to eat, but if you keep shoving things under his nose I expect he'll get back into the habit. But don't overdo it, or by the time he goes back he'll be fit to play only Falstaff."

"I don't think there's much danger of that," I said. "Raffy seems to be his only visitor — or the only one he ever lets in. I expect he's been able to open up to him and it will help him come to terms with his wife's death."

"Well, he's certainly rebuffed all Hebe Winter's attempts to rope him into the Friends of Winter's End, hasn't he?" Bella giggled, because I'd told her about the scene up at Winter's End.

"I have spotted a few people trying his doorbell recently and some of them looked like the actors in that *Cotton Common* series, so Marcia must have let slip about him being here."

"Pity she didn't also tell them he was here for some peace and quiet, then. But I suppose eventually he'll go back to Stratford and his career," she said. "Didn't he tell you he was on a six-month sabbatical?"

I nodded. "And time is ticking past. I've quite got used to having him living next door now, though I can't say I like the classical music he plays in the evenings. But hearing it and knowing there's someone just the other side of the wall is sort of . . . companionable. And if he's not just grief-stricken at losing his wife, but also upset about whatever she'd written in her diaries, then it's easier to forgive his short fuse."

"Tansy, you're not falling for him all over again, are you?" Bella asked, anxiously scrutinising my face. "I mean, he is rather gorgeous, in his way!"

I laughed. "Of course not! He's barely been civil to me since he moved in and I know he belongs in a different world entirely — and soon he'll be part of it again."

"He's done a lot to the cottage and garden for someone who doesn't intend staying."

"That occurred to me, but if he keeps it as a holiday cottage that would figure. But he might have decided Sticklepond is just too noisy for him and is making it look better because he intends to sell it."

"Neil's got one of those nice old red-brick terraced cottages in Middlemoss, with a Victorian cast-iron fireplace and polished wooden floors. It's lovely," Bella said absently. I didn't ask her how she knew!

When I popped down to the Spar later for some butter, everyone was talking about the proposed retail park and it appeared that Hebe had been very busy indeed.

She'd already discovered that planning permission hadn't yet been granted. The phone lines must have been *smoking*.

One of the gardeners from the hall had cycled round the village sticking photocopied posters up everywhere, summoning the villagers to an emergency meeting that was to take place in the village hall early the following evening. When I got back to Cinderella's Slippers, I found he'd also called in and delivered a personal invitation, too.

"He's going round all the business people in the area, to make sure every single interested party turns up — and I expect they will," Bella said. "I'll go, too, if Mum and Dad will keep an eye on Tia."

"Well, I'll certainly be there!" I declared.

I'd had a very long phone call from the fraught mother-of-a-bride-to-be who wanted to book a private evening visit to the shop, so I got to the village hall for the meeting much later than I had intended.

The place was crammed. I'd hoped to slip in at the back, but Hebe had stationed several Friends of Winter's End at the door and I was firmly escorted to some reserved seats near the front, where I found myself sitting next to Florrie Snowball, right in the thick of the Sticklepond business proprietors. There was Gregory Lyon, with Chloe and Zillah; Felix and his very pregnant wife, Poppy; Poppy's mother Janey (they run Stirrups riding stables together); Seth and Sophy, with her daughter from her first marriage, Lucy; and Val Priestly from the Green Man. I didn't know some of the newer shop and café owners, except by sight, but they all appeared to have turned out.

Florrie silently passed me an Everton Mint from a small paper bag.

Hebe was up on the stage chairing the meeting, with her steward and henchman Laurence Yatton sitting just behind her. The vicar was there too and Mike, the village policeman, though his wife, Anya, who runs the Winter's End gift shop and café, was down with the rest of us. I could see her pink dreadlocks two rows in front of me.

Hebe declared the meeting open and started by introducing the planning department officer the council had sent as a sacrificial lamb. Indeed, his name *was* Lamb, so you might as well have painted a target on the poor man. There was a sharp-eyed legal representative for the consortium who owned the Hemlock Mill site, too.

"So, why weren't we notified of this development plan?" demanded Hebe, getting right down to it with an opening shot across the bows.

"It wasn't in Middlemoss borough," the legal representative said quickly.

"That's right, all the notices were correctly posted in the Ormskirk paper and, of course, affixed to the perimeter of the mill," Mr Lamb agreed.

Hebe pointed out that since the site was only a few miles from Sticklepond, the proposed development would have a profound effect on the village and the surrounding area, not least to the thriving businesses already established there, and so we *should* have been consulted.

"Hear, hear!" Janey, Florrie and several others called loudly.

Hebe got them to outline the proposals in more depth than they evidently wanted to divulge and then threw the meeting open to questions from the room and the resulting discussion — or interrogation — got pretty lively!

One or two people *did* suggest that the retail park might create new jobs, but since the site was nearer to

Ormskirk than Sticklepond, local people would probably lose out anyway.

"And think of all those students in Ormskirk," Janey said. "I bet lots of them would take part-time jobs at minimum wage!"

"Good point," agreed Hebe.

"But jobs will definitely be *lost* in the village if everything closes up, and since Grocergo stocks clothes, gifts, books and practically anything else you can think of, that will hit us all," Felix pointed out. "The new delicatessen and bakery, my bookshop, the Spar — not to mention the projected reopening of the old butcher's shop in the High Street — might all go to the wall."

"And don't forget the retail park will have a huge branch of One Stop Bridal Shop," called Bella loudly from the back of the hall. "That's going to hit Cinderella's Slippers, too."

"*And* the fast food outlets will take some of *our* business," shouted someone else angrily, presumably one of the new café owners. "I bet it will have huge car parks that can take coaches, so they'll drop off the tourists there for lunch and tea!"

The discussion became loud and lively but eventually, in a small lull, Raffy spotted the timidly waving arm of Mr Glover, Hebe's Shakespeare, and asked him what his question was.

"Has the site been checked for rare species of plants and animals?" he asked, timidly.

"It's a brownfield site, a former factory," the planning officer told him defensively. He was sweating quite a lot and looked as if he would really prefer to be somewhere else. Anywhere else.

"Not all of it's brownfield, is it? Only where the factory stood. There's a large stretch of river bank and some woodland, and it's a haven for wildlife. I often go there for poetic inspiration and I expect I'd have seen the notices you put up, had I not recently been having car problems," he explained.

"Is there anything unusual there?" asked Seth.

"I'm not sure, not being a wildlife expert," Mr Glover confessed. "But I have seen a kingfisher on the river by the mill, and dragonflies. It's full of birds too, in the woodland."

"I'm sure there's nothing out of the ordinary up there, and isn't there a guard to stop the public getting onto the site?" asked the consortium representative.

"To stop vandals, of course," Mr Glover agreed. "But there's a public footpath through part of it, so you often find people walking there."

"We'd better do our own survey to find out exactly what flora and fauna are there, and if there are protected plants and creatures. Then you'll have to think again, won't you?" Hebe told the official representatives, and they looked even more worried.

A small hubbub had broken out, but Hebe clapped her hands for silence and announced, "I propose that as many of us that are free to do so should meet at the site of the Hemlock Mill tomorrow to look the place over. *You,*" she added to the planning officer, fixing him with a piercing cerulean-blue gaze, "can meet us there!"

"Oh, but I can't —"

"You can be there or not, as you please," Hebe interrupted him, and then also rode roughshod over the protestations of the consortium's representative, who was appealing to Mike, the village policeman, to prevent this incursion.

"I can't see any reason to prevent it," Mike said placidly — he is possibly the most laid back policeman in the country. "If there's a public footpath through part of the property, you can't do a lot about people viewing the site from it."

"I don't care who owns the site and I have no intention of asking for permission to visit it," Hebe stated regally. "We'll meet there at ten tomorrow, everyone!" she finished.

"Should the local press be informed?" someone suggested from the hall.

"Good point," Hebe said, and I could see Laurence Yatton just behind her, jotting that down.

"Now, one final point before we end the meeting and this is particularly addressed to those among you running shops and businesses in the area. I propose that we set up a Sticklepond Chamber of Commerce to protect our interests."

"Hear, hear!" called Florrie, through a mouthful of Everton Mint.

"Good: those of you in the front three rows stay behind and give your name to Laurence."

Raffy got up and declared the meeting closed, and then everyone else filed out while Laurence enrolled us business folk as founder members of the Sticklepond

Chamber of Commerce, with the first meeting to be convened later that week.

I hadn't realised that Ivo had been at the meeting until I went out and spotted him chatting to Raffy. I suppose it was good that he was taking an interest in village affairs — or then again, maybe he hoped that the new bridal boutique would get the go-ahead and put me out of business!

He caught me up as I set off across the green and fell into step beside me.

"I may as well come back with you and collect Flash. It's getting late for his walk," he said, and when I looked up at him he gave me that wonderful, heart-breaking smile. I fell over my feet, and he put a hand on my arm to steady me.

"Only if you still feel like it," I said, when I regained the power of speech.

"Oh, I enjoy it. Are you going to visit this mill site tomorrow?"

"Yes. I can leave Bella in charge of the shop and I'll be really interested to see it."

"I think I'll have a look, too," he said, to my surprise. "I seem to be being sucked into the life of the village whether I want to be or not. In fact, we might as well both go in my car. You can direct me," he added, and I was too surprised to protest.

When he returned Flash later he came in without any urging, much like a cautious vagrant cat. He didn't say much, just sat drinking a glass of Meddyg and eating fruit cake accompanied by a slice of crumbly

Lancashire cheese, while watching me hand-feed the insane dog, who'd had a sudden onset of Fear of Dinner Bowl syndrome again.

If I had a family crest, my motto would be "If it has a pulse, feed it."

CHAPTER
TWENTY-SEVEN

Late Calls

Violet's husband finally got back, but he'd had the malaria badly and he was never that well afterwards — quite yellow he looked, a lot of the time, and would sweat and sweat, burning up. He was much older than Vi too, of course. Still, he was happy that Vi had settled down in her ways a bit and that she'd adopted the little girl, who she called Imogen. In fact, he doted on her and I'm afraid she got rather spoiled. And he was always kind to me — never even hinted that he knew what had happened. He was a good man. Too good for Vi.

Middlemoss Living Archive
Recordings: Nancy Bright.

Revelations were coming thick and fast and I was quite tempted to call Immy in California and ask her if she knew she was adopted. She'd certainly never even hinted at it to me, so I was pretty certain she didn't know. Perhaps the facts had been so well hidden that Violet hadn't felt the need to tell her.

Peter, the grandfather I had never met (and I had no recollection of my grandmother either, since she had died when I was two), sounded like a really nice man. He'd certainly made Aunt Nan welcome in their Devon home so that she'd been able to see the little girl from time to time, even if they had turned her into a "spoiled little madam"!

It was odd to think that she had grown up into my mother . . .

I left Bella minding the shop until it was time to close, this being our half-day, and drove out to the Hemlock Mill site with Ivo, feeling very conspicuous roaring out of the village in his old red Jaguar.

In case of rough ground I was wearing patchwork dungarees tucked into yellow Wellington boots, but since Ivo was neat in leather jacket and dark cord trousers, a fringed silk scarf wound round his neck, I didn't exactly match the soignée image he was projecting. He should have looked old-fogey in that get-up, but somehow he didn't, just very attractive in a slightly edgy way . . .

I reminded myself firmly that falling for a grieving widower who had already broken my heart once was *not* a good idea.

"I've been here once before, I remembered late last night," I told him as I directed him off the Ormskirk road and up a single-track lane that had a tall strip of grass up the middle, like an eco-friendly Mohican haircut. "There was a Sunday school picnic in the woodland."

"So it's true that some of it's open to the public?"

"Yes, of course, there's a footpath across it. Oh, I do hope we can find a way of fighting off this retail park, even if I can see you think we're a lot of not-in-my-back-yarders."

"I'm just trying to see both sides and I don't think the new place would necessarily hit local businesses, just give some competition and bring in even more visitors."

"You're quite wrong, and anyway, it would be completely out of place in such a lovely spot," I told him firmly. "But we've already successfully fought off the threat of a huge housing development in the village, so I'm sure we can knock this one on the head too."

"Oh yes, Raffy told me about all that — how you nearly lost the tennis courts and the Lido field."

"I'd have hated to lose the Lido field. Aunt Nan taught me to swim in the river pool there, just as her father taught her . . . and probably his father, too. And we used to picnic there sometimes on a Sunday. But luckily someone discovered that the Lido field had been a plague pit."

"*Luckily?*"

"Well, not lucky for the plague victims buried there, of course," I conceded, "but it certainly wasn't a good selling point for new houses."

There were a lot of cars parked up the side of the lane leading to the mill, but one of the universally useful Friends of Winter's End, wearing a fluorescent orange tabard, waved us on through the open big wire-mesh gates. Evidently the guard had given in to force majeure and opened them, for he stood by, looking gloomy and talking into a mobile phone. The planning officer and the consortium's representative,

299

who had been at the meeting, were huddled deep in conspiratorial-looking conversation just behind him.

Inside, where the mill itself used to stand, many more vehicles were parked, including Hebe's distinctive white Mini. Ivo pulled carefully into the last parking space.

We joined everyone outside the old mill manager's house, which was the only building still standing. It was a fine four-square Victorian structure, even if it did look a bit sad with the doors and windows boarded up and a rampant weed growing out of the gutter next to the chimney stack.

There were a couple of unmistakable journalists with photographers in tow, and I also spotted George Turnbull, a reporter on our local paper. They were clustered around Hebe, who must have been bringing them up to speed on the situation. Then she was assisted onto a stone mounting block to address the troops.

"Thank you for such a great turn-out, everyone!" she called loudly in her clear, patrician voice. "Now, *I've* been here since early this morning but Caz Naylor —" she indicated a slightly furtive, foxy-looking young man standing nearby, who was wearing combat trousers, a khaki vest and big, lace-up boots — "who you may know is the gamekeeper at Pharamond Hall in Middlemoss, has been here since before dawn and already made several important discoveries."

She listed them. Caz had identified otter prints by the river, the pellets of barn owls, and evidence of a thriving newt community. There were also at least two species of bats roosting in the attic of the manager's house and, in the woodland at the top end of the proposed site, a colony of red squirrels.

Caz Naylor looked even shiftier as Hebe mentioned this final rare inhabitant (though I thought it was probably just his natural expression) but of course everyone cheered, because we all like to hear good news about our native Squirrel Nutkin. I was surprised it was managing to resist the greys in this isolated patch of woodland, even though I knew the grounds of Pharamond Hall, only a few miles the other side of Sticklepond, was a haven for them.

Hebe sent everyone to see the site and with all of us trooping about we didn't exactly spot a lot of wildlife, endangered or otherwise. It was all very overgrown but pretty, especially down by the river Ches, which formed one boundary to the plot. A botanist among us identified several quite uncommon plants too, so it was looking promising for *us*, and less so for the retail park.

By the time we had all reconvened and given our findings, the planning officer and the consortium's representative were looking very worried, and even more so when Mr Glover, our Sticklepond Shakespeare, suggested timidly, "The whole area would make a wonderful nature reserve with a visitor centre, wouldn't it?"

"Of course — the very thing!" Hebe exclaimed enthusiastically. "Good man!"

"It would be another local visitor attraction, drawing tourists to the area — an asset rather than the opposite," Chloe agreed. There was no sign of Raffy, who must have had other business, but the toddler, Grace, was in a baby carrier on her mother's back.

"I don't think my clients would consider developing it as a nature reserve, rather than a retail park. That's quite ridiculous!" the consortium's representative said. "There could be no profit in it."

"But if planning permission for a retail park is turned down because of all the endangered species, then the land won't be worth much anyway, will it?" Laurence Yatton pointed out.

"But part of it is a brownfield site, and there's already one building here," he retaliated.

"It can only be brownfield where the actual mill stood, which is quite a small area that could be used to erect a visitor centre on, perhaps incorporating the manager's house," Hebe suggested. "Or the house could be restored with Victorian furnishings as another visitor attraction, though Caz tells me that a bat occupation of any premises must be notified and arrangements put into place to protect them, before any renovation or rebuilding of a property can take place."

"That's right," Caz Naylor drawled laconically.

Anya, Mike the policeman's wife, really put the boot in (red leather, painted with purple daisies — I was very envious!) by saying that she knew lots of travellers who would immediately come and camp at Hemlock Mill if there was any threat to the trees and wildlife.

"Yes, you know lots of tree huggers, don't you, dear?" Hebe said graciously.

"I've heard on the grapevine that the local animal rights group's become part of Force for Nature now,"

Anya added. "They're less about guerrilla tactics and more about applying political pressure and lobbying, so we can get *them* involved, too."

"Excellent thinking: I am sure they would take it amiss if any animal habitats were destroyed in order to build shops," Hebe said. "As would we all." She swept her autocratic and withering gaze over the representatives of the council and consortium representatives and added, "*Almost* all."

At this point, Mr Lamb gave in to force majeure and defected to our side.

"I have a feeling there isn't going to be a retail park," Ivo remarked, as he drove me home again. "I'm totally stunned at the number of rare or endangered species in one small area."

"Yes, so am I." I was also slightly suspicious, especially about the red squirrels, but I decided not to share that with him . . .

"Hebe Winter is a force to be reckoned with."

"You certainly don't want to mess with her," I agreed.

Then he surprised me by suggesting we go somewhere for a pub lunch before he dropped me back.

"To pay you back for all those food parcels," he said, with one of those rare but charming smiles. "I can't resist them, so I'll feel less guilty if you let me buy you lunch."

"I'm always baking anyway; I like it," I said. "But they're really payment for giving Flash some exercise."

Bella would lock up the shop if I wasn't back in time, so there was no reason why I shouldn't have lunch with Ivo . . . Anyway, I thought, it would probably do him good to get out.

I knew a good place in Rainford, not too far away, and over lunch he opened up a bit about his acting career and all the Shakespearian roles he'd played.

"You must miss it and be dying to get back," I said sympathetically.

"Strangely enough, the longer I'm away, the less I feel like returning," he replied thoughtfully. "I mean, it's a whole separate world and it's pretty well been my life for most of my working career, but there *are* other things . . ."

Like your Nicholas Marlowe novels, I thought, but fortunately didn't say out loud.

"I expect you'll feel differently when you've recovered from your breakdown."

He gave me a sharp look from his lovely clear grey eyes. "Tansy, I haven't *had* a breakdown!"

"Right," I agreed, though if he hadn't had a breakdown, I thought he had come pretty close to it. "You just needed the space to grieve and instead went back to work too soon."

He ran his hands through his dark chestnut hair. Mine would have stood up on end like Medusa's curls if I did that, but his just settled softly back around his head, silky smooth. "Well, that's what they said when I kept drying on stage. It had never happened to me before and it was such a vicious circle. The more I worried about it, the more it happened."

"That must have been really difficult," I said sympathetically.

"Anyway, I thought if I spent six months somewhere quiet I could come to terms with everything . . ."

"And then you didn't get the peace you expected." I felt a bit guilty.

"No, quite the opposite. My nerves *have* been a bit on edge," he conceded, which was the understatement of the century, "so I expect you thought you'd got the neighbour from hell!"

"You were a bit ratty," I said frankly, "but you're looking more unwound with each passing day, so I hope your sabbatical is working anyway and you're starting to feel better."

"I *was*, until I started reading Kate's diaries . . ." The haunted expression came back to his eyes and he went all monosyllabic again until we got back to Sticklepond, so I wondered exactly what she had been writing in them. I was *dying* to ask.

Still, at least Ivo had opened up a bit and didn't seem to regret it, because later, when he brought Flash back from his walk, he came into the kitchen without even being asked, and stayed for a glass of Meddyg and a fairy cake, though he didn't say much, except about the progress Seth was making with his knot garden.

Later he was back playing the mournful music, but I'm becoming accustomed to it, just as I hoped he was becoming accustomed to the merry peal of wedding bells!

★ ★ ★

Cheryl was being increasingly firm about dragging Aunt Nan back to her life story when she made one of her sideways digressions, so I suspected she was almost dying from curiosity by that point, and that she'd drawn the same conclusions I had . . .

I told Bella all about it in a rare quiet moment in the shop. It had been so busy that earlier she'd had to buzz for me to help her. "So I strongly suspect that my mother was really Aunt Nan's daughter, though I don't think Immy can have any idea, or I'm sure she'd have said something, or been different with Aunt Nan," I finished.

Bella thought my suspicions had to be right, because it all fitted. "But if so, it's a tragedy that Immy and Aunt Nan were never close, isn't it?"

"Yes, my mother's never seemed especially fond of anyone except herself," I said sadly, "and Aunt Nan was such a warm, loving person. It's all terribly sad!"

"Still, at least Nan did have that relationship with you; she *adored* you," Bella consoled me.

"And I adored her right back. She was more than a mother — or even grandmother — she was *everything*."

"And she'd be so proud at how successful the shop's becoming," Bella said.

Business was certainly increasing rapidly and I'd had to order a lot more shoes, especially brightly coloured ones. I was still ploughing most of the profit back into new stock, but it was building up nicely.

During another brief lull I unpacked some vintage shoes that Timmy had found for me in London, including a fun pair of sixties pale pink silk booties by Pucci, unworn and in their original box. I had to decline the online offer of a pair of lovely strappy sandal Manolos, though. They simply weren't built to stay pristine for more than one wedding, unless you have fairy feet, and you don't want worn-out soles on your big day, do you? Or re-soled shoes, because the sole is part of the whole wonderful Manolo package, so replacement soles simply wouldn't be the same.

I always think Flash walks with little springy fairy feet, though his, of course, are also *very* hairy.

That Friday night was the first time I opened late by appointment, though it was only about an hour after my normal closing time of four thirty. Bella, of course, had long gone home.

I had the shop lit and ready well before my potential customers were due and it looked like an Aladdin's cave of loveliness. I'd put out a bottle of pink fizz in an ice bucket and a plate of fairy cakes iced in white and sprinkled with silver edible stars. I wanted to make the bridal shoe selection process *really* special.

The bride arrived with both bridesmaids and they all chose shoes for the wedding, including, to my surprise, her mother.

"Belinda's father's paying for her wedding — he divorced me last year, the bastard," she confided, after selecting an expensive pair of cream high-heeled shoes. "He said Belinda could have anything she wanted — guilty conscience, I suppose — so we might as well get our money's worth."

Then she triumphantly added chocolate shoes, and silver and pearl shoe necklaces for the bridesmaids to the heap.

"What about one of these tiny enamelled silver bluebird charms, to sew inside your wedding dress for luck, Belinda?" I suggested.

"Oh, yes! I need something blue."

"Bluebirds mean happiness, too," I told her.

In fact, as soon as I'd got them into stock I'd taken to wearing one on a long silver chain around my neck every day and also adopted Clinique's Happy as my signature perfume: I thought I might as well aim for the state I wanted to be in.

I'd given Bella a bluebird too: she deserved all the happiness she could get and it was starting to look as if Neil might be the man to provide it. I only hoped he was as nice and genuine as he seemed.

When my customers had left, laden down with parcels and full of fizz and cakes, I decided it was fun having these sessions and well worth opening up when I could make more in an hour than in an entire afternoon!

Saturday was turning out to be our busiest day of the week, which I supposed was not surprising. I did spare a thought or two for Ivo every time the doorbell pealed, but perhaps he was getting so used to it he barely noticed any more . . .

Brides in search of the perfect shoe seemed to bring either their mothers or their bridesmaids (who are usually their best friends), to support them, but hardly ever the prospective spouses.

We had a lot of tourists in, too, who made many small purchases, from handbag charms to umbrellas and purses and even some of my *Slipper Monkey* books. I was now stocking them all, not just the Cinderella one. The chocolate shoes were selling really well, too. Chloe was making her third big batch.

I was really tired by the time we shut, and more grateful than ever that Ivo would give Flash the long and tiring walk he so desperately needed, because I think it would have finished me off.

That evening Aunt Nan steamrollered right over Cheryl's prods and questions and rambled on at length about Bonfire Night and the nutty, half-charred taste of potatoes and chestnuts roasted in the ashes.

I told Ivo when he brought Flash back that I longed for some roast chestnuts right now, even if it was the wrong time of the year, and he said, "'*At Christmas I no more desire a rose than wish a snow in May's new-fangled mirth; but like of each thing that in season grows*'."

"With the supermarkets flying in food and flowers from all over the globe, it's a rare thing when you can't find something when you want it, but I think you're right, and anyway, things always do taste better in season. Have a meringue," I added, pushing the plate nearer to him.

"I thought you'd be too tired to cook anything today — your shop door tune seems to have been alternating with the church bells for the entire day," he said slightly tartly, but it didn't stop him taking a meringue, which I'd liberally daubed with cream and blackberry jam.

"We have been very busy and I'm shattered, but I've got a miraculous five-minute microwave meringue recipe and I thought if I couldn't have chestnuts, then I'd have a sweet treat as a consolation prize."

I could see he liked the meringues and wondered if perhaps low blood sugar was part of his problem?

I went to bed really early and fell deeply and instantly asleep, only to be awoken by the phone ringing in the middle of the night. I'd insisted Aunt Nan had an extension installed in her bedroom, so it went off right in my ear.

I always think it's bad news in the middle of the night, so it was both a relief and an anticlimax when I heard Justin's voice slurring thickly,

"Tanshy darling — you there?"

"Yes, but I was asleep. Why on earth are you ringing me at this time of night? Are you drunk?"

"S'not that late and I'm jusht shelebrating a poshibility."

"Poshibility?"

"Shomething that'll change everything — make you shee . . . shee things in a new light."

"Short of a frontal lobotomy, that *really* isn't going to happen, Justin," I snapped crisply. "Good night!" And I slammed down the phone.

I couldn't imagine what he was on about, but he rarely got totally plastered, so something must have happened to engender this unusual bout of intoxication.

He'd be sorry in the morning, when it would be a case of "physician, heal thyself"!

CHAPTER
TWENTY-EIGHT

Mixed Messages

The child, Imogen, grew up tall and fair, taking more after my mother than the darker Bright side like me. Father and I often invited her to stay with us, but she was never keen, being like Vi in that way. We weren't good enough for her, especially after Vi sent her to a smart boarding school, and she was easily bored.

Middlemoss Living Archive
Recordings: Nancy Bright.

Not surprisingly, I awoke on Sunday morning still tired and a little grumpy, but I felt better once I'd taken Flash out for a short walk, partly because it was one of those lovely bright April mornings when you could really feel the warmth in the sunshine.

I gave the shop a good clean out as usual, then did a little baking before I went upstairs to my studio in the back bedroom to dream over ideas for the next book . . . but found myself watching Ivo gardening, instead.

His knot garden was now planted out, much larger and more intricate than mine. Rather than start with small box cuttings and await the slow process of their growing together to define the outline of the knot, he'd gone for more of an instant effect: the hedging was

312

quite thick and without gaps, and there were four large box pyramids at the corners *and* a spiral in the middle. It must have cost him a fortune!

I felt a bit jealous: it was almost as lovely as the one in the back courtyard of the Museum of Gardening in London! Timmy and I had often met there for lunch, later with Joe, too . . . and I thought how much I missed seeing my friends. I often emailed them, or rang for a chat, but it wasn't the same thing at all.

Ivo usually gardened in the afternoon, because he wrote in the mornings, so I wondered if he had had a bad night, too. If so, he was likely to be snappy, so I resisted the urge to go out and admire his new garden and firmly hauled my mind back to ideas for the new book. I'd already twisted several new pipe cleaner Slipper Monkeys into existence while watching Ivo, without even realising it.

Slipper Monkeys Ahoy! would be the next title, I decided suddenly, and then spent the rest of the morning folding boats out of old magazine pages and seeing how they looked floating in the bath with Slipper Monkeys aboard.

After lunch I felt really restless and, since Ivo was still gardening, I went out and called him over.

"Ivo, I feel as if I need a really good walk, so I'm going to take Flash up through the woodland footpaths at the back of the Winter's End estate. That should be enough, if you want an evening off dog walking?"

"I expect he'd enjoy both . . . and so would I, really. I think I've had enough gardening for one day!"

"What, you want to come with me?"

"Yes, if you don't mind? But perhaps you want to be alone?" he said diffidently.

"No, of course not," I assured him quickly, "I'd be glad of some company," and went to fetch Flash and lock the back door while he quickly changed out of his muddy clothes.

We had a quietly companionable walk, neither of us saying much until we turned for home, when he asked me how I was getting on with Aunt Nancy's recordings.

"Do you think you've guessed her secret right?"

"Yes, but she still hasn't come right out and said so: I expect she's saving that for the personal recording she did for me. At the moment I'm just reading between the lines, but I can't get it out of my head. What about you?" I enquired cautiously. "Are you still working your way through your wife's diaries?"

"Oh, yes," he admitted heavily. "I don't want to, but Pandora never managed to get the lid back on the box once she'd taken a peek, and neither can I."

"I'm sorry," I said gently. "But I expect you have lots of happy memories to look back on, too."

"Happy memories?" he repeated blankly, as though this was a foreign concept to him. Then he sighed heavily and said darkly, "All Kate's secrets are escaping, but I expect that's my punishment for doing something that felt so wrong."

"It seems natural enough to me, to want to read them after she was gone," I told him, still in the dark about what it was that his late wife had done that had upset him. "And who doesn't have a few secrets?"

He didn't reply to that one, and we walked on in silence once more, with a wet, muddy and happy Flash, who seemed a lot bolder when out with both of us.

I thought Ivo would simply sheer off into his own garden when we got back, but to my surprise he accepted my impulsive invitation to come in and have tea, though I don't think he was expecting a proper high tea, just a cup and a biscuit.

He dried Flash off with his special towel, then sat at the pine kitchen table and watched me preparing it with widening eyes: ham sandwiches with English mustard, cut into triangles, the Dundee cake I'd baked that morning and thin slices of buttered malt loaf. Then I added a large chunk of crumbly Lancashire cheese, a pot of spicy apple and raisin chutney, a jar of piccalilli and a plate of rough oatcakes to the spread.

"There, that should do it," I said, handing him a flowery tea plate. "Get stuck in."

"I should think it *will* do: there's enough to feed an army here!"

"Aunt Nan always cooked Sunday dinner at lunchtime and then would spread out a cold high tea around four, so I got the habit, too. Anyone was welcome to drop in. Her friend Florrie often used to pop round from the pub, for instance. Aunt Nan used to wear her wedding dress to Sunday tea," I added. "Her fiancé was killed early on in the war so I think it gave her a feeling of being near him and also, she used to reminisce about him a lot. He was certainly the love of her life, whatever else happened."

"She was quite a character, wasn't she? I can understand why you miss her so much."

"Yes, though really I don't feel that she's that far away from me. Chloe — the vicar's wife — believes we all have guardian angels, and Aunt Nan is mine and taking care of me."

"I think *I* could do with one of those," Ivo said, still looking fairly morose, but once he'd consumed several sandwiches and a slice of cake he seemed much cheered. Perhaps I was right about the low blood sugar thing.

"I used to do most of the cooking, Kate couldn't even boil an egg," he said suddenly. "But actually, I like cooking — or I did. I seem to have got out of the habit of that, along with having regular meals."

"I enjoy all cooking, but I like baking best — cakes, bread and biscuits, *and* eating them," I told him. "But weirdly enough, even though I'm eating much more than before I moved back to Sticklepond, I'm actually losing weight!"

"You're probably a lot more active. If you're not in the shop, then you're baking or gardening."

"True, though I do spend a lot of time sitting working on my books in the mornings."

"But after you've taken Flash for an early walk."

"We don't go far, just up the lane and back usually, but he's so energetic he's always ready to go out."

When we'd finished eating and Ivo had helped me to clear away and wash up, he admired the fresh row of brightly coloured Slipper Monkeys swinging along the edge of the Welsh dresser. (I didn't remember hanging them there, so I think they really do have a life of their own!) He said how much he liked my books.

I told him about the new idea and the paper boats, and he turned out to be a whiz at origami, conjuring up a really neat little ship from the back page of the Sunday paper magazine.

By then, somehow, a couple of hours had slipped pleasantly past and Flash really was starting to look hopefully at his lead again.

"Look, I'll just take him for a quick walk round the green now," Ivo offered. "I don't mind, and I ate too much so I need to work some of it off or I'll have indigestion."

While he was out I made him a takeaway supper of leftover sandwiches and a piece of cake, and then had just sat down again in the old armchair by the stove that had been Aunt Nan's favourite, when, of all people, Marcia rang me.

"Tansy," she began eagerly, without preamble, and higher-pitched than a bat, "I'm in London —"

"I really don't care where you are, Marcia," I interrupted, and was about to put the phone down when she said quickly, "No, don't hang up on me. I've just done you a good turn."

"That'll be the day!"

"I wish you'd stop butting in and just listen — you'll thank me for this," she said. "I went to commiserate with Justin yesterday, but really I wanted to see if there was anything I could do to smooth things over between you both."

"Then you wasted your time, because this isn't exactly some little hairline crack you can wallpaper over," I said, wondering why she'd really gone. It was probably just curiosity and a ravening desire to find out all the details I hadn't given her.

"Justin wasn't exactly pleased to see me."

"You surprise me."

"Well, I didn't see why he *shouldn't* be; he can't blame *me* for his fling with Rae, can he? I didn't make him do it! Anyway, he thawed after a bit when I said I'd seen you and you were really missing him."

"But I'm not!" I protested angrily. "I'm *totally* over him!"

"Oh, come on, I know you're mad about him, so you don't have to lie to me," she said with a short laugh. "Justin opened up and started talking about why you'd split and how sorry he was, and he assumed you'd told me that Rae's little boy was his. That was a stunner!"

"Of course I wouldn't have told you: is he mad? Your fiancé getting your stepsister pregnant isn't exactly something you'd want to broadcast from the rooftops!"

"Well, then, it just goes to show that you *should* have told me everything, because I know Rae rather better than you do."

"I'd be quite happy never to have known either of you at all," I said bitterly, but she ignored me and swept on with her story.

"The thing is, when Rae got pregnant she told me that she wasn't sure *who* the father was, but it didn't matter because one of the possibles was in a serious relationship and would pay through the nose to keep the baby secret, so she'd tell him it was his."

"What? She said *that*? Do you think it was true?"

"Why not? She's always slept around, that's why her marriage went belly up, and she likes fair-haired blue-eyed men, so Justin might be the father — or he might not."

I was silent, trying to take this in, and she added, thoughtfully, "Come to think of it, I know she had a fling with Ritch Rainford about the time she got pregnant and I've always thought Charlie had a look of him."

"Isn't that the *Cotton Common* actor?"

"Yes, that's the one . . . but then, who *hasn't* had a fling with Ritch Rainford?" she murmured reminiscently.

"Have you told Justin this?"

"Well, I didn't mention Ritch Rainford, obviously, but yes, I told him Charlie might not be his and he should get a DNA test. He was absolutely stunned."

"He would be. He's paid out thousands to Rae in support and hush money for the last five years!"

"But it would be really good if he wasn't the daddy, wouldn't it? Then you could be all forgiving and magnanimous, without any risk of tripping over the evidence any time you're out shopping locally. And it will be entirely due to me that you got back together again!" she ended triumphantly.

"Marcia, this isn't a rom com film! Here in the real world he still had an affair with Rae, so it wouldn't make it any easier even if he wasn't Charlie's father."

"Of course it would! I bet he isn't, and once you know for sure you'll feel entirely different. Justin's going to go round to her house when only the nanny's there and get the DNA sample, so Rae doesn't know what he's doing."

"So Rae doesn't know you've told Justin?"

"No, of course not — are you mad? I've sworn Justin to secrecy about my telling him, too."

"What I don't understand is why on earth Rae wanted so much more money anyway? I mean, I know Lars gives you both a good allowance."

"Well yes, good, but not hugely generous, because he has this old-fashioned idea that we should work for our livings. Of course, I'm the blue-eyed girl because I've got my acting career, but Rae only played at the modelling for a year or two before she married, and she goes through money like a hot knife through butter."

"She's certainly always spent it as if she's got it."

"It's all pretence. When that dodgy marriage to her fitness instructor broke down, he had to be paid off and Daddy's had to bail her out over and over again, so now he's lost patience. Eventually he said he wouldn't do it again, so if she couldn't manage to spend within her means she would have to live in New York and move in with him."

My mind had been shocked into numbness by Marcia's bombshell, but was now up to working things out again. Joining up the dots was easy in retrospect. "So then Rae thought up this . . . scam?"

"Of course. She was living in the London house, way above her means, so I suppose when all her friends decided that babies were the latest designer must-have, it seemed like a good idea, and the rest followed as the night does the day."

"I think you're forgetting there's an innocent child at the heart of all this — poor Charlie," I pointed out. "One day he's going to learn the truth and then he'll want to know who his father is."

"At least he might know by then who he *isn't*! And in that case, perhaps she can pinpoint who else it might be," Marcia said, but not as if it was of any importance. "I don't really think you've grasped that if Charlie isn't Justin's, you won't have a permanent reminder that he slipped up a bit, so there'll be nothing to stop you getting back together again."

"Marcia, I'll never forgive either of them for what they did! Don't forget that while he was paying out all that money to Rae, he was telling me we couldn't afford to get married and have children," I said bitterly. "And now I've probably left it too late to have a baby."

"Did you really want to ruin your figure with sprogs?" she asked incredulously, before adding bitchily, "Not that you've got much of a figure left to ruin!"

"*Yes*," I snapped.

"Then I'd get back with Justin and give it your best shot, pronto," she advised. "Don't bother waiting for the DNA test results, because the more I think about it, the more sure I am that Charlie's Ritch Rainford's."

She rang off, leaving me in turmoil. In fact, I broke into harsh, bitter sobs as soon as I'd put the receiver

321

down, and that's how Ivo found me a few minutes later when he walked back in with Flash.

I'd tried to stop crying but somehow, once opened, the floodgates proved impossible to shut again, a bit like Ivo's Pandora's box.

"Tansy, what's happened?" he exclaimed, but seeing I was too choked by tears to reply, put his arms around me and gave me a wonderfully comforting hug instead. I relaxed into his arms and cried into his shoulder for ages, but eventually I calmed down enough to explain that something Marcia had just told me had upset me.

"She was here?" He darted a look towards the door, as if she might be hanging on the back of it with the coats, like a bat.

"No, she called me from London. She'd been to see my ex-fiancé — *she* said to try and get us back together, but since I broke up with him after I found out that he'd had a fling with my other stepsister, Rae, she had a wasted journey because that was *never* going to happen!"

"Right," he said slowly.

"Actually, there's more to it than that. I found out recently that Rae's little boy is Justin's too."

"I'm so sorry," he said sincerely. "That must have been a terrible shock."

"It was, though it also explained a lot. When we got engaged we planned to get married the same year and start a family, but then suddenly Justin kept putting me off and saying we couldn't afford it . . . though part of it was my weight, I think, because once the initial rosy glow had worn off, he said I should lose a couple of stone, so he could be really proud of me on the big day!"

"There's nothing wrong with your weight!"

"I am a bit plump."

"Pleasantly plump," he insisted. By now we were both sitting on the cushioned settle by the stove and I'd broken out some emergency Meddyg.

"He'd got a bit critical about me generally about then — my clothes, friends, everything. But anyway, I found out he'd not only been paying Rae maintenance the last few years, but also hush money so she didn't tell me. He said it was because he loved me and didn't want to lose me, but if that was true, why did he sleep with Rae in the first place?"

I didn't wait for him to reply. "No: Marcia might think that if the child isn't Justin's it'll make it all right, and I can forgive him and carry on as if nothing ever happened, but it *did* and it'll always be between us. Do you understand?"

"I certainly do," Ivo said. "When you look back at what you thought was a happy relationship and discover that underneath it was all built on lies, it shakes you to the very core. 'I thought her as chaste as unsunn'd snow'," he added.

"Your wife was unfaithful to you?"

"From almost the moment we married. She just jotted them all down in her diary, as if they were lunch engagements — the where, when and how often, with stars for performance!"

"That must have been an awful shock. I'm so sorry!"

323

"Don't be; I think reading it in the diaries, inch by slow inch, is my penance," he said bafflingly, because he didn't say what for and I couldn't ask, since his face was getting that familiar shuttered look again.

"I see what you meant about the Pandora's box now," I told him, with a long sigh. Ivo still had one arm draped around me for comfort, but gave my shoulders a brief squeeze and then got up to go.

Upset or not, I made sure he didn't leave without his supper box.

"You deserved much better than that fiancé of yours," he said, before vanishing into the night.

Flash, who had been leaning against my legs while I was sitting on the settle, poking a sympathetic wet nose into my hand from time to time, gave a brief howl and I had to make a real effort not to follow suit.

CHAPTER
TWENTY-NINE

Describing Circles

Peter died while Imogen was still young, and Violet had another go of the pneumonia not long after Immy had Tansy, and that was that. Though between you, me and the lamp post, she'd undermined her health with heavy drinking for years.

Middlemoss Living Archive
Recordings: Nancy Bright.

While we were opening up the shop, I told Bella about Marcia's call and how much it had upset me all over again.

"But it's really weird that Marcia's so keen to get me and Justin back together when I know she's never even liked me! Yet there she was, stirring things up and telling Justin I still missed him."

"Do you think it might be jealousy, because she really fancies Ivo and she's worried that you will get off with him again, now you're living next door to each other."

I stared at her. "One of the Ugly Sisters, jealous of me?"

"Why not? You and Ivo obviously had chemistry first time round."

"Well, there might be one or two reasons. Let me see . . ." I ticked them off on my fingers. "One, we're not Romeo and Juliet any more, a lot of water's passed under both our bridges; two, he's still grieving for his wife; three, after what Justin did with my stepsister I'm never going to trust another man with my heart ever again; and four — now, what could that be? Oh, yes, we don't fancy each other."

I left Ivo's revelation about his wife's unfaithfulness off the list, which I expect had put him as firmly off future relationships as much as Justin's affair had done to me. Bella and I shared most things, but I felt that these were Ivo's personal secrets . . .

"How do you know he doesn't fancy you?" she asked.

"You just do, don't you? He's only just started talking to me a bit — in an old-puppy-love-turned-to-friend kind of way. At least, I *think* we're slowly becoming friends. He was really kind last night when he came back with Flash and found me crying after Marcia's phone call."

"How kind?" she asked, with interest.

"Just *nice* — gave me a big hug and let me cry all over him, nothing else. What about you and Neil?"

"Friends too," she said firmly, but I suspected he was slowly creeping into her heart.

It would be all too fatally easy to let Ivo creep back into mine . . .

Neither Ivo nor I had mentioned anything deep and dark since that evening, but that was often the way:

you'd confide something important and then sort of step back and not mention it again for ages. I even did it with Bella sometimes, so maybe that was why she didn't know much about when I broke up with Ivo all those years ago.

But I did think it helped our burgeoning friendship, for we were slowly getting to know each other again. So much so, in fact, that I'd given him my back door key so he could come in and fetch Flash for his walk on Thursday, when I was finally planning a day trip to London to visit the RubyTrueShuze showroom.

Bella would let out and feed the hens and take Flash for a little walk before she opened the shop, but after she left at lunchtime it would be a long stretch until I got home again, so I was more than happy when Ivo said he'd let Flash out into the garden in the afternoon, and then take him for an extra long walk.

"And could you possibly feed the hens in the afternoon — I'll show you what to give them — and then shut them up before dusk?" I asked.

"OK. Not that I know anything about hens."

"You don't need to. They put themselves to bed. You just have to shut and put the catch down on the door, to stop the foxes getting in."

"Sounds easy enough."

"That's great — thank you! I know Bella would come back and do it, but she gets little enough time with Tia as it is. And I won't be too late back — probably before you return from walking Flash," I told him. "I'm going to the RubyTrueShuze showroom to look at new styles and put in a much bigger order than before, and then I'll lunch with friends and come back again."

"The shop is doing really well, then, if you're putting in bigger orders?"

"Yes, business is building much faster than I thought it would. I think it helps that on the RubyTrueShuze website it names me as the only stockist in the Northwest!"

"Your aunt would be proud of you," he said, and I nodded, my eyes suddenly welling with tears.

On the Wednesday evening the first official Sticklepond Chamber of Commerce meeting was convened in the village hall, and there was a good turnout.

Hebe had already got up a petition against the retail park and contacted Force for Nature, who campaigned against experimenting on animals, but also for any domestic or wild creature in danger of any kind, and they had promised to back the campaign.

But there was a surprising amount of support for the retail park being stirred up in Ormskirk, mainly based on the promise of new jobs. Laurence Yatton thought the consortium who owned the Hemlock Mill site were behind it, and was trying to find out who they were.

"And perhaps you might see who the shareholders of Grocergo are, when you have a moment," Hebe suggested, "since they would be the main retail outlet on the site. We might find that someone concerned in the application for the retail park had a vested interest."

Hebe seemed to have everything organised and we were really all there just as supporting cast and occasional Greek chorus, though when I suggested that we might get together to produce some kind of village trail leaflet, which would guide visitors on a tour of the village and surroundings (including, of course, Winter's End and all the shops, cafés and pubs) she said it was an idea of great genius.

"Well, it's not original; lots of places have them. We could make it a circular walk, starting at Winter's End and the big car park, through the fields to the village, taking in the Witchcraft Museum, then back by way of the Lido field, with its new Plague Pit Tourist Information board, and the church, to the path again. But they could start at any point on the circle."

"Stirrups is a little too far from the village to walk to," Janey put in.

"But it could be marked on the map, with information about it and contact details," Laurence suggested, busily making notes. "In fact, every point of interest within, say, a five-mile radius, could be numbered and information displayed about them on the back of the leaflet. It would all add interest."

"I think it is an idea of great possibility," Gregory Lyon said, "and if we all share the costs of the printing it will not be a huge expense. The local printer who does my pamphlets for sale in the museum is very reasonable."

So that was agreed, and also that Hebe would convene further meetings of the Chamber of Commerce as and when needed.

★   ★   ★

I left for London early next morning in smart black jeans teamed with a bright red and black ikat-weave jacket and my hair pinned up high and secured with colourful butterfly pins. Flash looked anxious and even though I told him he wouldn't have long to wait before Bella would be in to talk to him, I still felt very mean driving off to the station.

I'd forgotten what London was like. I enjoy the museums and the bustle and buzz of the city, but I love the peace and quiet of my home a lot more. I went to the RubyTrueShuze showroom first, where I finally got to meet Ruby herself briefly and then was handed over to an assistant who helped me order a scary amount of wonderful new stock.

I think I got a bit carried away, so I felt excited, nervous and a bit wrung out by the time I arrived at Timmy and Joe's tiny terraced house in Battersea. Joe was at work, but Timmy had taken the day off in my honour and cooked me lunch.

"An omelette and a glass of wine," he said. "Very Elizabeth David!"

Timmy admired my red and black jacket and the pins I'd secured my hair up with . . . or maybe unsecured it with, since the whole bird's nest seemed to be unravelling as the day went on.

"Do you think it's a bit much? People were staring at my head on the tube."

"No, it looks as if a cloud of butterflies has landed on your hair. You be yourself — you can get away with it," he assured me.

We settled down for a good catch-up over lunch, and I told him how well the shop was doing. "There's a steady stream of brides-to-be of all ages and I try to find them the shoes of their dreams. Luckily, there seems to be a style of RubyTrueShuze for practically everyone! One or two have gone for real vintage shoes, and I've promised to buy them back later if they're still in very good condition."

"Trade sounds flourishing!"

"I hope it'll do even better after the article and my advert come out in *Lively Lancashire*. That should be any minute now."

"Brides will be beating a trail to your door," Timmy assured me. "We'll be up again soon and we'll come over and visit."

"I seem to be selling lots of odds and ends to visitors. I think I ought to go to some trade fairs next year, in search of more shoe-shaped trinkets . . . But one step at a time."

After lunch Timmy showed me the vintage shoes he'd bought on my behalf: a pair of unworn palest pink linen platform shoes dating from the seventies, still in their original box, which were very wearable; and a pair of early nineteenth-century white satin shoes, which would be for display only.

"Too lovely to resist!" he said, pointing out the fine silk flowers hand-stitched to the front. "They have obviously been worn, so you couldn't sell them."

"No, they are a bit too fragile, anyway, but they will look lovely on display."

"Wait till you see what else I've got for you!" he said mysteriously, producing a plain white shoe box. "I'm not sure that you could really describe them as wedding shoes, and they really blew the budget, but if you don't want them, I'll keep them myself."

He opened the lid with a flourish, revealing a pair of see-through pumps with black patent toe-and-heel detail, and I gasped:

"Aren't those Chanel? I've seen them only in pictures!" I picked one up, admiring the transparent Lucite heels. You really would look as if you were wearing glass slippers in those.

"Yes, though the original box is missing."

"They're wonderful, and I'll have to have them — but I don't think I could bear to sell them, so they will have to be display only, too."

We packed the shoes back into their boxes and a sturdy paper carrier bag and then I brought Timmy up to speed on what was happening in Sticklepond: Bella and her resistance to Neil's advances, Tia's riding lessons, which had totally diverted her mind from ballet and given her a new circle of little pony-mad friends, and what happened at the Chamber of Commerce meeting. I'd already told him about the retail park.

"But what about you — are you getting pally with the handsome actor next door, yet? I'm assuming you've forgiven him for dumping you first time round?"

"Yes, especially after I found out that was really Marcia and Rae's doing. He's not quite as tense and bad-tempered these days, so I suppose you could say we're becoming friends."

"*Only* friends?"

"You're as bad as Bella!" I felt my face going pink. "There's nothing more and never will be, because not only is there no spark between us now, he's still coming to terms with his wife's death — and when he does, he'll be off back to the stage again! But Bella thinks Marcia's afraid I will snap him up, when she wants him herself!"

I told him about Marcia's meddling visit to Justin. "She's really put the spanner in the works. Justin called me late the night before, drunk and hinting he'd found something out that would change everything, which must have been after Marcia suggested Charlie might not be his son. But he'd have to be *really* drunk if he thought that would make any difference to the way I felt about him cheating on me with Rae!"

"Have you spoken to him since then?" asked Timmy. "Go on, this is just like a soap episode!"

"He texted me next day to say he was sorry for waking me up, but other than that there have been only the usual random texts and emails about what he's doing and how his mother is driving him mad — which serves him right!"

"I'm assuming you didn't tell him you were coming down today?"

"No, or he'd have wanted to see me. I'm only hoping he didn't take Marcia seriously when she assured him I was desperately missing him and sorry we had broken up, because I'm finding it very hard to hammer into his thick skull that there is no going back!"

I travelled back feeling tired but happy, and with two of Timmy's cinnamon and raisin loaves in my folding silk shopping bag. I was so hungry that when I found there was no buffet car and a promised trolley failed to materialise, I ate the better part of one of the loaves, tearing off great soft, fresh and delicious chunks.

The fat businessman opposite me watched in fascinated horror, as if I were some feral scavenging creature. Or maybe that was my ensemble? Timmy might have thought I looked wonderful, but I was still turning heads, so I dare say it wasn't to everyone's taste.

Flash was still out with Ivo when I got back, though they returned soon afterwards and Flash seemed very relieved to see me.

"You've been cruel and mean to him, haven't you?" I asked, as the dog held up a beseeching paw.

"Yes: first I tried to get him to eat his dinner, and then I dragged him round the lanes for miles. Or maybe he dragged me? Nice outfit, by the way — and I like the little butterflies in your hair."

"Really? You don't think they're a little too over the top?"

"No. In fact, the whole ensemble is quite restrained for you. I like all the bright things you wear."

Ivo was obviously sincere, so in reward I buttered some of Timmy's lovely bread and we toasted my return with Meddyg while Flash devoured his neglected dinner.

★　★　★

I could hear him playing miserable music later, even though I'd picked out a CD of *The Rite of Spring* in London in the hope it would give his musical tastes — and his thoughts — a bit of a lift, so I expected he was back to his diary reading. It's as if he is punishing himself for something, but I have no idea what: loving not wisely, but too well, perhaps?

If so, I too have been guilty of that.

CHAPTER
THIRTY

Bananas

You've no idea how long rationing went on for after the war and when bananas suddenly appeared, some of the younger children had no idea what they were! Father and I were always partial to a banana custard, but when we got our first ones after the war, we gave them to a family in the village — their baby was ill, and the doctor said bananas would be excellent for her. Everyone did it — there's always been a sharing spirit in Sticklepond.

> Middlemoss Living Archive
> Recordings: Nancy Bright.

I'd enjoyed my day in London, but the way my spirits lifted with every passing mile bringing me nearer to Sticklepond had made me realise even more clearly that my heart — and my life — now lay there.

It had crystallised my feelings for Justin too. Somewhere deep inside, part of me had still been mourning and missing the man I'd loved, yet that man hadn't ever really existed — or not after the first few months together. It was the attraction of opposites, and perhaps we were too different for it ever to have worked out anyway, but our life together

336

was built on a shaky foundation of lies once Rae came back from America and settled in London.

Bella said if I felt like that I should stop answering his texts and emails altogether, because even my occasional brief replies might give him false hope, and I could see she was right. So after some deliberation I sent him one last email spelling out exactly how I felt and telling him in the plainest terms that there was no possibility of us ever getting back together and I didn't want him to contact me any more.

However, he came bouncing right back with a long, long email saying he knew he had betrayed my trust and understood how hurt that had made me, but he hoped to win my forgiveness eventually and would in any case always be my friend.

Bella said it looked like the message that he'd done the unforgivable would *never* filter through his thick skull, and I was inclined to agree with her. I suspected I'd have to continue deleting all his texts and emails unread.

Life settled into a pleasant routine, my tranquillity only occasionally slightly disturbed by messages arriving from Justin, like brief flashes of lightning far away — vaguely troubling but not of any great importance.

Each morning I let out the hens, walked Flash and worked in my studio (unless Bella needed me), conscious that Ivo too would be working away next door on his novel. Then in the afternoons I would take over the shop once Bella had gone, and for the occasional evening opening by appointment. Saturdays were always busy, especially after my advert appeared in *Bonnie Brides* magazine, so we were both usually needed in the shop.

In the late afternoons I often gardened, and Ivo, who now obviously had the gardening bug, would be there too and would open the gate between our plots so Flash could come and go. Luckily he and Toby seem to have decided they can't see each other at all, even when only feet apart, so life is much quieter!

Though Ivo complained about the withering effect of dog pee on plants, I'm sure he enjoyed Flash's company, and that of the hens, which I sometimes let out in the afternoon for an hour or two. They loved to forage in Ivo's freshly dug garden.

Although naturally pale, Ivo was looking much healthier, which I put down entirely to my food and exercise, but I couldn't do much about the haunted look in his eyes or his state of mind . . .

But when he brought Flash back from his evening walk he came in for a glass of Meddyg, a bite of whatever I'd been baking, and a companionable chat, and I found myself looking forward to this quiet hour or so . . . And now we'd both opened up a little about the discoveries we'd made about our loved ones, the shared secrets had made a bond.

I was still spinning out Aunt Nan's memoir, as Ivo was with Kate's diary, though in his case it seemed to be more of a dogged determination to punish himself; I didn't know why, or what for. Perhaps grief can take you like that?

★ ★ ★

That Sunday afternoon, Ivo and I took Flash for another long walk together and then he came back for high tea — even higher than usual, since I'd embarked on a sudden frenzy of both sweet and savoury baking early that morning.

We'd almost finished when Bella and Tia unexpectedly arrived the back way, with Neil in tow, having been to a car-boot sale where Bella had bought me a hardy bay tree to replace one in Aunt Nan's garden that had not survived the winter.

"I got a riding hat of my own, so I don't have to borrow one from the riding school," Tia said.

"Yes, I noticed you were wearing one," I said, since she'd arrived with it jammed firmly over her long, floss-fine pale hair. "That was a good find!"

"Yes, it was a bargain," Bella agreed. "It didn't look as if it had been worn at all."

They didn't linger, but after they'd gone, Ivo raised one dark eyebrow and asked, "Is that Bella's boyfriend?"

"*Friend*, certainly. I'm sure he'd like to be more, but Bella's been through a lot so she's a bit wary."

"'He capers, he dances, he has eyes of youth, he writes verses, he speaks holiday, he smells of April and May'," Ivo said.

"You think he's got it *that* badly?"

"It's unmistakable. I couldn't make out how your friend felt, though."

I explained how Bella's partner had run up such huge gambling debts, unbeknown to her until after his death.

339

"He'd never even got round to divorcing his wife like he'd promised, so under the terms of his will everything went to her — not that there was much anyway."

"So then she moved back here, presumably?"

"Yes, her parents had a tiny granny flat over the garage, which was empty, but it's not ideal being so close to her parents, especially since her mother's become so house-proud it's practically an illness. Her parents have their own lives, too, and she feels she's really intruding."

"Couldn't she get her own place?" Ivo suggested.

"She's saving for a deposit, but I can't pay her much yet, though I'll put her wages up as soon as I can. She's really glad of the extra work you give her."

"It's been a godsend finding her. And it's another strange coincidence that you and I are both writing away every morning, only a wall apart, isn't it?"

"I often think that," I agreed, then asked brightly, "How *is* your autobiography coming along?"

He gave me a look. "Stop pretending you don't know that I'm Nicholas Marlowe, because I saw you with a stack of my novels in Marked Pages and realised that Bella must have told you."

"She did," I admitted, "but only because we've been best friends for ever and we know whatever we tell each other will remain secret. Your books are brilliant!"

"Thank you. I usually enjoy writing them, it's just that with everything else, it's taken me a while to get back into the routine and my publisher's pressing for the next one."

"I know the feeling," I agreed. "Now I've read them, I understand why you want to keep your writing name a secret."

He nodded. "I was afraid everyone would think I was basing my characters and plot on real people and situations, even though I've created a second smaller company of players in the books."

"The murders all take place when the company's on tour, rather than in Stratford, though," I said.

"You must have read a few!"

"Felix has been trying to find them all for me."

"And I admire your children's books — I think you're very talented indeed."

"We should set up a mutual admiration society then," I said with a grin.

"I think we already have," he said, helping himself to a last slice of apple upside-down cake before I could clear the plate away.

The following Tuesday was particularly busy, for not only did I approve an exciting new range of *Slipper Monkeys* merchandise — pencils, bags, lunch boxes, soft toys and lots of other things — but all the lovely shoes I'd ordered from RubyTrueShuze when I was down in London arrived too.

There were so many that Bella thought I'd gone quite mad — and perhaps I had.

"It's a gamble, but I think having a much larger stock might increase the sales even more," I explained. "We'll see!"

But there was one pair of the shoes that I'd picked out in London specially for me: medium-heeled pumps of soft white leather with pale blue crystal butterflies on the toes. I'd fallen in love with them and thought I'd wear them when I had high tea on Sundays, just as Aunt Nan had worn her wedding dress: a family tradition. She had worn her wedding finery to feel closer to her fiancé, Jacob, and I wore my beautiful shoes to feel closer to Aunt Nan.

I teased Bella that if she got married I'd give her the shoes of her choice as a wedding present. "Neil looks very smitten. Even Ivo noticed."

Her fair face clouded. "I'm not ready for another relationship, though it's good for Tia and me to escape from the flat. Neil takes us out to nice places, or back to his cottage." Then she added, pointedly, "You and Ivo looked very cosy when we dropped in on Sunday!"

"We do seem to be becoming friends," I admitted. "I'll miss him when he goes back to his acting again — and by the way, *he* knows that *I* know about him writing those novels."

"Well, that's a relief! I don't have to pretend any more," she said.

The inner sanctum where the RubyTrueShuze were displayed looked like an Aladdin's cave of treasures by the time we'd finished pricing and setting out the new stock. The artfully placed ceiling spotlights sparkled off diamanté and Swarovski crystal trimmings and added a soft sheen to silk embroidery and smooth satin.

342

I added to the stock some of the vintage shoes Timmy had found, and the rest on the "display only" shelf, then Bella took some pictures and put them on the vintage page of the website, adding an announcement that we'd just had a huge delivery of wonderful new bridal shoes.

Hebe Winter convened a Chamber of Commerce meeting, but it was much like the first, in that she mainly just wanted to tell us all what she had organised, rather than consult us.

Laurence Yatton was still delving into the affairs of the Grocergo supermarket chain and the consortium who owned the land, with Lucy Winter's help — they were both brilliant with computers.

Meanwhile, Force for Nature was now spearheading the campaign against the retail park and had even drawn up new proposals for a nature reserve instead, with a café and information centre, bird hides and walkways.

"We are aware that there's still a certain amount of support for the retail park, though," Laurence Yatton said.

"I expect it's because of the jobs it would generate," Poppy sighed. She seemed to have given up on the jodhpurs and was wearing maternity trousers with a flowing flowered top over her bump.

"But wouldn't a nature reserve generate quite a few jobs too?" I asked.

"Yes, though not as many, of course," Hebe replied. "But you would have to balance that with the number of jobs lost due to small businesses closing, if the retail park is approved."

Then she passed round the proofs of the Sticklepond village trail leaflet for our approval, and they looked very good, with a discount ticket attached that gave half-price entry to either Winter's End or the Witchcraft Museum, if you bought a full-price ticket for the other.

Later, I told Ivo about the meeting but he still wasn't entirely convinced that a retail park wasn't a good idea.

"After all, it wouldn't occupy the whole site; there could still be a nature trail around the rest of it."

"But everything would be disturbed by the building, and then all the cars and noise later," I pointed out. "But it's looking very doubtful they'll get permission anyway, what with all these rare plants and animals on the site, and Force for Nature involved."

"Well, we'll see," he said, taking a slice of banana bread. "Where has your aunt got to currently in her story?"

"She hasn't got anywhere. She's diverged from the plot altogether again, so it's back to rationing and cooking. She mentioned the first bananas appearing after the war and it made me remember this recipe."

"Kate's diary entries are increasingly angry that she's not getting any of the parts she's auditioned for. She thought it was because she was getting too old for some of them, but to be honest, although she was beautiful, she wasn't that good an actress . . . and I think, deep down, she knew it."

344

"In that case, perhaps she had very low self-esteem, and that's why she had the affairs?" I suggested cautiously, emboldened by the glass of Meddyg I'd just drunk.

"You could have a point," Ivo admitted thoughtfully. "She constantly needed reassurance that she looked good, that I still loved her . . ." A spasm of emotion crossed his face.

"Then I'm probably right, and she was just using the affairs to prove to herself she was attractive," I said. "They didn't mean anything to her. You were the significant man in her life."

"I think . . . that's made me feel slightly better," he said slowly. "Not that I deserve to, really . . ." he added, but I decided not to delve into what he meant by that.

"Justin had the opposite problem, because his self-esteem was bloated by his mother forever assuring him how wonderful he was," I told him, then poured us both another fortifying glass of Meddyg and passed the plate of buttered banana bread again.

CHAPTER
THIRTY-ONE

Lovers All Untrue

Imogen took up modelling right after she left her expensive finishing school, which was something Vi wasn't too keen on her doing. Rightly so, because she fell in with some artist and had my great-niece Tansy out of wedlock, which was still quite a scandal, even then . . . not that much had changed since I was a girl.

Middlemoss Living Archive
Recordings: Nancy Bright.

A couple of evenings later, while Ivo was out with Flash and I was just about to melt some chocolate to cover a sponge cake, Justin rang me and the moment I heard the strange mixture of triumph and anger in his voice, I guessed what he was going to say.

"Tansy, I've just got back from the hospital and the results of a DNA test on Charlie were waiting for me: I wanted to tell you right away."

"He's isn't your son, is he?" I said flatly, not knowing what I felt, except it probably wasn't what he was expecting.

"Can you believe it?" he exclaimed. "It means I've been paying Rae for nothing all these years, because even if she'd tried to blackmail me over our affair, I could just have denied everything and she couldn't have proved it."

"Oh, well, that would have been all right then, wouldn't it?" I said sarcastically, but he wasn't listening.

"All these years — all these years!" he repeated. "And all that money! I'm going to get it back, though, you'll see."

"Can you do that?" I asked, startled.

"Why not? I'll take her through the courts for it, if necessary, because it was extortion. She must have been pretty sure the baby wasn't mine."

"But there was also a chance that it was and I don't think there's any point in trying to get your money back, because apart from the allowance she gets from her father, she hasn't got any. It's you who's been subsidising her expensive lifestyle the last five years."

"If *she* can't pay me back, then maybe her father will," he said stubbornly. "Especially if I threaten to give the story to the papers!"

"You wouldn't do that, would you? You'd hate the publicity, and it would be a sort of blackmail too, so you'd be almost as bad as Rae!"

"Oh, I'm sure it wouldn't come to that: he'd pay up first. He's loaded, isn't he?"

"No one is as well off as they used to be and he was never any kind of Onassis," I said dampeningly. "Please, Justin, don't tell him what Rae did. He loves her and he'll be devastated."

"I'll only tell him if she refuses to pay me back," he said stubbornly. "Can't you see that I'm doing this for *us*, darling? On a nest egg like that we'll be able to get married, move out of London and start that family you want. I've conferred with colleagues about who's the best man to consult about IVF if we have any problems, though I'm sure that clinic you went to was just being alarmist and —"

"Just hold it right there," I broke in furiously. "This changes *nothing*, Justin! Can't you see that it's all too late — for us, for a family . . . for *everything?*"

"Of course it changes everything. You'll realise as soon as it's all sunk in. You're just a bit stunned by the news at the moment," he said, so soothingly that I would have hit him if he'd been in the room. "I'll call you again tomorrow, darling, when you've taken it in."

"Don't bother — I already have!" I snapped, but he'd rung off.

The cake never got its chocolate topping and I'd comfort-eaten a big chunk out of it by the time Ivo brought Flash back. He walked in the kitchen door — we don't stand on ceremony now — took one look at my face and asked me what was the matter.

"It's Justin. He just rang to say he'd had the DNA test result back for Charlie, the little boy I told you about — my stepsister's child. And he isn't his."

"That must have been a bit of a shock," he said, pulling out a kitchen chair and sitting down next to me. Flash, who had pushed a sympathetic wet nose into my hand and seemed to feel he had done his bit in the empathy line, went to inspect his dinner bowl for signs of scariness.

348

"It wasn't totally unexpected," I explained to Ivo, "but I just went numb when he told me! And now he seems to think it makes everything right between us, when really it changes nothing, because he still betrayed me with Rae!"

"Yes, just because the evidence isn't there any more, it doesn't take away the fact," he agreed.

"I wish he could see that, but no matter what I say, he carries on thinking we can get back together and play happy families as if nothing had ever happened! And he doesn't accept that it's probably too late for me to have a baby now, even if I could forgive him, which I can't." I felt hot tears trickle down my face and wiped them away with my fingers.

"Oh, come here!" Ivo said softly, pulling me up out of the chair and into his arms, to have my cry out against his shoulder . . .

I found myself suddenly thinking that if this got to be a habit, I really wouldn't mind!

"I honestly do understand," he said, "because I wanted children too. Kate was the reluctant one, though when the roles dried up, she came round to the idea. In fact, we'd just found out she was pregnant when she was offered the *Cotton Common* role out of the blue . . ."

My own woes forgotten, I pulled away to look up at his face, shadowed by that haunted sadness again. "The papers didn't mention that, though I'm sure they said she'd just joined the cast."

"Yes, she had, but she was convinced they could write the baby into the script, so she wasn't going to

349

turn the part down. She'd come up to stay with Marcia in Middlemoss to see the production company — we'd only just started renovating the cottage then, so she couldn't stay here — and then the accident happened when she was on her way home."

"I'm so sorry, Ivo!" I told him, hugging him back and thinking that to lose his wife and baby in the crash had been much worse than anything Justin had done to me.

"There's no way of knowing now whether the baby was mine or not, but I'd have loved it anyway."

"I was fond of little Charlie, too," I said, thinking how our shared secrets were slowly winding ties of friendship and consolation around us.

His embrace tightened slightly crushingly before he released me. "Well, 'there's nothing either good or bad, but thinking makes it so,'" he said heavily. "I'd better get back."

But before he went I poured us both a large glass of Meddyg and we drank a toast to old tragedies, new tragedies and unfaithful lovers.

When he'd gone, I went back to listening to Aunt Nan, hoping she had by now digressed into some soothing description of local traditions, or her favourite subjects of food and cooking. But no, she was still on about my mother, Immy, and it was all a bit painfully relevant.

"Immy came here when she discovered she was pregnant — which was a bit too late to terminate it, or I'm sure she wouldn't have hesitated, because she's never been the least bit maternal. Then off she went

leaving me literally holding the baby. I came downstairs in the morning and she'd left me a note and gone."

That was a detail I hadn't known before, but I wasn't surprised in the least.

"But it turned out well, because Tansy's been the greatest gift anyone could have given me," Aunt Nan added, and tears filled my eyes again.

Ivo playing his melancholy music didn't help, either, though when I went to bed I fell asleep feeling comforted by the idea that he was just the other side of the wall. In fact, I put my hand flat against it and imagined that he was doing the same . . . then told myself I was an idiot, and cast myself adrift into a sea of strange and confusing dreams.

I think Ivo's wife sounded very like my grandmother Violet (or Viola, as she always called herself) and Immy: not very maternal and probably afraid of ruining her figure.

As soon as Bella arrived to open the shop next morning I told her about Justin's phone call and the DNA test, and his threat to tell Lars, but of course I didn't share what Ivo had confided in me — and she, I was convinced, was holding something back too, though I was so full of my own woes that it took me a while to notice.

I suspected it was about Neil, but there was no time to try to persuade her to open up since it was yet another hectically busy Saturday and we didn't even close the shop for lunch any more, just took it in turns to grab a bite and a cup of coffee.

When we'd finally closed and cashed up, I cornered Bella and asked her what was the matter.

"You've been like a wet weekend all day."

"Neil asked me to move in with him," she confessed.

"He *did?* I didn't think you'd got to that sort of stage yet."

"Well . . ." she blushed slightly, "I have seen a lot of him lately, though only as a friend, and I keep telling him I'm not looking for a serious relationship. But last time I saw him, when he dropped me back home he said he could see how difficult living with my parents must be and he'd love it if me and Tia moved into his cottage."

"As . . . lover or lodger?"

"On any terms I liked, but I think he was hoping if it was as a lodger that the relationship would turn into the other anyway. I think he's a stealthy sort of person, really, quietly devious. I turned him down flat."

"I can see where you're coming from," I said, not really surprised: I mean, look what happened last time she fell in love and moved into her boyfriend's house. "But you do like him a lot, don't you?"

"Well, yes. But once bitten, twice shy," she said. "I'll keep saving towards a deposit on a little place of our own, where no one can kick us out."

"You could both move in here with me anytime."

"I know, and it's very kind of you, but if I did, I'd scupper your budding romance with Ivo Hawksley!" she teased. "I'm sure you're not telling me the half of it, because he seems to be coming and going in the cottage as he likes."

"Don't be daft, there's no romance! I don't think he's over his wife yet, though it's complicated . . ." I sighed. "And I'd like to move on and try to forget Justin ever existed, except that he won't let me."

I'd texted Justin early that morning, asking him again not to tell Lars about the whole sorry business, but just let it go, though the only reply was a message on my answering machine telling me to leave everything to him.

CHAPTER
THIRTY-TWO

Chicken Run

I've encouraged Tansy to see her mother over the years, of course, and she's even spent holidays with her, when it's taken Imogen's fancy to have her to stay for a while, but they're chalk and cheese, and Tansy's always been more than happy to come home to Sticklepond and her old aunt Nan again

Middlemoss Living Archive
Recordings: Nancy Bright.

Ivo had volunteered to help me move the chicken house and run to a different spot on Sunday afternoon after our high tea, and we'd just finished when damned if a hired car didn't pull up at the back of the house and disgorge Mummy Dearest, as unannounced and unwelcome as Lady Catherine de Bourgh in *Pride and Prejudice*!

"Justin's mother — what on earth is *she* doing here?" I whispered to Ivo, as Mrs Garvey paused and looked at the back gate and slightly muddy path uncertainly, then caught sight of us and came on through. Flash, who had been lying on the grass ignoring the hens, slowly rose to his feet and looked as if he didn't know whether to attack or flee. Ivo caught hold of his collar.

354

"This is a surprise, Mrs Garvey," I said, then introduced Ivo, though she spared him hardly a glance.

"I have come all this way in order to talk to you, Tansy! It shouldn't have been necessary, but I hope I know my duty as a mother."

"I only wish you did," I said, squaring up to her, "because he's all grown up now, and it's long past the time you cut the leading reins and let him toddle off on his own."

"I'll shut Flash in my garden with me for a while," Ivo said tactfully, and dragged him off while I reluctantly invited my almost-mother-in-law into the cottage.

"I can't imagine why the driver brought me to the back of the house rather than the front," she said, looking around the kitchen as if she was not quite certain what it was for.

"You can't drive to the front, it's accessible only by a passage from the High Street," I explained.

"How quaint — but very inconvenient, I would have thought."

"Do sit down and I'll make some tea," I suggested, wondering if several teaspoons of sugar in it might sweeten her up slightly.

"Please don't bother: I want nothing and what I have to say won't take long."

She did unbutton her camel cashmere coat and sit down, though, fixing me with her beady stare. "I know *all*!" she said, with great significance.

"Really?" I replied cautiously. "Justin has told you . . . everything?"

"If you mean about the child, then I've known about it for years," she said, and then it came out that Rae had actually visited her with little Charlie soon after he was born, spinning some tale about Justin promising to marry her but then falling for me instead!

"She swore me to secrecy, but of course we both hoped Justin would eventually come to his senses, see where his heart truly lay and do the Right Thing!"

I wondered if Mummy Dearest was secretly addicted to Mills and Boon novels, despite her unyielding aspect, though perhaps this plot was more suited to a Victorian melodrama. It struck me dumb, anyway.

She continued "I did tell him I had met Rae accidentally once or twice and that she was much more the kind of girl I'd hoped he would marry, but he was too besotted with you to see it. And now poor Rae tells me he refuses even to support the child because you have persuaded him Charlie isn't his after all, which is manifestly absurd: he's the image of Justin at that age."

"I haven't persuaded him of anything," I protested. "Rae's sister, Marcia, put the idea into his head, which made him decide to have a DNA test done — and Charlie really isn't his."

"Such utter rubbish! They must have got the result wrong. I don't trust these things."

"I don't see what Rae had to gain from telling you about Charlie," I said, puzzled, "because she met him for the first time only after I got engaged to him and I'm sure she never wanted a long relationship with him, let alone marriage! She was just piqued and scoring points off me." I paused, thinking it through, and then asked incredulously, "*You* haven't been giving her money too, have you?"

She looked defensive. "I have made her a small loan from time to time. What Justin was giving her was barely adequate for the child's needs, and he is a Garvey, after all."

"That's complete rubbish," I said, but when I told her exactly how many thousands of pounds Justin had actually paid out, she didn't believe that either — or that I had no intention of ever getting back together with him.

"You must have given him some encouragement, because he's planning to transfer to a hospital up here and set up home with you. I understand that you are carrying on your aunt's business and refuse to live in London any more."

"In his dreams!" I said forcefully. "I keep telling him we are over and I certainly don't want him to move up here. It would be entirely pointless."

"I don't believe you, or he wouldn't be so set on it. Promise me you will phone him today and tell him you will *never* marry him."

"I've told him repeatedly."

"And that there is therefore no reason for him to move North."

"If you can tell me a way of getting that message into his thick skull, I'd like to hear it," I said drily.

"You must promise me that you will call him as I have directed, then never speak, write or contact him in any way again."

"I'd love to, but your son seems so chronically unable to take no for an answer that he's quite likely to turn up here uninvited anyway. He's the one constantly contacting me, not the other way round."

But Mrs Garvey was not listening to a word I said. "So you *won't* promise?" she demanded angrily.

"I'll happily promise not to contact him, but if he catches me on the phone, or turns up uninvited, I *can't* promise to maintain a Trappist silence — that's unreasonable."

She got up. "I see I have wasted my time!"

It seemed she'd also been wasting her money on Rae too, but I tactfully didn't say so. I only hoped Justin didn't find out or I expect he'd be threatening to take Rae to court to get his mother's cash back, too.

Mrs Garvey was looking pale, tired and cross. She was no spring chicken and had had a long fruitless journey, so I said more gently, "Look, let me at least make you a cup of tea. Did you stop for lunch on the way up?"

"I was not hungry, nor do I want anything now," she declared grandly, but then had to admit that she would like to use the bathroom before she left, which rather spoiled the effect.

When she finally came down (just as I had begun to think she intended roosting up there for ever) she'd entirely resurfaced her face and painted her thin lips scarlet. She still looked like an elderly Bacchae disguised as a matron, but a sharper-edged version.

I'd made her a cup of tea anyway and put out a plate of fruit fairy cakes, but she refused my gesture and

358

tittupped off down the crazy paving path again in her smart camel-coloured city coat and stiletto-heeled court shoes, which, like Mummy Dearest, were not built for the country.

She totally ignored Ivo, who was standing by the gate in the fence holding on to Flash, shied violently away from Cedric, who was leading his ladies on a foraging expedition up the garden, and practically flung herself into the awaiting car.

" 'Exit, pursued by a bear'," Ivo said.

I'm sure Justin had no idea his mother was going to come up here and he *certainly* didn't know she'd been giving Rae money, so I hoped he didn't find out about either. Her visit did stiffen my resolve to continue ignoring his many texts and emails and to let the answering machine pick up any phone calls first. Perhaps even my occasional terse, discouraging replies have given him hope.

When I told Ivo what Rae had been doing, he said she was quite a piece of work, but I'm not sure he realised that Marcia was not that much better!

As far as I knew he'd let no visitors into the cottage except for Raffy, and Marcia must have been getting quite frustrated, for one morning she sneakily came up the back lane and caught him in his garden. I was up in my workroom, looking out from time to time, so I spotted her — and he should have been writing anyway, so it served him right, really . . .

From the body language I thought he didn't really want to invite her in, but had no alternative, but she still hadn't emerged when I went down to make Bella some lunch.

Later he told me she'd pressingly invited him over to her flat in Middlemoss. "She means well, but she doesn't understand that I'm here to get away from the acting world for a while and I don't want to hear all the gossip. And, of course, being Kate's best friend, seeing her brings everything back again . . ."

"Yes, but she's never been one to take a hint," I said.

"No, she certainly isn't," he agreed. "She wanted to take me out to lunch because she thought I needed feeding up, so I told her she didn't need to because you were a brilliant cook and already doing your best. That really seemed to annoy her."

"I expect it would."

"But she said she was sorry about you and Justin breaking up because you were really the perfect couple," he said, looking at me keenly.

"A perfect couple of opposites," I said. "I only hope she doesn't try any more meddling, because she's done enough harm."

"I think she means well. Her heart's in the right place," he said.

He truly hadn't got the measure of my sweet stepsister yet.

When I related all this to Bella later she said she was sure Marcia was still hoping I'd take Justin back, because she suspected Ivo was getting interested in me and she wanted him herself. "And she's probably still

360

keeping Justin's fires and hopes stoked high and that's why he's so impossible to get rid of," she added.

I expected she was right (though of course Ivo *wasn't* getting interested in me in that way, we were just becoming friends and good neighbours).

But, unsettlingly, I *had* felt a pang of something akin to jealousy when he'd taken Marcia into the cottage, where I had only ventured once or twice, and then only as far as the kitchen . . .

You'd think I'd had enough recriminations with the visit of Mummy Dearest, but no — my very own mother (if she merited that title) called me from California specially to tell me to stop being silly and take Justin back, then persuade him to stop suing Rae for the money.

"Rae's told me everything and it's a bit of a mess, but we all make mistakes, don't we?" she said.

"Most of us manage to avoid the mistake of sleeping with our stepsister's fiancé," I pointed out coldly.

"Oh, get over it, Tansy! Just take Justin back and persuade him to drop the lawsuit threats and keep it all to himself. Lars would be furious if he found out."

"Look, you're talking as if it's *me* who did something wrong and not Rae! She seduced my fiancé and then told him she was pregnant by him — how easy is that going to be to forgive?"

"He's a man — they have weak moments — and Rae genuinely thought the baby was his." I could almost see her shrugging her bony shoulders.

"Justin's mother wouldn't agree. She just came all the way up here to persuade me not to marry him. Not that she had to, because it's all finished, as far as I'm concerned; he just won't accept that."

"He really needs to get away from her, she's such a domineering smother-mother!"

"Well, he isn't getting away with me."

"You are *so* hard-hearted, Tansy!"

I was hard hearted? "I can't imagine why Justin is so set on having me back anyway, when he seemed determined to change everything about me."

"Neither can I," she said frankly. "Look, I'll have to go. You think about what I've said before it's too late and you end up a sad old spinster like Nancy."

"Aunt Nan was *not* a sad old spinster!" I began indignantly, but she ignored me.

"Sorry I couldn't get over for her funeral, only I'd just had a little nip and tuck round the derrière, as I explained, and sitting on a plane would have been quite impossible — I knew you'd understand."

You know, I think I'd much rather have had Bella's mother than mine, because, for all her strange little ways, deep down she did love Bella and Tia and at least she was there for her when she needed her!

Hebe had called another Chamber of Commerce meeting that evening, but I skipped it because I had a headache, which was hardly surprising. But she got Laurence to send me the minutes next day and it appears that the consortium who own the Hemlock Mill site have now put in an amended proposal, keeping part of the surroundings as a nature reserve and promising to rehouse any rare fish, flesh, fowl or flora that needed it.

However, a representative from Force for Nature had gone to the meeting and pointed out that most of the site would be under a huge car park, leaving very little indeed, so the new proposal didn't seem likely to curry much favour.

But also on the table was an offer from a wealthy and anonymous benefactor to buy the site and preserve the whole of it as a nature reserve, if the consortium would sell it. But, of course, *they* would have much preferred to make huge profits from a retail park.

Still, if we managed to overturn the plan for the retail park, I imagined they would settle for what they could get.

"What is this, national Besieged by Harpies Week?" I demanded incredulously. "I can't believe you've had the nerve to call me, Rae!" I wished I hadn't picked up the phone in an incautious moment. "It was bad enough that you went running to my mother and she took your part — as usual."

But Rae wasn't listening, being incandescent with rage because Mummy Dearest had mulled over what I'd said to her and then told Justin she'd been giving Rae money.

"So now he's even more hellbent on the idea of getting his money back *and* hers too — either from me or from Daddy. I don't want Daddy to know, and I haven't got the money to pay Justin back."

"You've brought all this on yourself, but I did ask Justin not to tell Lars," I said. "He's just not listening to anything I say."

"He'd listen to you if you asked him the *right* way — and promised to have him back again," she said. "Look, we only had a little fling, so aren't you cutting off your nose to spite your face? He didn't love me, he loved you all the time, isn't that enough?"

"No, not really."

"You are *so* hard! But he's convinced you'll take him back."

"He's wrong," I said wearily.

"His mother says he's coming up to see you again because he's got an interview in a Manchester hospital, so you must have given him some encouragement."

"None at all — the opposite, in fact.

"I don't believe you," she said flatly. "I think you're just making him suffer for a while, but now you have to stop it, take him back, get him out of his ghastly mother's orbit, and persuade him not to prosecute me for the money or tell Lars. This should all be kept in the family."

"I don't have any family any more," I snapped and put the phone down, trembling slightly. Flash shoved his wet nose into my hand in his usual gesture of sympathy, but I felt angry rather than upset at that moment.

I sent Justin a terse text telling him I didn't want to see him, so if he was planning to call in, to forget it.

He didn't reply. I wasn't sure if that was good or not.

CHAPTER
THIRTY-THREE

Mayday!

Immy's first husband didn't care for children so we didn't see a lot of her while she was married to him, but her second was a different kettle of fish. Lars, he was called, a Norwegian name I think it is, though he was American. Well, he still is American, but Imogen's married to someone else now and lives in California, where the raisins come from.

When I was a little girl we had Snapdragon at Christmas, a dish of raisins soaked in spirit and set on fire. You had to snatch one without burning your fingers . . .

No, lovey, I don't suppose Health and Safety would be very keen on people doing things like that these days, but we all thought it great fun and no one set themselves alight that I ever heard of.

Middlemoss Living Archive
Recordings: Nancy Bright.

On the first day of May I set the alarm clock before dawn so I could go and watch the Maypole-dancing on the green, just as I'd done so often with Aunt Nan.

But I didn't go alone, for I'd told Ivo about it and he walked beside me down the dark High Street, and we

365

stood and watched the dancers together as the sun rose.

"Did you do this kind of thing with your wife?" I asked without thinking.

"No . . . Kate's interests were very different from mine," he said, glancing down at me, his face inscrutable as always at the mention of his wife's name.

"Justin's, too. He'd have thought me mad even to suggest he got up early to watch Maypole-dancing!" I said. "We were complete opposites in practically everything."

"They say opposites attract, but I think what first drew me to Kate was that she was small and dark and reminded me of you," he said unexpectedly.

"Really?" I thought that perhaps he hadn't quite forgotten me after all! Of course, going by her photos online, Kate had been very beautiful, which I am not . . .

"Not that she was anything like you in character, though, when I got to know her," he added, and then we were silent for a while, watching the rising sun slanting across the grass where some very vigorous Morris dancing was now going on. "'More matter for a May morning'," as Ivo put it, before we turned home again, him to work on his book and me to help in the shop.

"I've nearly finished the first draft, so I'm going to crack on and do that today," he said.

"I wish I could work on mine, but Saturdays are way too busy," I said. "I enjoy being in the shop though, especially selling wedding shoes. I want *every* bride to feel like a princess on their wedding day!"

"You do seem to be especially busy on Saturdays, going by the endless repetitions of 'Here Comes the Bride' and so does Raffy, conducting marriages up at All Angels," he said grumpily, though he didn't complain quite as much about the noise by then, and secretly I suspected he even rather liked Cedric and his strangulated crowing.

"Does Raffy give a discount on Saturdays, or something?" Ivo asked.

"No, he's just very popular. I mean, who wouldn't want to be married by Raffy Sinclair, former front man of heavy rock band Mortal Ruin?"

"Good point," he conceded. "Do you fancy taking Flash out to the Hemlock Mill site for a walk tomorrow afternoon? It's a nice spot and it would make a change."

"I'd love to, but I'm half expecting Justin to turn up. Apparently he's got an interview at a hospital in Manchester. He's an orthopaedic consultant, did I say?"

"No . . ." Ivo paused. "So . . . he'll be staying over with you?"

"Over my dead body! Aunt Nan wouldn't let him stay in the house until we were married and she'd be horrified by the very thought!"

"Right," he said. "I'll keep out of the way and leave you to it, then."

"I don't want him to come, and I've done my best to dissuade him, so I'm hoping perhaps he's finally got the message."

Ivo looked unconvinced, so I hoped he didn't suspect me of still harbouring any feelings for Justin.

I'd so much rather have spent Sunday as I usually did, tidying the shop up, working on my book or in the garden, walking Flash with Ivo and then coming home to a high tea. Later, we'd share a companionable glass of Meddyg and chat . . .

"Even if Justin does arrive, I'll get rid of him," I told Ivo with great determination, though that might be easier said than done.

Inevitably, like a bad penny, Justin appeared on my back doorstep late next morning looking like any fairy-tale maiden's dream: tall, blue-eyed, tawny-haired and clutching the biggest bouquet of red roses you'd ever have seen in your life. A whole tree, practically.

"Tansy darling! I knew the moment Mummy told me you wouldn't promise never to see me again that you'd forgiven me!" he cried, unexpectedly throwing his arms around me, which sent me staggering back.

"I didn't!" I cried, trying to fight my way out and feeling suffocated, cross and flustered — even more so when I spotted Ivo standing on the other side of the wall, with Toby in his arms.

He turned on his heel and headed off before I'd even managed to uncling Justin's hands and avoid the kiss he was trying to press on me, but I expect he'd heard what Justin had said. The whole village probably had.

"Get off me!" I snapped just as Flash, slightly late to the rescue but willing, began to skirmish round Justin's legs, trying to nip him. It finally dawned on Justin that

368

I was not entirely compliant and he released me, though Ivo had vanished by then, thinking goodness knew what.

"Justin, read my lips: we are *not* getting back together *ever*," I stated, pushing him further off. "Flash — quiet! Down — good dog!"

"But you told Mummy —" he bleated, following me into the cottage uninvited, though with one wary eye on Flash.

"I told your mother that you were the one trying to stay in contact with me, not the other way round, so it would be hard to promise never to speak to you again, if only to tell you to go away! And I also told her that it was definitely all over between us so there was absolutely no point in your handing in your notice and moving north. In any case, you'd hate it."

"Too late," he said, like a big, sulky schoolboy. "The interview tomorrow is just a formality."

"Un-hand your notice, then!"

"No. Look, Tansy, I can see that Mother's visit upset you —"

"Yes, not to mention Rae having the cheek to ring *my* mother and get her to tell me to take you back," I said. "And when that didn't work, Rae rang me herself!"

"*Rae?* What did she say?"

"She wanted me to persuade you not to sue her for your money back — or to tell Lars, which would be the same thing, because she's obviously blown the cash. And I'd really hate Lars to find out about this whole

369

sordid affair, so can't you just write it off as a penance you have to pay for lust and stupidity?"

Justin's chin jutted out in the ominously stubborn way I recognised. "I'm getting my money back — but it's for *us*, darling! We can buy a lovely house near Manchester somewhere — Wilmslow and Knutsford are very nice, I hear — and settle down. It's not far away, so you can still run your little shoe shop if you want to . . ."

"Gee, thanks," I said. "But no thanks. My little shoe shop is building business amazingly well and I'm going to do Aunt Nan proud."

He tried the soft soap-touch. "And so you can, but that friend of yours could run it, couldn't she? You'll need someone to manage it, because I'm sure with the best medical advice we can start a family, and I really *want* that, Tansy."

"It's a bit late to decide that — probably too late altogether for me, good advice or not. And even if it wasn't, I still wouldn't marry you. I *mean* it," I added. "It's O.V.E.R. — over. Got it?"

Justin went into a deep and profound sulk, which would probably have got him his way with Mummy when he was a little boy, but never did anything to soften my heart. He wouldn't leave, though, until I agreed to go to the Green Man with him for lunch.

He was still being sulky and misunderstood afterwards, when we were walking back to the cottage, but also dropping hints about my home baking in the hope, presumably, that I'd let him back into the cottage and offer him tea later. Instead, I told him to stay by his car while I fetched him a slab of ginger parkin wrapped in greaseproof paper, a small price to pay to get rid of him.

Goodness knows what the upmarket hotel he was booked into would make of that.

Unfortunately, he seemed to regard the parkin as some kind of peace offering or love token, for on my return with it he landed a kiss on my cheek and, getting back a bit of bounce, said in a horribly understanding way that he'd obviously chosen the wrong time of month to visit me and it had always made me ratty.

"But I love you anyway, darling," he declared understandingly, while I was still rendered speechless with anger.

As he reversed out and drove off, waving, I wished I'd thrown the parkin at him, because it was pretty solid. He was beyond healing himself now, in my opinion: he needed a psychiatrist.

I hoped Ivo would have noticed that the car was gone and come in for high tea later as usual, but he didn't turn up until he came to collect Flash for his evening walk, and then he was monosyllabic, so I didn't even try to explain the scene he had witnessed . . . or why I'd been crying since (rage, mostly). I'd tried to hide the traces, so perhaps he hadn't noticed.

Nor would he come in when he brought Flash back, saying he had something to do. I expect he meant going into a total black gloom and playing the most miserable classical music you ever heard in your life, because that's what came through my walls for the entire evening.

I could have done with his quiet companionship — I missed it. Instead, I comforted myself with an extra-long session of Aunt Nan, though knowing how she felt about my living with Justin all those years instead of marrying, her first words didn't exactly lighten my mood:

"*Tansy lives down in London now, with her fiancé, though why they don't get married decently I can't imagine. He goes home to his mother most weekends, and Tansy comes back to me, which seems a strange how-do-you-do. Not that I'm not pleased to see her, of course, and I know she'd rather live up here than down there.*"

She was quite right: I should never have left. There was no mistaking her pride in the way she talked about me and I let her voice, with its familiar flat vowels and common-sense observations, wash soothingly over me like loving syrup.

"*When Tansy went to art college down in London, Immy's second husband, Lars, who was a widower with two grown-up daughters, wanted her to make his London house her home and she did for a while, though she didn't get on with her stepsisters and went to a flat with friends. Lars still takes an interest in her — more than her mother ever did!*

Now she writes and paints her children's books and does some foot modelling too. Her mother got her into that early, when she was living with them.

No dear, I said foot modelling, not food modelling! They take pictures of Tansy's feet for adverts and suchlike — did you ever hear of such a thing?"

★   ★   ★

You had to give it to Rae: she never lay down and gave up, no matter how the cards were stacked against her. Beleaguered, she'd made a sudden pre-emptive strike and told her father some whitewashed version of the truth.

Of course, Lars was horrified and rang me at dawn to apologise for her. "She knows she did a really bad thing, Tansy: but when Charlie came along she truly thought he was Justin's and it was right to ask him to help support the baby. But to have an affair with your sister's fiancé . . ." He tailed off, sighing heavily and, being fond of him, I refrained from pointing out that she was merely a stepsister.

"Now I know why you broke up with Justin, but it was like your kind heart not to tell me. I'm flying over on Friday to sort this whole mess out as best I can and I'll come to see you just as soon as I have."

Lars was now into his seventies, but was never one to let the grass grow under his feet.

"I'll see Justin and arrange to pay back the money *and* have a few words about the way *he* behaved, because it takes two to tango, as they say."

"It certainly does," I agreed. "Has Rae told you who the real father is yet?"

If she knew, that was!

"No, but I hope to get it out of her eventually, because Charlie will want to know, one of these days. Rae says Justin is still dead set on making it up with you, though I can't imagine there's any possibility of that?"

"None at all; he's done the unforgivable. And I've no idea why he still wants to marry me anyway, when I know for sure that he'd soon start going on about my weight and my clothes and all the rest of it again. He's very, very stubborn, though, and also, perhaps I'm just the first woman ever to turn him down?"

"You always look perfect to me," Lars assured me.

"Rae and Marcia used to call me the little goblin in the fairy family."

"Did they?" he said, sounding taken aback. "I suppose, all of us being tall and fair and you small and dark, you did look kind of different."

"Yes, even my mother looked like one of the family and she always had lots in common with Rae and Marcia, and nothing at all with me."

"They were more like sisters," he said. "I don't think your mother's ever quite grown up and she was never much good in the mothering department."

"But you were as close to a father as I've ever had, Lars, and I've always been grateful for what you've done for me — the allowance when I was at college, all the rest of the help you've given me."

"I'd have given you more, if you'd let me, as if you were one of my own. But you just tell me if you need a bit of money behind you in your new business. How's it going?"

"It's doing really well. I'll tell you all about it when I see you."

"I'll visit Marcia when I come up, too. Has she been over?"

"Just the once," I said, with restraint, not telling him that it was Marcia who had thrown the spanner in the works by telling Justin that Charlie might not be his, and then encouraging him to think I still loved him.

I couldn't get back to sleep after the call, though it was a Bank Holiday Monday so the shop was shut and I'd intended having a lie-in.

Ivo appeared mid-morning, just as I'd finished experimenting with a kind of home-made version of Reese's peanut butter cups (the great thing about experimenting with cooking being that you can generally eat your mistakes). He apologised for his grumpiness yesterday, which he ascribed to having had a visitor himself the previous afternoon: Marcia had sneaked into the garden and caught him, again.

"Why don't I take you for a run out somewhere?" he suggested. "I think we probably both need a change of air."

I suggested we visit a National Trust property nearby called Rufford Old Hall, since it also had Shakespeare connections that I thought might interest him.

"But we won't tell Hebe Winter we've been," I added. "She would count it as treachery!"

So we went there, and after we had toured the lovely old house we went for coffee in the tearoom and I told him about my ex-stepfather calling me and that he would be coming to see me. "He's horrified and ashamed to think one of his own daughters would sleep with my fiancé."

"Marcia said she felt like that too, and surprised at Justin, because she knew he really loved you all the time and was sure he'd never looked at another woman since he'd got engaged to you."

I was pretty certain that Marcia, far from feeling anything like shame at what Rae had done, was merely intent on getting me back with Justin and out of Ivo's orbit, so she could snaffle him herself! Not, of course, that Ivo and I were about to pick up where we left off so long ago, but at least we seemed to be friends again today.

"Marcia must have arrived after Justin finally left, because I didn't see her car," I said. "She wouldn't have tried to see me, because I more or less threw her out last time."

"She was so kind after the accident that I feel guilty that I don't want to see her now. But it just brings everything back, and I'm sure she knew Kate was unfaithful."

"Then she also probably knew that Kate loved you despite the affairs," I pointed out gently.

"And I am sure Justin must still love you, despite what he did," he said. "Marcia's sure of it."

Marcia's obviously been telling him how right Justin and I are for each other, as well as telling Justin himself that I still love him and will forgive him eventually. She is so devious!

"It doesn't matter to me whether he does or not, because I can't forgive and forget what he did!" I said. "I didn't want to see him yesterday and I certainly don't want him moving up here and haunting me!"

376

"But his visit upset you, so clearly you must still have some feelings for him?

"I was just angry," I snapped, but Ivo didn't look entirely convinced. I don't know how I can make him believe I'm over Justin . . . or why it should matter. Perhaps Ivo still loved Kate, despite what he was finding out about her.

But soon he would have finished torturing himself by reading her diaries — his act of penitence and self-flagellation, and returned to his acting profession. On this thought, Ivo suddenly told me the Management were coming up to see him in a few days.

"The Management?"

"Of the RSC."

"Oh — then I expect they want to persuade you to come back early?"

"They certainly want to make sure I'm going back 'and 'tis no sin for a man to labour in his vocation'," he agreed, so I really didn't think he would take much persuading, especially with his next novel almost finished. My heart sank a little at the thought of losing him. I'd got used to having him around to talk to, especially in the evenings. But perhaps he would come back for weekends and I could look forward to seeing him then . . .

Ivo said the cakes in the teashop didn't look a patch on any of mine, so we went back to my cottage for tea later. The air might not have been totally cleared of misunderstandings after Justin's visit and Marcia's Iago-like innuendoes, but I was happy that we appeared to be back on our usual friendly footing again.

Over tea he asked me where I'd got to with Aunt Nan's recordings.

"I listened to a bit this morning while I was cooking breakfast. She was saying how the rumours about her died down eventually, but in any case, her friends had stood by her. Then after that, she was into the home straight with happy memories of when I was growing up. I'm really enjoying this part so I don't want it to end, especially when I know what she's going to say in her personal message at the end. It'll be so sad and poignant, hearing exactly what happened in her own words."

"I'm finding Kate's diaries not so much poignant as appalling and harrowing," he confessed. "She might keep saying how much she loved me, but it didn't stop her having her flings with other men, especially after she'd been turned down for a part, or been written out."

"It must have made her feel better."

"It certainly doesn't make me feel better, knowing about it! And in last night's entries she said I was pressing her to have children, but she was afraid it would destroy her figure and end her career."

"That was a bit pessimistic, but I expect her looks were very important to her."

"She certainly spent a fortune on clothes, beauty products and treatments — much more than I ever knew about at the time! But perhaps all women lie about that kind of thing."

"I don't know, because I've never bought expensive things. Mine are mostly from a Swedish company who do unusual stuff, mixed up with charity shop and vintage finds."

"It works and I like your style — it's very distinctive."

"And Helena Bonham Carter?" I said pointedly.

"I'm sure she must have spotted you somewhere and be copying you, rather than the other way round," he said with a straight face, but the laughter lurking in his clear grey eyes reminded me of the boy he had been when I first met him, so that my heart skipped several beats just as if I were a love-struck teenager!

CHAPTER
THIRTY-FOUR

Porkers

I've carried on with the shop, but it doesn't do a lot of business these days, even though I've a nice sideline going in bride's satin shoes. It was getting a bit much for me, I have to admit, but providentially, Bella, Tansy's best friend, has moved back to the village and runs it for me now. I don't want centuries of tradition to die with me — Bright's shoes have been here forever — but it will be Tansy's choice what she does with it after I'm gone.

Middlemoss Living Archive
Recordings: Nancy Bright.

I got an email update from Hebe, in her role as chair of the Sticklepond Chamber of Commerce, all about the latest developments and plans. Force for Nature had come up with an exciting plan for a nature reserve with café and visitor centre, and the mill owner's house as a living history museum. Public opinion seems to be favouring that one.

We'd got enough shops already round here, what with St Helens and Ormskirk, and if anyone wanted more than those, they could go to Liverpool, Southport or Manchester easily enough.

I'd already found a bundle of the village walk leaflets on my doorstep that morning, so presumably Hebe had dispatched one of her minions at dawn to drop them off. I didn't remember discussing calling it "A Saunter Round Sticklepond", but then again, I did miss a meeting because of a headache, so I expect it was discussed there.

Neil Seddon paid me a surprise visit just after I'd closed the shop up in the afternoon and said he wanted to talk to me about Bella, so I took him through into the kitchen and, after priming him with tea and chocolate cake, and prodding him a bit, he said, "You're Bella's oldest friend so I thought you might be able to tell me what she's thinking. I mean, I've obviously said the wrong thing, asking her and Tia to move in with me, but I did mean it for the best!"

"She's afraid history will repeat itself," I explained. "When she moved in with Robert, Tia's father, he was separated and promised they'd get married as soon as he'd got his divorce, only it never happened. In fact, it was a bit like me with my fiancé: we got engaged and I moved in, then nothing happened for years!"

"Right . . ." he said thoughtfully.

"Robert was a really laid-back type so I think he just didn't get round to it, and then he died suddenly and it was then Bella found he'd run up huge gambling debts she'd no idea about. And then, to cap it all, his wife got whatever was left, because he'd never divorced or changed his will."

"But surely Tia was entitled to something?"

"Possibly, but by the time the debts were paid off, there wasn't much to fight over. Bella lost everything and that's when she had to move back in with her parents, so it's hit her hard and made it difficult for her to trust anyone again. She certainly wasn't looking for another relationship when she met you."

"I did get that message loud and clear, but I was taking it slowly and I thought she was getting a little bit fond of me."

"Yes, I'm sure she is and you were doing fine until you suggested she move into your house. She wouldn't want any chance of the whole cycle happening again."

"Well, it wouldn't. I'm no gambler, for a start! How can I persuade her I'm different from this Robert? I do love her," he confessed, going slightly pink as if it was some shameful secret.

"You haven't got a wife secreted away anywhere, have you? Only if not, and you do love Bella, I wondered why you didn't ask her to marry you — only to move in — and you weren't too specific about the terms, either!"

He looked surprised. "I didn't think she felt like that about me, but I hoped if she moved in she'd get fonder of me and things would go from there. I've been trying to sneak up on her."

"Then if you're serious, why don't you just tell her you love her and suggest you have a proper, old-fashioned courtship, the sort where you have a long engagement getting to know each other properly before you set a wedding date? It's a lot more romantic and likely to succeed than saying, 'How about moving in with me, love?'"

"I've been an idiot, haven't I?" he said sheepishly.

"Just a bit," I agreed. "One more thing — she told me that you had an old pigsty at the bottom of your garden and a small field and wood beyond it?"

"Yes, it's one of those odd parcels of land that come with old cottages sometimes."

"Bella has a thing about pigs."

"*Pigs?*"

"Loves them," I told him. "I'm surprised you haven't noticed. She collects ornamental ones like I collect shoes, and she's always longed to keep real ones. That's not something you can do in a granny flat!"

His eyes lit up. "I wished she'd mentioned it before, because I really fancy keeping pigs, only I didn't think I'd be able to give them enough time while I was getting the business going."

"I think you may find a porky way to her heart," I suggested, and he went off looking as if he'd had a major light bulb moment — or even the full neon tube.

I may end up going down the aisle yet, I decided, even if only as a bridesmaid!

Neil clearly hadn't wasted a moment, but had gone straight from my cottage to Bella's flat and insisted she go out to the pub with him so they could have a serious talk.

"Luckily Mum was in and said she didn't mind keeping an eye on Tia — she seems to like Neil — so I did," she said, and I guessed what was coming, from her glowing eyes and cheeks.

"Tansy, he wants to marry me! But he said since he could see I'd been hurt in the past he didn't want to rush me into anything and then he suggested we have the sort of proper, old-fashioned engagement and courtship that they had in your aunt Nan's day — it's so romantic!"

"Walking out, getting engaged, and setting a wedding day and all the rest of it? Sounds lovely to me!" I said innocently.

"Yes. No pressure to move in with him or anything, until we're married."

"So what did you say?" I asked, though I'd already guessed the answer.

"Yes! And since we've done a lot of walking out already, we're going to go and look at engagement rings this afternoon!"

"So, you love him, then?"

She nodded, the smooth wings of her ash-blond hair swinging. "I wasn't admitting it to myself — but yes, I do!" She giggled suddenly. "I knew he was the one when he shared a bag of Percy Pigs with me and said he longed to see some piglets in that sty in his back garden. I hadn't realised he was so keen on them before!"

"Oh, is he?" I said innocently. "What a coincidence!"

Her eyes were shining and I thought perhaps things might not stay quite so proper and old-fashioned for very long!

I told Ivo about it that evening and he said I was positively Machiavellian, but he hoped they would be very happy.

"She deserves a second chance at love," I said, "and I really like Neil."

"Are you going to give Justin a second chance too?" he asked, looking at me directly and seriously with those large, translucent grey eyes, just as if the answer was really important to him.

I shook my head. "No way. I keep telling you, he's done the unforgivable."

I wanted to ask if he could ever have forgiven Kate if he'd known about the affairs, but I was afraid the answer would be yes. Would he be suffering so much if he didn't still love her?

But Ivo was coming out of himself more lately and had been to have his dark chestnut hair cut, so that it lay close and satin-smooth to his head, emphasising the lovely bone structure of his face. I could only too easily imagine him wearing a princely coronet in some Shakespeare play . . .

It was no wonder I had my Cinderella dream again that night, though this time Justin suddenly appeared and snatched the slipper off my foot at the last moment, just when it was all going so well . . .

Lars arrived in London on the Thursday morning and by Friday had not only sorted everything out but had had himself driven up to have lunch with me.

Bella, who was wearing a modest antique sapphire band on her left hand, had her lunch early while I covered for her, and then said she would buzz for me if she got really busy while Lars was there.

Lars, who is tall and white-haired, with eyes of a much brighter blue than either of his daughters, is kind and good-natured, but with a core of steel. I remained fond of him despite his ghastly daughters and he always seemed to consider me an errant child, wilfully refusing most of his help. But just because he was married to Immy for a few years, I didn't see why he should have to subsidise her daughter by another man.

Flash liked him too, which I'd come to think was a very good sign.

He gave me a hug and kissed my cheek, then held me away from him and apologised sincerely for the way Rae had behaved, even though it was hardly his fault!

"I'm so sorry, honey, *and* ashamed of her, now I've managed to find out the whole truth! I've seen Justin and that god-awful ma of his, too — and Marcia."

"You know . . . everything?" I asked cautiously.

"I know Rae was taking money from both Justin and his mother, and I've paid them back every penny. Rae's behaved very badly, but she really did think Justin was Charlie's father."

"Of course she did," I agreed, though I was sure of no such thing!

"She wouldn't tell me who else Charlie's father could be, but Marcia was there and she said she thought it was some actor called Ritch Rainford."

"Oh, yes, she told me Rae had been seeing him around the time she got pregnant."

"Well, Rae didn't deny it, but she didn't want to tell him either, so we will leave that one there at the moment. It doesn't mitigate the fact that she had an affair, however brief, with your fiancé and then told Justin's mother she'd met him before you got engaged to him and he dumped her for you, which I know very well wasn't the case at all."

His jaw set and you could see the ruthless businessman in him. "I didn't believe any daughter of mine could tell such a pack of lies or behave like that with her sister's fiancé!"

Stepsister, I thought — not that it made it any better. "Justin behaved just as badly."

"That's what I told him, and that he didn't deserve you. He said he hoped you'd forgive him eventually — and he was taking a post at a hospital up here?" he added, with an enquiring glance at me.

"I told him not to, because there is absolutely no chance of us getting back together again, but he simply won't listen to me!"

He looked dubious. "Marcia thinks you'll get back together eventually too. I didn't think you would, after what you said, and it would sure make things awkward in the family if you married him now, but if you still love him . . ."

"I don't," I said firmly, "and I can't imagine why no one believes me, because not only did he kill my love stone dead in one fell swoop, but now I'm out of the relationship I can see just how much he undermined my self-confidence over the last couple of years, too!"

"Marcia must be wrong then," Lars said, then added, "she's upset because she says you'd had an argument about something she did years ago, and she was trying to bring you and Justin back together to make up for it, though I told her she'd be better off not meddling."

"Yes, I wish you'd tell her not to keep sticking her oar in! I'm sure Justin would have given up on me by now if she hadn't kept feeding him lies about my missing him."

"Justin's mother sure still seems against the idea, even though she knows the truth now. She was dead set on getting the money back she gave Rae, too. What a harridan!"

"She'd certainly have been the mother-in-law from hell," I agreed. "I think Justin had forgotten what life was like before I moved into the flat, when she could demand even more of his attention and use the flat as if it was hers."

"You could be right there, and it might be part of the reason why he's so keen to move far away."

"Perhaps. So let's hope that once he has, he'll fall for someone else in Manchester."

I'd made us a lovely lunch of soup, quiche and salad, followed by apple pie and ice cream, which I knew to be Lars' favourite dessert. Over it he made it clear that he'd paid off Justin and his mother and cleared off a whole load of Rae's debts, only on the strict understanding that she and Charlie moved back to the States to make their home with him.

"I can make sure Charlie's brought up right, then, seeing he's the only grandchild I'm likely to have."

"Will she do that?"

"She has to. That was the price of sorting this mess out."

She had bamboozled him only a very little, then, and she was certainly going to have to watch her step from now on! But he'd been right about the whole thing being just as much Justin's fault as Rae's in the first place.

"I'm thinking about selling the London house, now I haven't so many business interests over here," Lars told me. "It was just Rae and Charlie living there that was stopping me before."

"Won't you need a base in London, for when you come over to see Marcia, at least?"

"There're hotels, or maybe I'll get a small flat — and it would be nice if my two girls over here could make up, so we could all have dinner together when I do come over?" he suggested hopefully.

I gave in. "If Marcia stops winding Justin up so that he thinks there is the slightest possibility that I'll take him back, then I will."

"I'll tell her, and maybe she'll drop by so that you can make it up," he said. "She seems to be keen on the actor in the cottage next door to you, the widower of her friend. She says he's still very down and she's trying to cheer him up, but I can read between the lines."

"Mmm . . ." I said noncommittally. Then I showed him the shop — he was pleased to see Bella again — and he listened carefully while I told him about our marketing strategy and the rapidly increasing sales, asking the sort of sharp, businesslike questions that had got him his empire. He made one or two good suggestions too, like taking a stand at wedding fairs.

"They're big business; it could really increase your turnover."

"I see what you mean, and it's so obvious I should have thought of it myself," I agreed. "I suppose I've just been too busy getting the shop off the ground to see beyond the end of my nose."

"I'm thinking more of the future, Tansy: it's something you could plan for next year, once Cinderella's Slippers is well established. You'll need to find a way of making yourself stand out against your competitors, though."

"A display of genuine vintage shoes might do the trick," I said thoughtfully. "Thanks, Lars, that's a great idea!"

All too soon it was time for Lars' car to collect him. "I'm having flights back arranged for Rae and Charlie on the same plane and I left her packing," he said. "I'm not going back without them, or I might have trouble getting her home again."

He did seem to have more of her measure than he used to!

I walked down the garden to the car with him and he admired my knot garden. And then, since I could see Ivo staking his tomatoes, I called him over and introduced them.

They shook hands and appraised each other frankly, then briefly chatted, seeming to get on.

Then, before he got into the back of his waiting car, Lars told me he was glad that someone sensible was living nearby to keep an eye on me! Little did he know that Ivo would have dwindled to a sad wraith of his former self if I hadn't been feeding him up for weeks!

CHAPTER
THIRTY-FIVE

Shared

Yes, now the family has just dwindled to me and Tansy — and soon it'll be just Tansy. I don't count Immy, for all I've encouraged Tansy to keep in touch with her mother, because she's never really felt like part of the family, despite everything . . .

So there you are, lovey — a quiet life, with not a lot happening. I've done my duty and my best, and I hope my Maker will understand when I go to meet Him.

Middlemoss Living Archive
Recordings: Nancy Bright.

Lars must have told Marcia I'd forgiven her (sort of) because she kept trying to ring me all day Saturday from London. But of course we're frantically busy now on Saturdays, so I hadn't even checked for messages until after we closed, when I was bone-weary.

"At last — I've been trying to get you all day. Are we friends again?" she asked cautiously.

"We were never that, but I'm prepared to put up with you for your father's sake — or I will if you stop telling Justin that there's the remotest possibility that I'll ever take him back."

"Oh, good," she said, ignoring the proviso, "Daddy's really cut up about Rae, which means I'm the blue-eyed girl at the moment, so *something* good has come out of it!"

"Every cloud has a silver lining," I agreed drily.

"Did he tell you he's selling the London house? It's a bit of a bummer, because I need somewhere to stay when I'm in town, but I think I've persuaded him to buy a small flat instead."

"Well, I'm sure that's really riveting, Marcia, but I've had a long, busy day —"

"Yes, Daddy said you were making a big success of the shop. I've dropped in to see Ivo a couple of times, but I didn't think you'd be pleased to see me, so I haven't called in. I will next time, though, so we can kiss and make up," she promised.

I sighed. "I'll count the seconds."

"Ivo's really missing theatre life, I can tell, because he's always happy to hear any gossip. I didn't think he'd like being in a backwater like this for long, so it's a pity he and Kate didn't buy a place over in Middlemoss, where most of the *Cotton Common* cast are. Has he told you the Management are coming up on Monday, hoping to persuade him to go back early? He's looking much better and doesn't seem to mention Kate at all now, so he probably will."

"I knew they were coming up, but not when," I said, "and I expect he *is* missing his old life by now."

Just as I would miss his companionship after he'd gone, especially now that Bella and Neil were an item. Bella would always be my best friend, but things were bound to change. Even now, I realised that there were confidences I'd shared with Ivo, instead . . .

But his time here was running out, and I knew that he was nearing the end of his wife's diaries, too, just as I was almost on the brink of hearing Aunt Nan's confession about what really happened just after the war.

It looked like Bella's would be the only truly happy ending.

Ivo and I went for one of our Sunday afternoon walks with Flash, and I told him an edited version of what Lars had said.

"So now I'm having to be friends with Marcia, who I've never got on with, even if you two are best buddies, and she's threatening to drop in next time she comes to see you."

"Not best buddies, she was just very kind after Kate died, which makes it hard to avoid inviting her in when she sneaks up the lane and catches me in the garden," he said gloomily. "And she always brings some nasty shop-bought cakes with her, not a patch on anything you make."

I felt a warm glow of something or other in my stomach — and no, it wasn't indigestion, because this was before we went back for high tea.

"She means well," he continued. "She thinks I want to know all the acting world gossip but actually, I don't . . . but she does genuinely seem to have *your* interests at heart."

"If you mean she's still trying to get me and Justin back together, then I told Lars I wished she wouldn't give him false hope. He's determined to move up here now!"

Ivo gave me a searching look from his lovely, smudgy-edged grey eyes and I wasn't entirely sure he believed me . . . *or* why it was so important to me that he did.

Once Flash had happily rendered himself wet, muddy and rank with river weeds we turned for home and walked back in companionable silence. We were halfway before I'd realised I'd slipped my arm through his and I left it there, feeling suddenly and quite unreasonably happy and content.

Today's high tea included sherry trifle, which Ivo had let fall was a secret weakness of his — and it was true, I'd never seen anyone eat so much in one go. In fact, he seemed happy to eat anything I put in front of him these days, so it was no wonder he looked so much better! He would always have a bony, hollow-cheeked face with deep-set eyes, but at least he wasn't gaunt any more.

I gave him two kinds of cake to take back, ready for his Management visit the following day: a Dundee and a Victoria sponge. That should refuel them during their pit stops.

Next morning, while I was working on my latest illustration, I could hear loud male conversation through the adjoining wall, so even though I couldn't make out any of the words, the Management must know how to project their voices like actors.

I looked out later, just before I went down to cover for Bella's lunch break, and caught sight of a large, dark car reversing out from the parking space next to Ivo's Jaguar. I expect they were all off somewhere swish to get their trotters in the trough.

And speaking of trotters, Neil's declared interest in keeping pigs had endeared him to Bella even more, so that she'd allowed herself to fall properly in love. The brakes were off and she'd plummeted headlong as a teenager . . . like I once fell for Ivo.

Only, of course, Neil wouldn't dump Bella and break her heart — he wasn't like that. And if he was, I'd go round there and break his legs.

No, they'd get married, raise Tia and a family of pigs, and live happily ever after.

I wasn't sure if Ivo would be able to take Flash out that evening, or still be occupied with his visitors, but he showed up at dusk as usual, though in a very quiet and thoughtful mood. He wouldn't come in when he returned either, saying it had been a long day, but I made him hang about while I put some cheese scones in a box, in case he felt peckish later, though he said there was a bit of Victoria sponge left. The remains of the Dundee cake had apparently gone back to London with the Management.

Ivo didn't volunteer any information about his meeting and I didn't like to ask . . . except for

396

suggesting that the Management probably wanted him to go back early from his six-month sabbatical, that is.

"They do — but I'm not going to."

"Oh, good!" I exclaimed unguardedly and he shot an inscrutable look at me from his clear grey eyes before turning to go.

Next afternoon I began filling the first fermenting jars of Meddyg of the year, using a mix of fresh and dried herbs, green speckles swirling in the green-gold honey. The rate Ivo and I were knocking it back in the evenings, my stock was dwindling rapidly: it had become our comfort drink of choice.

I wondered if Aunt Nan's secret ingredient was addictive? Or maybe it's the *combination* of all those herbs that was addictive, even though they are strained out after a few days.

The May weather continued warm and fine, an idyll, and when Ivo and I were both working on our gardens in the late afternoons, the gate between the two was open so that Flash could come and go between us. It was much more peaceful now he and Toby were pretending they couldn't see each other. The hens, too, loved to range beyond their own garden when they got the chance and Ivo has now stopped looking measuringly at Cedric and muttering about *coq au vin*.

As the month progressed Ivo seemed to do more and more of the work in my garden, for since the big article and photographs of the opening of Cinderella's Slippers finally appeared in *Lively Lancashire* magazine,

397

business was booming. And then, of course, it *was* peak wedding time.

I was forever ordering new stock from RubyTrueShuze — and at a better rate, now I could buy more at a time — and even the vintage shoes Timmy found for me were vanishing quite quickly. Then there were all the tourists doing the Sticklepond Saunter and buying up trinkets, which helped the bank balance, too.

Bella was wonderfully happy and I found myself feeling quietly content. Although I still missed Aunt Nan, life suddenly seemed almost perfect. I was living in the place I loved most in the world, an idyllic existence divided between the shop, my writing and illustrating, gardening and cooking, with Ivo to chat to, to stop me feeling lonely . . . Or it *would* seem idyllic, if I didn't have to keep reminding myself that Ivo would vanish back to his old life when his six-month sabbatical was up, except perhaps for brief weekend visits. I was like a butterfly dancing in the last days of summer, except that *I* was aware that winter would come one day, while the butterfly was not.

Marcia, who was no Cabbage White but merely the fly in the ointment of my life, popped in and out, though it was Ivo she really came to see, of course. He was never visibly cheered by her visits, and seeing her must have rubbed salt into his wounds, for he was still punishing himself for goodness knew what by rationing out Kate's diaries each evening, inch by inch . . .

Not that he said much about them . . . but when we'd had a drink and a bite to eat in the evenings and he got up to go, a mask seemed to fall across his face.

" 'Once more into the breach . . .' " he muttered the other night, which gave me some idea of his state of mind.

Meanwhile, Justin had gone totally silent. I wasn't sure if that was a good sign or not, but I relished his absence from my life and hoped it was permanent.

Harmony was shattered one morning when Hebe called me early, before the shop opened, and announced that Ivo was a major Grocergo shareholder!

"Oh, no, I'm sure you must be mistaken," I said, stunned.

"Not at all. Laurence found out and Ivo Hawksley is not exactly an ordinary run-of-the mill name, is it?" she pointed out. "No, it is your neighbour — and I do recall that he has more than once suggested that the retail park might be a good idea."

"Well, yes," I conceded, "but surely he wouldn't be so devious as to have had a hand in the proposals and not have told me?"

"He's certainly kept the shares secret," Hebe pointed out, which was undeniable.

I was shaken: I'd thought we'd become such good friends that he totally understood how important it was for me to keep the tradition of Bright's Shoes going in the form of Cinderella's Slippers, and how worried I was that the advent of the One Stop Bridal Shop might stop my fledgling business in its tracks . . .

Furiously I marched off through the garden gate and burst through the back door into his kitchen without even knocking.

He was sitting at the pine table over a croissant and *The Times*. "Come in, why don't you?" he said mildly.

"I know!" I cried accusingly. "Why didn't you tell me?"

"'Her voice was ever soft, gentle and low, an excellent thing in a woman,'" he said with mild sarcasm, putting his croissant down. "Are you all right, Tansy? Do you want a cup of tea?"

"No, I don't want a cup of tea! I want you to explain how you happened to forget to mention that you're a major shareholder in Grocergo! Slipped your mind, perhaps?"

He stared at me blankly, then said slowly, "*Am* I? How do you know?"

"Laurence Yatton found out and told Hebe, and she's just rung me up. She thinks you're a mole."

"I feel more of a rabbit in the headlights at the moment," he said. "Look, if this is true, then I think I can explain."

"I *trusted* you!" I said accusingly. "I told you how worried I was about the retail park, and you kept arguing for the other side!"

"No, I just wanted to consider it fairly," he insisted. "And I had no idea I was a Grocergo shareholder until you told me."

"Tell that to the marines!"

"No, really. I inherited a load of shares from my father, but his financial advisor kept on handling all that for me, and I left him to it. I did say I only wanted shares in ethical companies."

"I wouldn't call the plans for the retail park ethical."

"I think that's going a bit too far, but I really had no idea — honestly, Tansy. I mean, do I look like a mole?"

I stared at him and he looked back at me from clear, challenging grey eyes.

"No, I suppose not. So — you really had no idea all this time?"

"No, none. But I have to go down to Stratford soon for a few days, so I'll make an appointment with the financial advisor and talk to him about it."

Now the shock and my temper had calmed down a little, I could see he was telling me the truth.

"I'm sorry," I apologised, "it was a bit of a bombshell, hearing that from Hebe and I didn't stop to think about it."

"Yes, you were a bit quick to judge me, weren't you? I thought you knew me better — that we'd become good friends."

He sounded hurt and I said hastily, "I do, really . . . it's only that I've had one or two knocks in the trusting-men department lately."

I sank onto the nearest kitchen chair and he got down a cup and poured me some tea.

"Croissant? I have another one without a bite out of it."

"No, thanks, I've eaten — and you ought to have something more solid in the mornings."

"I can't even manage a whole croissant most days, not after the supper you give me!" he said. "The birds get at least half my breakfast. I must have the fattest sparrows in Sticklepond."

I sipped my tea and eyed him over the cup and he suddenly smiled at me, like the sun coming out from behind a darkly watercolour cloud.

"Will *you* try to persuade Hebe that I'm not subverting her campaign before she has me run out of the village on a hurdle, or must I?"

I called Hebe right back and did my best, though I'm not sure her suspicions were entirely allayed. She said *someone* locally was still stirring up pro-retail park support, and if it wasn't Ivo, then who was it?

"I don't know, but I'm sure it's not him," I assured her, and she made a *harrumph* noise and rang off.

I wondered why Ivo was going down to Stratford? Had he changed his mind, so wanted to arrange about his return to the stage now, before his six-months sabbatical was even up? I knew he'd go eventually, but I'd prefer it later rather than sooner.

Aunt Nan had been on the point of winding up her narrative for ages in the penultimate archive CD, but each time she approached some kind of conclusion she would suddenly about-turn and vanish into a cloud of anecdotes.

But finally one evening, after she'd been rambling on about making rhubarb wine and the best way to tighten up sagging canework furniture, she suddenly paused and heaved a heavy sigh.

"*Well, lovey, I can't avoid it any more, so I'd better tell what happened just before VJ Day, all those years ago. There isn't anyone left to be hurt by the truth any*

402

more — and moral codes have gone totally out of the window these days, so I don't expect anyone will blink at what I'm about to say. Whether Tansy will be surprised or not, I don't know, but hers will be the decision as to whether this part of the story goes into the public archive or not."

And with that, the CD ended. I switched it off and sat there thinking about Aunt Nan's life till Ivo brought Flash back from his evening walk and I could tell him what she'd said.

"So now I've just got the last one, the one she recorded especially for me. I'll have to brace myself for that a bit, even though I've guessed what's coming. And . . . I don't really want to get to the end of them, anyway. It's a bit like letting go of her altogether."

"I've almost got to Kate's final diary too," Ivo said. "It's unfinished, of course — it was returned to me with her effects after the accident and I just put it in the box with the others. I don't suppose there'll be any new revelations in it . . . only things I already know about, and they'll be painful enough to read . . ."

I supposed he meant more of her infidelities — or maybe just the poignancy of her excitement at being offered the *Cotton Common* role, when he knew what was to come.

Whatever it was, we each seemed equally reluctant to bring our self-imposed journey into the life of our loved one finally to an end.

CHAPTER
THIRTY-SIX

Wishes

I wanted to listen to Aunt Nan's final explanation ... and yet, I didn't. I certainly couldn't settle to anything else the following day, and Bella said I was like a cat on hot bricks and why didn't I just get it over with?

"You don't have to wait till evening, do you?"

"I suppose I've just got into the habit. I like to listen to it while Ivo is out with Flash, though I have listened to bits here and there, late at night or in the morning, when the temptation has been too much for me. But the evening is good, because it's ... nice to have someone to discuss what she's said with, to talk about Aunt Nan, even though he never knew her."

"You save it then," Bella said kindly, but with a worried look at me. I'm sure she thought I was getting too reliant on Ivo's company, when he was a bird of passage, about to take flight back to Stratford, and I'm afraid she is right.

Ivo understood — he left me to listen to it that evening with an encouraging, "Go for it!" before vanishing into the night with Flash.

Mind you, I thought that was a bit rich coming from him, since he appeared to be spinning his diary reading out indefinitely!

But for me, it was time to hear the truth.

"Here goes, Tansy my love, and don't judge your old aunt Nan too harshly," said her beloved voice. As if I would judge her at all!

"Violet sent me a letter at the same time as she sent one to our parents. Theirs said she'd been ill again and needed me to go down and nurse her, but that wasn't the truth, because the one she wrote me swore me to secrecy and confessed that she was pregnant — with a husband who'd been in the Far East at the relevant time! She'd hatched this crazy plan that we could make it appear that the baby was mine. We'd no phone then, so I rushed out to the village call box as soon as I could and rang her, but she'd already written to her husband, telling him that I was having an illegitimate baby, and she was going to adopt it."

"What!" I exclaimed to the empty air, sitting bolt upright.

"Well, I was that upset!" Aunt Nan said. *"Not to mention furious that she expected me to give up my good name so she could keep hers for, whatever she said, I knew rumours would soon fly round the village. But what was done, was done, so in the end I had to accept it."*

Oh, poor Nan!

"Of course, her husband never suspected the truth, for although Imogen was tall and fair like Violet, while I was small and dark, Immy looked just like our

mother, so it was easy enough to say she took after that side of the family in her colouring."

I could see that Aunt Nan hadn't really been left with any alternative, but there wasn't anything at all to forgive her for. She was the blameless one in all this. And when she described how some people in the village cut her dead when the rumours went round, including the curate with whom she'd thought she might have a second chance at marriage and a family, I just wept and wept for her.

When Ivo returned I walked straight into his arms, seeking solace there as I had done before — and how that comforting embrace came to turn into a long, slow kiss, I have no idea . . . But it felt so natural, familiar and right that *I* certainly didn't resist — in fact, I enthusiastically participated — and *he* was the one finally to pull back.

"I'm *so* sorry, Tansy, I shouldn't have done that," he apologised, all pale and taut, as if he'd committed some heinous crime.

"That's all right," I said slightly shakily — and not just from Aunt Nan's story, either. "I know it's just a luvvie thing and actors kiss each other all the time."

"Well, perhaps not quite *all* the time," he said, with one of those fleeting, fugitive smiles. "But I'm sorry if your aunt Nan's story has upset you, though I suppose it was likely to, hearing it in her own words."

"It wasn't that. It was because it was an entirely different story from the one I thought it would be! I suspected she was my grandmother and actually, she really *was* my great-aunt, after all."

I explained what had happened and the terrible position that Violet's actions had put Aunt Nan into. "And the upsetting thing is that some people believed the rumours, including the man she'd thought she might marry, so Violet destroyed all hope of that, too."

"He can't have been worthy of her, in that case," he said.

"No, she does say that her eyes were opened to his true character and she'd had a lucky escape. He was moved to another parish soon afterwards."

I sniffed and dabbed my eyes. "I'm glad I know, but it's just all so sad."

"*I'm* not expecting any surprises in Kate's last diary, but it won't make for easy reading," Ivo said heavily. "I'd tried to persuade her to turn the *Cotton Common* part down because of the baby, but she wouldn't listen, and then she called me from Marcia's and told me she'd miscarried. It was so early and it often happens, she said . . ."

"Oh, Ivo, I'm so sorry!" I cried.

"She sounded quite calm about it, but in retrospect that must have been shock. And instead of being understanding, I blamed her and said perhaps if she'd listened to me and stayed at home, she wouldn't have lost the baby. Our last words to each other were angry."

"But that was natural, and you weren't to predict the accident," I said, and this time it was me who put my arms around him.

He rested his cheek against my hair and sighed heavily. "Even though I was so angry, I wanted to go up and fetch her home, because I didn't think she should

407

drive herself back, but she wouldn't hear of it. If I'd been kinder and more understanding, the accident might never have happened."

I understood now that he'd blamed himself for her death, and guilt had been eating him up, but sharing this awful secret with me obviously had a cathartic effect (just as that kiss had had a strangely cathartic effect on *me*) for he released himself and declared resolutely, "I'm going straight back to read the last diary! I've punished myself for months by prolonging the torture, but now it's time to finish with it, burn them, and try to move on."

When he'd gone I sat there turning it all over in my mind, not least the way I had reacted to his kiss, and finally admitted to myself that I could all too easily fall in love with Ivo all over again . . . in fact, I was more than halfway there already.

And that was so not a good idea, for I thought it likely he would always blame himself for Kate's death and never quite get over her loss. She'd always be the unwelcome ghost at any future wedding feast.

I must have fetched two chocolate shoes and eaten them without conscious thought, for the evidence lay all around me in Cellophane and silk ribbon — and two paper Wishes.

The first read, "Don't be afraid to step through the door and find what is on the other side," which would have been useful encouragement had I read it before embarking on the last of Aunt Nan's memoirs.

408

The other said cryptically, "All things will come to she who waits," and I sincerely hoped that didn't mean that Marcia is about to snaffle Ivo in a weak moment when he's at his lowest ebb.

I poured myself a generous slug of Meddyg, hoping Ivo was doing the same to dull whatever mixed emotions he was feeling — for the dismal music was by now swelling and eddying next door — and began to listen to Aunt Nan's final words.

CHAPTER
THIRTY-SEVEN

Wrecked

"*Since Immy has never mentioned anything to me, and Tansy seems to have no idea that her mother was "adopted" at all, I suspect Violet may not have told her anything about it. In that case, all this might be a bit of a surprise to her, should Tansy decide to tell her!*"

There was a pause and then Aunt Nan said, directly to me, "*I've sent that Cheryl out of the room for a bit, our Tansy, so it's just you and me. I want you to remember that I've always been proud of you, lass, you're a good girl, and it was a blessed day for me when Immy upped and left you here.*

"*I never thought that Justin was the right man for you, so I hope by now Mr Right has come along — and don't you be stubborn if he has, because where would Cinderella have been if she'd told Prince Charming where to put his glass slipper? No, if you get another opportunity, which I pray you will, then grab it with both hands.*"

Well, I'd certainly grabbed Ivo with both hands earlier, I thought! My reactions had been so automatic and it had opened my eyes to the realisation that once Justin had been expunged from my heart, Ivo had

410

rapidly taken his place. But *he* wasn't free. His heart belonged with an unfaithful ghost and probably always would.

Aunt Nan finished with her familiar, "*Good night, lovey!*" just as if she was off to bed, rather than to some longer sleep, and then there was just silence . . . apart from the faint, sad strains of music from Ivo's cottage.

I turned the machine off and sat there for ages just thinking — and then even when I went to bed I couldn't sleep, because everything was whirling round in my mind like a merry-go-round: all that Ivo had let fall about Kate, my realisation of my true feelings for him and the sure knowledge that falling for a man still yearning for his dead wife was not the sort of second chance Aunt Nan had had in mind.

I gave up on sleep in the end and went downstairs in my dressing gown, where Flash seemed mildly surprised to see me again so soon, but asked to go out.

When I let him back in, the light from the kitchen sent out a bright beacon into the darkness, drawing Ivo from the darkness like a moth towards the flame until he stood before me, eyes wide open and staring — not at me, but inwards, at some terrible vision.

"Ivo?" I said, afraid and concerned. "What is it?" I took his arm and drew him in, unresisting, closing the door on the night but not the dark miasma of thoughts he'd brought with him.

"It's . . . Kate," he said with difficulty. "She thought they wouldn't give her the *Cotton Common* part if they knew about the baby and so . . . she aborted it!"

"Oh my God!" I said blankly.

"She said she didn't want it anyway and she'd just tell me she'd miscarried . . . and Marcia — *she* knew! She even took her to the clinic, helped to arrange it. Yet all this time . . ." His voice broke.

"Yes . . . I see. She pretended she didn't know and let you suffer." Right then, I'd have loved to have made my ex-stepsister suffer a little too — or more than a little!

"All this time I've blamed myself because I wasn't kinder to Kate when she lost the baby," he said brokenly. "But she *chose* not to have it, chose her career above a family *and* lied to me. I've tortured myself over it and now —"

"Don't — *please* don't look like that, Ivo!" I begged, laying a hand on his arm and looking up into his anguished face. "I can't bear you to be so upset!"

For the first time he seemed to be really aware of me and his grey eyes focused. " 'Put forth thy hand, reach at the glorious gold,' " he said obscurely, taking me by the shoulders and staring down into my face. Then his grip tightened and changed intent and when we kissed, this time there was no drawing back on either side.

I awoke on the echoes of a scream that was my own, bathed in cold sweat from a very Brontëan nightmare, where Kate had been clawing at the bedroom window to be let in, while singing that "Wuthering Heights" song. Her face had been white and framed in clammy curls, and her malevolent dark eyes had been fixed on me. I just knew her blood-red fingernails had been itching to get at me, too . . .

It took me several minutes to realise that there was only birdsong and early sunshine on the other side of the familiar flowered curtains at the window . . . *and* why my guilty mind had conjured up Ivo's dead wife.

"*My love*," he'd whispered at one point last night . . . but whether to me or a ghost woman, I had no way of knowing.

We'd clung together like two drowning people — but now I was aware without even checking that I was alone in the shipwreck of my bed and had been for a considerable time, for there was no warmth where he'd lain, limbs tangled with mine.

"*That's what you get for fornication outside marriage — and under my very roof, too!*" I heard Aunt Nan's voice say in my head, though more in sorrow than in anger. I expect she knew I couldn't help myself last night — and neither could Ivo.

Then something — some instinctive knowledge of loss — made me spring out of bed and rush to my studio window overlooking the back garden. The red Jaguar had vanished.

Downstairs Flash looked at me accusingly.

"Not you, too!" I told him, fondling his ears. "I've already been ticked off by Aunt Nan. I don't suppose Ivo told you why he left so early or where he's gone?"

Flash thumped his tail then asked to be let out, and that's when I spotted the note Ivo had left, stuck with a dolphin magnet to the front of the fridge.

It said he'd left for Stratford for a few days because he needed to be alone to think things through and he was so, so sorry about what happened . . . but not as sorry as I was when I read it! If he ever apologised for touching me again, I'd *hit* him.

And just to add insult to injury there was a PS: "Could you possibly go in and feed Toby while I'm away?"

Just as well I knew where he hid the back door key. The key to his heart was another thing entirely. I think he'd thrown that one away.

CHAPTER
THIRTY-EIGHT

Uninvited Guests

"'Tansy darling, I'm so, so sorry — I really didn't mean that to happen!'" Bella read aloud. "'I wasn't thinking straight and I need some time on my own to work things through, so I'm going off to Stratford and I'll ring you later — if you can forgive me. Ivo.'"

She looked up at me. "He does call you 'darling'," she offered consolingly, but she was clearly clutching at straws. I'd poured the whole sorry tale into her ears the moment she'd arrived, of course, and we were still sitting in the kitchen, even though the clock was inexorably ticking towards opening time.

"He's a luvvie," I pointed out. "I expect actors call each other 'darling' in every sentence. No," I sighed heavily, "I've fallen in love with him all over again, but he's made it plain he only sees me as a friend, and I know last night it was only the shock making him look for comfort."

"Yes, and *what* a shock! I can't believe you've been holding out on me about his wife being unfaithful all this time — or exactly how much you were seeing of each other."

"We saw an awful lot more of each other last night," I said, with a slightly hysterical giggle.

"Tansy!"

"Yes, OK — I didn't tell you about his wife, because it didn't seem like my secret to tell."

"I can't imagine why she ever looked at another man when she had Ivo," she said frankly. "He may not be my type, but still — *phwoar!*"

"That puzzled me too, but she seemed to have been a very insecure person and I think she just needed the reassurance that she was attractive, because she kept putting in the diary that she loved Ivo and didn't want him to find out."

"But then to abort the baby just so she could get a part in a soap series — it beggars belief!" Bella exclaimed.

"It may not even have been his baby, but that doesn't make it any easier for him." I paused. "Bella, I was sure he was still in love with her, despite being angry when he found out about the affairs, but now I don't know what he's feeling."

"Probably neither does he, that's why he's gone away," she suggested. "It's just a pity he didn't hang around long enough to talk to you before he left."

" 'Goodbye' " would have been quite nice," I agreed, "but if sleeping with me was just a search for oblivion, then he probably regretted it as soon as it was over and couldn't wait to get away. Now I expect he'll tell the Management he's moving straight back to Stratford and he may not even keep the cottage on at all."

416

"That's it, look on the bright side! But I'm sure you're wrong," Bella said, even though I thought she secretly agreed with me.

Then something occurred to her. "Did you . . . you know, use *protection* last night?" she asked.

"I — no! I never even thought of it! It was all a bit . . . sudden. And Ivo wasn't thinking at all. But I'm hardly going to get pregnant from a one-night stand after what they said at my fertility MOT, am I?"

"I suppose not," Bella agreed, "but there's more than pregnancy to worry about and you should be more careful."

"It's not exactly like I make a habit of sleeping around!"

"No, of course not," she said, then added dreamily, "Neil would like children and the sooner the better really, so Tia has some siblings before there's a huge age gap."

"I thought you were going to breed pigs, instead?" I said, and she laughed.

"Yes, those too! We're going to have a day out at a rare-breed farm on Sunday with Tia, but I think we know what kind we'd like best."

A faint hammering could be heard and she started and looked at the clock. "It's well past opening time, and that sounds like a frantic bride on the doorstep!"

My *Slipper Monkeys* illustration turned into a giant doodle and was crumpled up and thrown forcefully into the wastepaper bin. In the end, I gave up altogether and went down and made tomato chutney, then racked the Meddyg. I'd just finished when Ivo finally rang me . . .

The conversation, such as it was, cannot be said to have gone well, partly because he began by apologising for sleeping with me.

"Will you *stop* apologising?" I snarled through gritted teeth.

"But I know you must have felt as terrible as I did next morning," he said, adding insult to injury. "I don't know what came over me."

"Probably too much Meddyg," I suggested.

"I had knocked a lot back while reading the diaries, but that's no excuse. And I'm really fond of you, Tansy. I wouldn't hurt you for the world."

Too late, I thought, but didn't say.

"Look, I'll be back on Sunday and we'll talk it through then."

"I don't think we need to talk about it at all," I suggested. "Much better if we just forget about it and move on."

"*Forget?*" he repeated, as if this was a concept he found hard to grasp. Then he said, "At the moment I just need space, to sort things out in my mind. It's like a kaleidoscope — you know, when you shake it and all the bits fall into an entirely different pattern from the one you started out with?"

"Well, good luck with that, then," I said, wondering if he might be trying to shake *me* out of the kaleidoscope altogether.

"How's Toby?" he asked after a slight pause.

"He's hardly noticed you've gone," I lied, because Toby had looked pretty put out by the time I'd remembered to go and give him his breakfast.

"You'll have to give him space," Bella said.

"I know, but I wish he'd stop damned-well apologising for touching me! Anyway, I don't suppose he'll be in Sticklepond much longer and we can just pretend it all never happened until he goes."

"Easier said than done," she said, looking at me doubtfully as if she knew that the events of that night tended to replay themselves in my head at the oddest moments . . .

Florrie and Zillah Smith paid me a surprise visit after the shop had shut, so it was just as well I'd thrown myself into a frenzy of baking earlier and had fresh bara brith and some Fat Rascals made.

"Zillah saw something in the leaves, and she said to me that we ought to come and see you," Florrie explained, settling herself comfortably at the kitchen table and reaching for the plate of Fat Rascals.

Zillah smiled, gold teeth flashing. "That's right. There's trouble at the moment, I could see that, but it'll pass, eventually. Here are some chocolates Chloe sent, so you can stop eating the stock!"

"How did you know I ate some chocolate shoes —" I began, amazed, but Zillah just shook her head, big gold hoop earrings swaying.

"Florrie, give her the . . ." she paused, "*tonic*."

"Tonic?"

Florrie produced a little phial of some greenish substance. "It's not for you, it's for that actor next door that you're so friendly with. He needs it."

I took it dubiously and the contents shifted viscously when I tilted the phial.

"What's in it?"

"Oh, heartsease, that kind of thing," she said vaguely.

"I think *I* could do with some of that," I commented without thinking, then went slightly pink.

"Oh, no, you'll do — just be patient," Zillah said, and suddenly I was sure they knew what I'd been up to!

"You want me to give this to Ivo when — *if* — he comes back?"

"He will come back and I don't mean you should *hand* it to him, of course, but bake it into something. It would make a nice cheese and herb scone."

"You're quite sure it won't do him any harm?"

"On the contrary. Trust me, I'm a witch," Florrie said with a cackle of laughter. Then she dipped her slice of buttered bara brith in her tea, so that a fatty sheen spread across the surface.

Florrie reminded me before they left that Hebe had called a Chamber of Commerce meeting at seven that evening, which I went to more in search of distraction than anything.

And actually, it *was* distracting, because Hebe told us that to her deep regret (and obvious chagrin) she'd discovered that her nephew Jack Lewis was one of the members of the consortium proposing the Hemlock Mill retail park, and he was behind all the campaigning.

This made everything clear, since Jack, Sophy Winter's wicked cousin, was a bad lot who had been exposed on TV a year or two ago, swindling elderly people out of their property. There was a big rumpus and he hadn't been seen much in Sticklepond since.

"Once Laurence had told me, I spoke to Jack," Hebe continued, then paused while we all imagined *that* scene.

"The outcome is that he has now persuaded his fellow members of the consortium that selling the land to Force for Nature, so that it can be turned into a nature reserve, is much the best option. I have it on good authority that planning permission will not be passed for the retail park, particularly in regard to the fact that the expert the council brought in has now identified the site as a habitat of the rare blue-toed newt."

"I didn't know there was such a thing," Felix said.

"That is because it *is* so rare," she said.

Then we tossed a few promotional ideas around before Felix's mobile went off and he had to dash off home. Poppy had gone into labour.

I had to go, too: I had a dog expecting a decent walk, and a peeved cat to feed.

It was noon next day before we heard that Poppy had had a little girl and both were doing well.

"Yet another little girl in the village!" Bella pointed out.

"Perhaps Aunt Nan was right about there being something strange in the water," I agreed, and then we

421

decided to club together to buy the baby something pretty in pink, since it seemed likely that once it started to toddle it would be inevitably attired in jodhpurs, gilet and paddock boots.

"And so is Tia these days; she's pony mad now," Bella said.

It distracted my mind from my own woes for a bit, because I'm already missing Ivo — and so is Flash, who doesn't understand where he has vanished to. I did want Ivo to come back, yet I also dreaded seeing him again. I didn't know how we could get over what we'd done and resume our friendship, which was clearly all that is on offer . . . and which seemed even more precious in retrospect.

And I'd hoped that Justin had *finally* given up on me, but no: he emailed to say he was now flat-hunting in the North because his move was imminent and he hoped to see me soon — there was no reason why we couldn't still be friends and he missed me.

I hadn't given him even a passing, irritated thought for ages, so that was hardly mutual. Besides, one old-lover-turned-friend was more than enough to cope with, and Justin had been pushed right out of both my head and my heart.

Toby moved in with us, though he did eat his meals in his own home. He'd simply appeared out of the darkness on Wednesday evening after we'd got back from our walk and stalked past us into the kitchen, where he took possession of a cushioned basket chair.

Flash and I were both disconcerted at first, but soon got used to the situation, though I was sure he'd abandon us when Ivo returned . . . if he ever did return.

But, his six-month sabbatical would soon be up, so he'd be off again soon, anyway, and presumably take Toby with him.

I felt restless and edgy on Saturday night, wondering if Ivo really would come back next day, and if so, what we could say to each other . . .

It meant it was late before I asked Toby and Flash if they would care to avail themselves of the garden before I locked the kitchen door for the night and went to bed, so it was a shock when, before I could lock it again, it was suddenly flung open and Justin barged straight in!

Flash leaped at this unwelcome intruder and in the ensuing pandemonium it became pretty obvious that Justin had had considerably too much to drink — especially when he stumbled and fell heavily into the basket chair on top of Toby.

Cat scratches seem to take for ever to heal, don't they? But luckily Toby seemed unhurt, except in his dignity.

I calmed Flash down and he retired under the table with Toby. Then I turned to my unwelcome visitor, who was sitting staring owlishly at me from the depths of the basket chair, while sucking his bleeding hand.

"What on earth are you doing here — and at this time of night?" I demanded. "You didn't drive here in that state, did you?"

"No, Marcia dropped me off."

"*Marcia?*"

"She's putting me up and she's been looking for flats for me too. I'm going to rent for a while, then we'll see . . ."

"That makes sense, because I think you'll find yourself heading back to London in pretty fast order," I said. "Why've you come here?"

Justin got up again with an effort, towering over me. His face had more than a healthy glow and his eyes were not quite focused — goodness knew what alcohol Marcia had been pouring into him! It quickly became apparent she'd been pouring more lies into his ears, too.

"Marcia said you were getting close to that widowed actor next door and I came to tell you I won't have it," Justin slurred, with a menacingly jealous look.

"Don't you tell me what you will or won't have!" I told him angrily, and then gave him such a sharp push that he stumbled back into the basket chair again. "Get a grip! I'm friends with my neighbour, nothing more, and Marcia's just spinning you lies because she has the hots for him herself."

"I don't believe you," Justin said, narrowing his bleary, slightly bloodshot blue eyes at me.

"I don't care if you believe me or not. And in any case, what I do is no longer any business of yours."

Well, that did it. He heaved himself up, saying he was going to teach me a lesson I wouldn't forget and trying to grab me. This would have been scary, since he's so much bigger than I am, but fortunately he wasn't

424

entirely in charge of his legs and fell backwards into the chair even as I was reaching for a handy frying pan to defend myself with.

He'd never been violent, so I wasn't quite sure what he had in mind, but this was an unpleasant side of him I'd never seen before, presumably buried deep and brought out by the drink.

"You try anything and I'll ding you one with this pan," I threatened, then told him to get out.

He refused to go, though, crossing his arms across his broad chest and staring at me with bleary belligerence, so I left Flash and Toby watching him intently while I went into the parlour and phoned Timmy. It was providential that he and Joe were staying in Ormskirk this weekend and I prayed they were not out somewhere. Luckily they were home.

"Justin's drunk and stubborn and he says he's staying here with me tonight. Marcia dropped him off, so I need to get him into a taxi back to her: she got him in this state, so she can cope with him."

Timmy quickly grasped the situation and he and Joe turned up half an hour later, by which time I'd given Justin a slug of the cooking brandy in the hope it would render him slightly more malleable while we all wrestled him into a taxi. It did — in fact, almost comatose.

The driver was not too keen on his drunken passenger, but relented when I removed Justin's well-stuffed wallet and paid him double in advance.

"It's well after midnight: no wonder he turned into a pumpkin," Timmy said, as the taillights receded up the lane.

"Now he's gone somewhere else to vegetate," Joe put in.

"Enough with the vegetable jokes," I said, grinning, "or we'll never get to the root of it."

"What a turnip for the books!" Timmy said, irrepressibly.

CHAPTER
THIRTY-NINE

June Bug

Ivo came back on Sunday afternoon, while I was in his kitchen feeding Toby. I'd left the door open to the garden and he walked in and dropped his bags just inside the door before standing and looking at me with a very odd expression on his face. I mean, I'd expected embarrassment, or worry, maybe, but this was more . . . accusatory.

Toby ignored him because he was in the middle of one of those cat mimes, trying to tell me he'd prefer a different flavour cat food to the one I'd opened.

"Hi, Tansy," Ivo said finally. "I've been to see Marcia, that's why I'm late back. I wanted to tell her I knew about Kate having the abortion and that she'd helped her."

"What did she say?" I asked. I'd been edging towards the door, ready for flight, but now I waited.

"That she'd tried to persuade Kate out of the abortion and there hadn't seemed any point in telling me afterwards . . . but she was wrong. It would have made a big difference."

"Yes, of course it would," I agreed. "Well, I'd better be off, I've —"

"Don't go yet," he said. "Look, I really am sorry for what happened and I'm hoping you can forgive me — and that it hasn't mucked things up with Justin?"

I stared at him. "*What* things?"

"Come on, you don't need to pretend. Marcia told me she'd been putting him up while he was flat-hunting, but he spent last night with you — you'd invited him over."

"I had not, and no — he didn't!" I declared indignantly.

Ivo eyed me closely. "He *wasn't* here?"

"Well, yes, he did turn up late and drunk — but uninvited," I admitted. "Then he refused to leave."

"So he stayed the night?"

"He certainly *didn't*! I got Timmy and Joe over from Ormskirk to help me get him in a taxi and we sent him right back to Marcia, as she knows very well!"

He frowned. "But if that's so, then why would she lie to me?"

"Because she's jealous, of course, you numbskull! She thinks you and I have a thing going and that's why she's been stirring Justin up and encouraging him to think I really want him back. She was probably peeved because you'd found out about her helping Kate, too."

"I did make it clear I'd rather not see her ever again," he said slowly. "But surely she wouldn't —"

"If you don't believe me, I'll give you Timmy's phone number," I offered coldly.

"Yes, of course I believe you. In fact, I don't know now why I even listened to Marcia. It was just that when I thought you and Justin . . ." He stopped and rubbed his hands over his tired face.

"There is no 'me and Justin' and I'm hoping he's now shot his bolt and that's the last time I'll hear his name. And there's no 'me and Ivo', either, come to that, so as to the other night, we'll just forget it ever happened. It was something and nothing."

"If that's what you want," he agreed, with a searching look from his grey eyes. "We can but try."

"You'll be moving back to Stratford soon, so we won't have to try for very long, will we?"

"But I'm not moving back," he said, "I'm staying here. That's one of the reasons I went: to tell them straight I was retiring from the stage and to sort out a few things."

"You're . . . staying here?" I repeated, my heart making a sudden leap and then starting to race. "For ever?"

"Yes, '*my tale is done*' as far as acting's concerned. I just want an unquiet life here in Sticklepond, writing my books, gardening, being woken at unearthly hours by Cedric, driven mad by bells . . .'"

"*Seriously?*" I asked, still hardly daring to believe it, when I'd been expecting him to vanish out of my life as suddenly as he had reappeared.

"Seriously. So it would be pretty difficult if we couldn't get back to being friends, wouldn't it?" He ventured one of his rare charm-the-birds-from-the-trees smiles. "I missed you while I was away."

"I've got used to having you around too," I conceded grudgingly, which was the understatement of the year considering I felt as if the sun had just come out and an entire Welsh male-voice choir was singing "The Hallelujah Chorus" in my head.

"Oh, and I told my broker to sell the Grocergo shares," he added, which reminded me about the Chamber of Commerce meeting and I told him about Hebe finding the true Sticklepond mole — her nephew, Jack Lewis.

"So all your deep dark suspicions about me were unfounded," Ivo pointed out.

"Hebe's too — and when she hears you're going to live here permanently, she's bound to try to persuade you to join the Friends of Winter's End again," I said, and he groaned, so I don't rate her chances of succeeding with that very highly.

Bella and I visited Poppy's baby on Thursday afternoon when the shop was shut, to give her the little shell-pink vests and dress we'd bought. The baby was a sweet little thing and I think both Bella and I felt equally broody afterwards, though of course in Bella's case she has some hope of having another baby or two while I haven't even passed the starting post and never, it seems, will.

Bella and Neil's leisurely courtship suddenly seemed to have wheels, for they were now planning a wedding. I'd promised to buy them a pig as a wedding present if I could be bridesmaid, though of course I knew Bella would ask me anyway.

She'd already chosen her RubyTrueShuze wedding shoes — palest lilac suede high-heeled pumps with flower and silver hummingbird detail!

430

★　★　★

Of course, Ivo and I didn't easily fall straight back into our old friendly ways. Things were a bit stiff at first and sometimes embarrassing. We'd forget what we'd done and be easy together and then suddenly catch each other's eye and it was clear we were remembering the same thing.

Ivo was careful not to touch me and vice versa . . . but one day we accidentally bumped into each other and Ivo went so still I thought he'd turned to stone on the spot, while I felt as if I'd received an electric shock. We gazed into each other's eyes for a long moment — and then Bella came into the kitchen from the shop and the spell was broken. We sprang apart, slightly self-consciously.

Bella said later that she despaired of us, but it did get easier as the days went on and I decided I'd so much rather have Ivo next door as a friend, than not there at all. I've already got his cat: Toby went home only for meals by then.

Strangely, things seemed to become easier between us right after our first high tea together following his return, when I remembered Florrie's well-meaning herbal tonic and made Ivo two special scones, which he ate with great relish.

"These are different," he said, and oddly enough *he* seemed a little different after he'd eaten them, too . . . more relaxed, his spring not quite so tightly wound, nor his eyes so haunted. Perhaps they'd given him amnesia? I ought to have eaten one.

I told Florrie next time she called in and she said he'd be a changed man, just wait and see . . .

As May turned to June I relied on Ivo more and more, for the shop was hectically busy but the garden didn't stop growing and fruiting, and the dog still needed walking. When I had any free time, I seemed to spend it jamming, chutneying and brewing away . . .

Ivo was in and out of the cottage and we shared the cat, the dog and the produce. In fact, the only thing we *didn't* seem to be sharing was a bed.

Raffy was still visiting him, and I assumed Ivo had told him what he had discovered about Kate and received some good advice. Raffy called in on me one day too, and said Ivo needed a lot of time and understanding, and when I said I had an infinite supply of both, he laughed.

Far from finally vanishing from my life, as I'd hoped, Justin emailed and texted a couple of times insisting we had something to talk about and saying he was sorry if he'd been a bit drunk the other night. (A bit!) It became apparent that he had no recollection of anything that had happened after he'd arrived at my cottage!

I didn't reply to any of them: we had nothing to talk about. He was my past, an uncomfortable dream I would rather forget, if only he would let me.

New plans for the nature reserve had been submitted and approved in record time, so all the Chamber of

Commerce members could relax, but not rest on our laurels, for it was getting into peak tourist season and the village is Sticklepond Saunter busy.

While Bella and I both found the hectic shop very exhilarating, as the month went on I began to feel a little . . . *odd*. I went right off coffee, for a start — and then even Meddyg, which I could have done with just to keep me going.

"I wonder if I'm sickening for something?" I said to Bella eventually. "I just feel weird, and funnily enough, although I haven't put weight on, my clothes don't seem to fit me the same."

Bella's eyes widened slightly. "Have you thought . . . you might possibly be *pregnant?*"

The question and all its possibilities hung shimmering on the air for a moment, then I said with a shaky laugh, "Don't be daft!"

"At least think about it — that clinic didn't say you *couldn't* get pregnant, did they?"

"No, just that my window of opportunity was about to vanish. And that was months ago, too." But now I came to think about it, my erratic cycle seemed to have stopped entirely and we'd been so busy I hadn't even noticed.

"I *can't* be pregnant!"

"Do a test and then you'll know one way or the other," she urged.

I looked at her blankly.

"Look," she said, "you mind the shop and I'll pop out to the chemist in your car and get one."

★ ★ ★

I did the test next morning after a largely sleepless night — I'd been so distracted the previous evening that Ivo had asked me if I was feeling well!

So did Bella, when I rang her at dawn to say the test was positive.

"I don't know how I feel," I replied. "Happy, sad, over the moon, afraid, delighted . . . you name it. This isn't how I wanted it to be, but then, I thought it was never going to happen to me at all!"

"It'll be fine, you'll see," she said soothingly. "But you'll have to tell Ivo at some point, won't you?"

"I suppose so, though I don't think this will be news he wants to hear. But it's early days yet, so I'd like to keep it to myself in case anything goes wrong. And why would he believe it was his anyway? He'd probably think I really *had* slept with Justin!"

"I'm sure he knows you better than that," Bella assured me. "And you'll have to tell him. I mean, he's *entitled* to know."

"I don't know how he's going to take it — especially when you think about what happened with Kate . . ."

"It's tricky, but *you* aren't Kate and you want the baby, don't you?"

"Yes, I do! I really, really do," I confessed.

It might shatter the friendship with Ivo that we'd been so carefully building up again, but I would risk all to hold this lovely, unexpected and fragile gift I'd been so carelessly given close to my heart.

Of course I was totally distracted for the rest of the week and I know Ivo was puzzled, but whatever Bella said I was determined to keep the news from him as long as I could. I simply couldn't guess how he'd take it.

Then Justin, the last man on earth I felt like talking to, managed to catch me on the phone one afternoon just after the shop was shut, when Bella and I were having a sit-down and a cup of coffee. She didn't have to dash off and fetch Tia for once, since she'd gone to tea with a friend.

"Tansy?" Justin said, "I've been trying to get you for ages, because I really wanted to apologise for the other evening. I wasn't myself."

"Well, whoever you were, it wasn't an improvement," I said. "Far from it. I accept your apology, but I'd prefer that you never contacted me again, Justin. Please, just let me go now."

"Come on, Tansy! I can't remember much about that evening, but Marcia says I only went back to her flat in the early hours, so I wanted to know — I mean, I can't remember whether we —"

"There was no 'we'," I interrupted, astonished. "You were drunk and aggressive and wouldn't go away. In the end, I got Timmy and Joe over and they managed to get you in a taxi. And it was only about one in the morning, so Marcia was exaggerating."

"So . . . nothing happened?" He sounded disappointed.

"What, you really thought I might have leaped into bed with you?" I exclaimed incredulously. "Of course nothing happened! Now, I think we've said everything we need to say and —"

"But I love you, Tansy. I've even moved up here for you!"

"No, you finally decided to move as far away from your mother as you could, and I was a handy excuse. And don't keep telling me that you love me, because I'm not sure you ever did, you're only obsessed with me now because I turned you down."

"I can see what's happened," he snapped angrily, "and Marcia is right. You'd have come back to me like a shot if you hadn't fallen for that actor next door, that's what it is. But she says he's not interested in you, he's still grieving for his wife, so maybe it's time you came to your senses and realised that we —"

"Justin, not only am I never coming back to you, but I'm expecting another man's baby!" I yelled, entirely losing it. Then I slammed down the phone with a trembling hand.

I was sorry I'd blurted that out the moment it was said — and even more so when I turned round and saw Ivo framed in the doorway, his face deathly white.

Behind me I heard Bella put her cup down in its saucer with a small clink.

"Is that true?" Ivo demanded. "And — is it *mine*?"

"Of course it's yours, you prat," Bella said helpfully, getting up to go.

Ivo glared at me, ignoring her. "And you were going to tell me . . . when, exactly, Tansy? Or not at all?" He suddenly paled. "You weren't going to —"

"Oh, for goodness' sake!" Bella exclaimed impatiently. "Tansy's over the moon about it and she was only waiting till she got safely past the three-month stage

436

before she told you. She doesn't know how you're going to take it — and neither do I. Now, I'm off. Play nicely, children."

She whisked the packet of manuscript he'd brought with him out of his hands as she went past him, but I'm sure he didn't notice, for his merman-grey eyes were fixed on my face.

"Are you really over the moon about it, Tansy?" he enquired softly.

"Of course I am! I *desperately* want this baby — *your* baby," I confessed. "But don't worry, I know you don't love me and I'm not expecting —"

Ivo took two quick steps and seized me in a rough embrace. "I do love you! Why on earth would you think I didn't? I've been torturing myself thinking you'd never get over Justin."

"But I thought you still loved Kate, despite everything, and probably always would!"

"Kate?" he said incredulously. "No, I'd stopped loving her long before she was killed, but . . . well, I stayed fond of her and she needed me . . . or so I thought. And then I felt responsible for the accident and terribly guilty . . ."

"I think you've paid any penance now, with interest," I said, nestling into his arms. "I didn't want to fall in love with you, if her ghost would always be there with us."

"It won't be. It's more than time for both of us to put the past behind us and move on. And you're so precious to me I don't want ever to let you out of my sight again. Let's get married!"

437

"You've run mad!" I said, then voiced my greatest fear. "This is a miracle baby but . . . I'm only just pregnant, and what if something happened and I lost it?"

"Nothing will happen, you'll see," he assured me, stroking my hair tenderly, so that a scatter of multicoloured butterfly clips pattered round our feet like rain. Then we kissed, one long, slow kiss leading to another . . .

This time, there was no disapproving voice in my head, just a sense of absolute bliss.

CHAPTER
FORTY

A Delightful Plot

When we told Raffy we wanted to get married, he said,
"'Consideration like an angel came, and whipp'd the
offending Adam out of him,'" then flashed a quizzical
grin at Ivo, so he'd obviously caught the Shakespeare
bug too. Or maybe he'd seen the occasion coming and
mugged a quote up specially? I wouldn't have put it
past him.

He managed to squeeze us into a wedding slot in not
much more time than it took to put up the banns, for as
Ivo pointed out, if I didn't have a white wedding, then
Aunt Nan was going to be very disappointed.

Bella would be my bridesmaid and then I would be
hers not long afterwards, for she and Neil have now
fast-forwarded their engagement: they long to live
together with Tia in the little cottage with the pigsty in
the garden.

Of course, I had to ring Immy and tell her I was getting
married, for however little it felt like it, she *was* my
mother (though I'd decided to let sleeping dogs lie as
regards Nan's revelations). She said I'd done all right

for myself, even if she thought I was mad turning Justin down.

She must have passed on the news, too, because Marcia had the gall to call me and tell me I was welcome to Ivo, because she and Justin were now engaged!

"I'm at that age when a gal might as well settle for the best she can get," she explained.

"But don't you think it's all a bit incestuous, what with him having been my fiancé and then having an affair with your sister?"

"Not really. Why not keep him in the family?" she said unrepentantly. "Daddy's mad about it, but he'll come round eventually when he sees how I keep Justin in line."

"'Oh what a tangled web!'" Ivo exclaimed in astonishment when I told him, and then said he thought he could tie some of that plot in nicely with his latest novel and vanished back to work. Now he's left the acting profession he's really thrown himself into writing his books and is going to come out as Nicholas Marlowe, the author.

One hot, sunny, bee-drowsy afternoon when we were in the garden picking herbs, I offered to have "Here Comes the Bride" permanently silenced. The back door was open, and we could *just* hear it, even from so far away!

"There's no need, I've got used to it — and when we knock the two cottages back into one, I'll be part of the business too," Ivo said. "I've ordered the full church peal for our wedding, by the way: no half-measures. And I'll see if I can get the organist to play you up the aisle with 'The Wedding March', rather than a fugue."

"Lovely!" I said contentedly. "It's just as well Toby and Flash are friends now too, isn't it?" I looked over at where they lay in the shade and thought that perhaps "friends" was going a little too far, since Toby seemed to be using Flash as a kind of furry hammock.

"I'd still quite like to have Cedric fitted with a silencer," Ivo admitted, as the hens came high-stepping cautiously through the arch in the holly hedge. "'Hence home, you idle creatures, get you home: is this a holiday?'" he added.

I find it strangely sexy when he goes all Shakespearian . . .

"Yes, go and lay a few eggs," I encouraged the hens, then slipped my arm through his and uttered a blissful sigh.

"From now on, let's just remember the happy hours, like the sundial in the courtyard says," I suggested.

"As You Like It," he replied, with that irresistible smile — and kissed me.

Exclusive Recipes from Trisha Ashley

Recipe 1: Fat Rascals.
Fat Rascals are a Yorkshire delicacy somewhat akin to rock cakes and no-one can come close to those baked to a secret recipe by Betty's Café in Harrogate. However, this is author Angela Dracup's quick, easy and delicious version with one or two tweaks of my own.

Ingredients.
8oz/200g self-raising flour.
Pinch of salt.
A quarter teaspoon each of ground cinnamon, grated nutmeg and mixed spice.
3oz/75g margarine or butter
3oz/75g castor sugar
3oz/75g mixed dried fruit with peel.
2oz/50g currants
One large egg lightly beaten with two tablespoons of milk.

Method.

1) Preheat the oven to gas mark 6/200C/400F and cover an oven tray with baking paper.

2) Put the butter, flour, salt and spices into a large bowl and mix together using the rubbing-in method until it looks like very fine breadcrumbs.

3) Add the dried fruit and sugar and mix well.

4) Start to stir in the egg/milk mix a spoonful at a time until you have a stiff dough.

5) Divide into either two big rounds or four smaller ones and place on the baking tray. (You can decorate the top with glace cherries for eyes and slivered almonds for teeth to make smiley faces if the fancy takes you.)

6) Bake for fifteen to twenty minutes.

7) Best eaten warm, with butter!

Recipe 2: Microwave Meringues.

There are lots of recipes for these but they are all more or less the same — just sugar and egg white. Easy to whip up in minutes, you can then use them to base other dessert recipes on.

Ingredients.
One large egg white.
12oz/300g icing sugar

Method.
1) Cover a microwaveable plate with baking paper.
2) Lightly beat the egg white in a large bowl and then sieve the sugar over it.
3) Stir well until you have a thick mixture a little like soft fondant icing. You may have to add a little more sugar or beaten egg whites to get this consistency, but if so, do it a tiny bit at a time.
4) Roll into 8 balls and microwave them on the paper-covered plate two at a time for about a minute — watch them swell up like magic!
5) Let them cool, then eat as they are or sandwich together with whipped cream.

Variations:
1) Break the meringue into pieces and mix with whipped cream and strawberries to make Eton Mess, the perfect summer dessert.
2) Make a Pavlova. Cover two plates with baking paper

and form the mixture into two balls. Place one in the centre of each plate and microwave for about a minute, which should give you a large round disc of meringue. Do the same with the other.

Spread a layer of whipped cream on the bottom layer, sprinkle on strawberries or other fruit, cover with a little more cream and then put on the top circle of meringue.

Recipe 3: Fairy Cakes.

Who needs a big, heavy, greasy muffin when they can have a delicious little morsel like this? And don't slather on an inch-thick layer of sugary "frosting" until you have eaten one straight from the oven to remind yourself just how good home-baked cake can taste.

Ingredients.

You will need paper cake cases — you can get small ones for fairy cakes and even tinier, bite-size ones. If you haven't got a cake or muffin tin, just stand them on a baking tray.

4oz/100g butter or margarine
4oz/100g castor sugar
4oz/100g self-raising flour
2 medium eggs
Half level teaspoon baking powder.

Method.

1) Preheat the oven to gas mark 6/200C/400F
2) Soften the butter (a minute on very low in the microwave will do it) and place in a large mixing bowl.
3) Sieve the flour into it, and then stir in all the other ingredients.
4) Mix well for a couple of minutes until you have a smooth mixture.
5) Divide between about eighteen paper cases for normal sized fairy cakes (the mixture will rise a lot,

so don't overfill!). If using the tiny ones, then a level teaspoon of mixture should be more than enough.

6) Bake for about fifteen minutes, until a nice golden-brown colour, then leave to cool on a wire rack.

Variations.

1) To make chocolate fairy cakes, add a level tablespoon of cocoa powder when stirring the ingredients. You could also decorate the top with a little melted chocolate.

2) To make butterfly cakes, slice off a disc from the top of the cakes and cut them into two halves.
   Put a blob of jam and another of butter cream or whipped cream on top of each cake.

3) Place two half-circles of cake on top of each one to make butterfly wings.

4) Fruit fairy cakes: add about an 1oz/25g of currants to the mix while stirring.

5) Decorate each cake with a little water icing (literally icing sugar mixed with water).